$\mathcal{D}$INA'S
BOOK

DINA'S BOOK

A Novel by

H. WASSMO

*Translated from the Norwegian
by Nadia M. Christensen*

Arcade Publishing • New York

Translator's Note

I wish to thank Joe Hognander for his invaluable editorial and processing assistance in completing this translation.

Copyright © 1989 by Gyldendal Norsk Forlag A/S

Translation copyright © 1994 by Nadia Christensen

FIRST ENGLISH-LANGUAGE EDITION

Originally published in Norway under the title *Dinas bok*

The characters and events in this book are fictitious. Any similarity to real persons, living or dead, is coincidental and not intended by the author.

Library of Congress Cataloging-in-Publication Data

Wassmo, Herbjørg, 1942–
    [Dinas bok. English]
    Dina's book / Herbjørg Wassmo ; translated from the Norwegian by Nadia M. Christensen.
      p.   cm.
    ISBN 1-55970-243-5
    I. Title.
PT8951.33.A8D5613   1994
839.8'2374 — dc20   93-47397

Published in the United States by Arcade Publishing, Inc., New York
Distributed by Little, Brown and Company

10 9 8 7 6 5 4 3 2 1

BP

PRINTED IN THE UNITED STATES OF AMERICA

To Bjørn

Prologue

Many a man proclaims his own loyalty,
but a faithful man who can find?
A righteous man who walks in his integrity —
blessed are his sons after him! . . .
Who can say, "I have made my heart clean;
I am pure from my sin"?

— Proverbs 20 : 6–7, 9

I am Dina who sees the sleigh with the person on it rush headlong down the steep slope.

At first I think I am the one lying there tied to the sleigh. Because I feel pain more terrible than any I have ever known.

Through crystal-clear reality, but beyond time and space, I am in touch with the face on the sleigh. Moments later, the sleigh crashes against an ice-covered rock.

The horse actually loosed the carriage shafts and escaped being dragged down the slope! Amazing, how easily that happened!

It must be late in the fall. Late for what?

I do not have a horse.

A woman found herself at the top of a cliff in cold morning light. The sun was not shining. Around her, the mountains rose dark and watchful. The cliff was so sheer that she could not see the landscape below.

Across a wide gorge, an even steeper range of mountains stood in silent witness.

She followed every movement of the sleigh. Until it finally came to a stop against the trunk of a large birch tree at the very edge of a precipice.

The sleigh teetered slightly toward the sheer drop. Beneath were steep bluffs. And, far below, thundering rapids.

The woman looked at the trail leveled by the sleigh as it plum-

1

meted down the slope. Pebbles, snow, clumps of heather, broken brushwood. As if a giant carpenter's plane had swept down, taking with it every protruding thing.

She was wearing leather trousers and a long, fitted jacket. Had it not been for her hair, one might have taken her for a man from a distance. She was very tall for a woman.

The right sleeve of her jacket hung in shreds. It had blood on it. From a wound.

Her left hand was still clenched tightly around a short-bladed knife, the type Lapp women wear in their belts.

The woman turned her face toward a sound. A horse's whinny. It seemed to awaken her. She hid the knife in a pocket of her jacket.

She hesitated a moment, then resolutely stepped over the stone wall at the side of the road. Toward the sleigh. It teetered less now. As if it had decided to save the person with the battered face.

She climbed down the slope quickly. In her haste she dislodged loose stones. They formed a small avalanche, which rushed past the sleigh and over the edge of the precipice. She stared out into the unseen. As if she were in touch with the stones and followed them, even when she could no longer see them. As if she watched them until they reached a deep pool beneath the thundering rapids below.

She paused for a moment as new stones tumbled past the sleigh that bore the unmoving body. But only for a moment. Then she continued her descent until she could put her hand on the sheepskin robe covering the man and lift a corner of it.

Something that must once have been a handsome male face came into view. One eye was pushed in. Fresh blood flowed thick and evenly from many wounds on his head. During the few seconds she stood there, the man's head became completely red. The white sheepskin at his neck soaked up the blood.

She raised a long, narrow hand with well-formed pink nails. Lifted the man's eyelids. One after the other. Thrust her hand onto his chest. Was the man's heart still beating? Her fumbling hand could not tell.

The woman's face was a snow-covered world. Immobile. Except for the darting eyes under her half-lowered lids. Her hands became bloodstained, and she dried them on the man's chest. Then covered his face again with the corner of the sheepskin.

She crawled over the sleigh to the carriage-shaft fastenings. From each fastening she quickly pulled the remains of a worn piece of rope. She gathered them together carefully and put them into her jacket pocket along with the knife. Then she took out two frayed leather straps and coaxed them into the places where the ropes had been.

At one point she straightened up. Listened. The horse whinnied from the road. She hesitated, as if deciding whether her task was completed. Then she crawled back over the sleigh. The battered figure was still between her and the precipice.

The solid birch tree creaked from the cold and from the added weight of her body. She found a footing among the icy stones, then thrust her weight against the sleigh. Calculated the force needed, as if she had performed the same movement many times before.

As the sleigh left the ground, the sheepskin slid away from the man's face. He opened the eye that was not pushed in and looked straight at the woman. Speechless. A helpless, incredulous look.

It startled her. And an awkward tenderness flashed across her face.

Then everything became movement and air. It went quickly. The sounds echoed through the mountains long after everything was over.

The woman's face was blank. The landscape was itself again. Everything was painfully good.

I am Dina who feels the downward pull when the man on the sleigh reaches the deep, foaming pool. Then he crosses the vital boundary. I do not catch the final instant, which could have given me a glimpse of what everyone fears. The moment when time does not exist.

Who am I? Where are space and place and time? Am I doomed to this forever?

She drew erect and began resolutely to climb back up the slope. It was harder going up than down. Two hundred yards of icy terrain.

At the point where she could see the torrential autumn river, she turned and stared. The river curved before thundering out of view. Foaming masses of water. Nothing else.

She continued climbing. Rapidly. Gasping for breath. Her injured arm was giving her pain. Several times she nearly lost her balance and fell as the sleigh had.

Her hands grasped for heather, branches, stones. She made sure she always had a firm grip with one hand before moving the other upward. Strong, swift movements.

As she took hold of the stone wall by the roadside, she looked up. Met the large, shining eyes of the horse. It was no longer whinnying. Just stood there looking at her.

They faced each other, resting a little. Suddenly the horse bared its teeth and, angrily, bit into some tufts of grass at the side of the road. She had to use both arms to pull herself up onto the road, grimacing in pain as she did so.

The animal bowed its large head over her. The carriage shafts splayed at its sides. An empty decoration.

Finally, she reached for the horse's mane. Firmly, almost brutally, she pulled herself up to the resisting horse's head.

This woman was eighteen years old. With eyes as old as stones.

The shafts scraping against the ground were sounds outside the picture.

The horse stamped frozen blades of grass into the ground again.

She took off her jacket and rolled up the sleeves of her sweater and blouse. The injury appeared to be a knife wound. Perhaps she had been injured in a fight with the man on the sleigh?

She bent down quickly and dug into the frozen gravel road with her bare hands. Picked up sand and ice, grasses and debris. Rubbed them energetically into the knife wound. A look of intense pain crossed her face. Her mouth opened and let out dark, guttural sounds.

She repeated the movements. Repeated the sounds at regular intervals. Like a ritual. Her hand dug. Found gravel and sand. Picked them up. Rubbed them into the wound. Time after time. Then she tore off her heavy sweater and her blouse and rubbed them on the road. Ripped and tore the sleeves. Rubbed and rubbed.

Her hands became covered with blood. She did not wipe them clean. Stood there outlined against the autumn sky in a thin lace bodice. But she did not appear to feel the cold. Calmly, she put on her clothes again. Examined her injury through the holes in her clothing. Smoothed her tattered sleeve. Grimaced with pain as she straightened her arm and tested if she could use it.

Her hat lay at the side of the road. Brown, narrow-brimmed, trimmed with green feathers. She gave it a quick glance before beginning to walk north along the rough sleigh road. In dim, silvery light.

The horse trudged after her, dragging the shafts. Soon caught up with her. Put its muzzle over her shoulder and nibbled at her hair.

She stopped walking and moved close to the animal. With a tug of her hand, she forced the horse down on its two front legs as if it were a camel. And seated herself astride the broad, black back.

The sound of horse's hooves. The shafts weeping against the gravel. The horse's easy breathing. The wind. Which did not know. Did not see.

It was the middle of the day. The horse and the woman had taken the steep road down the mountain and had come to a large estate. Tall, swaying rowan trees lined a broad lane, which stretched from the white main house down to the two red warehouses that faced each other near the stone pier.

The trees were already bare, with crimson berries. The fields yellow, sprinkled with patches of ice and snow. There were frequent breaks in the clouds. But still no sunshine.

As the horse and the woman entered the courtyard, the young man named Tomas came from the stable. Stood like a post in the ground when he saw the empty shafts and the woman's disheveled hair and bloodstained clothing.

She slid off the horse slowly, without looking at him. Then she staggered step by step up the wide stairs to the main house. Opened one of the double doors. Stood motionless with her back to him while the light enveloped her. Then suddenly she turned around. As if she had become afraid of her own shadow.

Tomas ran after her. She stood in light from the house, warm and golden. From outside, cold, with bluish shadows from the mountains.

She no longer had any face.

There was great excitement. Women and men came running. Servants.

Mother Karen hobbled with a cane from one of the parlors. Her monocle dangled from an embroidered ribbon around her neck. A gleaming lens that tried in vain to make things cheerful.

The old woman creaked laboriously through the elegant hallway. With a gentle, omniscient look. Did she know anything?

Everyone flocked around the woman at the front door. A servant girl touched the woman's injured arm and offered to help remove the torn jacket. But she was brushed aside.

Then the clamor broke loose. Everyone talked at once. Questions poured over the woman without a face.

But she did not answer. Saw nothing. Had no eyes. Simply took hold of Tomas's arm so tightly that he moaned. Then she stumbled over to the man named Anders. A blond fellow with a strong chin. One of the foster children on the estate. She took his arm, too, and made both men accompany her. Without saying a word.

Two horses from the stable were saddled. The third horse had no saddle. Was tired and sweaty after the ride down the mountain. The animal was unhitched from the shafts, wiped down, and watered.

The horse's large head lingered in the water bucket. People had to wait. It drank in well-deserved slurps. From time to time, it tossed its mane in the air and let its eyes glide from face to face.

The woman refused to change clothes or to have her wound bandaged. Just swung herself onto the horse. Tomas offered her a homespun coat, and she put it on. She still had not said a word.

She led them to the spot where the sleigh had skidded over the cliff. There was no mistaking the tracks. The ravaged slope, the flattened small birches, the uprooted heather. They all knew what was below. The sheer rock. The rapids. The gorge. The deep pool. The sleigh.

They summoned more people and searched in the foaming water. But found only the remnants of a crushed sleigh with frayed straps in the carriage-shaft fastenings.

The woman was mute.

The eyes of the Lord keep watch over knowledge,
but he overthrows the words of the faithless.
— Proverbs 22 : 12

*D*ina had to take her husband, Jacob, who had gangrene in one foot, to the doctor on the other side of the mountain. November. She was the only one who could handle the wild yearling, which was the fastest horse. And they needed to drive fast. On a rough, icy road.

Jacob's foot already stank. The smell had filled the house for a long time. The cook smelled it even in the pantry. An uneasy atmosphere pervaded every room. A feeling of anxiety.

No one at Reinsnes said anything about the smell of Jacob's foot before he left. Nor did they mention it after Blackie returned to the estate with empty shafts.

But aside from that, people talked. With disbelief and horror. On the neighboring farms. In the parlors at Strandsted and along the sound. At the pastor's home. Quietly and confidentially.

About Dina, the young wife at Reinsnes, the only daughter of Sheriff Holm. She was like a horse-crazy boy. Even after she got married. Now she had suffered such a sad fate.

They told the story again and again. She had driven so fast that the snow crackled and spurted under the runners. Like a witch. Nevertheless, Jacob Grønelv did not get to the doctor's. Now he no longer existed. Friendly, generous Jacob, who never refused a request for help. Mother Karen's son, who came to Reinsnes when he was quite young.

Dead! No one could understand how such a terrible thing could have happened. That boats capsized, or people disappeared at sea, had to be accepted. But this was the devil's work. First getting gangrene in a fractured leg. Then dying on a sleigh that plunged into the rapids!

Dina had lost her speech, and old Mother Karen wept. Jacob's son from his first marriage wandered, fatherless, around Copenhagen, and Blackie could not stand the sight of sleighs.

The authorities came to the estate to conduct an inquiry into the events that had occurred up to the moment of death. Everything must be stated specifically and nothing hidden, they said.

Dina's father, the sheriff, brought two witnesses and a book for recording the proceedings. He said emphatically that he was there as one of the authorities, not as a father.

Mother Karen found it difficult to see a difference. But she did not say so.

No one brought Dina down from the second floor. Since she was so big and strong, they took no chance that she might resist and make a painful scene. They did not try to force her to come downstairs. Instead it was decided the authorities would go up to her large bedroom.

Extra chairs had been placed in the room. And the curtains on the canopy bed were thoroughly dusted. Heavy gold fabric patterned with rows of rich red flowers. Bought in Hamburg. Sewn for Dina and Jacob's wedding.

Oline and Mother Karen had tried to take the young wife in hand so she would not look completely unpresentable. Oline gave her herb tea with thick cream and plenty of sugar. And advice against everything from scurvy to childlessness. Mother Karen assisted with praise, hair brushing, and cautious concern.

The servant girls did as they were told, while looking around with frightened glances.

The words stuck. Dina opened her mouth and formed them. But their sound was in another world. The authorities tried many different approaches.

The sheriff tried using a deep, dispassionate voice, peering into Dina's light-gray eyes. He could just as well have looked through a glass of water.

The witnesses also tried. Seated and standing. With both compassionate and commanding voices.

Finally, Dina laid her head of black, unruly hair on her arms. And she let out sounds that could have come from a half-strangled dog.

Feeling ashamed, the authorities withdrew to the downstairs rooms. In order to reach agreement about what had happened. How things had looked at the place in question. How the young woman had acted.

They decided that the whole matter was a tragedy for the community and the entire district. That Dina Grønelv was beside herself with grief. That she was not culpable and had lost her speech from the shock.

They decided that she had been racing to take her husband to the doctor. That she had taken the curve near the bridge too fast, or that the wild horse had bolted at the edge of the cliff and the shaft fastenings had pulled loose. Both of them.

This was neatly recorded in the official documents.

They did not find the body, at first. People said it had washed out to sea. But did not understand how. For the sea was nearly seven miles away through a rough, shallow riverbed. The rocks there would stop a dead body, which could do nothing itself to reach the sea.

To Mother Karen's despair, they gradually gave up the search.

A month later, an old pauper came to the estate and insisted that the body lay in Veslekulpen, a small backwater some distance below the rapids. Jacob lay crooked around a rock. Stiff as a rod. Battered and bloated, the old fellow said.

He proved to be right.

The water level had evidently subsided when the autumn rains ended. And one clear day in early December, the unfortunate body of Jacob Grønelv appeared. Right before the eyes of the old pauper, who was on his way across the mountain.

Afterward, people said the pauper was clairvoyant. And, in fact, always had been. This is why he had a quiet old age. Nobody wanted to quarrel with a clairvoyant.

Dina sat in her bedroom, the largest room on the second floor. With the curtains drawn. At first she did not even go to the stable to see her horse.

They left her in peace.

Mother Karen stopped crying, simply because she no longer had time for that. She had to assume the duties that the master and his wife had neglected. Both were dead, each in his or her own way.

Dina sat at the walnut table, staring. No one knew what else she

9

did. Because she confided in no one. The sheets of music that had been piled around the bed were now stuffed away in the clothes closet. Her long dresses swept over them in the draft when she opened the door.

The shadows were deep in the bedroom. A cello stood in one corner, gathering dust. It had remained untouched since the day Jacob was carried from the house and laid on the sleigh.

The solid canopy bed with sumptuous bed curtains occupied much of the room. It was so high that one could lie on the pillows and look out through the windows at the sound. Or one could look at oneself in the large mirror with a black lacquered frame that could be tilted to different angles.

The big round stove roared all day. Behind a triple-paneled folding screen with an embroidered motif of beautiful Leda and the swan in an erotic embrace. Wings and arms. And Leda's long, blond hair spread virtuously over her lap.

A servant girl, Thea, brought wood four times a day. Even so, the supply barely lasted through the night.

No one knew when Dina slept, or if she slept. She paced back and forth in heavy shoes with metal-tipped heels, day and night. From wall to wall. Keeping the whole house awake.

Thea could report that the large family Bible, which Dina had inherited from her mother, always lay open.

Now and then the young wife laughed softly. It was an unpleasant sound. Thea did not know whether her mistress was laughing about the holy text or if she was thinking about something else.

Sometimes she angrily slammed together the thin-as-silk pages and threw the book away like entrails from a dead fish.

Jacob was not buried until seven days after he was found. In the middle of December. There were so many arrangements to be made. So many people had to be notified. Relatives, friends, and prominent people had to be invited to the funeral. The weather stayed cold, so the battered and swollen corpse could easily remain in the barn during that time. Digging the grave, however, required the use of sledge-hammers and pickaxes.

The moon peered through the barn's tiny windows and observed Jacob's fate with its golden eye. Made no distinction between living and dead. Decorated the barn floor in silver and white. And nearby lay the hay, offering warmth and nourishment, smelling fragrantly of summer and splendor.

One morning before dawn, they dressed for the funeral. The boats were ready. Silence lay over the house like a strange piety. The moon was shining. No one waited for daylight at that time of year.

Dina leaned against the windowsill, as if steeling herself, when they entered her room to help her dress in the black clothes that had been sewn for the funeral. She had refused to try them on.

She seemed to be standing there sensing each muscle and each thought. The somber, teary-eyed women did not see a single movement in her body.

Still, they did not give up at once. She had to change her clothes. She had to be part of the funeral procession. Anything else was unthinkable. But finally, they did think that thought. For with her guttural, animal-like sounds, she convinced everyone that she was not ready to be the widow at a funeral. At least not this particular day.

Terrified, the women fled the room. One after another. Mother Karen was the last to leave. She gave excuses and soothing explanations. To the aunts, the wives, the other women, and, not least of all, to Dina's father, the sheriff.

He was the hardest to convince. Bellowing loudly, he burst into Dina's room without knocking. Shook her and commanded her, slapped her cheeks with fatherly firmness while his words swarmed around her like angry bees.

Mother Karen had to leave. The few who remained kept their eyes lowered.

Then Dina let out the bestial sounds again. While she flailed her arms and tore her hair. The room was charged with something they did not understand. There was an aura of madness and power surrounding the young, half-dressed woman with disheveled hair and crazed eyes.

Her screams reminded the sheriff of an event he carried with him always. Day and night. In his dreams and in his daily tasks. An event that still, after thirteen years, could make him wander restlessly around the estate. Looking for someone, or something, that could unburden him of his thoughts and feelings.

The people in the room thought Dina Grønelv had a harsh father. But on the other hand, it was not right that such a young women refused to do what was expected of her.

She tired them out. People decided she was too sick to attend her husband's funeral. Mother Karen explained, loudly and clearly, to everyone she met:

"Dina is so distraught and ill she can't stand on her feet. She does nothing but weep. And the terrible thing is, she's not able to speak."

First came the muffled shouts from the people who were going in the boats. Then came the scraping of wood against iron as the coffin was loaded onto the longboat with its juniper decorations and its weeping, black-clad women. Then the sounds and voices stiffened over the water like a thin crusting of beach ice. And disappeared between the sea and the mountains. Afterward, silence settled over the estate as though this were the true funeral procession. The house held its breath. Merely let out a small sigh among the rafters now and then. A sad, pitiful final honor to Jacob.

The pink waxed-paper carnations fluttered amid the pine and juniper boughs across the sound in a light breeze. There was no point in traveling quickly with such a burden. Death and its detached supporting cast took their time. It was not Blackie who pulled them. And it was not Dina who set the pace. The coffin was heavy. Those who bore it felt the weight. This was the only way to the church with such a burden.

Now five pairs of oars creaked in the oarlocks. The sail flapped idly against the mast, refusing to unfurl. There was no sun. Gray clouds drifted across the sky. The raw air gradually became still.

The boats followed one another. A triumphal procession for Jacob Grønelv. Masts and oars pointed toward ocean and heaven. The ribbons on the wreaths fluttered calmly. They had only a short time to be seen.

Mother Karen was a yellowed rag. Edged with lace, it is true.

The servant girls were wet balls of wool in the wind.

The men rowed, sweating behind their beards and mustaches. Rowing in rhythm.

At Reinsnes everything was prepared. The sandwiches were arranged on large platters. On the cellar floor and on shelves in the large entry were pewter plates filled with cookies and covered by cloths.

Under Oline's exacting supervision, the glasses had been rubbed to a glistening shine. Now the cups and glasses were arranged neatly in rows on the tables and in the pantry, protected by white linen towels bearing the monograms of Ingeborg Grønelv and Dina Grønelv. They had to use the linen belonging to both of Jacob's wives today. Many guests were expected after the burial.

Dina stoked the fire like a madwoman, although there was not even frost on the windows. Her face, which had been gray that morning, began slowly to regain its color.

She paced restlessly back and forth across the floor with a little smile on her lips. When the clock struck, she raised her head like an animal listening for enemies.

Tomas let the armload of wood drop into the wrought-iron basket with as little sound as possible. Then he took off his cap and clenched it between his strong hands. Embarrassed beyond all belief, because he was in the master bedroom, the room with the canopy bed and the cello, where Dina slept.

"Mother Karen sent me because I'm to stay at Reinsnes when the servants and everybody take Jacob to the churchyard," he managed to stammer.

"I'm to give Dina a hand. If she needs it," he added.

Tomas did not tell her, if he knew, that the sheriff and Mother Karen had agreed it was best to have a strong fellow there who could prevent Dina from harming herself while everyone was away.

She stood by the window with her back to him and did not even turn around.

The moon was a small pale ghost. A deformed fetus of a day tried in vain to break out to the north and west. But the windows' surfaces remained dark.

The boy took his cap and left. Realized he was not wanted.

However, when the funeral procession was far out on the sound, Tomas came to the room again. With a pitcher of fresh water. Would she like some? When she did not say thank you or give any indication that she saw him, he set the pitcher on the table by the door and turned toward her.

"You don't want help from me on the day of the funeral?" he asked in a low voice.

At that, she seemed to awaken. She went toward him quickly. Stood close to him. Half a head taller.

Then she lifted her hand and let her long fingers glide over his face. Like a blind person trying to see with her fingertips.

He felt as if he were being strangled. Because he forgot to breathe. So close! At first he did not understand what she wanted. Standing beside him exuding her fragrance. Tracing the lines in his face with her forefinger.

He slowly turned crimson. And found it impossible to look at her. He knew her eyes were waiting. Suddenly he took courage and looked straight at her.

She nodded and looked at him questioningly.

He nodded in return. Simply to have nodded. He wanted to leave.

Then she smiled and came even closer. Used the index and third fingers of her left hand to open his worn vest.

He retreated two steps toward the stove. And did not know how he would escape before he got strangled or burned, or disappeared from the face of the earth.

She stood for a moment, sniffing his stable odor. Her nostrils were everywhere. They vibrated!

Then he nodded again. In utter confusion.

It was unbearable. Time stood still. He leaned over abruptly, opened the door of the stove, and threw a chunk of wood into the flames. Then he added three damp, sputtering birch logs. To stand up and meet her gaze again was a test of manhood.

All at once her mouth was on his. Her arms were stubborn willow branches filled with spring sap. Her aroma was so powerful that he had to close his eyes.

He could never have imagined it. Not in his wildest fantasies under his worn wool blanket in the servants' quarters. So he stood there, and all he could do was let it happen!

The colors of the embroidery on her dressing gown, the yellow walls with a vinelike design, the beamed ceiling, the deep-red drapes — they all fluttered into each other. Material merged with material. Limbs with limbs. Movements, furniture, air, skin.

He stood outside himself. And yet was inside. The smell and sound of bodies moving heavily. And deep, two-part breathing.

She put her hands on his chest and undid his buttons. Then she drew off his clothing. One piece after another. As if she had done it a thousand times.

He stood hunched forward, his arms hanging uselessly at his sides. As if ashamed that his underclothes were not completely clean and his shirt was missing three buttons. Actually, he did not know where he was, where he was standing, or how he was behaving.

She kissed the naked boy, opened her dressing gown, a
in to her large, firm body.

It made him warm and brave. He felt the sparks from her skin as
a physical pain. His skin tingled against hers, created a picture of her.
He stood with closed eyes and saw each curve, each pore on her white
body, until he went out of his mind completely.

When they were both naked, sitting on the sheepskin in front of
the round black stove, he thought she would begin to speak. He was
dizzy with embarrassment and desire. The seven lighted candles in
the candelabra on the dressing table troubled him like a warning of
hell. Their flickering light on the mirror's surface revealed everything.

She began to explore his body. Quite gently at first. Then wilder and
wilder. As if driven by a great hunger.

At first he was simply frightened. He had never seen such intense
craving. Finally, he gasped and rolled over on the sheepskin. Let her
pour oil on a fire greater than anything he had ever imagined.

In quick flashes he came to his senses again and to his horror felt
himself pull her close and do things no one had taught him.

The air was dense with a woman's body.

His terror was vast as an ocean. But his desire, enormous as the
heavens.

At the churchyard, the coffin decorated with wax flowers was lowered
into the grave. Containing the earthly remains of innkeeper and cargo-
boat owner Jacob Grønelv.

The pastor tried to speak words that would allow the deceased to
slip easily into paradise and not end up in hell's fire and brimstone.
Yet the pastor knew that even though Jacob had been a good man,
he certainly had not lived like a wax flower. Or he would not have
met such an end.

Some of the funeral guests stood with their gray jowls drooping
in genuine sorrow. Others wondered what kind of weather they would
have on the trip home. Still others just stood there. Took in everything
halfheartedly. Most of them felt bitterly cold.

The pastor pronounced his ritual words and tossed his paltry
spadefuls of earth in God's name. Then it was over.

Behind furrowed, serious faces, the men looked forward to the
liqueur. The women, with tear-filled eyes, thought about the sand-

wiches. The servant girls wept openly. For the man in the coffin had been a loving master to them all.

Mother Karen was even more pale and transparent than in the boat. The eyes behind her black fringed shawl were dry as she stood supported by Anders and the sheriff. Each with his hat under his arm.

The hymn had an endless string of verses and was far from beautiful. In fact, it was barely endurable, until the deacon joined in with his untrained bass voice. He had a need to save every situation, the deacon.

In the large bedroom, behind drawn curtains, Tomas, the cotter's son, burned and blazed. In seventh heaven. Yet totally alive.

Moisture from human bodies collected on the windows and mirror. A faint odor clung to the sheepskin on the floor, the seats of the chairs, and the curtains.

The room welcomed Tomas the stableboy. Just as it once had welcomed Jacob Grønelv, when he was hospitably received for the first time by the widow of Reinsnes.

The widow was named Ingeborg. And she died one day when she leaned over to pet her cat. Now she had company where she was.

The bedroom was filled with heavy breathing, skin, and heat. Blood thundered through veins. Pounded against temples. Bodies were horses on broad plains. They galloped and galloped. The woman was already a practiced rider. But he rode to exhaustion after her. The floorboards sang, the beams wept.

The family portraits and drawings swayed slightly in their black oval frames. The linen sheets in the bed felt abandoned and dry as dust. The stove stopped roaring. Just stood in its corner and listened openly, without embarrassment.

Downstairs, sandwiches and glasses stood waiting. For what? For Dina, the mistress of Reinsnes, to come sliding down the banister? Naked, her black hair like a half-opened umbrella above her large fragrant body? Yes!

And following her — half terrified, half in a dream — a powerful young boy clad in a sheet edged with French lace? Yes!

Tomas ran down the stairs on bare, hairy legs and sturdy toes with very dirty nails. He reeked so powerfully of plowed fields that the demure inside air drew back.

They fetched sandwiches and wine. A large glass and a large carafe. A sandwich stolen here and there from the platters so it would not be noticed. They pretended they did not have permission to eat.

16

After they helped themselves from the platters, Dina gently rearranged the empty spaces. With long, quick fingers that smelled of salty earth and newly cleaned fish. Then she covered the plates again with the monogrammed cloths.

They stole up to the bedroom again like thieves. Sat down on the sheepskin in front of the stove. Tomas left the stove's double doors ajar.

Leda and the swan on the folding screen were a weak reflection of these two. The wine sparkled.

Greedily, Dina ate smoked salmon and salted meat. Bread crumbled across her firm breasts and down onto her round stomach.

Tomas realized he was in his mistress's room. He ate his food politely. But drank in Dina's body through his eyes, with watering mouth and many sighs.

Their eyes glistened over the same glass. It had a long green stem and had been a wedding present to Ingeborg and her first husband. The glass was not of the highest quality and had many bubbles in it. Bought before wealth entered the house through large cargo boats, dry fish, and powerful connections in Trondheim and Bergen.

Well before the funeral guests were expected to return, the glass and the remaining wine were hidden away, far back in the clothes closet.

Two children, one worried and one wild, had fooled the grownups. Jacob's Chinese dice game was replaced in its silk-lined box. All traces were obliterated.

At the end, Tomas stood at the door completely clothed, with his hat in his hand. She scribbled some words on the black slate that she always kept close by, let him read them, then carefully erased them with a firm hand.

He nodded, looking nervously at the window. Listening for the sound of oars. Thinking he heard them. Suddenly he understood what he had done. Took all the guilt upon himself. Already felt the Lord's scourge upon his shoulders. Many deep lashes. Tomas's mouth trembled. But he could not feel regret.

Standing in the dark hallway, he knew he was no longer under anyone's protection. Like a gladiator who had fought joyfully against great odds. For one single experience! Important beyond words.

He was doomed to lie on his straw mattress each night for months, feeling a woman's breath on his face. To lie with open eyes, reliving. The room. The smells.

And the thin blanket would rise in youthful, dreamlike ardor.

He was doomed also to the image of Jacob's coffin. That had to sway right along with them. And the great wave within him would combine all the impressions and send him straight to the northern lights. The wave would empty into his wretched bed, and he would not be able to prevent it.

Dina was calm and powdered pale when the boats glided in to the rocky beach. She lay in bed, thereby avoiding any fuss about putting in an appearance with the funeral guests downstairs.

Mother Karen came down from the bedroom and gave everyone complete details about Dina's condition. Her voice was honey on the sheriff's disposition. It blended lightly and sweetly with the liqueur.

Now that Jacob had been properly laid to rest, the somber, sorrowful atmosphere lightened and improved. As the evening wore on, a sense of calm descended, and thoughts of temporal things and the hard day tomorrow crept into the quiet conversations.

Everyone went to bed early, as was fitting on such a day. Dina got up and played solitaire on the walnut table. After the third try, she broke the game. Then she sighed and yawned.

Book One

Chapter 1

In the thought of one who is at ease there is contempt for misfortune;
it is ready for those whose feet slip.

— Job 12 : 5

*I am Dina. Who is awakened by the screams. They stay in my head.
Sometimes they gnaw at my body.*

*Hjertrud's image is split wide open. Like the belly of a slaughtered sheep.
Her face is the screaming, where everything comes out.*

It began with the sheriff bringing him along when he returned from
the autumn Assembly session. The smith was a real find! From Trondheim. A magician at his trade.

Bendik could forge the most unusual things. Things that could
be used in so many types of work.

He forged a device for the grinding wheel that would pour seven
spoonfuls of water on a scythe blade for each ten turns of its crank.
Made locks that stuck if someone who did not know the mechanism
tried to open a door from the outside. And he also forged the most
beautiful plows and fittings.

People called the smith Long Jaw.

The moment he arrived at the sheriff's estate, everyone understood why. He had a long and narrow face and two enormous eyes.

Dina, who had just turned five, raised her gray eyes when he
entered the room, as if wanting to forestall him. She did not seem
exactly frightened. There was just no need to become acquainted.

This dark-eyed man, who was said to be a gypsy, gazed at the
sheriff's wife as if she were an expensive object he had purchased.
And she obviously did not mind.

After a while, the sheriff wanted to stop giving the smith more
work. He thought things were taking too long.

But Bendik remained under Hjertrud's gentle smile.

He forged ingenious locks for doors and cupboards, and the water-

21

ing system for the grinding wheel. Finally, he forged new handles for the huge kettle in which the women boiled the laundry in lye.

Onto the handles he fastened a device that made it possible to tip the kettle forward, notch by notch, so the lye ran out gradually. The entire operation could be done easily, controlled by a lever on the kettle's hanger.

Now the women had no worry about maneuvering the frightening black pot. It could be lowered, turned, and tilted with miraculous ease, thanks to the smith's wonderful ingenuity.

One could stand on the floor and control the entire operation with no fear of getting near the steam or the boiling contents of the pot.

Dina followed her mother into the washhouse one day just before Christmas. It was a big washday. There were four women working, and a hired man to carry water.

The buckets filled with slush and ice were brought in and dumped into large barrels by the door with a cheerful splash. Later everything melted in the huge laundry kettle, and steam filled the room like a night fog.

The women wore only shifts with unbuttoned bodices. They swayed and splashed and gestured. Had bare feet in wooden shoes and rolled-up sleeves. Their hands were as red as newly scalded baby pigs.

Below their tight kerchiefs, their faces were covered with sweat. It ran in rivers down their cheeks and necks. Then flowed into larger riverbeds between their breasts, and disappeared into their damp clothing, down to the underground.

It was while Mistress Hjertrud was giving orders to one of the servant girls that Dina decided to look more closely at the mechanism that made everyone so proud.

The kettle was already boiling. The odor of lye was anesthetizing and familiar, like the smell of the toilet buckets in the upstairs hallway on warm summer mornings.

Dina clasped her small hands around the lever. Just to know how it felt.

In a flash Hjertrud saw the danger and rushed over.

Dina had not known enough to wrap a rag around her hand as the servants did. She burned herself badly and quickly pulled her hand back.

But the lever had already moved. Two notches down.

The angle, directed at the lowest point on the kettle, determined Hjertrud's fate.

The pot emptied the amount specified by the lever's position. Neither more nor less. Then it stopped. And continued boiling on its hanger.

The stream of lye first reached her face and breasts, with absolute precision. Then rapidly sent scalding rivers down the rest of her poor body.

They came rushing from everywhere. Pulled off Hjertrud's clothing.

Dina was inside fluttering steaming images. They showed large patches of skin and scalded flesh coming off with the clothing, which reeked of lye.

But half of her mother's face was spared. As though it were important that Hjertrud come to God the Father with sufficient face so that He could recognize her.

Dina shouted, "Mama!" But no one answered.

Hjertrud's own screaming was enough.

The pink opening spread and covered nearly all of her. She was glowing red. More and more, as they gradually pulled off her clothing and her skin accompanied it.

Someone poured bucket after bucket of icy water over her.

Finally, she sank to the rough wooden floor, and no one dared to help her up. You could no longer touch her. No one could reach her. For she had no surface.

Hjertrud's head tore open more and more. The screaming was newly sharpened knives. Which cut into everyone.

Someone took Dina into the yard. But the screams were in the outer walls too. Rattled in the windowpanes. Trembled in the ice crystals on the snow. Rose with the greasy smoke of the chimneys. The entire fjord listened. There was a faint pink stripe in the east. Lye had also spilled on the winter sky.

Dina was brought to a neighboring farm, where people stared at her. Intently. As though there were a crack in her that could be opened and searched.

One of the servant girls spoke baby talk to her and gave her honey straight from the jar. She ate too much and vomited on the kitchen floor. With disgust all over her face, the girl cleaned it up. Her scolding sounded like a frightened little magpie shrieking under the gable.

For three days, the sheriff's daughter stayed at the home of people she had never seen before. Who stared at her the whole time as if she were a creature from another planet.

Now and then she slept, because she could no longer endure all the eyes.

At last the sheriff's farmhand came to fetch her in a two-seated sleigh. Wrapped her well in a sheepskin rug and brought her home.

At the sheriff's estate, everything was silent.

Later, in the servants' quarters, when they had forgotten her under a table, she learned that Hjertrud had screamed for an entire day before she became senseless and died. Half of her face had no skin. Also, her neck, right arm, and stomach.

Dina was not sure what it meant to become senseless. But she knew what sense was.

And she also knew that Hjertrud had personified sense. Especially when Dina's father raged and shouted.

"Our wisdom is received from God. . . . All gifts come from God. . . . The Holy Scripture is the word of God. . . . The Bible is the merciful gift of God." Hjertrud said such things every day.

That she died was not too bad. Her screaming, and that she did not have skin, were worse.

Because animals died too. On the sheriff's estate they always got new animals. Which resembled one another to the extent that they could be mistaken for one another. And which, in a way, were the same year after year.

But Hjertrud did not come again.

Dina carried around the image of Hjertrud as the split belly of a slaughtered sheep. For a long time.

Dina was very tall for her age. And strong. Strong enough to let go of her mother's death. But perhaps not strong enough to exist.

The others had command of words. Easily. Like oil on water. Reality existed in the words. The words were not for Dina. She was nobody.

*   *   *

24

Conversations about the "terrible thing" were forbidden. But still they occurred. Servants had the right to do precisely that, to talk in low voices about forbidden things. Suitably low voices. When children seemed to be sleeping angelically and one was not responsible for them.

It was said that Long Jaw never again forged ingenious mechanisms for wash kettles. He took the first boat south to Trondheim. With all his unfortunate, clattering tools in a chest. Reports preceded him. About the smith who forged objects that scalded people to death. They said he became a bit odd because of it. In fact, downright dangerous.

The sheriff had the smithy and the washhouse, including the chimney and stove, leveled to the ground.

It took four men with large sledgehammers to do the job. Four additional men carted the stones down to the old jetty, which was a breakwater for the pier. It was now several yards longer.

As soon as the frost left the ground, the sheriff had the plot seeded. From then on, the raspberry bushes grew wild and unrestrained.

During the summer he traveled to Bergen on Jacob Grønelv's cargo boat and stayed away until he had to attend the autumn Assembly session.

So Dina did not exchange a word with her father from the day she scalded her mother to death until he came back from the Assembly more than nine months later.

At that time, the maid told him Dina had stopped talking.

When the sheriff returned from the Assembly he found a wild bird. With eyes that no one could capture, hair that never was braided, and bare feet, even though there had been frost at night for some time.

She ate food wherever she happened to find it, and never sat at the table. She spent her days throwing stones at people who came to the estate.

Naturally, she often got boxed on the ears.

But in a way she controlled people. She could just throw a stone. And they would rush to her.

Dina slept several hours in the middle of the day. In a manger in the stable. The horses, who accepted her, carefully ate around her sleeping body. Or brushed their large muzzles against her momentarily to pull hay from beneath her.

*   *   *

She did not move a muscle when the sheriff's boat landed. Simply sat on a rock, dangling her long, thin legs.

Her toenails were incredibly long, with ingrained strips of dirt.

The servants could not manage her. The child simply refused to be in water. She would scream and escape out the door, even with two people trying to hold her. Nor would she go into the kitchen when anything was being cooked on the large black stove.

The two housemaids made excuses for each other. They were overworked. It was hard to get help. It was hard to control such a wild, motherless child.

She was so filthy that the sheriff did not know how to act. After a few days, he overcame his aversion. Tried to touch her stinking, snarling body to see if he could make contact and turn her into a Christian human being again. But he had to give up.

Besides, in his mind, he saw his unfortunate Hjertrud. Saw her poor, burned body. Heard her mad screams.

The fine German doll with a porcelain head was left lying where it had been unwrapped. In the middle of the table. Until the maid was ready to set the dinner table and asked what she should do with the doll.

"God knows!" said another servant, who was in charge. "Put it in little Dina's room."

Much later, a farmhand found the doll in the dungheap. Ruined almost to the point of being unrecognizable. But its discovery was a relief. There had been anxiety about the doll for several weeks. The sheriff had asked Dina about it. When she gave no sign of knowing its whereabouts, it was presumed lost. Everyone was under suspicion.

When the doll was found, the sheriff took Dina to task. Sternly demanded to know how the doll ended up in the dungheap.

Dina shrugged her shoulders and started to leave the room.

Then she was spanked. For the first time in her life. He put her over his knee and spanked her bare bottom. The hardened, cursed child bit his hand like a dog!

But something good came out of it. After that experience she always looked people straight in the eye. As though she wanted to know immediately whether they would hit her.

It was a long time before Dina received another present from the sheriff. To be precise, the next gift was the cello given at Mr. Lorch's request.

26

But Dina owned a small, shining mother-of-pearl shell, the size of her little finger. She kept it in a tobacco tin in an old shaving box.

Each evening she took it out and showed it to Hjertrud. Who sat with her face turned away to hide her disfigurement.

The shell had suddenly caught Dina's eye one day when she was walking on the beach at low tide.

It had tiny, gleaming pink grooves and was delicately multicolored at the lower part. And it changed colors according to the time of year.

In the lamplight it gave out a faint, shimmering glow. While in daylight, by the window, it lay in her hand like a small star. White and transparent.

It was the button in Hjertrud's heavenly kirtle. Which she had thrown down to her!

It would not do to miss Hjertrud. You could not miss somebody you had sent away yourself.

No one ever mentioned that it was she who started the tilting mechanism on the laundry kettle. But everyone knew. Including her father. He sat in the smoking parlor. Like the men in the old pictures on the walls. Big, imposing, serious. With an utterly flat face. He did not talk to her. Did not see her.

Dina was sent away to a cotter's farm called Helle. They had many children there and not much of anything else. So it was good they got a child in the house who yielded a profit.

The sheriff paid handsomely. In money, in flour, and in the reduced work required of the cotter.

The idea was that the child should learn to speak again. That it would be good for her to be with other children. And that the sheriff would avoid being reminded of poor Hjertrud's death every single day.

The people at Helle tried to approach little Dina, each in turn. But her world was not theirs.

She seemed to have the same relationship to them as she had to the birch trees outside the house, or the sheep that grazed on the twice-mown meadows in the fall. They were part of the physical landscape in which she lived. Nothing more.

Finally, they gave up and went back to their normal routine. She became part of their everyday life, like the animals, which required a minimum of care and otherwise managed by themselves.

She did not accept any of their overtures and rejected every attempt at human contact. And she did not speak when they talked to her.

When she was ten years old, the pastor took the sheriff to task. Urged him to bring his daughter home and give her the proper environment for her social status. She needed both upbringing and education, the pastor said.

The sheriff bowed his head and mumbled something to the effect that he had, in fact, been thinking along those lines himself.

Once again Dina was brought home in a two-seated sleigh. Just as mute as when she left, but with considerably more meat on her bones. Clean and presentable.

Dina was given a tutor who had the dignified name of Mr. Lorch and who did not know Hjertrud's story.

He had interrupted his music studies in Christiania to visit his dying father. But when his father died, no money remained for him to return to school.

Lorch taught Dina to read numbers and the alphabet.

Hjertrud's Bible, with its millions of complicated signs, was diligently put to use. And Dina's forefinger went along the lines like a Pied Piper, causing the small alphabet creatures to follow it.

Lorch brought with him an old cello. Wrapped in a felt blanket. Carried ashore like a large infant in secure arms.

One of the first things he did was to tune the instrument and play by heart a simple hymn.

Only the servants were in the house at the time. But they later told the details to anyone who wanted to know.

When Lorch began to play, Dina's gray eyes rolled as if she were about to faint. Tears streamed down her cheeks, and she pulled at her fingers so the joints cracked in time with the music.

Mr. Lorch stopped in alarm when he saw how the music affected the child.

Then it happened. The miracle!

"More! Play more! Play more!" Dina cried out. The words were reality. She could say them. They existed for her. She existed.

He taught her the fingering. At first her hands were far too small. But she grew quickly. After a while she had mastered the instrument so well that Lorch found courage to suggest to the sheriff that Dina ought to have a cello.

"And just what would the girl do with a cello? She should learn to embroider instead!"

The tutor, who was outwardly frail and anxious but inwardly tough as an unopened nut, modestly pointed out that he could not teach Dina to embroider. But he could, on the other hand, teach her to play the cello.

That is how a cello, which cost many *speciedaler*, came into the house.

The sheriff wanted the instrument kept in the parlor so that visitors could clasp their hands in admiration.

But Dina had a different idea. The cello was to be kept in her room, on the second floor. For the first few days she carried it back upstairs each time her father ordered it moved to the parlor.

The sheriff soon tired of this. And an unspoken compromise was reached. Whenever cultured people or other important guests came to visit, the cello was brought downstairs. Dina was summoned from the stable, bathed, dressed in a long skirt and bodice, and required to play hymns.

Mr. Lorch would sit nervously twisting his mustache. It did not occur to him that no matter how many were in the room, he was probably the only person capable of hearing Dina's small mistakes.

Dina early understood that Mr. Lorch and she had one thing in common. Namely, they took responsibility for each other's inadequacies. This became a comfort to her.

When the sheriff raged above Lorch's bowed head because, after three years of tireless instruction, Dina still could not read properly except in Hjertrud's Bible, she would open the door to her room, take the cello between her knees, and send the notes of her father's favorite hymns streaming down into his office. It had an effect.

That she learned arithmetic very quickly, that she embarrassed the young clerk at the warehouse when she added numbers of several digits in her head faster than he could write them down — these were things nobody mentioned. Except Mr. Lorch.

Each time Dina read her catechism aloud for the sheriff, Lorch defended himself with seeming humility against accusations of being incompetent in his work.

For Dina made up the words she did not know how to read. So the text often was unrecognizable but considerably more colorful than the original.

The servants stood listening, the corners of their mouths twitching, not daring to look at one another for fear of bursting into unrestrained laughter.

"Not arithmetic! That's not natural for a girl! Her younger brother should have learned arithmetic," the sheriff countered in a broken voice. Then he rushed from the room. Everyone knew the sheriff's wife was several months pregnant when she was scalded to death.

To be honest, though, this was the only time the sheriff even indirectly reproached Dina for that.

There was an old organ at Fagerness. Far back in the main parlor. Covered with a jumble of mugs and platters.

It was such a poor organ that Mr. Lorch refused to teach Dina on it. He gently suggested to the sheriff that in a house that had so many prominent guests, from both home and abroad, it might be nice to have a proper grand piano. Which was, in addition, a beautiful piece of furniture.

Moreover, a piano would need to be in the parlor. This would be a way of compensating for Dina's obstinacy regarding the cello.

A black English grand piano arrived at the house. It was a hard, sweaty job to unpack it from the sturdy crate and remove the rags and wood shavings.

Mr. Lorch tuned it, pulled up his trouser legs, which were threadbare at the knees, and slid carefully onto the solid swivel stool.

There was one thing Mr. Lorch could do better than anything else. Play the piano!

With eyes like doves that had just been set free, he began to play Beethoven. The *Appassionata* Sonata.

Dina sat tightly pressed against the velvet back of the chaise lounge. Her feet dangled in the air. Her mouth opened with a deep sigh as the first notes filled the room.

Dina's face was rivers and streams. A loud sound came out of her and knocked her to the floor.

The sheriff ordered an immediate halt. The girl was sent to her room. She was twelve years old and should know how to act properly.

At first Mr. Lorch did not dare to go near the piano. No matter how much Dina begged, scolded, and coaxed.

But one day the sheriff left for the Assembly and was to be away a week. Then Mr. Lorch shut all the windows and doors in the parlor, despite the warm May weather.

Once again he pulled up the worn knees of his trousers and carefully seated himself at the piano.

He let his hands pause for a moment over the keys and then touched his fingers to them with all the love he possessed.

He hoped Dina's reaction to the *Appassionata* would not be repeated. Today he chose Chopin's *Tarantella* and a *Valse*.

But he could just as well have played his entire repertoire. Because Dina wept and howled.

This continued for the whole week. The girl was so red-eyed by the time the sheriff returned that they did not dare to let him see her. She complained of feeling ill and went to bed. Knowing her father would not come into her room. He was deathly afraid of possible infection. He got that from his dear, departed mother, he said. And made no secret of it.

Mr. Lorch had a plan. One afternoon he mentioned it to the sheriff as the two men sat in the parlor and the sheriff talked at great length about the Assembly.

It was a shame about that expensive piano not being used. And did the sheriff think Dina's weeping might stop if she just practiced listening to music? In fact, someone he knew owned a dog that slowly but surely had become accustomed to music. For the first month, the animal only howled. It was terrible. But gradually the dog became calmer. In the end, it would just lie down and go to sleep. Of course, that had been violin music. But still . . .

The sheriff finally confessed to Lorch that he could not stand crying. He had heard enough crying when his wife passed away so tragically. She had screamed for an entire day before she was released. Ever since then, such sounds were very painful for him.

And at last Mr. Lorch heard Hjertrud's story. About how Dina had moved the lever that caused the huge kettle to pour boiling lye over her poor mother.

Mr. Lorch, who was not accustomed to having people confide in him, had nothing comforting to say. He had been in the house three years without knowing why he was teaching a wolf cub.

The sheriff's details sickened Lorch. But he listened with a musician's tough discipline in distinguishing art from sentimentality.

And various ideas went through the tutor's sensitive mind. Some had to do with his belief that the sheriff had accepted the tragedy to a degree. Despite his outer sorrow.

Mr. Lorch ventured to suggest, in a gentle way, that it still would be too bad if no one played that expensive piano. He could teach Dina when the sheriff was not around.

Now that the sheriff had finished his story, cleared his throat, and smoked another pipe of tobacco, he agreed to Lorch's idea.

Afterward, Mr. Lorch took a long walk. Along pale springtime shores. Dry grass poked through the snow, and homeless seabirds soared overhead.

In his mind he kept seeing Dina's hardened face. Heard her glib, defiant mental arithmetic and her frantic weeping when he played the piano.

He had actually been planning to go to Copenhagen that summer to study music. He had saved a considerable amount at the sheriff's estate. But he stayed. A shriveled young man. Who already had thin hair and a worn face, although he was not yet thirty.

He somehow felt a calling.

Dina continued to talk. At first only to Lorch. But then gradually to the others with whom she came in contact.

She learned to play the piano. From Lorch's music. First small pieces and finger exercises. Then hymns and light classical selections.

Lorch was very particular about the music. He wrote to Trondheim, Christiania, and Copenhagen for music that would be appropriate for beginners. This also put him in touch with his old musical friends.

Dina learned to both play and listen without howling like a wolf. And the sheriff's home became known for its music. Visitors sat in the parlor listening to the cello and piano. And drank *punsj*. It was an atmosphere of decorum and brilliance. The sheriff was extremely satisfied.

Mr. Lorch, with his haggard, unattractive appearance, his awkwardness and dull reserved manner, became known as an artist.

Lorch told Dina many strange things from the great world. As well as many stories about music and magic.

One day as they rowed for pleasure on a calm sea, he told her about a man who asked a headless sea specter, called a *draug*, to teach him to play the violin. The music had to sound so beautiful that a princess would weep and want to marry him!

The *draug* agreed to teach the man. And, in return, he wanted some good fresh meat.

The ghost did as he had promised. The violinist learned his art so well he could play even while wearing thick gloves. But then he realized he did not have any meat. So instead he threw a bare bone into the sea.

"Then what happened?" asked Dina eagerly.

"He should never have tried to fool the *draug*. For the ghost sang to him night and day: 'Because you gave me a meatless bone,/You'll play the strings but make no tone.' "

"What does that mean?"

"He became a very good player, but the princess wasn't moved by his music. So he didn't win her hand."

"Why not? When he was so talented?"

"Being able to play music well isn't the same as the art of making sounds that touch people's hearts. Music has a soul, just like human beings. It also must be heard. . . ."

"You have that art," Dina said firmly.

"Thank you," said the tutor with a slight bow. As though he were in a concert hall, with a princess in the front row.

To Dina, Lorch was a person to whom she could turn when anything went wrong. And when she was present, nobody dared to make fun of him.

He learned to deal with her eager caresses and embraces. Simply by standing straight and letting his arms hang at his sides. His eyes were spiderwebs in the brush, with raindrops in them.

That was enough for her.

Mr. Lorch took Dina to Hjertrud's grave. It was covered with lovely flowers. A whole bed, edged with round moss-covered pebbles.

Lorch spoke to Dina in a soft voice and explained things she had never asked about.

That Hjertrud did not bear any resentment. That she sat in heaven and was happy to have escaped this world's hardships and sorrow.

That everything was somehow predestined. That people were tools in one anothers' lives. That some people did things that seemed horrible in their own and others' eyes but that could become a blessing.

Dina turned her moist eyes toward him, as if she realized that she had exalted Hjertrud. In fact, set her free! That she had actually done what nobody else dared, or wanted, to do. Delivered Hjertrud to God the Father in heaven. Where there were no sorrows or servants or children. And in gratitude, Hjertrud sent the fragrance of dog rose and forget-me-nots.

Dina's look made Lorch change the subject. He explained a little breathlessly about the different parts of the flowers.

The summer that Dina turned thirteen, the sheriff came home from Bergen with an unusually well-trimmed beard and a new wife.

He exhibited her with pride, as if he had created her himself.

The "new one" moved into Hjertrud's room after a week. Everyone on the estate, as well as the neighbors, thought it happened somewhat suddenly.

Two maids were assigned the task of removing dear, departed Hjertrud's things and scrubbing the dormer room. It had been closed all these years. Like a chest for which no one had a key and therefore everyone had to forget.

Poor Hjertrud no longer had any use for the room, after all, so no harm had been done. Everyone understood that. But nonetheless, there was something about the manner in which it was done.

People spoke in low voices. Said that as time went on, the sheriff had felt such a need for women that the maids at his estate did not stay long. If they wanted to avoid trouble. So when Dagny arrived in the house, it was not entirely an ill wind that blew no good.

She was a genuine Bergen woman. With three layers of petticoats, a waist as thin as a knitting needle, and hair piled elaborately on her head. She should have been a blessing to them all, but it was not to be that way.

One of the first faces to greet the sheriff's new wife was a homemade plaster mask.

Dina had gone to great lengths. Had dressed up in the plaster mask and a white robe to surprise her father.

She had made the face herself. According to Mr. Lorch's instructions. A cast of his face, which was not wholly successful. It looked more like a dead person than anything Dagny had ever seen. More grotesque than humorous.

The sheriff roared with laughter when the figure appeared in the parlor doorway. Dagny clapped a hand to her forehead.

From the first day, Dina and Dagny waged a cold, implacable war. In that war, the sheriff had to accept the role of intermediary if there was to be any contact between the two females.

I am Dina. Hjertrud has thrown down to me a small button from her coat. Before, she did not like that I had dirty fingernails. Now she never mentions them.

Lorch says I have a gift for calculating numbers quickly in my head. He dictates and I add. Sometimes I subtract digits too. Or divide. Mr. Lorch figures it out on paper. Then he draws a deep breath through his teeth and says: "Prima! Prima!" Then we play music together. And do not read anymore from the catechism or the book of sermons.

Hjertrud's screams shatter the winter nights into tiny shreds that flutter past my window. Especially just before Christmas. Or she pads about in felt slippers, so I do not know where she is. She has been thrown out of her room.

All the pictures are packed away. The dresser has been emptied. The books were placed in my room. They move in and out of the shelves in the moonlight. Hjertrud's black book has soft edges. And contains many adventure stories. I borrow her magnifying glass and pull the words up to me. They flow through my head like water. I get thirsty. But do not know what the words want of me.

Hjertrud has moved out completely. An eagle keeps circling above us. They are afraid of it. But it's only Hjertrud. They do not understand.

Chapter 2

He delivers the innocent man.

— Job 22 : 30

*T*omas! Do you know why the horse has to sleep standing up?" Dina asked one day.

She cast a sidelong glance at the short, stocky boy. They were alone in the stable.

He was a cotter's son, from the home where Dina had stayed for some years. Now he was big enough to earn an extra skilling on the sheriff's estate, besides the labor regularly imposed on a tenant farmer.

He tossed some fodder into the manger and let his arms fall to his sides.

"Horses always sleep standing up," he said.

"Yes, but don't they also stand up when they're awake?" asked Dina with her peculiar logic, as she jumped into the warm horse manure and began pressing it between her bare toes like greasy worms.

"Yes."

Tomas gave up.

"Don't you know anything?" Dina demanded.

"Aww!"

He spit and wrinkled his forehead.

"Do you know that I burned my mother to death?" she asked, looking straight at him.

Tomas just stood there. He did not even manage to put his hands in his pockets. Finally, he nodded. As if saying a prayer.

"Now you have to sleep standing up too!" she insisted, with the strange smile that was uniquely hers.

"Why?" he asked in bewilderment.

"I told the horses what I did. They sleep standing up! Now you know what I did. So you have to sleep standing up too! You're the only ones I've told."

She turned on filthy heels and ran from the stable.

It was summer.

That night Tomas was awakened by someone entering his small room. He thought it was the stableboy, who must have changed his mind about taking the rowboat to go fishing for coalfish.

Suddenly she was standing over him, breathing. He looked into two wide, accusing eyes. Gray as polished lead in the dim light. Set heavily in her head. Threatening to roll down onto his bed.

"You cheated!" Dina accused, and lifted the blanket. "You were supposed to sleep standing up!"

She looked at the boy's naked body, which he instinctively tried to cover with his hands.

"You're funny-looking!" she decided. Pulled the blanket off him completely and began to examine his inner thighs.

He defended himself with an embarrassed grunt and reached out an arm for the trousers hanging at the edge of the bed. Before he knew it, he was standing in the middle of the floor. Then she was gone. Was it all just his imagination? No. Her smell remained. Like wet lambs.

He did not forget the experience. Sometimes he awoke in the middle of the night, certain that Dina was in the room. But he never had any proof.

He could have bolted the door from the inside but told himself that the other fellows would find that strange. Would think he was locking someone out.

The horses seemed to look at him strangely when he fed them. Sometimes, when he offered them bread crusts and they opened their huge jaws with yellow rows of teeth, he was sure they were laughing at him.

She was the first person who had seen him. Like that. Since then, everything was somehow confused.

He began to go to the pond behind the grove. He guessed that she bathed there. Because he suddenly realized he had seen her with wet hair on warm summer afternoons.

He thought he heard something rustling in the haymow during the light summer evenings when he was busy in the stable.

He could swear someone moved in the bushes when he bathed in the pond after evening chores.

One evening he did it! Trembling with chills and excitement, he walked from the cold water to the rock where he had left his clothes. Calmly, not running with his hands in front of him as he usually did. And he had laid his clothes on a rock much nearer the grove. As if he wanted someone to see him.

The wish exploded in him when he noticed that there actually was someone in the bushes. He caught just a glimpse. A shadow! Light-colored fabric? For a moment he scarcely dared to look around. Then, trembling all over, he began to put on his clothes.

The whole summer, she was in his blood. She flowed through all his thoughts. Like a torrential river.

I am Dina. I do not like raspberries. They are picked in the thicket where the washhouse stood. Thickets like that hurt more than nettles.

Hjertrud stands in the middle of the pond, where water lilies are floating. I walk into the pond toward her. Then she disappears. At first I swallow much water, until I notice that she is holding me afloat. Now I can float in the lakes and sea, because she holds me. Tomas cannot do that. Nobody holds him.

Dagny let out her waistband before she had been the sheriff's wife for even a month.

The cook remarked that the sheriff obviously had not spared gunpowder when he fired his cannon. To her close friends, she expressed a hope that he had fired so well that from now on the servant girls would be left in peace. And she would no longer need to find new maids both in and out of season.

The sheriff became downright cheerful. He took strolls through the woods on the estate and held Dagny's parasol high above her head. So high that she complained because sunlight reached her and birch branches tore holes in the silk.

Dina laid traps. After much serious thought.

Sometimes the door to Dagny's room would get locked and the key would disappear without a trace. Only to be found, later, inside the room!

She slipped into the room unseen when Dagny was downstairs, locked the door, and left the key inside. Then crawled through the open window.

She made her body a pendulum, as on the old grandfather clock. After six or seven vigorous swings, she gained a footing in the large weeping birch tree outside.

It was always Tomas who had to fetch a ladder and climb through the pale, valanced curtains to open the door.

Suspicion focused on Dina.

Dagny's shrill, offended voice fell like winter snow over the entire estate.

But Dina said nothing. She looked straight into her father's furious eyes and said nothing.

He pulled her hair and thumped her shoulders.

She denied everything, until he was completely exasperated. And the sheriff gave up. Until the next time.

Sometimes Dagny's book or sewing disappeared. And everyone in the house searched for it. To no avail.

But after a day or two, the book or sewing lay exactly where it belonged.

If Dina said she had been with Tomas or the young kitchen maid, it was so. They lied, for reasons they hardly understood themselves. The boy because, once, Dina had torn off his blanket and seen him naked. And because, since then, he burned with a fire he could not quench. He intuitively knew he would lose all chance of quenching that fire if he denied she was in the barn when Dagny's things disappeared.

Large, long-legged Dina had solid knuckles and a hot temper. She had never used them against the kitchen maid. But still, the girl was afraid.

Dagny gave birth to a son. In contrast to the quiet wedding in Bergen, the christening was a royal event.

For days, the sideboard and the buffet were covered with gifts of silver mugs and silver candlesticks and crocheted blankets.

The maids wondered if they were expected to set the food and serving dishes on the floor.

The child, who was named Oscar, cried a great deal. And that was something the sheriff had not foreseen. His delicate nerves could not tolerate crying.

But Dagny had gained weight attractively and became beautifully buxom and blithe as soon as a nanny was hired. She ordered stylish clothes and children's outfits from Trondheim and Bergen.

At first the sheriff generously denied her nothing. But when the shipments and packages continued to arrive, he grew impatient. Reminded her that their financial situation was not so good at the moment. He had not yet received full payment for the fish he had sent to Bergen.

Dagny began to cry. Oscar cried too. And when the next shipment arrived from Trondheim, the sheriff sighed and kept to himself for a few hours.

But that evening he emerged from his study quite transformed and was like his old self. Those in the main house could swear to that. Because there was a rhythmic creaking in the wooden floor between Mistress Hjertrud's bedroom and the room below.

"They could have waited until we had gone to bed," the eldest maid said, sniffing disdainfully.

However, the sheriff limited himself to the one woman. He left all the others in peace. So they did not complain. Some even found it entertaining to listen to the unmistakable sounds from upstairs.

They had never heard sounds like that in Mistress Hjertrud's time. She was an angel. A saint. No one would ever think she had done such things with the lewd, vulgar sheriff. But after all, they begot this girl . . . this poor Dina, who bore such a heavy sin. What an unfortunate soul!

The women did not feel it was beneath them to talk about dear, departed Hjertrud. In whispers. Yet loud enough that Dagny heard them. But not the sheriff.

They described her. Her tall, proud figure. Her bright smile and remarkably narrow waist. They quoted her wise words.

When Dagny appeared in the doorway, the room grew silent. As if someone had blown out the candles. But by then nearly everything had been said and heard.

Dagny tolerated the portraits of Hjertrud. For several months. One picture gazed at her with a slight smile from the velvet wall-covering above the wainscoting in the main parlor. Another looked at her somberly from the stairwell. And one stood on the sheriff's desk.

But one day she could tolerate them no longer. She removed the portraits from the walls herself, put them into an old pillowcase, and placed them in a chest containing things from Hjertrud's room.

Dina came upon her as she was taking down the last picture from the wall. The moment was an open crock of sour whey.

The girl followed her, step by step. To the linen cupboard in the upstairs hallway to get the pillowcase. Into the dark corner where the Hjertrud chest stood. Dagny acted as though the girl were air.

Not a word was spoken.

They had eaten a good dinner.

The sheriff was leaning back in his green plush wing chair. He had not noticed that the portraits were gone.

Then Dina struck.

She was the leader of an army sweeping across the battlefield. The banner she carried was the old pillowcase with its rattling contents.

"What's that?" asked the sheriff, clearly annoyed.

"I'm just going to hang the portraits," Dina replied in a loud voice, looking pointedly at Dagny.

She stood before the sheriff and drew one picture after another from its hiding place.

"Why did you take them down?" the sheriff asked brusquely.

"I didn't take them down. I'm going to hang them up!"

The room became very, very quiet. The footsteps in the house became mice scratching in the pantry.

Finally, Dagny spoke. Because the sheriff had discovered that Dina's eyes were fastened on her like live coals.

"I took them down," she said cheerfully.

"And why did you do that?"

He had not meant to be so gruff. But something about women irritated him to the bone.

The sheriff believed an unwritten rule: Address servants and women as if speaking to an intelligent dog. If that does not work, "chain" the dog. Then talk to the creature as if to an intelligent horse. In other words, do not raise your voice, but lower it an octave. So it resounds from your chest and fills the entire room.

But he seldom managed to follow his own rule. He did not manage this time either.

"I refuse to explain!" Dagny declared.

The sheriff understood the yelp of a tormented dog and ordered Dina to leave the room.

She took her time, arranged the three portraits at her father's feet, tucked the pillowcase under her arm, and left quietly.

41

The next morning, the portraits were back in their usual places.

Dagny stayed in bed with a headache, so little Oscar had to be downstairs the whole day.

The sheriff grew weary of the quarrels between his wife and daughter. He found himself wanting to be somewhere else. On a solitary voyage in his boat, with a few crew members, his pipe, and a dram. He caught himself wishing his daughter were far away. Married. But she was only fifteen years old, after all.

Future prospects did not look particularly bright either. Not that Dina was bad-looking. She was not. She was tall and solid for her age. Well developed.

But there was a wildness about her that did not exactly attract men who were looking for a wife.

Still, the sheriff did not despair. He took it as a mission. Whenever he met unmarried men from good families, he immediately thought: Could this be something for Dina?

Dagny eventually had enough of being sheriff's wife, mother, and stepmother. She wanted to go to Bergen to visit "her own," as she put it. At that point, the sheriff realized something must be done, and done quickly.

He tried to send Dina to school in Tromsø. But no one who knew the family was willing to provide housing. People offered a multitude of good excuses. Everything from tuberculosis to emigration. And the girl was too young to live alone in a boardinghouse.

It made him furious to think of all those for whom he had done favors at one time or another. Obviously, they had forgotten. He grumbled about this to anyone who would listen.

Dagny declared in exasperation that it was impossible to have "that one" in the house.

So the sheriff's daughter was "that one," eh?! He burned with rage and injured pride. Wasn't she the only girl who could play the cello? Didn't she wear shoes? Didn't she ride better than anyone in the whole parish? Couldn't she add figures faster than the best store clerk? Was there anything wrong with her?

No, there was nothing wrong with Dina, except that she was wild and malicious and difficult to the core!

Dagny hurled her judgment at the sheriff straight between the eyes, and clutched her little son, who was whimpering in fright from all the uproar.

"And who's going to take her mother's place?" the sheriff demanded. By now his temper had reached the boiling point.

"Not me," Dagny replied firmly. She plunked the baby on the floor by his feet and stood with arms akimbo.

At that, the sheriff left. Walked out of the sitting room, down the wide, elegant front steps, across the yard, and down to his beloved storehouses by the wharf.

He longed for Hjertrud's gentle presence and her cool hand on his forehead. Since her death, her reserved angelic serenity had increased, if that was possible.

The sheriff stood in the twilight and prayed that dear, departed Hjertrud would take her daughter, because things were too difficult for him. Surely she saw that. He hurriedly explained that he did not want the girl to die; he just wanted her to learn some good manners.

"Talk to her, please!" he prayed earnestly.

He blew his nose with his monogrammed handkerchief, lit his pipe, and sat down heavily on a mooring buoy.

When the dinner bell rang, he realized he felt hungry. Nevertheless, he waited a long time.

No one could begin the meal before the sheriff was seated at the head of the table. That was the law when he was at home.

Dina did not come to the table at all. She sat in the old birch tree behind the small *stabbur* storehouse. From there she had a falcon's view. And she could easily hear the sounds from the courtyard.

She could sit there unseen.

In the treetop hung Dagny's light-blue knitting. Twisted in all directions, with gaps where the stitches had unraveled.

Her knitting needles lay in the magpie nest high under the *stabbur* roof. They gleamed and glistened when the sun struck them.

Chapter 3

And she said, "I will surely go with you; nevertheless, the road on which you are going will not lead to your glory, for the Lord will sell Sisera into the hand of a woman."

— Judges 4 : 9

*J*acob Grønelv from Reinsnes was the sheriff's close friend. They went hunting together in the winter and traveled to Bergen in the summer.

Nearly twenty years before, Jacob had come from Trondheim to help the widow at Reinsnes, Mistress Ingeborg, with her cargo boats.

At that time, Reinsnes was already one of the best trading centers in the county and had two splendid small sailing vessels.

It was not long before Jacob moved into the large bedroom on the second floor. But Ingeborg married her young seaman all the same.

This proved to be a good choice. Jacob Grønelv was a capable young man. Soon afterward, he applied for an innkeeper's license. And to the envy of many, the license was granted.

Everyone spoke highly of Ingeborg Grønelv. And of Jacob's mother, Karen. The women at Reinsnes had always been distinctive. Although the family lineage had gradually changed, the women were always those one remembered best.

People said you could never walk through the door at Reinsnes without being served refreshments, regardless of your social status. If the women of the estate had any defect, it was that they did not get pregnant every year. On the other hand, they kept their delicate, youthful complexion.

The southwest wind and the great western sea seemed to have cleansed them of wrinkles and old age. It must have been something about the place itself. Because it was nothing inherited. The bloodlines shifted constantly at Reinsnes.

*   *   *

Jacob Grønelv was a hard worker and a man about town. He had come from the outside world with sea winds in his hair. Had married Ingeborg, fifteen years his senior, along with all her possessions. But he squandered nothing.

Since Ingeborg was forty years old when Jacob arrived, no one expected heirs.

But that was a miscalculation.

Ingeborg, who had been barren with her first husband, began to bloom.

Like Sarah in the Old Testament, she became fruitful in maturity. At forty-three, Ingeborg of Reinsnes gave birth to a son! He was named Johan, after Jacob's father.

Jacob's mother, Karen, came from Trondheim to see her grandchild. Before long, she had sent for her bookshelves and her rocking chair and had settled for good at Reinsnes.

No mother-in-law could have been better to have in the house. So the Reinsnes women's rule entered a fine new phase. A gentle, all-incorporating rule. The entire household developed tolerance and good working habits. To be under Reinsnes's domestic discipline was a blessing.

The fact that Ingeborg had two foster sons living with her could have presented problems. But they grew up and conducted themselves well. Niels, the eldest, was dark-haired and serious and managed the general store. Anders was blond, lighthearted, and restless. He sailed with the cargo boats.

Ingeborg negotiated business dealings and divided the work. Always in a congenial manner.

Jacob possessed the legal rights of husband and master, but Ingeborg's talents directed and decided. She asked Jacob for advice. And sometimes she followed it.

Nobody minded that Jacob was actually a stranger. And it seemed natural that he wanted to sail to Bergen with the cargo each year and always liked to be on the move.

Abusive language was never heard between Jacob and Ingeborg. They had separate lives.

Jacob's life was the cargo boats. Anders became his apprentice in everything.

Thus Jacob and Ingeborg each had a foster son. Tasks and responsibilities were unwritten laws. Carefully defined according to what was best for the large estate. Anything else was unthinkable.

The crystals dangling from the chandelier were not jarred by noise and commotion in the house. Voices were calm and cultivated.

Ingeborg's spirit spread even into the barn and the warehouses. Swearing was never heard.

Jacob got that out of his system when he was at sea. It had all blown away by the time he felt the solid ground of Reinsnes under his feet.

Before entering Ingeborg's bed, he always made himself presentable. Both inside and out. And he was never rejected.

Although sometimes he might satisfy his appetite at inns along the shipping lane, he still sought the mature woman on his return to Reinsnes. Was always glad to be home in the high bed with its curtains and white canopy.

People saw a slight blush spread across Ingeborg's freckled cheeks when the cargo boat sailed into the sound. The blush might last for weeks. Until Jacob left again.

Early evenings and late mornings became the rule. But nobody minded the new rhythm. It meant longer nights for everyone.

Jacob Grønelv did not spit in his liqueur glass. Nor did the sheriff.

When the sheriff became a widower, it was Jacob who comforted him. Who introduced him in good society in Trondheim and Bergen. And who arranged a meeting with Dagny.

They were mutually helpful. In business and with regard to women. For a short time, each in turn visited the same bedchambers in Helgeland county, without causing the least disagreement between them.

Then one day Ingeborg died as she leaned down to pet her black cat under the larch tree in the garden. She fell to the ground like an apple. And was no more.

No one had imagined that Ingeborg would pass away, although death regularly visited all generations. At any rate, no one had imagined that Our Lord would deny her the chance to see her son ordained in the church. She who cared about every frail person along the coast and always came to the defense of others.

From the day of Ingeborg's death, the larch tree and the black cat were regarded as sacred relics.

Jacob could not be comforted. He was like many people who are bereaved suddenly. Realized that love cannot be weighed, neither with scales nor with steelyards. It appears when one least expects it.

This realization did not hit Jacob until he was watching over the corpse. He had thought it was a matter of business and bed. Instead it was incredibly much more.

For a year, he tormented himself sleepless and thin because he had never shown Ingeborg his real love.

He neglected his inn and drank more whiskey than he sold. This not only resulted in a poor profit; it also made him listless and indifferent.

The capable foster sons had much to do, but they also had all the power and praise.

People both at home and abroad would surely have found Jacob disgusting had he not been such a handsome man.

He projected an aura of sensuality. It affected every living thing, just as it had affected Mistress Ingeborg.

Jacob was a sailor and a vagabond. And Ingeborg's talents as a businesswoman quickly came to light once she was gone.

The foster sons treaded water and stayed afloat. But soon realized they must either assume the management completely or send Jacob to sea, to do business where he knew the rules. Otherwise their entire enterprise could go bankrupt.

Jacob was tolerated and forgiven. And protected. Even when he carried the canopy bed into the garden one night.

He had drained several whiskey glasses and missed Ingeborg in every way and in every place. Probably thought he would be closer to her in the garden. At least he could see her heaven.

But obviously, heaven did not care about him. Rain fell like cannonballs. And thunder and lightning punished the brave man in the canopy bed.

It had been hard work to dismantle the bed, haul it outside, and then reassemble it properly.

He had not hung the silk canopy. Which was fortunate. The rain was hard enough on the wood. It would have been a catastrophe for the silk.

But Jacob got sober. As if by a miracle.

Chapter 4

The two angels came to Sodom in the evening; and Lot was sitting in the
gate of Sodom. When Lot saw them, he rose to meet them, and bowed
himself with his face to the earth, and said, "My lords, turn aside, I pray
you, to your servant's house. . . ." But he urged them strongly; so they
turned aside to him and entered his house. . . . The men of the city, the
men of Sodom, both young and old, all the people to the last man,
surrounded the house; and they called to Lot, "Where are the men who
came to you tonight? Bring them out to us, so that we may know them."
Lot went out of the door to the men, shut the door after him, and said,
"I beg you, my brothers, do not act so wickedly. Behold, I have two
daughters who have not known man; let me bring them out to you, and
do to them as you please; only do nothing to these men, for they have
come under the shelter of my roof."

— Genesis 19 : 1–8

Whenthe sheriff heard about the canopy bed being dragged outside,
he decided to invite his friend to Fagerness. They would hunt, play
cards, and have a few drams together.

The widower arrived at Fagerness in a white boat with a deckhouse
and blue railings.

The air had an autumn crispness, but during the day the weather
was warm and pleasant. Ptarmigans had been sighted. Motley, as was
to be expected so early in the fall. And since there was no snow, the
men expected hunting to be poor.

But that did not matter.

Their meeting was warm and friendly.

Jacob praised Dagny's dress, her hair, her figure, and her embroidery. He praised the food, the liqueur, the warmth of the stove,
and the hospitality. He smoked cigars and did not bother anyone with
talk about himself and his unhappy situation.

Dagny joined the men after dinner and vivaciously described the

48

Swedish man who had visited them for a week. He had scurried around studying birds, for whatever good that might do.

"Didn't you have a wild bird in your house last year?" asked Jacob with careless good humor.

The hosts became uneasy.

"She's probably in the stable," the sheriff replied at last.

"Yes, she was there the last time too," Jacob chuckled.

"It's hard to get her to grow up," said Dagny.

"Well, she was pretty long-legged the last time I saw her," said Jacob.

"Oh, it's not that," sighed the sheriff. "It's that she's wilder and more unmanageable than ever. She's fifteen years old and should have been in school or in a good foster home. But that's just asking for trouble. . . ."

Jacob was about to remark that being motherless could not be easy, but he refrained. That would not be an appropriate thing to say.

"But doesn't she eat?" he wondered, glancing into the dining room, where the maids were clearing the table.

"She eats in the kitchen," replied the sheriff with some embarrassment.

"In the kitchen!"

"She always causes so much trouble," explained Dagny, and cleared her throat.

"Besides, she enjoys being in the kitchen," the sheriff added quickly.

Jacob glanced from one to the other. The sheriff felt uncomfortable. They turned to other subjects. But the atmosphere was not the same.

Mr. Lorch said nothing. He had an ability to be invisible and not present. It caused both irritation and pleasure.

This particular evening it made the sheriff break out in a cold sweat.

Jacob and the sheriff went hunting at daybreak.

Dagny demanded that Dina get dressed properly and play the cello after dinner, threatening dire consequences if she disobeyed. For some reason, which could only have been Lorch's master strategy, Dina did as she was told. Despite the fact that Dagny had given the order. She even endured sitting at the table with the adults.

The men were in good humor and helped themselves to the lamb roast. Wine flowed. There was laughter and conversation.

Mr. Lorch did not join in the masculine topics of conversation. Hunting was not his strong point. He was a scholarly man and a good listener.

The men held forth at great length about the hunter's excitement.

Then they remarked that perhaps hard times had ended here in the north. The price of dried cod had risen. In fact, the price of raw fish had risen two *speciedaler* per *storhundre*.

The dried-cod business was booming, said the sheriff. He was planning to clear his hills for drying racks all the way to the moors. The heather cover was so thin that he could hire children to do the clearing if necessary.

Jacob did not know anything about dried cod.

"But the hills at Reinsnes are marvelous! You have hills all around you!"

"That may be, but it takes people to do the work," Jacob noted. He clearly had no intention of getting involved in such a thing.

"I'm better off in ship chandlery and small cargo trade," he insisted.

"But you'd increase your profit if you made the products yourself instead of buying them."

Dina, following the conversation, noticed only facial expressions and voices. What was said was not very important.

She sat opposite Jacob and stared openly at the "old widower." Otherwise she ate her dinner with surprisingly good manners.

Her firm young body was decently fitted into a bodice and a long skirt.

"You've turned gray, Mr. Grønelv," she observed in a loud voice.

Jacob was obviously embarrassed, but he laughed.

"Dina!" said Dagny, quietly but sternly.

"Is there anything wrong with having gray hair?" Dina asked stubbornly.

The sheriff, who knew this could be the beginning of a quarrel, hastily gave a brisk order, even though they had not yet eaten dessert:

"Go and get your cello!"

Dina obeyed without protest.

Mr. Lorch hurried to seat himself at the piano. He held his hands and body over the keys for the minutes it took Dina to find her correct position.

The bordered green velvet skirt divided itself as she placed the cello between her knees. This was no womanly gesture. Neither neat nor elegant. A heavy sensuality filled the room.

It blurred Jacob's vision.

Two buxom young breasts presented themselves as she leaned over the instrument and drew the bow.

Her face became tranquil beneath the dark, unruly shock of hair. Which was more or less brushed and free of straw dust for this occasion. Her large, slightly greedy, girlish mouth was half open. Her eyes looked past everything. Dully.

Jacob had felt a hard pulse in his groin when she leaned forward and began to play. He knew what it was. Had certainly felt it before. But this was more powerful than anything he could remember. Perhaps because it came so unexpectedly?

Jacob's head became a swallows' nest, all the eggs shattered by the music. Yokes and whites ran down his cheeks and neck. Instinctively he leaned forward, letting his cigar go out.

Dina's clothing was suddenly thick foliage covering a young woman's body. That the same woman had certain problems interpreting Schubert to Mr. Lorch's satisfaction was far beyond Jacob's reality. He saw the fabric in her skirt quiver over her thighs as the notes trembled.

Jacob became the strings under her fingers. The bow in her soft, strong hand. He was the breath beneath her bodice. He rose and sank with her.

That night, Jacob Grønelv could not sleep. It was all he could do to keep from rushing naked into the frosty night to put out the torch.

One door away lay Dina. He undressed her with all the ardor he possessed. Was about to burst with the image of her large young breasts. With the picture of her knees hospitably spread wide, the brightly lacquered instrument between them.

All night long, Jacob Grønelv did not know what to do with himself.

He was to leave the next morning.

When the boat was ready to sail, he took the sheriff aside and said with a determined look:

"I must have her! I . . . I must have Dina . . . as my wife!"

The final words came out as if he had just then discovered that this was the only solution.

He was so distraught about how to present his message that he forgot to speak civilly. The words stumbled out of his mouth as though

51

he had never heard them. Everything he had decided to say was forgotten.

But the sheriff understood.

As Jacob's boat left the shore, snow began to fall. Very gently at first. Then heavily.

The next day, Dina was summoned to the office and informed that Jacob Grønelv wanted to marry her as soon as she turned sixteen.

Dina stood with trembling knees in the middle of the room, wearing her old homespun trousers. She had already created a pool of melted snow, manure, and straw on the floor.

When her father called her into the office she had thought she was going to be reprimanded for her latest trick on Dagny or for letting her little half-brother into the pigsty earlier that day.

She no longer had to look up when she talked with her father. She was as tall as he.

She gazed at him as though observing that his hair was rather thin or that he needed a new vest. The sheriff's waist had grown large during the past year. Life had been good to him.

"You've gained weight! You've gotten fat, Father!" she said matter-of-factly, and was about to leave.

"Didn't you hear what I said?"

"No!"

"Jacob owns the best trading center in the area. He has two cargo boats!"

"He can wipe himself front and back with his cargo boats!"

"Dina!"

The sheriff roared. Set off an echo that rang from rafter to rafter, room to room, throughout the house.

At first he tried gentle words, a form of mediation. But Dina's raucous response was more than he could tolerate.

The slaps resounded loudly.

What no one saw was that the slaps came from both sides. Dina went after her father at the first blow. With the fury of someone who had nothing to lose. Who did not care about limits. Was not restrained by either fear or respect.

The sheriff emerged from the office with a gash on his cheek and a torn vest. He staggered to the little outhouse with the heart on the door and thought he was about to end his days, the victim of an overexerted heart.

His breathing came in heaves and gasps.

A loud whinny and hooves thundering against the ground did not make things better.

It was hard to be the father of a devil.

He never admitted it to a living soul. His grown daughter had given him quite a battle.

They were more or less equal. What Dina lacked in brute strength was more than compensated for by her teeth and nails, her vicious tactics, and her physical agility.

The sheriff could not understand what he had done to deserve such a fate. As if things were not already bad enough. A child who hit her father! Oh, God!

To tell the truth, it was the first time anyone had laid a hand on the sheriff. He had grown up with an authoritarian but loving and absentminded father and had been his mother's only son.

He was not a hard man. Now he sat in the outhouse and wept.

Meanwhile, Dina galloped along the rocky beach and across the heath to the other side of the mountain.

Intuitively, she sensed the right direction.

Late that afternoon, she rode down the steep slope to Reinsnes.

The path zigzagged among large rocks, shrubs, and clumps of juniper. A bridge spanned the swiftly flowing autumn river. Here and there, the path was reinforced with stones to protect it against spring floods.

Clearly, the best approach to Reinsnes was by boat. The slope was so steep that from the top it appeared there was nothing but sea below.

On the opposite side of the broad sound, a somber ridge of mountains rose toward the sky.

But to the west, the sea and sky offered all the freedom an eye could need.

As she descended farther, the fields spread out to the left and right. Flanked by luxuriant birch forest and the pounding gray sea.

Far in the distance, the sea and sky merged in a way she had never seen.

When she rode out of the last crevice, she reined in her horse.

The white buildings. There must be at least fifteen! Two piers and two warehouses. This estate was much larger than the sheriff's!

Dina tied her horse to the white picket fence and paused to look at a small octagonal summerhouse with stained-glass windows. Each corner was decorated with elegant carvings, and Virginia creeper arched over the front door.

The entrance to the main house was solid and imposing, with ornate leaf carvings above the doorway. Its broad slate steps had wrought-iron railings and a pair of facing benches by the door.

It gave such a lavish impression that Dina took the path leading to the kitchen entrance.

She asked a shy, bewildered maid if Mr. Grønelv was at home.

Jacob Grønelv sat dozing in his large rococo chair by the iron stove in the smoking parlor. His vest was unbuttoned, his shirtfront missing. His curly graying hair was rumpled and hung down on his forehead. And his mustache drooped.

But he was not conscious of his appearance when he saw Dina standing in the doorway.

She came straight out of his wildest dreams. Albeit without her bodice or her cello. She was already fluttering in his veins. So it took a moment before he realized that she was actually standing there.

Jacob Grønelv's neck and ears turned slowly crimson. The effect of seeing her was overpowering.

His first impulse, before fully awakening, was to take her. Then and there. On the floor.

But Jacob had a sense of propriety. Moreover, Mother Karen might come into the room at any moment.

"Father says we have to get married!" she hurled at him without saying hello. Then she pulled off her sheepskin cap with a boyish movement and added:

"It's not going to happen!"

"Won't you please sit down?" he said, getting to his feet.

He cursed the sheriff's manner. The girl had undoubtedly been frightened out of her wits by commands and harsh words.

Jacob reproached himself. He should have said that he would ask her himself first.

But it had happened so suddenly. And since then, he had thought of nothing else.

"Your father surely didn't say we have to get married. Didn't he say I wanted you to be my wife?"

A sudden uncertainty crossed her face. A kind of precocious curiosity.

Jacob had never seen anything like it. It made him awkward and young. He gestured again toward the chair in which he had been sitting. Helped her remove her jacket. She smelled of fresh sweat and heather. Had small droplets on her hairband and upper lip.

Jacob smothered a sigh.

Then he ordered coffee and cookies to be served and said they were not to be disturbed otherwise.

With controlled calm, as if Dina were a business partner, he took a chair and seated himself opposite her. Expectantly. He was careful to look into her eyes the whole time.

Jacob had done this before. But not since he proposed to Ingeborg had so much been at stake.

The whole time they were drinking coffee, which Dina slurped from the saucer, angry furrows remained between her eyebrows.

She had partially unbuttoned her heavy cardigan, and the front of her outgrown blouse could not keep her breasts or his gaze in place.

Jacob dutifully sent for Mother Karen and introduced Dina. The sheriff's daughter. An unkempt figure who had ridden across the mountain with a message from her father.

Mother Karen looked at Dina through her monocle and a veil of goodwill. She clapped her hands and ordered the maids to prepare the south dormer room. Warm water and clean sheets.

Jacob wanted to show her the entire estate. Needed to have her to himself.

He looked at her. Spoke earnestly in a low voice. About everything he would give her.

"A black horse?"

"Yes, a black horse!"

Jacob showed her the stable. The warehouses. The store. Dina counted the trees along the avenue.

Suddenly she laughed.

Early the next morning, a hired man was sent back across the mountain with Dina's horse.

Before Jacob loosed the moorings of his boat to bring her home, they were agreed. They would get married.

On the sheriff's estate, everything was in an uproar. No one had any idea where Dina could have gone.

They had searched the surrounding area on horseback. When the hired man from Reinsnes came with his message and Dina's horse, the sheriff fumed in relief and rage.

But when Jacob Grønelv's boat beached at high tide and Dina jumped ashore with the manila hawser, the sheriff became calm.

I am Dina. Reinsnes is a place where the sea and the sky become one. A line of twelve tall rowan trees leads from the store to the main house. In the garden is a big chokecherry tree that one can climb. There is a black cat. And four horses. Hjertrud is at Reinsnes. Under the infinitely high roof of the washhouse.

Wind. There is always the sound of wind.

The wedding would take place in May, before the cargo boats headed south.

On the sheriff's estate, trunks and chests were filled with the trousseau.

Dagny busily rushed here and there with flushed cheeks. Packed and gave orders. The women sewed and knitted and made lace.

Dina usually stayed in the barn and stable, as if all the activity had nothing to do with her.

Her hair absorbed the strong animal scents. You could smell them from far away. She bore the stable odors like a shield.

Dagny warned her that a young woman who was to be mistress of Reinsnes must not smell bad, but the reprimand evaporated like rain on sun-warmed rocks.

Dagny took her aside in a motherly way to confide what life would be like as a married woman. Began cautiously with the fact that she menstruated each month. Said that it was a duty and a joy to be a wife and mother.

But Dina showed little curiosity, seemed almost condescending. Dagny had the unpleasant feeling that the girl was watching her surreptitiously during the explanation, and that she knew more than Dagny about the hardships of life.

Each time she saw Dina unfasten her skirt and climb the large birch tree by the *stabbur*, Dagny could not understand how a fifteen-year-old girl could be so incredibly childish and yet have such a poisoned mind.

This girl was not the least coquettish, did not realize the impression she made on people. She still handled her body as though she were six years old. She showed no diffidence in her attire or her remarks.

To marry off someone like that was not quite right. That much Dagny understood. But to tell the truth, she did not know who would suffer most: Dina or Jacob.

She allowed herself the luxury of malicious pleasure. And she eagerly awaited the day when, at last, the estate would be hers. Without the strife and stress of having this crazy girl in the house.

But she hid her relief at Dina's approaching departure behind fevered activity and concern. And thus she salved her conscience with self-pity, as women do.

The sheriff had been in excellent humor since the day Jacob arrived in his boat with Dina aboard. Everything had turned into a blessing, the sheriff said.

He mentioned this over and over again. It did not occur to him that he placed his own interests above concern for his only daughter. She would marry the best possible husband.

Yet oddly enough, he sometimes worried that he might be doing his best friend an unintentional disservice by giving Dina to him. Jacob was basically a good fellow. . . . But since the man wanted this marriage, he would certainly manage.

Without realizing it, the sheriff felt grateful for the mountains and air and long coastline between Reinsnes and Fagerness.

Mr. Lorch was sent south. To Copenhagen. At the sheriff's expense. The tutor had received unmistakable indications that he was no longer needed. They were as good as a letter of dismissal.

It made little difference that Dina flew into a rage and slashed her father's elegant Louis XVI card table with a knife. The sheriff gave her a sound scolding. But he did not hit her.

During the years Lorch was charged with Dina's education, she had received a thorough knowledge of music and learned to play the piano and cello. "Her piano playing is still somewhat inferior, considering her ability. But her performance on the cello is most satisfactory for an amateur," he wrote in his final report for the sheriff.

The report could serve as a certificate, should that prove necessary. It stated that Dina had received suitable instruction in both modern and ancient history. She had learned German, English, and

Latin to some degree. But did not show much interest in these subjects. On the other hand, she had an impressive intellectual bent for mathematics. She could add and subtract five- or six-digit numbers rapidly and easily, and also multiply and divide multidigit numbers.

The report did not contain much about Dina's reading ability. It simply noted that she had no patience for this pastime. On the whole, she preferred things she could do in her head.

"She can recite almost the entire Old Testament by heart," Lorch added as a mitigating factor.

On several occasions he mentioned to the sheriff that Dina might need glasses. She should not have to squint each time she opened a book or wanted to see something at close range.

But for some reason, the sheriff forgot that comment. A young girl with a monocle was too unappealing.

When Mr. Lorch left, with his cello packed safely in cotton blankets and his modest belongings in a cardboard suitcase, the sheriff's estate seemed to lose its spice.

There were many small details about this dry, quiet man that one did not notice when he was present. But they were evident as soon as he had gone.

Dina did not enter the house for three days. And for long afterward she lived and slept in the stable. She grew even taller. Within a month, her face had become pinched and thin. As though Lorch had been the last human being to be taken away from her.

She would not talk even to Tomas. Regarded him like dung and air in an old sheepskin.

But no one reproached Dina, since things were more peaceful for Dagny when the girl was not in the house.

Now and then the cook stood in the doorway and beckoned to Dina. As if to a stray dog. Except this creature was not so easily enticed.

She wandered around like a wolf. Trying to conjure up Lorch. He was there. In the air she inhaled. In the fragile sounds of nature. Everywhere.

I am Dina. When I play the cello, Lorch sits in Copenhagen, listening. He has two ears that hear all music. He knows all the musical notes in the world. Better than God. Lorch's thumb is bent and completely flat from pressing the strings. His music is in the wall. One needs only to free it.

*　　*　　*

"What can you do with a child who isn't afraid of punishment?" the sheriff asked the pastor who confirmed Dina.

"The Lord has His ways," said the pastor expressively. "But those ways are beyond an earthly father's domain."

"You understand that it's difficult, Pastor?"

"Dina was a headstrong child and is a headstrong young woman. She may need to bow her head deeply in the end."

"But she isn't a bad girl?" the sheriff asked earnestly.

"Our Lord must be the judge of that," replied the pastor. He had taught her in confirmation class and preferred not to pursue the subject.

She was confirmed in 1841, although she was not questioned about mathematical formulas or asked to figure the sheriff's business profits.

It was good to get that accomplished. For the next spring she became a bride.

Chapter 5

A prudent man sees danger and hides himself;
but the simple go on, and suffer for it.

— Proverbs 22 : 3

Dina's marriage to Jacob took place at the end of May the year she
turned sixteen in July.

She sailed from Fagerness to the church in an outrigger decorated
with leafy branches. In bright sunshine across a gentle sea. Nonetheless, sitting on a wolfskin the sheriff had bought in Russia, she
shivered with cold.

At the church they dressed her in Hjertrud's white muslin bridal
gown trimmed with narrow lace. The draped skirt had four wide rows
of cording at the bottom. Lacework in the shape of a heart was sewn
across the front of the fitted bodice. The delicate puffed sleeves were
transparent as a spiderweb.

The gown smelled of moth repellent and storage, despite having
been carefully washed and aired. But it fit exactly.

Although they had dressed her in a bridal gown and sent all her things
to Reinsnes in trunks and chests, she acted as if the whole thing were
a game.

She shook herself and stretched, she laughed at them as they
dressed her. Just as when she and Lorch had played theatrical games
with plaster-of-Paris masks and memorized lines.

She had the body of a well-developed animal. The day before the
wedding, she climbed the large birch tree and sat there a long time.
And she had two skinned knees because she had fallen while running
on the rocky beach looking for seagull eggs.

The bridegroom arrived in a longboat with a large company and much
commotion.

Forty-eight years old, with a graying beard, he looked younger than Dina's father, although he was older. The sheriff had grown stout from alcohol and good living, whereas Jacob was still lean.

They had decided to celebrate the wedding at Reinsnes. Because it was closer to the church and had more space for guests. Besides, they had the best cook in the parish. Oline.

It was a lively wedding.

After dinner, the groom wanted to show his bride the house. Upstairs. Show her the master bedroom with the wonderful canopy bed. He had ordered a new canopy and bed curtains. Above the wainscoting there was new velvet wallcovering with a vinelike border. She had to see the small alcove and the bookshelves with glass doors. Which had a key to turn and then hide in a Chinese vase on the writing table. The linen cupboard in the wide, dark upstairs hallway. The stuffed male ptarmigan. Shot by Jacob himself. Stuffed in Copenhagen and carried in a hatbox by Mother Karen. But first and foremost: the master bedroom and the canopy bed. With trembling hands, he turned the key in the lock. Then he walked over to her with a smile and pressed her against the bed.

It had long been an obsession. To find her opening. Penetrate her.

He tugged at the hooks in the bridal gown.

Breathing heavily, speaking childishly and incoherently, he told her she was the loveliest creation in Jacob Grønelv's life.

At first she appeared to be somewhat curious. Or she wanted to protect Hjertrud's dress from the man's greedy hands. At any rate, the dress came off.

But suddenly the bride seemed unable to make Jacob's words correspond to his actions.

She went at him tooth and claw. And she had brass tips on her silk shoes. It was a wonder that her kicks did not debilitate him for life.

"You're worse than a stallion," she hissed. Tears and mucus ran down her face.

Clearly, she knew what a stallion could do.

She was already in wild flight toward the door when Jacob realized her intentions. The moment he understood what was happening, all his rutting instincts evaporated.

For a while, they stood breathing hard, measuring each other's strength.

She refused to put on the clothes Jacob had torn off her.

He had to pull on her pantalets with as much force as when he tried to remove them. And the ribbons on one leg got torn. He was very clumsy.

Despite all his efforts, the terrible thing happened. She finally wrenched herself free and fled downstairs. To the sheriff and all the guests. Wearing nothing more than underclothes, silk stockings, and silk shoes.

It was the first time he sensed that Dina had no limits. That she did not fear other people's judgment. That she swiftly added up the balance sheet — and acted! That she had an inborn ability to ensure that any calamity that struck her would strike others too.

This first time, he became sober immediately. Somehow she made him a criminal on his own wedding day.

Dina came rushing down the stairs, making an extraordinarily loud racket. She ran through the rooms wearing only pantalets, past thirty pairs of eyes that stared at her aghast.

She knocked the *punsj* glass from the sheriff's hand, splattering its contents and causing unpleasant stains. Then she climbed into his lap and declared loudly and clearly, so everyone could hear:

"We're going home to Fagerness. Right now!"

The sheriff's heart skipped several beats. He asked the maid to put the bride in "proper condition" again.

He was furious, because he realized Jacob had shown no restraint, had not waited until the bridal night, after people had properly gone to rest. He was furious at Dagny, who had not told the girl what was expected of her. She had promised to do so. He was furious at himself for not anticipating that Dina would act exactly as she had. Now it was too late.

Brusquely, the sheriff swept Dina out of his lap and straightened his shirtfront and tie. Both were dotted with *punsj* stains.

Dina stood there wild-eyed, like a trapped animal. Then she ran into the garden. Quick as a lynx, she climbed the large chokecherry tree by the summerhouse.

And there she stayed.

By now Dagny was weeping openly. The guests sat or stood, immobile as statues. No one had moved since Dina rushed into the room. And they had forgotten they knew how to speak. Fortunately, the pastor was already out on the sound and could not see or hear anything.

Only the sheriff showed some practical sense. He went outside and bellowed abusive words at the tree where the white, thinly clad figure sat.

What was to have been a celebration and a triumph, when the sheriff gave his daughter to his best friend, became a nightmare.

Later, after the servants and guests had gathered under the choke-cherry tree in the garden, the bridegroom and master of Reinsnes came downstairs.

He had allowed himself plenty of time to tidy his clothes and hair and beard. Feared the worst. From fatherly rage to icy condescension from all the prominent guests.

He had observed parts of a threatening picture from the bedroom window. Behind the curtains.

A blush of shame spread across his face. His organ hung helplessly in his trousers when he met Mother Karen's worried eyes on the stairs.

She had remained at a dignified distance from the spectacle around the tree and was on her way upstairs to find her son.

Jacob looked at the group under the chokecherry tree. Dina was a large white bird with dark drooping feathers on her head.

He stood on the wide flagstone steps with wrought-iron railings and saw a picture unlike anything he had ever seen. It was incredible! The clump of people milling around the tree. The sheriff's shouts and gestures. The evening sun through the thick green foliage. Daisies in a heart-shaped bed. The girl in the tree. As though she had been sitting there a thousand years and intended to remain for years to come. She looked down at the people as if watching a bothersome caravan of creeping ants. Jacob began to laugh.

He was still laughing as he brought a ladder from near the barn and ordered everyone into the house so he could work in peace. Had forgotten he should be ashamed. Chuckling, he waited until the last guest disappeared inside.

Then he leaned the ladder against the tree and climbed up.

"Dina," he called. Slowly and bubbling with laughter. "Won't you come down to this bad billygoat of a man? I'll carry you into the house as carefully as if you were the Bible."

"You filthy animal!" snarled the bride from above his head.

"Yes, yes!"

"Why do you act like a stallion?"

"I couldn't help it. But things will be better. . . ."

"How can I be sure?"

"I swear it!"

"Swear what?"

"That I'll never force myself into you like a stallion."

She sniffed. It was quiet for a moment.

"Will you witness to that?"

"Yes, by God!" he replied quickly, afraid the sheriff's daughter would demand actual witnesses.

"You swear?"

"Yes! And if I break my promise, I'll die!"

"You're saying that so I'll come down."

"Yes! But you can believe me. . . ."

She leaned forward so both breasts nearly spilled out of her shift. Her dark hair was a tangle of sea kelp whose magnificence shadowed the sky for him.

It occurred to Jacob that he was too old for this bride who fled into treetops. She might demand more stamina than he possessed. But somehow he could not confront that. Not now.

"Get out of the way so I can come down," she commanded.

He climbed down backward and held the ladder for her. Closed his eyes and inhaled her aroma as she brushed past him. Close, close.

Jacob was a happy clown. Before God and the wedding guests. For the rest of the evening he satisfied himself with Dina's scent. Still, he felt like one of the Lord's elect. He would get closer, without her escaping into a tree!

The sheriff did not understand much about the matter. It amazed him that his friend was more foolish in dealing with women than in business. He regarded the episode as a painful personal insult against the sheriff of Fagerness.

Widow Karen Grønelv, on the other hand, had serious misgivings. She felt uneasy about Dina's being given the keys to the Reinsnes estate and managing Jacob's home.

At the same time, she was concerned about this girl, of whom she had heard so many strange stories. It was not right that a young woman from a good family was so uninhibited. And had so little understanding of what was proper!

Mother Karen thought Jacob had bitten off more than he could chew with this impulsive marriage. But she said nothing.

Johan Grønelv was twenty years old. Had just arrived home from school to celebrate his father's wedding. He sat in a corner for hours and stared at a crack in the floor.

*   *   *

Jacob kept his word. He approached very carefully. They were to sleep in the large canopy bed in the master bedroom. Everything was ready. Cleaned and decorated. The embroidered sheets had been bleached on the snow in April. Had been cooked in lye, rinsed, and hung on clotheslines in May. Smoothed with a mangle, folded neatly, along with small bags of dried rose petals, and placed in the large linen cupboard in the upstairs hall, awaiting a bride.

Midnight sun and delicate lace curtains. Long-stemmed, glistening green goblets. Crystal carafes filled with water and wine. Flowers in vases and urns. Freshly picked from the garden and the meadows. The fragrance of spring leaves through the window. Distant sounds of mountain winds and roaring rapids.

Jacob used all his wisdom. He approached her with soft down in his hands. First, he took off her shoes, which had caused him such pain earlier in the evening.

He still ached in unmentionable parts of his body. He still sensed the nauseating dizziness he had felt when Dina's shoe hit its target.

She sat on the high, wide bed and looked at him. Braced herself with her arms behind her. Gazed until he began to feel embarrassed. Could not remember the last time a woman had made him shy.

As he knelt at her feet, tugging her shoe, he was once again a clown and a servant. Humbly, he felt his heart skip several beats when she straightened her instep so he could remove her shoe more easily.

What was worse, he had to maneuver her into a standing position to take off her clothes.

The shade was not drawn completely. There was too much light.

And he saw those pale, watchful eyes! Slightly slanted. Wide open, expectant. Far too observant of his every movement.

He cleared his throat. Because he thought she expected him to talk. He did not normally talk with women in such situations.

If only there were winter darkness in all the corners, instead of this accursed light! Beneath her clear gaze he felt naked and on display.

With his forty-eight-year-old body and its ordinary, but very visible, stomach he was as shy as a sixteen-year-old.

The deep lines in his face. His years as a widower, with their worries and carousing. His gray hair. They gave him no experience for moments like this.

Suddenly he remembered that she had noticed his gray hair. The day at the sheriff's estate when he first saw her with the cello between her thighs.

Jacob went to pieces. He hid his head in Dina's lap. Wantonly, and with a certain shame.

"Why are you doing that?" she asked, squirming impatiently.

Jacob lay motionless.

"Because I don't know what to do," he replied at last.

"You were undressing me. You've taken off my shoe. . . ."

She yawned and leaned back heavily on the bed. Which left him lying like a forgotten dog.

"Yes," was all he said, as he emerged from her lap. First just one eye, then his whole gray, tousled head.

He surveyed all the splendors. The hilltops. As she lay there, her skirt sank into the crevices. It drove him wild. But he kept himself under control.

"You're slow," she said dryly, and began to undo her buttons.

He fumbled feverishly. Helped her remove one piece of clothing after another.

The closer he got to her, the stronger grew the smell of stable, hay, and spices.

He stood behind her and gently filled his hands with her breasts. Savored the effect of fabric and warm skin. A breathless moment. Before he took off her dress, petticoats, corset, and pantalets.

Her eyes followed his movements with curiosity. A few times she closed them and sighed. While he summoned all the tenderness within him and gently stroked her shoulders and hips.

Completely naked, she freed herself and walked to the window. Stood there. As if she were from another world.

He would not have believed it possible. A woman, a virgin! Who rose naked from the bed on a light summer night. And calmly strolled across the room to the window!

She stood there with gold on her shoulders and hips. Witch and angel. No one had possessed her! She was his alone! Strutting around in his room, in his house.

The midnight sun turned half of her body to honey as she turned toward him.

"Aren't you going to take off your clothes too?" she asked.

"Yes," he replied huskily.

And one piece of clothing after the other fell in quick succession. As if he were afraid something would happen before he reached his goal.

To tell the truth, it took a while before he reached his goal. He had never imagined it would be like that.

When they were in bed and he had spread the white sheet over them and wanted to press her close, she sat up and pulled the sheet off him.

Then she began an inspection. Greedily, with an air of having found an animal she did not fully recognize.

He got so embarrassed he covered himself with his hands. "It's different from a bull or a horse," she noted with interest. "But the bull's is completely different from the horse's too. It's long and thin and pink. The horse's is a big fellow!" she added with grave expertise.

He felt his lust recede and his maleness burst.

He had never met anyone so completely uninhibited. Images came to his mind. His few times with those who did it for money. But their mating rituals were a matter of time and training. Determined by the payment. He remembered how sad he was to see through the artificial passion and the empty, mechanical movements.

Their eyes had been the worst. . . .

He realized then that Dina — the mistress of Reinsnes — was a child. He was moved by the thought and filled with shame. And excited beyond belief!

It was a long, long ritual. In which she demanded her role. Insisted on playing all parts. Grew furious and punished him by turning away if he did not agree with her ideas.

Sometimes it crossed his mind that this was unnatural, animal-like. Breathing heavily, he comforted himself with the thought that nobody saw them.

And when she showed her pleasure, he took even more time. Played her games. Felt as if they were the first couple on earth. And everything was acceptable.

The graying man fought against tears a few times. It was too much for Jacob. To be a child making love among the trees.

When it came time for him to penetrate her, he held his breath. His rutting instinct was suddenly a black cat sleeping in the shadows.

Amid a crimson fog, he knew: she could utterly destroy him, if she grew to hate his ways. That helped him get through.

She barely moaned, although the sheet was more than spotted.

All the crude stories he had heard about wedding nights and weeping brides were contradicted.

This was unlike anything Jacob Grønelv had heard or seen. Everything he had learned and experienced had to be relearned.

His bride was a young mare. On lush green summer pastures. She pressed him against the fence. Stopped frolicking and drank from the deep pool when she became thirsty. Bit his flanks when he attempted an awkward leap. Until, unexpectedly, she allowed herself to be caught. And with the heavy calmness of a submissive mare, she hunched on her knees and arms. Let the trembling young body be opened, and received his careful thrusts.

Jacob was seized by a religiosity he did not understand. Release would not come. It was not his.

Jacob could not hide his feelings. He wept.

They did not go downstairs before late afternoon the following day. All the wedding guests had left. Including the sheriff and his family. Mother Karen had set a tray of food inside the bedroom door. And said good morning. With a mild expression and downcast eyes.

The servants smiled a little. They had never heard of a wedding night that lasted from two o'clock in the morning until five the next evening.

The reindeer steak was dry and tasteless and the potatoes had cooked to pieces before the newlyweds finally appeared.

Dina was impeccably attired in a new dress from her trousseau. But her hair still flowed down her back like an unmarried girl's. The smiling, freshly shaven bridegroom clearly had problems with walking and with his back.

At dinner they completely ignored Mother Karen, Anders, Niels, and Johan.

Eros dominated the room. Heavy and satisfied, it paraded up the wallpaper, frolicked in the wainscoting, and dulled the silverware.

The bridal pair was visibly drunk before the entrée. Dina had been introduced to port wine before they came downstairs. It was a new game, sweet to the tongue.

Mother Karen's gaze wavered, and Johan's eyes filled with disgust.

Niels stole curious sidelong glances at Dina and ate well.

Anders looked as if he had unwillingly entered a room where he was forced to sit at a table with strangers. He handled the situation best.

Dina had learned a new game. She knew it from the pasture. From the chicken house and from seagulls pairing in the spring. Jacob was her toy. She looked at him with polished glass eyes.

Chapter 6

You will be filled with drunkenness and sorrow.
A cup of horror and desolation,
is the cup of your sister Samaria.

— Ezekiel 23 : 33

As early as March 5, 1838, the steamboat *Prince Gustav* had made its first voyage north from Trondheim. At that time, many thought such a trip was a madman's journey. But miraculously, it became a regular coastal route.

The Lord had a say with regard to the sea's surface. But there were also dangerous reefs. And difficult fjord passages, currents, and eddies. Winds blew in every direction, and passengers did not board at scheduled times. There was also the sad fact that on the Fold Sea and Vest Fjord, nothing, except centrifugal force and the earth's rotation, occurred according to expectations.

Even now, several years later, not everyone along the shipping lane was convinced that the fire-and-smoke-spitting *Prince Gustav* was a blessing.

It could not be right for ships to travel against the wind and currents. Moreover, the steamboat frightened away the fish, according to those familiar with the subject. A conclusion difficult to disprove.

But people did reach their destinations. Those who traveled often praised the steamboat. It was pure paradise compared to an open Nordland boat or a crowded cuddy on an outrigger.

The gentry traveled first class, in the men's cabin with its ten bunks or the women's cabin with five. Second class had an unsegregated cabin with twelve bunks. Third class was on the open deck, where passengers had to manage as best they could among the boxes and barrels and other freight.

But in good weather, the common people in third class also traveled like nobility. Ticket prices were high: twenty, ten, and five

70

skilling per mile. But then, it took only one week to go from Trondheim to Tromsø in the summer.

Trading centers fortunate enough to have steamboat service had flourished during the last years. Despite the fact that, in keeping with Nordland hospitality, innkeepers did not take money for food or lodging when the gentry went ashore.

It might seem surprising, then, that the inns made such great profits. But business in Nordland was a chess game.

The chessmen were always openly displayed. And one could think in peace and quiet while eating and drinking. But eventually one learned that one's opponent also had playing pieces. Which attacked. Nordland hospitality could checkmate, if you were not careful.

One of the first things Jacob learned at Reinsnes was long-range planning. When the *Prince Gustav* arrived with business connections, Jacob was there with the patience of an angel and roast lamb that was pink near the bone. Deep wineglasses and good pipe tobacco. And generous portions of cloudberries brought from the cellar and served in elegant crystal bowls.

Jacob knew why he was grateful to the steamboat.

Dina had never seen such a vessel before her first week at Reinsnes.

She jumped out of bed the first time she heard the ship's whistle. May sunshine filtered into the room, although the shades were drawn.

The strange, hoarse sound came simultaneously from the sea and the mountains.

She rushed to the window.

The dark object glided into the sound. Its red wheel foamed and roared. The vessel looked like a huge, odd cooking stove: nickel and copper stovepipes and cooking pots made in giant proportions and set adrift on the fjord.

The floating black stove appeared to be stoked for all it was worth. It boiled and seethed and surely might explode at any moment.

She flung the window wide open, without fastening the hatch. Leaned out her whole upper body, half naked. As if she were the only person on earth.

People outside could not help seeing the lightly clad young wife in the window. Her bare skin had an amazing effect on them, even from quite a distance.

Their imaginations acted like telescopes. Enlarged each pore and each small nuance of color. The distant figure came closer and closer.

Finally, she plunged into the minds of those who saw her. They lost all interest in the steamboat.

Jacob was standing in the garden. He saw her too. Sensed her aroma. Amid sunshine and wind and the slow rustling of spring foliage. A provocative tingling, coupled with helpless wonder, took his breath away.

Niels and the store clerk had rowed out to meet the steamboat. Niels strictly prohibited boats from surrounding farms to "disturb the channel," as he put it. He did not want any commotion other than what he caused himself.

So when the steamboat whistled at Reinsnes, there was less noise and festivity than elsewhere.

Jacob did not interfere with Niels's discipline of the young people on neighboring farms and estates. Because he knew that Niels's refusal to allow boats on the sound was precisely why people congregated at the Reinsnes wharves to see who arrived and what cargo was loaded. And this, in turn, meant profits and helping hands for the estate.

Today there was not much cargo to unload. Just some sugar sacks for the store and two bookcases for Mother Karen. Then a bewildered-looking man climbed down the ladder and stood in the rowboat as if it were a parlor floor. For a moment, the small craft rocked dangerously.

Then Niels made the man understand that he must sit down so they could get safely ashore with the sugar.

The visitor proved to be an ornithologist from London, who had been advised to stop at Reinsnes.

"The steamboat just deposits people at Reinsnes?" Dina asked in amazement.

Mother Karen had come to the bedroom to help Dina dress more quickly, so she could go downstairs and greet the guest.

"This house is also an inn, as I'm sure Jacob told you," replied Mother Karen patiently.

"Jacob and I never talk about things like that," said Dina lightly, fumbling with the buttons on her bodice.

Mother Karen went to help her. But Dina drew back, as if a flaming cudgel had been thrown at her.

"We need to talk about dividing the household duties," said Mother Karen, ignoring the rejection.

"What duties?"

72

"Well, it depends on what you used to do at home."

"I was in the stable with Tomas."

"But indoors?"

"Dagny was there."

After a slight pause, Mother Karen asked:

"Do you mean you haven't learned to keep house?" She tried to hide her dismay.

"No. There were many others to do that."

Mother Karen brushed her hand quickly across her forehead and moved toward the door.

"Then we'll start with small things, my dear," she said pleasantly.

"Like what?"

"Like playing music for the guests. It's a great gift to be able to play an instrument. . . ."

Dina walked quickly to the window again.

"Does the steamboat come often?" she asked, looking at the black smoke in the distance.

"No; every three weeks or so. It comes regularly from about May to October."

"I want to travel on it!" said Dina.

"You must learn something about housekeeping and responsibility before you start traveling," said Mother Karen, her voice not quite so gentle.

"I'll do as I please!" said Dina, and shut the window.

Mother Karen stood in the open doorway.

Her pupils shriveled like lice in a flame.

Nobody spoke to Mother Karen like that. But she was a refined person. So she held her tongue.

And as if fulfilling a compromise between the two women, Dina played the cello for the household and its guest after dinner.

Mother Karen said they planned to buy an English grand piano. Dina could develop her talents at Reinsnes just as well as at the sheriff's estate.

Niels raised his head and commented that such instruments cost a fortune.

"So do outriggers and longboats," she replied calmly, and turned to translate the remark to the Englishman.

The man gladly allowed himself to be impressed, both by the price of outriggers and by the music.

*   *   *

Johan strolled through the garden with his books strapped together, or he sat reading and dreaming in the summerhouse on warm days. He avoided Dina like the plague.

He had inherited Ingeborg's narrow face. He also had her square chin and eyes that changed color according to the sky and sea. His hair was dark, like Jacob's, and straight, like Ingeborg's. Though still thin and ungainly, he showed good promise.

His head was the most important thing about him, Jacob liked to say with unconcealed pride.

Aside from wanting to be a pastor, the young man had no apparent ambitions. He did not share his father's interest in women and boats. And heartily disliked having the house constantly filled with travelers who came and went and did nothing more beneficial than eating, smoking, and drinking. They had so little education and culture it would almost fit in a schoolbag!

Johan's disdain for people — the way they behaved, and dressed, and moved — was merciless and uncompromising.

To him, Dina became the symbol of a whore. He had read quite a bit about whores but never had any direct contact with them. Dina was a shameless female who made his father look ridiculous and disgraced his mother's memory.

The first time he saw her was at the scandalous wedding. And afterward he could not meet people's eyes without wondering whether they knew, or whether they remembered. . . .

Despite his definite ideas about what kind of person his father had married, he sometimes awoke at night in a strange stupor. And little by little reconstructed his dreams. About riding a dark horse. The dreams might vary a bit, but they always ended with the horse tossing its large head as it became Dina's dark, defiant face. The flowing mane was her black hair.

He always awoke with a start and felt ashamed. Got up and washed himself in cold water, which he poured slowly from the porcelain pitcher into a chaste white bowl with a blue border.

Afterward, he dried himself carefully with the cool, smoothly ironed linen towel and was saved. Until the next time the dream awakened him.

Being a newlywed was a full-time job for Jacob. People never saw him — on the wharves, in the store, or in the drinking parlor. He drank wine with his wife and played dominoes and chess.

At first everyone just smiled. Nodded and said hello. But after a while the people at Reinsnes began to feel bewildered and uneasy.

It started with Mother Karen and spread as quickly as a grass fire.

Was the man bewitched? Would he ever put his hand to honest labor again? Would he waste all his time and energy on marital duties in the canopy bed?

Mother Karen reproached Jacob. Her eyes were downcast, but her voice was all the more determined. Surely he didn't want Reinsnes to fall apart? This was worse than the way he acted after dear, departed Ingeborg's sudden death. Then he had spent most of his time in the drinking parlor or roaming the shipping channel. But this was turning him into the laughingstock of the parish. They were laughing at him!

"As well they should," parried Jacob, and laughed himself.

Mother Karen did not laugh. The muscles in her face tightened.

"You're forty-eight years old," she admonished.

"God is many thousand years old, and He's still alive!" Jacob chuckled and went whistling up the stairs.

"I'm in such a wonderful mood these days, Mother dear!" he called down to her.

Soon afterward they could hear cello music from upstairs. But what they did not see was that Dina wore only her corset, was naked below, and held the cello between her strong, tensed thighs. She played very seriously, as if she were playing for the pastor.

Jacob sat by the window with folded hands and watched her. He saw the picture of a saint.

Many light-years ago, the ubiquitous sun had planned to splinter the air between them. In the cone-shaped beam of light, dust particles stood like a slumbering wall. They did not dare to lie down and sleep.

Jacob announced that he wanted to take Dina to Bergen that summer. The first cargo boat had already sailed. But Jacob's pride, the newest vessel, named after Mother Karen, was to leave at the end of June. Preparations for the trip had been under way since the wedding.

Mother Karen took Jacob aside again and explained that such a voyage was no place for a young woman. Besides, Dina needed to learn some basic things about housekeeping and proper behavior. The mistress of Reinsnes must be able to do more than play the cello!

Jacob thought those things could wait, but Mother Karen insisted.

Jacob gave Dina the sad news and gestured helplessly with his hands. As if Mother Karen's word was law.

"In that case, I'm going back to Fagerness!" Dina announced.

Jacob had learned that Dina always kept her word.

He returned to Mother Karen. He explained and begged. Until she relented.

It soon became clear to Jacob, Mother Karen, and everyone on the estate that Dina had no intention of learning to run a large home. She went riding, played the cello, ate, and slept. Once in a while she came home with a coalfish on a birch branch, without anyone having realized she had been out in the rowboat.

Mother Karen sighed. The only duty Dina performed gladly was raising the flag when vessels approached.

One had to be content with the thought that, as long as Mother Karen remained in good health, things would continue as always.

Before long, it was reported that the young wife at Reinsnes climbed to the top of the tallest tree in the garden to get a better view of the steamboat or to examine the mountains through binoculars. No one had heard of such things before.

People began to question her family background. Her mother had become a saint the day she escaped her pain and her scalded body and died. So they excluded her as a source of unfortunate traits.

But the sheriff's family got subjected to scrutiny and investigation, which brought to light the wildest stories. He was said to have both Lapps and gypsies among his forebears. And apparently some ship-wrecked Italians had dallied with a woman in his family years ago. Everyone could imagine what effect that had on the offspring. Yes, the punishment came now, many generations later.

Nobody could identify with exact names or places those who had had such a fateful effect on the sheriff's daughter. But that was not necessary.

A young woman who climbed trees after she was married, who paraded in nothing but her underclothes at her own wedding, who did not learn to read anything but Bible verses until she was twelve, who rode astride a horse and without a saddle — she must be the legacy of her forebears' misdeeds!

That she rarely exchanged a word with anyone and always appeared in unexpected places was sufficient proof that she was a "gypsy" now, in any case.

*   *   *

Johan heard all these stories. They bothered him, and he was eager to leave home and begin his studies.

Mother Karen helped him assemble what he would need. It was no small task. She packed the items herself and gave orders in every direction.

For two months, she gathered all sorts of things for the boy. Finally, three large trunks stood on the wharf, ready to be lowered into the longboat that would take him to the steamer.

Late one evening, as Johan sat in the summerhouse, he saw a figure walking among the trees in the garden. His whole body broke out in a cold sweat.

At first he thought he had been dozing, but then he realized she was real enough.

It had rained. The branches were dripping. The bottom of her chemise was heavy with moisture and clung to her hips.

He was trapped! With no chance of escape. And she came straight toward the summerhouse. As if she knew he was there. Hidden by hops and lilacs.

She sat down on the bench beside him, without a word.

Her aroma overpowered his brain. At the same time, he shuddered with disgust.

She swung her naked legs onto the garden table and whistled an unfamiliar melody. While she gave him a serious, scrutinizing look. The June light was dim in the summerhouse. Still, he knew he could not hide his reactions from her.

He rose to leave. But her long legs on the table blocked his way. He swallowed.

"Good night," he finally managed to say, hoping she would lower her feet.

"I just got here," she said contemptuously. And made no move to let him pass.

He was a package someone had forgotten.

Suddenly she reached out her hand and stroked his wrist.

"Write when you go south! Tell about everything you see!"

He nodded dully and sank to the bench beside her again. As though she had pushed him.

"Why are you going to be a pastor?" she asked.

"It's what Mama wanted."

"But she's dead."

"That's exactly why. . . ."

"Do *you* want to be a pastor?"

"Yes."

She sighed deeply and leaned against him. He felt her breasts through the damp, thin linen and got goose pimples all over his body. He could not move.

"Nobody told *me* to be a pastor," she said with satisfaction.

He cleared his throat and pulled himself together with great difficulty.

"Women don't become pastors."

"No, fortunately."

It started to rain again. Cautious small drops that fell in gossamer waves toward the lush green grass. The smells of earth and moisture filled their nostrils. And blended with the aromas of Dina. Which were deeply deposited, for all time. Wherever the scent of woman is found.

"You don't like me," she suddenly declared.

"I never said that!"

"No. But it's the truth."

"It's not. . . ."

"Oh?"

"You're not . . . I mean . . . Father shouldn't have such a young wife."

She laughed quietly then, as if she had thought of something she did not want to say.

"Shhh," he said. "People might wake up."

"Do you want to go swimming in the bay?" she whispered, shaking his arm.

"Swimming! No! It's nighttime!"

"Does that matter? It's warm outside."

"But it's raining."

"So what? I'm already wet."

"They might wake up . . . and . . ."

"Do you have someone who'll miss you?" she whispered.

Her whispers took a stranglehold on him. Bent him to the ground. Sent him into the air. Among the mountains. Knocked him onto the bench again with a clenched fist.

Later he could not distinguish between what had actually happened and what was his dream of the horse's head.

"But Father . . ."

"Jacob is sleeping!"

"But it's light out. . . ."

"Come on! Or are you a scared rabbit?"

She got to her feet and leaned close to him as she passed. Turned once and stood motionless for a second or two.

Her face had a sad expression that did not fit with her voice or her movements. She walked into a wall of wetness that absorbed her body and made her invisible. But there was no question which direction she had taken.

He was soaked to the skin when he reached the bay beyond the flag knoll. She stood among the beach rocks, naked. Waded into the water a few steps. Leaned over and picked up something from the bottom. Examined it carefully.

Then! As though feeling his gaze on her hips, she turned and stood erect. She had the same sad expression as in the summerhouse.

He wanted to think that was why he joined her. Removed his shirt and trousers. Embarrassed and excited at the same time. And waded out to her. The water was cold. But he did not feel it.

"Can you swim?"

"No; how do you do it?" he said, and could hear how stupid that sounded.

She came closer. A thundering pressure against his temples threatened to drown him, although he stood only knee-deep in water.

He suddenly realized how ridiculous he looked in his white underwear. Trembling.

She came over to him and held his waist and began pulling him into deep water. He let himself be drawn. Let himself be led so far that their bodies floated to the surface. Let himself be taken beyond the drop-off.

She moved for them both. With calm, rhythmic movements of her legs and lower body. Powerless, he let her keep him afloat. Keep them both afloat.

The icy water, the gentle mist, her hands that changed their grip and held him first in one place, then in another.

The horse from his dream! Dina, whom his father had married. She slept in the master bedroom, in his father's bed. And in the midst of it all, she was another being.

He wanted so much to tell her about the black hole in the churchyard. That had swallowed Ingeborg. And about the father who staggered around half drunk after the funeral.

But he had not learned the necessary words. They were so hazy and warm. Like this night.

He could have told her about the things he should have said to Ingeborg before she died. And about Christmases at Reinsnes. When Mother bustled back and forth. With flushed cheeks. About the needles that stuck him when he lost his mother's attention because his father entered the room.

He could have described to her the sadness that always overwhelmed him when he left home. Although that was what he wanted. To get away from home.

Dina became a Valkyrie from Mother Karen's mythology book. A being that kept him afloat. Who secretly understood everything he could not say.

Out in the deep water, Johan let go. His revulsion for Dina drowned. Her nakedness wrapped itself like a membrane around him.

I am Dina, who is holding a shiny fish. My first fish. Must take it off the hook myself. The hook got bent. My fish is not badly hurt. I will throw it into the water again. Then it must manage on its own. It is a blue day.

They had nothing with which to dry themselves. He attempted an uncertain role, that of a gentleman. And offered his shirt as a towel.

She refused.

They dressed in the rain, shivering and serious.

Suddenly, as if he were ready to board the steamboat for school, she said:

"Write to me!"

"I will," he promised, glancing anxiously at the path to the house.

"I never went swimming with anyone before."

That was the last thing she said before running up the path.

He wanted to call after her. But did not dare. She had already disappeared among the trees.

All the trees were dripping. He hung his desperation on the branches. And everything fell to the ground in wet drops.

"How did you learn to swim, if you never went swimming with anyone?" said the drops. Again and again.

For he did not dare to shout it to her. Someone might hear. . . .

He hid himself in it. Hid the lust that still lay on the ebb tide beach and floated among the seaweed. In the question: "How did you learn to swim?"

But in the end, that was not enough. He crept under a huge rock that had been his secret refuge all through childhood. There he took his stone-hard organ in his hand and went at it. Without thinking about God.

From that day on, Johan began to hate his father. Deeply and intensely. Still without consulting his God.

Jacob awoke when Dina entered the bedroom.

"Where have you been, for God's sake?" he said when he saw the wet figure.

"Swimming."

"At night?" he exclaimed in disbelief.

"There aren't so many people around at night," she said. She left her clothes in a heap on the floor and crawled into bed.

He was warm enough for two.

"Well, my little witch," he teased, half asleep. "Did you see the *draug*, that headless ghost who foretells drownings?"

"No, but I saw the *draug*'s son!"

He laughed softly and sighed about her being so cold. Jacob saw no sorrow. He did not know she could swim.

Chapter 7

Can a man carry fire in his bosom and his clothes not be burned?
Or can one walk upon hot coals and his feet not be scorched?
— Proverbs 6 : 27–28

*D*ina went to Bergen that summer.

Mother Karen realized that Dina's training would not be accomplished overnight, after all. And once the cargo boat was under way, she had to admit she had longed for the peace and quiet. But it was difficult for her when Johan left immediately afterward.

Dina was an unrestrained child who needed to be tended.

More than once she bothered the crew and hindered the work on board with her notions.

Anders took everything very calmly and good-naturedly.

First, Dina brought the sheepskin from the small aft cabin onto the deck. And there she sat, playing cards and singing worldly songs with a foreign fellow who had been hired at the last minute and who strummed a stunted version of a string instrument. The kind Russian seamen played.

The swarthy fellow spoke broken Swedish and claimed he had roamed the world for many years.

He had arrived from the north on a Russian ship one day and gone ashore at Reinsnes. There he had waited for a cargo boat to take him farther south.

Jacob shouted to the helmsman a few times, ordering him to quiet things down out there. But it did little good. He felt like an old sourpuss. And he could not stand that role.

Finally, he came out and joined the commotion.

Jacob ordered the vessel to land at Grottøy the following evening. There they received a warm welcome and good lodging.

Grottøy estate had recently become a stopping place for the *Prince*

Gustav, and the owner had big plans for building a new house, store, and post office.

Among the guests was an artist who was painting portraits of the master and his family. Dina immediately focused her attention on the easel. She scampered around like an animal, sniffing the oil paints and the turpentine. She hung on the painter's every move and practically crawled into his lap.

Her utter naturalness embarrassed people. The servants whispered about the young wife from Reinsnes. And they shook their heads over Jacob Grønelv. He certainly had his hands full. . . .

Dina's familiarity with the artist turned Jacob into a furtive watchdog. He felt ashamed of her indecent behavior.

He tried to even the score in bed. Set himself on top of her with all the strength and righteousness of a wounded, jealous husband.

But such loud coughing came from the other side of the thin wall that he had to stop.

Dina put her hand over his mouth and whispered, "Shhh." Then she raised her nightgown and sat astride her mistrustful Jacob. And led them, more or less silently, into the realms of bliss.

When they set sail again, she remained quietly in the cabin. And Jacob's world became brighter.

They headed toward Bergen, with no further skirmishes.

The throngs of people on the Bergen wharf! The fort, the houses, and the church. The carioles. Carrying elegant men and women holding parasols.

Dina's head seemed to be mounted on the hub of a wheel. She clicked along the pavement in new traveling shoes. And stared intently at each coachman who sat straight and proud with a whip resting against his knee.

The carriages looked like whipped-cream cakes, heaped with light summer dresses, capes, and ruches. And lace parasols. Which completely cut off their owners' faces and heads.

There were gentlemen too. Elegantly attired in dark suits and derbies, or young and dashing, with light-colored suits and straw hats on their foreheads.

An old officer in a blue coat with red lapels leaned against a town pump. His well-waxed mustache looked as if it had been painted on him. Dina walked up to him and touched him. Clearing his throat in embarrassment, Jacob took her arm and drew her away.

Farther on, a sign in a café window offered choice Madeira and Havana cigars. Beyond the curtains they saw a room with red plush sofas and tasseled lampshades.

Dina wanted to go in and smoke a cigar. Jacob followed. Sounding like a worried father, he made her understand that she could not smoke cigars in public!

"Someday I'll come to Bergen and smoke cigars, I promise you!" she declared angrily, and took a large gulp of Madeira.

Jacob bought an elegant double-breasted blue wool jacket with velvet lapels, and checked trousers. He wore a hat as though it were an everyday occurrence.

He spent a long time at the barber's and returned to their lodgings clean-shaven. He had good reasons for shaving his beard.

The hotelkeeper had asked if he wanted two single rooms: one for Mr. Grønelv and one for his daughter. Also, he remembered that almost a year ago Dina had observed he was turning gray. There was no need to have more gray hair than necessary.

Dina tried on hats and dresses with the same deep seriousness as when she had secretly tried on Hjertrud's dresses before leaving Fagerness.

The Bergen outfits did wonders. Dina became older and Jacob became younger.

They were two vain finches who admired themselves in every shop window and mud puddle they passed.

Anders smiled good-naturedly at all their profligate talk about clothes.

Dina estimated and counted, added figures and divided. Served as a living calculator for Jacob and Anders as they decided sales and purchases. She attracted attention.

One evening Jacob was drunk and jealous. She had talked with a cultivated gentleman who treated her with respect because she played Beethoven on the piano at the inn.

When she and Jacob were alone, he hurled at her that if she did not pin up her hair she would always look like a whore.

She did not respond at first. But when he persisted, she kicked his shins so hard he moaned, and she said:

"It's all just Jacob Grønelv's selfishness! You can't bear to have anyone see my long hair. God isn't selfish like you. Or He would stop my hair from growing!"

"You flaunt yourself!" he accused her, rubbing his leg.

"And what if I'd been a horse? Or an outrigger? Would I have the right to be seen then? Am I supposed to be invisible, like a ghost?"

Jacob gave up.

Their last day in Bergen, they walked past a wooden fence that had many notices nailed to it.

Dina was a fly that discovered the scent of a sugar bowl.

A Wanted poster for a pickpocket. The man might be dangerous, it said. Small homemade signs advertised seamstress services or inspirational religious gatherings.

An elderly, well-to-do man wanted a housekeeper.

In the midst of it all was a large black-and-white announcement that a man was to be hanged for murdering his sweetheart.

The picture of the man was mud-splattered beyond recognition.

"That's fortunate for the family," Jacob commented soberly.

"Let's go there!" said Dina.

"To the hanging?" asked Jacob in dismay.

"Yes!"

"But, Dina! They're going to hang a man!"

"I know. That's what the sign says."

Jacob stared at her.

"It's a horrible thing to see!"

"There's no blood."

"But he's going to die."

"Everyone's going to die."

"Dina, I don't think you really understand. . . ."

"Slaughtering is much worse!"

"Slaughtering is animals."

"Anyway, I want to go."

"It's not for women. Besides, it's dangerous. . . ."

"Why?"

"The mob might decide to lynch wealthy women who come just out of curiosity. That's the truth," he added.

"We'll rent a carriage. Then we can drive away in a hurry."

"We won't find a driver who'll take us there to be entertained."

"We're not going there to be entertained," said Dina angrily. "We're going to see how it's done."

"You frighten me, Dina. What do you want to see at such a place?"

"The eyes! His eyes . . . When they put the rope around his neck . . ."

"My dear, dear Dina, you don't mean that."

Dina's gaze floated past him. As if he were not there. He took her arm and wanted to leave.

"How he reacts, that's what I want to see!" she said firmly.

"Is that anything to watch, a poor man in all his misery . . . ?"

"That's not misery!" she interrupted impatiently. "That's the most important moment!"

She did not give up. Jacob realized she would go alone if he did not accompany her.

They hired a carriage and drove to the execution site the next morning at dawn. Contrary to Jacob's expectations, the coachman was not the least unwilling. But he demanded a large sum for staying there during the hanging so they could drive away at the least sign from Jacob.

A steady influx of people gathered around the gallows. Bodies pressed against one another. Tightly. Anticipation filled the air like nauseating cod-liver-oil vapors.

Jacob shuddered and stole a look at Dina.

Her pale eyes stared at the dangling gallows noose. She pulled her fingers, cracking the joints. Her mouth was open. Her breath hissed between her teeth.

"Stop that," Jacob ordered, placing his hand over her fingers.

She did not reply. But her hands grew quiet in her lap. Beads of sweat slowly appeared on her forehead and ran down the crevices by her nostrils. Two strong rivers.

There were no ordinary conversations. A constant mumbling filled the air. An anticipation. Which Jacob gratefully did not share.

He held Dina firmly when the man was driven on a cart to the spot beneath the gallows.

The doomed man did not have anything over his head. Was ragged, filthy, and unshaven. He clenched and unclenched his hands in the shackles.

He was the most down-and-out human being Jacob had ever seen.

His eyes stared wildly at the huge crowd. A priest arrived and said something to the poor fellow. Now and then someone spit at the cart and shouted abusive words. "Murderer!" was one of them.

At first the man tried to avoid the clumps of spit. But before long he seemed as if already dead. He stood passively as the hand and leg irons were removed and the noose was put around his neck.

Many people had pushed their way between the carriage where Dina and Jacob sat and the barrier in front of the gallows.

Dina stood up. Clung to the top of the cariole and leaned over the heads of the spectators below.

Jacob could not see her eyes. Had no contact with her. He rose to catch her if she fell.

But Dina did not fall.

The hangman's horse received a flick of the whip on its flank. The man dangled in the air. Jacob put his arms around Dina. The murderer's twitching was powerfully transmitted into her body.

Then it was over.

She did not say a word as they drove to the harbor. Just sat quietly. As erect as a general.

Jacob's scarf was wet with perspiration. He forced his homeless hands into his lap and wondered which was worse. The execution? Or Dina's desire to watch it?

"He was pretty calm, that fellow," commented the driver.

"Yes," said Jacob dully.

Dina stared blankly into space, as if holding her breath. Then she gave a loud, deep sigh. She seemed to have finished a huge task that had weighed upon her for a long time.

Jacob felt ill. He kept an eye on Dina the rest of the day. Tried to talk with her. But she just smiled with a strange friendliness and turned away.

The second morning at sea, Dina awakened Jacob, and said:

"He had green eyes that looked at me!"

He held her close then. Rocked her, as if she were a child who had never been taught to cry.

On the voyage north they stopped to see Jacob's friends at the old Tjøtta manor. It was like arriving at a king's palace. Because of its elegance, and because of the royal reception they received.

Jacob worried about how Dina might behave. At the same time, he was like a man displaying his rare hunting falcon. People would just have to accept that she reacted if you did not handle her carefully.

Dina did not seem particularly impressed that they were staying at an estate that had housed chief magistrates and members of the Royal Council and that, at its height of prosperity, had been as large as two or three parishes combined. She uttered no polite exclamations about the splendid rooms. Did not remark on the manor house itself, which was two stories high and sixty-eight feet long.

But she stopped each time they passed the remarkable old bautas at the entrance to the main courtyard. Showed almost respect for the tall, rough-hewn stone monuments and wanted to hear stories about them. She ran outside without shoes to watch as the evening light fell on them.

On their first night at Tjøtta, conversation was lively above the *punsj* glasses. The drawing room was crowded with young and old. Stories flew back and forth across the tables.

The host told how Nordland had once fallen into the hands of a powerful seventeenth-century Dane, Jochum Jurgen, or Irgens, as he was also called.

This royal property administrator in Jutland became chamberlain in King Christian IV's court. He was extremely cunning and sold endless quantities of Rhine wine and pearls to the royal household. But the treasury did not have money to pay for it all. So the king gave him all the royal property in Helgeland, Salten, Lofoten, Vesterålen, Andenes, Senja, and Troms — according to the deed of January 12, 1666. To settle a debt of 1440 *vag*.

This was more than half the land in North Norway. In addition, Irgens received Bodøgård manor and the Steigen estate, as well as the king's share of the entire region's tithe.

Dina found this story so shocking that she wanted Jacob to prepare his cabin boat immediately and take her through the district that had paid for the Rhine wine and pearls.

She also devised arithmetic problems for the young girls on the estate. How many flasks or small wine barrels would Irgens's property have been worth? How many large barrels?

But since no one could tell her the exact price of either pearls or Rhine wine in the 1660s, she could not figure the answers to these problems.

Jacob would have preferred to leave on the second day. But their host urged him to remain two more nights, as was customary.

Dina and Anders wanted to stay, so he agreed. Although the mate, Anton, was of the same mind as he.

During the whole trip, Jacob had been on guard about Dina's behavior. This had begun to take its toll on him. The nightly exercises were demanding too.

It was a welcome relief when Dina and the young daughters at Tjøtta spent two nights watching for a ghost.

The ghost usually appeared at night. Dina heard forewarnings. Several people on the estate had seen it. They talked as though this were an ordinary visit from a neighbor.

But Dina's eyes clouded, and her forehead wrinkled as if she had been given a difficult piece of music to play.

The second night, a little child floated through the main parlor and disappeared behind an old clock. The Tjøtta daughters agreed. They had all seen the child. Again.

Dina was silent. So silent it was almost rude.

Jacob felt glad the visit was ended but did not show it outwardly. They had slept three nights at Tjøtta.

On the homeward voyage, Jacob remarked that the belief in ghosts at Tjøtta was very strange.

Dina turned away, stared out to sea, and did not reply.

"What did it look like?" he asked.

"Like most lost children."

"And how do they look?" he asked impatiently.

"You should know."

"Why should I know that?"

"You've had several in your house!"

She was a hissing cat about to attack. The change so alarmed him that he said no more.

Jacob told Mother Karen about Dina's reaction to the alleged ghosts at Tjøtta. But he did not say he had taken her to see a hanging in Bergen.

Mother Karen had her own thoughts, which she did not voice to Jacob. She realized the girl was wiser than she appeared.

"You've had several in your house" was a remark Jacob should have taken seriously, without anyone having to tell him.

Jacob admitted to Mother Karen that he was more tired than usual after this trip.

She did not say it was because he had taken Dina along. In fact, she never made wise remarks in hindsight.

Besides, Mother Karen had concluded that Dina's trip to Bergen that summer had done much good.

The tall girl had a different bearing now. It seemed she had discovered, for the first time, that the world was larger than what the eye could see from the sheriff's estate or from Reinsnes.

Her face had changed too. Mother Karen could not say exactly how. Something about her eyes . . .

Mother Karen usually understood more than she expressed aloud. And she did not repeat to Jacob what she had said when he announced elatedly that fifteen-year-old Dina Holm would be the mistress of Reinsnes.

She just put her hand lightly on her son's shoulder and sighed sympathetically. And she saw that new clothes and a good haircut could not hide how much grayer Jacob's hair had become and that his incipient potbelly had shrunk.

His vest fit as if it belonged to someone else. There were deep wrinkles in his forehead and dark shadows under his eyes. Nonetheless, he was extremely handsome.

Resigned weariness seemed to suit him better than the arrogant manner he had had when Dina first came to Reinsnes.

Calm, heavy movements. The way he drew himself erect. The tall, agile figure so utterly lacking the ponderous bulk that wealthy men his age should have.

Mother Karen saw it all. From her perspective.

Oline moved to and fro in the kitchen. She saw the changes too. Was not sure if she liked this new Jacob, who bore the mark of such heavy responsibility. She did not particularly like Dina either. Oline wished everything had remained as before. Especially Jacob.

Dina wanted to sail the cabin boat throughout Nordland to see what Christian IV had given for some paltry pearls and firkins of Rhine wine.

She could not understand that it was impossible at this time of year.

Jacob said it gently but firmly: No!

He bore her fury like a calm father. And accepted her punishment. It meant he had to sleep in the alcove off the master bedroom, alone.

To be honest, his constant vigilance on the Bergen trip had so exhausted him that he slept soundly on the uncomfortable chaise lounge in the alcove. Secure in his conviction that the storm would clear and everything would turn out for the best. As long as he had health and vigor.

Chapter 8

For a harlot is a deep pit;
an adventuress is a narrow well.
She lies in wait like a robber
and increases the faithless among men.

— Proverbs 23 : 27–28

*T*he new marriage, which began with the sight of two strong thighs embracing the body of a cello and continued with the dramatic rescue of a bride in a tree, lost its glow with a trip to Bergen.

Jacob was always tired. He seemed to have a constant need to be in Dina's world. Never to lose her from sight or let her give too much to others.

He was not aware enough to call it jealousy. Simply knew that tragedy lurked around the corner if he left Dina for too long.

Something always stole her from him! Ghosts at Tjøtta. Painters or musicians. Even a crew member, whom they hired out of kindness because he did not have money for the steamboat, became an impossible, degrading threat.

Dina had played cards and even smoked a pipe with that bearded, unkempt young fellow!

Jacob had a vague sense that his final love would cost him more than he had initially anticipated. Not least, his rest at night.

He even had to forgo his trips along the channel to carouse with blood brothers of his youth. Could not leave Dina and could not take her with him. Her mere presence was disturbing where men were concerned.

She could be as crude as the worst riffraff in the servants' quarters on Midsummer's Eve, and as complicated as a judge.

Her femininity was not even worth mentioning, because it had nothing to do with usual, proper behavior. She moved her large, firm body like a young general. Whether sitting or riding.

The mingled aromas of stable and rosewater she exuded, and

her air of disinterested coolness, made men swarm around her like flies.

Jacob got enough of that on the Bergen trip. It made him sweat profusely and get terrible headaches.

And then there was the music. . . .

For Jacob, it was erotically exciting to watch Dina play, and he grew furiously jealous at the thought of anyone else seeing her with the cello between her thighs.

He went so far as to demand that she keep both legs on the same side of the instrument. That would be less offensive to observers.

Dina's laughter was rare, if not nonexistent. But it rang through the whole house when Jacob — his face as red as a Siberian poppy in August — demonstrated how she should sit. They heard her as far away as the warehouses and the store.

Then she seduced him, in bright daylight, behind an unlocked door.

Sometimes Jacob tortured himself with the thought that she had not been completely innocent the first time. That her utter lack of shyness, her trembling abandon and methodical examination of his hairy body, bore more resemblance to his experiences with professionals than to the behavior of a sixteen-year-old.

The thought tortured him even in his dreams. He tried to question her, letting his words drop casually. . . .

But she answered with sharp slivers of glass in her eyes.

Mother Karen and the foster sons allowed Jacob to be a newlywed until he returned from the autumn market. But then they made it clear, both in words and actions: Reinsnes needed him.

At first, he scarcely paid attention.

Mother Karen called him into her room and bluntly told him she did not know whether to laugh or cry about the life that he, a grown man, was living.

It had been bad enough when he was grieving for Ingeborg, but this was much worse. From now on, he must get up in time for breakfast and go to bed at a Christian hour. Or else she would leave. Because things had gotten completely out of control since Dina came to Reinsnes.

Jacob took it like a son. Bowed his head guiltily.

He had neglected both the farm and the businesses. Dina demanded all of him. The days went by unnoticed, like a circle dance in which Dina's whims, Dina's ideas, Dina's needs, blended with his.

Except for the difference that she was a child, with no other responsibility than to be Jacob's child bride.

Jacob had long felt tired and useless. Dina's ideas had become a strain. Her animalistic mating in the canopy bed, and wherever else it might occur, deprived him of the sleep and rest he sorely needed.

The evening Mother Karen spoke to him, he declined the usual wine and board games in a half-naked state by the bedroom stove.

Dina shrugged her shoulders and filled two wineglasses, undressed except for her chemise, and sat down to play a game.

She played against herself and drank from two glasses. Rattled the stove doors and hummed softly late into the night.

Jacob did not sleep a wink. At regular intervals he gently asked her to come to bed.

But she pursed her lips and would not even reply.

Just before daybreak, he got up. Stretched his stiff body and approached her. With the patience of an angel and the cunning of a snake.

It took a long time to soften her. Three board games, to be exact. The wine had been consumed hours before. He brought a crystal carafe from the night table and poured water into the empty glass intended for him. Then gave her an inquiring look.

She nodded. He poured some water for her too. They clinked their glasses and sipped the tepid contents. He knew she did not talk when her eyes were heavy with wine, but he still made an attempt.

"Dina, this can't continue. I need to get some sleep at night. A man like me has many things to do. During the day, I mean. You should understand that, darling. . . ."

She sat there with her little smile. But did not look at him. He moved closer. Put his arms around her and stroked her hair and her back. Tenderly. He was so tired that he did not dare to start anything that might result in hostility or quarreling. Besides, Jacob was a peace-loving man.

"The party is over, Dina. You must understand that the master and his family have to work on an estate. And then we need to sleep at night, like other people."

She did not answer. Just leaned heavily against him and lay quietly while he caressed her.

He sat there drinking tepid water and gently stroking her until she finally fell asleep.

She had been like a taut spring against him at first, but gradually she relaxed and gave in, like a child that had cried itself to sleep.

He carried her to bed. She was large and heavy. Even for a man like Jacob. It was as if the earth grasped for her and wanted to bring them both to their knees beside the canopy bed.

She whimpered when he pulled himself free and covered her.

It was time to get up. He felt stiff and old and more than a little lonesome as he stole down to all the tasks he had neglected.

Jacob ordered Oline to prepare the bedroom alcove, which had served as a dressing room until now. In it was a cognac-colored chaise lounge with worn upholstery that had fringes missing. He asked for bed-clothes and an extra chamber pot. This is where he would sleep now, he explained. Because his snoring kept Dina awake.

Oline looked at Jacob in surprise at his remark. But said nothing. Just drew her lips into a thin line that sent expressive wrinkles radiating from her strong mouth. So it had come to this at Reinsnes! The master of the house had to sleep on an uncomfortable chaise lounge, while a young girl lay in the canopy bed! Oline snorted and sent the maid upstairs with sheets, a comforter, and down pillows.

The night Jacob moved into the dressing room, Dina began to play the cello about midnight, when everyone was sound asleep.

Jacob awoke with a start, and even before being fully awake he felt a dangerous rage. He strode into the bedroom with blazing eyes, and hissed:

"That's enough! Now you've gone too far! You'll wake the whole house!"

She made no reply and continued playing. So he staggered across the room and grasped her arm to force her to stop.

She jerked her arm loose and stood up, so she was the same height as he. Carefully leaned the cello against the chair and laid down the bow. Then she put her hands on her hips, looked him straight in the eye, and smiled.

This made him furious.

"What do you want, Dina?"

"To play the cello," she said coldly.

"At night?"

"Music lives best when everything else is dead."

Jacob realized this was not leading anywhere. Intuitively, he did what he had done at dawn the previous day. He put his arms around her. Caressed her. Felt her become heavy. So heavy that he could get her to bed. He lay close to her and kept caressing her until she fell asleep.

He was surprised at how easily this happened. But realized that, over time, it might become a strain to have such a large child in the house.

The desire! The desire that had blazed in him day and night before the Bergen trip was gone. Everything was so different from what he expected at first. So much more complicated. He felt weary just thinking about it.

But he did not return to the dressing room.

Exhausted and confused, he lay with Dina's head on his arm the rest of the night. Stared at the ceiling and remembered Ingeborg's gentle ways.

They had lived in peace and forbearance and had given great pleasure to each other. But they had slept in separate rooms. He wondered if he should start using his old room again. But rejected the idea.

Dina would take some terrible revenge. He had begun to know her by now. Her way was to possess, without being possessed herself.

In the dark, he could see only the contours of her body. But he recognized the aromas and the naked skin.

He sighed deeply.

Then something happened.

It began when Mother Karen had a spring attack, as everyone called it. But this was October!

It was an attack of sleeplessness. This usually occurred when spring began to appear outside the two large windows in Mother Karen's room. The light was terrible in March, she complained.

Oline said nothing. But she drew the corners of her mouth into a scornful grimace and turned away. It was just like them! Those people from the south. Even when they came only from Trondheim, they still complained. About the dark fall and winter. And when the Lord flipped the coin, that was no good either! In her youth, Oline had been in Trondheim, which had daylight in the spring too.

But they always needed to complain about something. Women from Trondheim, who acted as if they came from Italy!

Mother Karen's attack, which everyone had thought was as reliable a sign as the oyster catcher, had come at the wrong time. It came in October this year.

So the nighttime creaking on the stairs began. And a saucepan with a ring of milk in it stood on the counter waiting for the kitchen maid in the morning.

For Mother Karen heated milk and honey. Sat at the table in the empty kitchen, watching the light illuminate the copper pans on the wall and the blue wainscoting and reveal that the rag rugs needed washing.

Mother Karen awoke just after midnight. She padded down to the kitchen and prepared herself for sleep with a cup of milk and the silence of the large, slumbering house.

But this time it was the wrong season, so she had to bring a candle.

As she walked past the hall window, she saw a lantern glowing in the summerhouse! At first she thought the moon was playing a trick on her by shining on the colored glass windows. Then she saw the light clearly.

Her first thought was to wake Jacob. But she pulled herself together. Threw her fur coat over her dressing gown and went to investigate the matter.

She had gotten no farther than the front steps when the door to the summerhouse opened and a tall figure in a wolfskin coat emerged. It was Dina!

Mother Karen hurried into the hallway and slipped upstairs again, as fast as her old legs could carry her.

This was no time to listen to Dina's loud explanations. But she promised herself she would talk with the girl the next day.

For some reason, the conversation was postponed.

Mother Karen became more sleepless than ever. Because she also had to keep an eye on Dina. It did not seem right for a young woman to sit in the summerhouse on a chilly night, even if she was wearing a fur coat.

Somehow she could not bring herself to talk with Jacob about it.

She discovered a pattern in Dina's wandering. When the nights were clear and cold, with stars and northern lights, Dina sat in the summerhouse.

Finally, one day when they were alone in the parlor, she remarked casually, while carefully observing the younger woman:
"You have trouble sleeping now too, don't you?"
Dina gave her a quick look.
"I sleep like a log!"
"I thought I heard . . . weren't you awake Thursday night, walking around?"
"I don't remember," said Dina.
That was the end of it. Mother Karen got no further. She did not want to argue or to make an issue of the fact that a person could not sleep. But she thought it strange that Dina wanted to keep it a secret.
"After all, you're used to the long dark months."
"Yes," said Dina, and began to whistle.
At that, Mother Karen left the room. She regarded it as the rudest provocation. Women from good families did not whistle.
But her indignation did not last long. She soon returned to the parlor. Looked over Dina's shoulder as she sat paging through some music, and said:
"Yes, play something for me instead. You know I can't stand whistling. It's a nasty habit and very improper. . . ."
Her voice was gentle enough. But her meaning was unmistakable.
Dina shrugged her shoulders and left the room. Slowly went upstairs to the master bedroom, where she began playing hymns with the door open.

Mother Karen made regular rounds to take stock of the household supplies and furnishings.
It took her great effort to walk down into the damp cellar. But it had to be done. She examined the shelves of canned preserves and the barrels of salted meat and fish. She made sure that old or perishable food was cleaned or replaced. Controlled everything with a strong, gentle hand. Always knew how many jars of currants and raspberries remained each spring. Decided how many were needed for the next year.
She replenished the wine cellar four times a year. That had usually met their needs until now. For aside from Jacob's mourning period a

few years before, wine was consumed in reasonable quantities at Reinsnes.

One Tuesday morning just before Christmas she went to the cellar to make an inventory. And discovered that not one bottle remained of the expensive dry Madeira that had cost seventy-eight skillings each! And only a few Hochheimer Rhine wine, at sixty-six skillings a bottle! Of the red table wines, she found only a scanty allotment of choice Saint Julien, at forty-four skillings. Two bottles!

Mother Karen left the cellar resolutely. Wound her shawl around her shoulders several times and marched down to the warehouse office to talk with Jacob in person.

He was the only person who had a key to the gate in front of the wine racks. She had had to ask for it herself that morning.

Mother Karen was more than dismayed. Jacob had shown no sign of a guilty conscience when he heard she was going to take inventory.

Oline had stern instructions to put a line in the household ledger for every bottle that they opened. And those numbers had to balance.

Jacob sat puffing his pipe when she arrived. His face was flushed and he wore no shirt collar, as was usual when he examined the ledgers with Niels. It was a task he did not enjoy.

The moment Mother Karen appeared in the doorway he knew something was wrong. The small, sprightly figure quivered under the fringed shawl.

"Jacob, I need to talk with you! Alone!"

Niels obediently left the room and shut the door behind him.

Mother Karen waited a few moments, then opened the door quickly to make sure he had left the warehouse and gone into the store.

"Have you started your bad habits again?" she demanded bluntly.

"What do you mean, Mother?"

He pushed the ledger aside and put down his pipe, to avoid upsetting her even more.

"I've been to the wine cellar! There is no dry Madeira left, and almost no Saint Julien!"

Jacob seemed taken aback. As he sat smoothing his mustache, some of the old guilt feelings returned. He almost believed he had drunk all that wine.

"That can't be true, Mother!"

"But it is!"

Mother Karen's voice was trembling.

"I haven't been down to the cellar without Oline's knowledge for a long, long time. Not since my trip south . . ."

He was an unhappy little boy, unjustly accused of vandalism he had not committed.

"Well, the bottles are gone," she declared firmly, sinking onto the visitor's chair by the large desk. She took a deep breath and gave him a searching look. Jacob avowed his innocence. They discussed possible explanations. But none sufficed.

When Dina returned from horseback riding she found great commotion in the kitchen. A harsh investigation was under way.

Oline was crying. And everyone was under suspicion.

Dina followed the sound of the excited voices and stood unnoticed by the pantry door. In the old leather trousers she always wore for riding. Her hair was tousled and her face flushed after riding against a sharp wind and blowing snow.

She looked from one person to another for a while. Then said calmly:

"I took the wine. There weren't many others Mother Karen needed it for, after all."

The room became extremely quiet.

Jacob's mustache quivered, as it did when he was unsure how to maintain his status.

Mother Karen turned even paler than she had been.

Oline stopped crying with a resolute thrust of her heavy lower jaw, which made her teeth chatter.

"You did? When?" Mother Karen exclaimed in astonishment.

"At different times. I don't really remember. The last time was one night when there was a full moon and northern lights, and everything was crazy. I needed something to help me sleep."

"But the key?" Jacob collected himself and took a few steps toward Dina.

"The key is always kept near the shaving chest. Everyone knows that. Otherwise the maid couldn't fetch wine when it's needed. Are you going to interrogate me here in the kitchen? Maybe we should get the sheriff."

She turned on her heels and left the room quickly. But the look she sent Jacob was not good.

"Dear God!" sighed Oline.

"Heaven help us!" added the kitchen maid.

Mother Karen immediately understood the situation and rescued the family honor.

"Well, that's quite a different matter," she said calmly. "Please forgive me. Oline! Everyone! I'm an old, suspicious woman. I didn't stop to think that Mistress Dina might have gone to the wine cellar, in her rightful concern for the welfare of the house and its guests."

She drew herself erect, crossed her arms over her breast as if protecting herself, and followed Dina at a dignified pace.

Jacob stood with his mouth half-open. Oline had an incredulous look on her face. The maids were wide-eyed.

No one knew what was said between Dina and Mistress Karen Grønelv.

But when they placed the next orders for wine and liquor, the young wife had her own allotment. Over which she had complete control.

However, the older woman always noted carefully how often the stock needed to be replenished, and exactly what was ordered.

When there was a full moon, and often other times as well, Dina did not come downstairs until late in the day.

Mother Karen kept her worries to herself.

Since only Dina used the summerhouse during the winter, no one but Mother Karen counted the row of half-empty, frozen wine bottles under the bench.

But when Dina sang hymns so loudly they could be heard both in the main house and in the servants' quarters, it was hard for dignity to be maintained the next day, as if nothing had happened.

She also held long conversations with herself, asking questions and responding.

To be honest, this did not happen often.

It was obviously connected with the phases of the moon.

Jacob and Mother Karen watched the developments with concern. Especially because they knew that when Dina was in this mood she would neither listen to reason nor agree to go to bed.

She could fly into a frightening rage if anyone tried to approach her.

Mother Karen hinted that sitting out in the cold in the middle of the night could make Dina ill.

But the girl laughed soundlessly in the old woman's face, insolently showing all her white teeth.

100

Dina was never ill. She had been in perfect health ever since she came to Reinsnes.

In the end, the wine-drinking excursions to the summerhouse became a well-guarded family secret. And since no family is without its peculiarities, everyone accepted that this must be the odd thing about the Grønelv family.

Chapter 9

The horse is made ready for the day of battle,
but the victory belongs to the Lord.
— Proverbs 21 : 31

*D*ina began wandering in and out of the two large warehouses at
the wharf, as if she were looking for something. She constantly went
to get the large iron keys.

People heard her pacing back and forth. First on the lower floor.
Then on the upper floor. Sometimes they saw her in the unloading
door of the cranehouse under the gable. Motionless, gazing toward
the horizon where sea and sky met.

*I am Dina. Reinsnes devours people. People are like trees. I count them.
The more the better. At a distance. Not inside the windows. Then everything
goes black.*

*I walk around Reinsnes, counting. The mountain range across the sound
has seven peaks. There are twelve trees on each side of the lane.*

*Hjertrud was with me at Tjøtta. She was the little girl who hid behind
the clock. She made herself so small because I was not alone. She needs a
place. It is so cold spending the winters on Fagerness beach.*

*What you are, you are forever. No matter how you have to walk through
a room.*

*Hjertrud breathes under the planks at the wharf. She whistles among the
beams when I open the unloading doors. Hjertrud always returns. I have
the gleaming mother-of-pearl shell.*

Dina roamed the huge notched-timber warehouses at all hours of the
day. Sometimes it was after dark, so she brought a lamp. People got
used to her rituals.

"It's just the young wife walking . . . ," they said, when they heard
sounds from the warehouse or saw light flickering through the windows.

*   *   *

102

The echo was not always the same. It depended on the floor where she was, the merchandise stored there, and the wind's direction. Everything blended with the constant yet shifting pull. Wind, high tide, and low tide.

In one section of the warehouse, the sparse timberwork was solidly reinforced with logs. Merchandise that could not tolerate much cold, dampness, or heat was stored here. Each stall had its particular contents. Barrels of salted herring, stocks of dried cod, salt, tar.

Flour and unmilled grain were also stored in this part of the building. As were furs and a wide variety of trousseau chests and travel chests. The tar smell was not as strong on the upper floors.

Masts and sails lay across the beams on the second floor. They were all different colors, depending on their age and condition.

The sails lay like grayed shrouds in airy coils of rope high under the roof on racks made from long wooden poles. Or they were hung to dry across the huge center beams and sent rhythmic, magical drops onto the scarred floor. It was stained with a variegated pattern. Of tar, fish oil, and blood.

The larger warehouse was called Andreas Wharf after a former owner who hanged himself there. Its walls were covered with fishing gear and innumerable small trawl nets. And it also contained the family's proudest possession. A new, dark-brown herring seine. That hung, high and airy, just inside the great double doors facing the sea.

The odors were alive and acrid but were constantly cleansed by salty sea winds. Which was a blessing for one's nostrils.

Shafts of sunlight slipped through the building's framework and crisscrossed one another. Here and there.

Hjertrud came to Dina at Andreas Wharf. In late autumn. Her first year at Reinsnes.

She stood suddenly at the intersection of three rays of sunlight. They came through cracks in three walls.

She was healthy and unscalded. Her eyes were alert and friendly. She held an invisible object in her hands.

Dina began to speak, in a child's high voice:

"Papa tore down the washhouse a long time ago. The one here at Reinsnes isn't dangerous. . . ."

Then Hjertrud disappeared into the folds of the herring net, as if she could not bear such topics of conversation.

But she returned. Andreas Wharf was the meeting place. The place most exposed to the winds.

Dina talked with Hjertrud about the little girl behind the clock at Tjøtta and about her new pastime of sitting in the summerhouse.

But she did not bother Hjertrud with trivial things that she had to deal with by herself.

Such as the fact that Jacob and Mother Karen were obviously unhappy about her disinterest in household tasks and that they wanted her to pin up her hair and plan the menus with Oline.

She talked with Hjertrud about all the amazing things in Bergen. But not about the man on the gallows.

Once in a while Hjertrud smiled broadly, showing her teeth.

"They walk around bundled in clothes and talk into thin air. People don't listen to one another. All they care about is selling their merchandise quickly and at a good price. And the women can't add the simplest numbers! They don't know what a long distance it is to Reinsnes. And they don't see anything around them, because they've got such big hats and parasols. They're afraid of the sun!"

At first Hjertrud replied in monosyllables. But little by little she revealed that she had her problems. With time and space. She did not like being driven from the little bedroom at the sheriff's estate.

She talked most about the glorious colors in the rainbow, for only a pale nuance was visible down here. And about the starry heavens spiraling around this small earth. It was beyond imagination.

Dina listened to the quiet voice she knew so well. Stood with her eyes half closed and her arms dangling.

Hjertrud's perfume penetrated the warehouse odors and the stubborn smells of salt and tar. Just when her fragrance grew so intense that it was about to shatter the air, Hjertrud disappeared into the folds of the fishing net.

I am Dina. When Hjertrud goes away, I become a leaf floating in the stream at first. Then my body stands alone, shivering. But only for a little while. Then I count the beams and the windowpanes and the cracks between the floorboards. And blood flows into my veins, one by one. I get warm.

Hjertrud exists!

Jacob feared Dina was unhappy. Once he came to get her in the warehouse.

But she put her fingers to her lips and said "Shhh!" as though he were disturbing an important thought. Contrary to his expectations, she seemed annoyed and not at all happy he had come.

Later he stopped following her wanderings. Just waited. Eventually he did not notice them.

During the first year with Dina, Jacob was lord and master in the canopy bed. Although sometimes the situation became too much for him and embarrassed and frightened him.

But as time passed, he realized sadly that the marital intimacy he had initiated with force and a widower's voracity had now become a horseback ride he could not take as often as he wished.

It came to the point where Jacob, who had enjoyed great pleasure in bed all his adult life, was forced to admit he was inadequate.

Dina had no mercy. Did not spare him. Sometimes he felt like a breeding stallion, where the owner and the mounted mare were one and the same.

He cast himself over the cliff as often as he could. But she was insatiable and unrestrained. Encouraged the wildest movements and situations.

Jacob did not get used to it. Became old and tired and lost his proud hunting instinct.

He began to wish for quiet days with a dignified, responsible wife. He thought about dear departed Ingeborg more and more. Sometimes he wept when he was rowing in a rough sea, where the spray kept others from seeing that it was mostly tears flying overboard with the wind.

Both he and Mother Karen believed for a long time that everything would be fine if only Dina would get pregnant.

But that did not happen.

Jacob bought a young black stallion. It was wild and untrained. They named it Blackie, a Norwegian word for devil. Because it was the constant object of oaths and curses in the stable.

Dina sent a message to the sheriff after Christmas, without asking Jacob's advice. She wanted Tomas to help her train the new horse.

It infuriated Jacob, who threatened to send the boy home.

Dina insisted a promise was a promise. You could not hire a cotter's boy one day and send him away the next. Did he want to disgrace

105

the family? Maybe he could not afford a stableboy? Maybe he was not as wealthy as he had told her father when he proposed?

Of course he was. . . .

Tomas stayed. He slept with the men in the servants' quarters. But he was ignored or teased. And envied more than a little. Because he was Dina's plaything. Rode with her in the mountains. Followed her whenever she was outdoors. Stood near her with downcast eyes when she boarded the outrigger wearing a tight bodice and fringed cape.

Dina of Reinsnes did not keep a dog. Had no confidant. She owned a black horse — and a red-haired stableboy.

Chapter 10

Has not man a hard service upon earth,
and are not his days like the days of a hireling?
Like a slave who longs for the shadow,
and like a hireling who looks for his wages.

— Job 7 : 1–2

Marriage is like eating a cucumber that was pickled in too sweet a brine. You must combine it with good, well-seasoned meat in order to endure it."

Oline was sure she was right. She had never been married. But she had seen it all at close range. Thought she knew everything about marriages. Knew them from the first engagement parties. Trousseau chests and dowries. Unexpected, pleasant sounds in the house, creaking beds, and chamber pots.

It began with her own parents, whom she never mentioned. Her mother, a wealthy farmer's daughter who married beneath her station, was disowned by her powerful family. And lived for years on a cotter's farm, with numerous children and a small rowboat for getting supplies.

Her husband disappeared at sea. And that was that. True, the boat drifted ashore and could be repaired. But what could the family do with the boat when there was no man to row it?

Her mother died early, and the children got scattered in all directions. Oline was the youngest. And the few small things her parents owned were gone long before it was her turn for an inheritance.

"If you have good health and good teeth, you can chew anything!" she often said. That did not stop her from conjuring up the tenderest bearberries in her sour-cream game sauce. Along with crushed juniper berries, rowan-berry jelly, and plenty of *snaps*. Pure gastronomic delights.

But that was not the whole story of Oline and her cooking pots.

She had learned her culinary arts "by a miracle" as a young cook's assistant in Trondheim. How she got there was no less miraculous.

Oline did not talk about herself. So she knew all about everyone else.

One day in Trondheim she had felt so homesick that she decided to take action. Of course, it had something to do with a man, who proved not to be a gentleman. . . .

She found a cargo boat going north. And like the woman she was, she managed to beg a trip home. Carried aboard a large, oval wooden box filled with *lefse*. Perhaps in exchange for the ticket.

It was a Reinsnes cargo boat. And her destiny.

Oline remained in the blue kitchen. Under many conditions and circumstances.

Ingeborg had appreciated her culinary arts and firm hand.

But after Mother Karen's arrival, there was a true connoisseur in the house.

She had dined at elegant tables in Hamburg and Paris! And understood that food should be prepared with love and generous measurements.

Mother Karen and Oline discussed a "menu" with as much seriousness as they prayed the Lord's Prayer.

The old woman had French recipe books in her bookcases. Which she translated, very precisely, into Oline's language and cookbook measurements. And when ingredients were not available in either Bergen or Trondheim, they devised good substitutes together.

Mother Karen put time and careful thought into planting a small herb garden. And Jacob brought back unusual seeds from his travels.

With the help of this garden, Oline produced such superb creations that people arranged to be weather-bound at Reinsnes, in both calm and stormy weather.

Oline's loyalty toward the master and his family showed itself concretely. God help anyone who tried to shame them in the parish! Those who did paid the consequences. Oline had connections. She heard everything worth hearing.

The servants at Reinsnes received no warning. They were simply ordered to pack their satchels and leave. Even if it was slaughtering time, or if preparations for a Bergen voyage were under way.

This happened to a young man and woman after poor Jacob moved the canopy bed into the garden to be near his dead Ingeborg. For Oline heard the story again.

"With the help of Our Lord and me, people have the position their talents deserve. If you're at Reinsnes, you don't walk around with your nose in your armpit and diarrhea on your tongue." That was the reference she gave them.

She had observed dear departed Ingeborg's first marriage. Childless, secure, and gray. Like an eternal late-autumn day, without leaves, without snow, without fruitfulness. She wept only the appropriate tears when the husband disappeared at sea.

But she cherished the widow like a jewel. Tended her through sleepless nights with toddies made from black currant wine and a cinnamon stick. Placed glowing hot stones wrapped in wool cloths in the canopy bed without being asked.

Oline's skepticism showed on her face the moment she got news of the arrival of Jacob, who was fifteen years younger than Ingeborg.

She had first heard about this man when her mistress mentioned having found a suitable coxswain while she was in Trondheim for a court hearing. The widow had a dispute with a tenant farmer regarding some bird rocks. The title to the property had been lost, and the farmer had laid claim to it.

Ingeborg won the case. And the coxswain came to Reinsnes. Wearing homemade boots and goatskin trousers that had belonged to a brother-in-law in Møre. And a leather hat, with a gray-flecked stocking cap inside, which he carried like a dead crow under his arm.

A coxswain who dressed like his crew and did not care for nautical finery.

The first nights he slept in the small guest room. But his wavy brown hair and dark eyes ignited sparks around him and attracted everyone's attention. It was a long time since Reinsnes had housed a truly handsome man.

Lithe and well-built, he came into his own once he discarded the leather outfit in which he arrived. Cloth trousers appeared, with wide legs and an exotic cut. Along with a short red brocaded vest and a fine white linen shirt that had no collar and was open at the neck, as though it were the height of summer.

Jacob captured many important fortifications. One of the first things he did was to stride briskly into Oline's large kitchen with two tender wild rabbits. Which he skinned himself.

He brought other gifts to the kitchen table as well. Direct from the great outside world. Small canvas and burlap bags containing coffee, tea, prunes, raisins, nuts, and citric acid for drinks and puddings.

With an easy naturalness, as if he never doubted who was in charge at Reinsnes, he laid his marvels on Oline's well-scrubbed table.

And as he stood skinning the rabbits, it happened. Oline gave him her unrestricted love. And through all the years ahead she would keep it alive and warm, like baby ptarmigans in late June. Hers was the kind of love described in the Bible: It endured everything. Absolutely everything!

Mistress Ingeborg also had fallen in love. The pastor could see that too. He talked about love in the marriage ceremony and in his speech at the wedding dinner.

Ingeborg even agreed to have Jacob's mother move to Reinsnes. Though all she knew about her mother-in-law was that she could not come to the wedding on three weeks' notice. She lived abroad and owned many bookcases with polished glass doors. She would bring them when she moved to Nordland, as she said in her first letter.

People formed an idea of Karen Grønelv long before she arrived at Reinsnes. Being the widow of a merchant skipper from Trondheim, and the owner of bookcases, gave her esteem and respect. But the fact that she had lived abroad for years, without even a man at her side, showed she was not just any Trondheim woman.

Ingeborg became a mother scarcely seven months after the wedding. To forestall comments from the pastor when her son was to be baptized so soon after her marriage, she mentioned that she had not had even a week to lose. She had been childless since her first marriage, at age eighteen, and now she was over forty. God would understand her eagerness.

The pastor nodded. He did not say it might seem to God that her haste had more to do with the young bridegroom than with eagerness to be a mother. Such words were not appropriate.

One did not say just anything to Ingeborg of Reinsnes. She gave generously to the poor. And two proud silver candlesticks in the church choir were inscribed from the Reinsnes family.

Instead he blessed her motherhood and told her to go in God's peace and teach her son all that the Lord had commanded.

And it was decided that the child would become the first clergyman in the family.

Niels was fourteen years old, and Anders twelve, when their parents died in a shipwreck. Since the boys were Ingeborg's distant relatives, they went to live with her.

After a while, it seemed they had always belonged there. They benefited from the lack of true heirs at Reinsnes.

But when this fellow named Jacob made Ingeborg fertile and blessed the estate with an heir, the foster sons' youthful dreams of inheriting manorial rights to Reinsnes sank like an overturned boat.

Oline took care of them all, even during Ingeborg's time. With her stolid devotion and untiring discipline.

She did not mind having two mistresses in the house, as long as they kept their peace and did not get in her way.

Jacob eventually became the most important person in her life. But if anyone had hinted even one word to that effect, it would have meant immediate dismissal.

Given her pride and her awareness of status, which were as strong as her belief in eternal life, she mourned genuinely, with red-rimmed eyes, when Ingeborg died.

Yet no one could have wished for a more beautiful death. All the signs were propitious. The lilacs burst into bloom the day of her funeral. And cloudberries were plentiful that fall.

Jacob's second marriage was a painful warning to Oline. It was not just that Dina never came to the kitchen to skin rabbits.

That she had table manners like a boy, climbed trees, and drank wine in the summerhouse at night were not the worst things either.

But that she did not "see" Oline at all was unforgivable.

Oline could not understand how this crazy girl could be at Reinsnes, even if she was Sheriff Holm's daughter.

For Jacob to make such an utterly ridiculous marriage seemed a catastrophe to Oline.

But as in so many other cases, she said nothing. And since she slept in the small room behind the kitchen, directly below the master bedroom, she knew all the sounds and vibrations that came from the canopy bed.

Such inordinate and shameless activity mystified her. It hurt her more than Ingeborg's death.

Amidst all her aversion was a quivering string. A curiosity. To discover what drove people to insane behavior such as Jacob's. To discover how a young girl could take control of an entire estate. Without lifting a finger, apparently.

Chapter 11

Drink water from your own cistern,
flowing water from your own well.
Should your springs be scattered abroad,
streams of water in the streets?
Let them be for yourself alone,
and not for strangers with you.
Let your fountain be blessed,
and rejoice in the wife of your youth.

— Proverbs 5 : 15–18

Jacob began taking "necessary" trips with the outrigger. He visited old friends. Did business in Strandsted.

At first, Dina wanted to go with him. But he refused, saying it would be boring for her. It would be cold. He would be back very soon.

He practiced what he would say. She did not get furious, strangely enough. Just withdrew.

He saw the heavy wolfskin coat lying by the stairs in the morning. Like the sloughed hide of a bewitched animal that had become a human again.

She never asked him where he had been. Not even when he was away all night. Never met him at the door.

She sat often in the summerhouse at night. But at least she did not play the cello.

One evening when Jacob returned late from Strandsted, he saw a light in the warehouse office window.

Dina sat paging through the account books. She had taken all the ledgers from the shelves and spread them on the table and floor.

"What are you doing?" he demanded.

"I'm trying to figure this out," she answered, without looking at him.

113

"You can't understand all that. We've got to put these things back, or Niels will be furious."

"I don't think Niels always knows how to keep correct accounts," she mumbled, biting her index finger.

"What do you mean? That's been his job for years."

"His numbers disappear. Lorch would say the arithmetic was wrong."

"Dina, don't fool with that. Come now, let's go to the house. It's late. I brought you a special *kringle* pastry."

"I want to go over these figures. Jacob, I want to start working here in the office!"

Her eyes shone, and she breathed through her nose. As was her habit when she occasionally showed enjoyment.

Niels, however, was adamant. The choice was either him or Dina. Jacob tried to mediate. Suggested that Dina might be a help with the books. In fact, she was an absolute genius when it came to calculating figures and that sort of thing.

But Niels, who usually never opened his mouth at the wrong time, said no!

Dina walked over to him with her special smile. She was half a head taller than he and brandished her words like a keen-edged sword.

"No, you wouldn't want anyone to see that you can't keep accounts! Numbers disappear in your books like dew in the grass. Don't they? But numbers don't disappear forever. It only seems that way to people who don't understand. . . ."

The office grew silent.

Then Niels turned on his heels and marched out, calling over his shoulder:

"This could never have happened in Ingeborg's day! Remember, it's either me or that one!"

Dina was not allowed in the office. But she shot looks at Niels during mealtimes.

He began to eat in the kitchen.

Jacob tried to make amends for siding with Niels in the matter. He brought Dina small gifts when he returned from his trips. Bars of soap, a brooch.

He tried to include her in activities and conversations.

One evening when they were all sitting in the parlor after dinner, he turned to Dina and asked her opinion of the new king, Oscar I.

"Maybe I can request the new king's permission to look for the lost numbers in the Reinsnes office!" she sneered.

Niels rose from his chair and left the room. Mother Karen sighed. Jacob lit his pipe abruptly.

Jacob knew a widow in Strandsted. She had heavy, but not unpleasant, features and a dignified graying knot of hair at the nape of her neck. Beneath her tight bodice was an attractive body. She lived alone respectably in a small house, where she took in lodgers and sewing.

With her, Jacob found some comfort. With her, he could unburden his heart and talk.

In Ingeborg's day he had taken the outrigger to look for social life — dancing and entertainment, and occasionally an embrace or two. Now he left Reinsnes to find peace and harmony.

A man's need! Inscrutable, and impossible to predict.

The summer of 1844 arrived. It was filled with ants and light and had no meaning.

Mother Karen gave Dina a collection of folk songs by a man named Jørgen Moe and a book of heathen folktales by Asbjørnson and Moe. But Dina had no interest in the latter.

Hjertrud's book contained better stories. And you could not predict the endings, as you always could with folktales.

"Folktales have a different moral, Dina dear," said Mother Karen.

"What do you mean?"

"They're based on human morals."

"What's the difference?" asked Dina.

"God's words are divine. They're about sin and the need for salvation. The others are just tales told by ordinary people. Where evil is punished and goodness triumphs."

"But Hjertrud's book is written by people too," said Dina.

"God has His messengers. His prophets who bring us His word," Mother Karen explained.

"I see. Well, at least God tells better stories than Asbjørnson and Moe!" declared Dina.

Mother Karen smiled.

"That's fine, Dina dear. But you must say 'the Bible,' not 'Hjertrud's book.' And you mustn't compare God's word with heathen folktales!" she added in a conciliatory tone.

"Hjertrud's book, the Bible, wins that comparison," the girl said dryly.

Mother Karen sensed that philosophical discussions or theological topics were not the way to train Dina. So she dropped the subject.

Dina played the cello and rode with Tomas. And she met Hjertrud at Andreas Wharf.

Each morning, red circles the size of a wineglass were drawn on the table in the summerhouse.

She watched the shipping lane from the chokecherry tree. The steamboat carried few passengers. And those who came ashore were from other worlds.

Dina drew conclusions about Jacob's frequent business in Strandsted. Rumors reached her through the walls of the servants' quarters and on random breezes. She heard a strophe now and then. Sometimes the whispering stopped when she entered a room or approached people. Even on the hill leading to the church.

And she put the pieces together.

Autumn came.

The dark sea frothed with whitecaps, and snow blew like icy needles from Blåflag Peak. The moon shone round and white, as the northern lights chased evil forces across the star-studded sky.

The weather had alternated between snow and rain, making the road across the mountain impassable for either humans or horses. Anyone who owned a boat felt fortunate. Although the sea was whipped by strange winds that nobody fully understood.

They entered the sound from the north at first. Then they came from the west, bringing heavy seas and cormorants with blue-black plumage.

Dina lay awake all night. But she did not follow her usual custom. Did not get up and sit in the summerhouse wearing her wolfskin coat.

The night was alive with rough weather. The clear sky and northern lights persisted, a protest against the storm sweeping past.

She lay in the canopy bed with its curtains open and stared through the tall windows until scant daylight turned the sky pale blue and infinitely distant.

Suddenly Jacob entered through the closed door. Came right through the door panels and toward the bed. Hobbling.

116

His ravaged face looked weary, and he held out his hands as if pleading for mercy.

He had removed just one boot and made a great racket that might awaken the whole house.

Infidelity was chiseled into his pale face.

She had called him. But he did not hear. So now it was too late. His pitiful specter appeared instead. She stared toward the sound, waiting for morning and a message from Strandsted.

I am Dina. Jacob says one thing and does another. He is a horse that refuses to be ridden. He knows he is mine. But he is afraid I will see that he wants to escape. Seven times he has lied in order to escape.

It is late. People are like seasons. Jacob will soon be winter. First I feel the blow. I think it hurts. But the feeling disappears in the enormous thing I always carry with me.

I float from room to room, among furniture and people. I can make people tumble over each other. They are so poor at playacting. Do not know who they are. With a mere word I can make their eyes waver. People do not exist. I will not count them anymore.

A cold, wet young man arrived ignominiously at the estate in a *faering* boat. Jacob had been hurt in an accident and needed to be fetched at the home of the widow at Larsnett, near Strandsted.

Dina showed no surprise. She just began putting on her wraps and ordered Blackie hitched to the sleigh.

Anders wanted them to take the boat. A woman should not travel across the mountains.

Dina was a snarling lynx and already leaping for her prey.

Anders shrugged his shoulders. Given the swift currents in the sound, perhaps this was not a bad solution.

It seemed as if she had gotten dressed that morning so she could just put on her fur coat and shawl, climb into the sleigh, and go to get Jacob.

Mother Karen and Oline sighed more deeply over Jacob than over the hazardous trip for Dina.

So it was Dina herself who came to fetch Jacob from the small bedroom in the widow's home.

He had been with a convivial group and planned to end the evening in peace and delight at his usual refuge.

But unfortunately, he slipped on some ice and fell down the steps. His leg snapped like a dry branch at the first gust of wind. The break was so serious that the bone shaft protruded.

Fortuitously, the doctor was at Strandsted. It took a whole bottle of rum to dull the pain while he cleaned the wound and applied a splint.

As usual, Dina was wearing leather pants and high boots like a man. She seemed overwhelming in the small house. Between her brows was an entire mountain chasm. Her words were like ice.

She treated the widow as a servant. And she ignored the good advice about letting Jacob wait until they could sail across the fjord.

She demanded help in getting Jacob lashed securely to the sleigh. Finally he lay in the sheepskin robes like a solid piece of rolled mutton.

"The woman must be reimbursed for the doctor's fee, and for my lodging," said Jacob meekly.

But Dina said neither thank you nor good-bye to Jacob's hostess. Just smacked Blackie to get him moving and swung herself onto the sleigh.

The horse was a devil. That fled from the flashing sleigh runners across the mountain.

Dina was a falcon above the man.

He felt deathly afraid as they sped down the steepest slope on frozen terrain.

The road had been partially washed away by fall floods. And his leg ached when they had to force their way into the deep, ice-covered ruts.

It was the first time he felt totally under Dina's control.

Jacob had limited experience with horses and roads. He was happiest at sea.

He tried to complain that she had not brought a crew to sail his boat home. But she did not give him even a glance in reply.

Jacob had not only seriously injured his leg; he had also fallen into disfavor. He knew that time was needed to heal both wounds. But had very little patience.

The break was serious, the bone was not set properly, and the leg would not heal.

It was as though evil forces had settled in the innocent limb. Jacob was confined to bed. He shouted and complained, whispered and begged for sympathy.

They moved him into the parlor, bed and all, to make him feel that he still belonged among the living.

The cleft between Dina's brows became deeper. And her sympathy for the sick man was well hidden.

When Jacob innocently asked if she would play for him instead of drinking so much wine, she rose from the elegant leather chair. So abruptly that her glass tipped, the stem broke, and the contents spilled onto the lace doily.

The wine formed a red flower that grew larger and larger.

"Ask the widow at Strandsted to play that shank into place in your old carcass," she hissed, and rushed out the door.

But Mother Karen and Oline nursed him tirelessly. And Anders sailed the outrigger back to Reinsnes.

After Dina's outburst, Jacob understood several things. But he did not know the situation was irreparable.

To him, nothing was irreparable when it concerned women. Not even the two years with Dina had destroyed this irrepressible optimism.

Jacob's wound did not improve. Gangrene developed. That was obvious from the color. The odor spread like an evil rumor, an inexorable warning of Judgment Day. Wrapped itself oppressively around each second.

Time became precious.

Mother Karen realized that Jacob required expert treatment. Soon!

Dina was the only one who actually had any idea what expert treatment would mean.

She had seen gangrene before. One of the sheriff's trawl fishermen had developed gangrene in a frostbitten foot. He survived but could only sit with his stump in the air and rely on charity. After a few years he was so shriveled with bitterness and hate toward everyone that the maids dreaded bringing him food.

Dina had visited him out of curiosity.

Even in the hallways you could smell Jacob's leg. Mother Karen sat by the bed. Oline added tears to the soup.

The ocean seemed the devil's own handiwork. Waves rose as high as boathouse doors.

Anders gave in once again when Dina announced that she and Tomas would drive Jacob across the mountain to the doctor.

Since she and her headstrong horse had managed to make the trip alone, she could probably do it with the help of a stableboy.

That was definitely the best plan. And was what happened.

Except for one thing: Tomas did not go along.

He gave her an incredulous look when she swung herself onto the sleigh and wanted to drive off alone.

Jacob nodded to him palely. As if uttering a prayer.

Tomas tensed his body. Prepared to jump onto the sleigh.

"No!" she snarled, lashing his knuckles with her whip. Then she barked a "Giddap!" to the horse and sped from the courtyard on squealing runners.

Tomas was left sprawled on the ice-covered ground. Gasping for breath. With bloody stripes on his right hand.

Later he defended Dina's actions by saying that three would have been too many on the sleigh. And she had no time to lose if she was to reach the doctor in time.

Like most things Tomas said, this seemed true enough to everyone. He had seen the fear in Jacob's eyes. But it was so terribly hard to remember.

Tomas was a trained dog. He did not howl while there was still time.

He drowned his thoughts in the water barrel in the courtyard. He rinsed his hand and his face in the ice-crusted water. Felt the pain from the whiplash go up his arm and into his armpit. Then he dried his face lightly with a wet hand and went inside to see Oline.

His face ruddy from the ice water, he commented that Jacob was indeed very ill.

Oline dried her eyes and sniffed the air imperceptibly. The smell of Jacob's leg was all they had now.

Three hours later, Tomas stood ready to receive Dina and the horse with the empty carriage shafts.

Book Two

Chapter 1

The heart knows its own bitterness,
and no stranger shares its joy.

— Proverbs 14 : 10

*C*hristmas was not celebrated at Reinsnes the year they laid Jacob
in the grave. No one felt tempted to visit the widows at Reinsnes.
Bad road conditions developed, as if specifically ordered for those
who needed an excuse to stay away.

Oline claimed that a damp misery came from the walls and settled
in both her hips, giving her no peace.

The bad roads lasted until the middle of January. People at
Reinsnes were idle and uncertain.

Tomas found pretexts to walk past the master bedroom windows.
Raised one blue eye and one brown eye. And did not realize he was
praying.

When occasionally he was sent upstairs with firewood, his hands
shook so much he dropped logs on the stairs.

Dina always sat with her back turned as he put the wood in the
basket behind the folding screen with a picture of Leda and the swan.

He offered prayers to her back, said "God's peace," and left.

No one knew when Dina slept. Day and night, she paced the floor
in travel boots with iron cleats on the heels.

The delicate pages of Hjertrud's Bible fluttered in the draft from
the window.

Mother Karen was a lovely little bird of passage that somehow had
remained for the winter.

Grief made her transparent, like delicate glass. The dark winter
days left their shadows on her gentle ways.

She missed Jacob. The curly hair and laughing eyes. Missed him as he was before life became so crazy at Reinsnes.

Age made it easy for her to cross the boundaries to the dead. The servants thought she was beginning to get senile. She hobbled around, talking to herself.

It was actually a symptom of great loneliness. And hopeless longing. For what had been.

People and animals, barns, sheds, and warehouses, were marked by this loneliness.

The whole estate held its breath, waiting for someone to fill Jacob's place.

Reinsnes had become a ship floating aimlessly, with no captain or crew.

It did not help matters that Dina never left her bedroom and paced back and forth in travel boots at night.

That she had stopped talking was discomforting.

Anders escaped from the house of sorrow and prepared to go fishing in the Lofoten Islands.

Mother Karen wrote a letter to Johan, saying he was fatherless but not homeless. She spent a week finding the right words. And spared him the details.

They had done everything possible to save his father's life, she wrote. But still, God had taken him. Perhaps in His great mercy He saw that it would be too hard for Jacob to live as a cripple with only one foot. Perhaps God in His wisdom understood he was not made for such a life.

After sending the letter with the sad news, Mother Karen climbed the stairs laboriously and knocked on Dina's door.

Dina was standing in the middle of the room when the old woman entered.

She was about to turn away toward the windows when Mother Karen's gentle voice burst out:

"You keep pacing back and forth in your room! But that won't accomplish anything!"

Perhaps it was Mother Karen's white, quivering nostrils. Or the restless fingers she kept hooking onto the fringes of her shawl.

Dina withdrew from her shell and showed a speechless interest.

124

"Life must go on, Dina dear. You should come downstairs now and get things under control. And . . ."

Dina gestured for Mother Karen to sit down at an oval table in the center of the room. It was covered by a gold plush cloth with tassels that fluttered gently in the draft from the open door.

The old woman seated her small, frail body on a high-backed chair.

The table and four chairs had been shipped from Bergen the first year she lived at Reinsnes. She herself had made sure the expensive furniture was carried carefully ashore.

Suddenly the old woman drifted into another world. As if she had never come to Dina's room because the loneliness and worry were too overwhelming to bear alone.

She sat staring at the curved table legs. As if they were unusual. Then, slowly and without introduction, she began to tell the story of the furniture.

Dina crossed the room and shut the door to the hall. Then she got her slate and sat down beside the old woman. With her smile as a shield at first. But then just as herself. Listened. It seemed she had been waiting all her life for precisely this story.

Mother Karen told about the oak furniture, about the chairs with elegantly upholstered seats. Jacob had thought they looked like women's bodies, with low-cut bodices and fine hips.

She let her fingers glide over the small heart-shaped opening carved in the back of the chair. Then her wrinkled, transparent hand smoothed the heavy tablecloth, lingering sadly where a cigar had left its mark.

"That's from Jacob's unhappy days as a widower," she said with a sigh.

With no beginning or end, she told the story of her wonderful life with Jacob's father. About the years in Paris and Bremen. About countless voyages with her beloved husband.

Until one time in Trondheim when she waited for him to return from Copenhagen. In vain.

His ship had sunk at a cursed spot on the southwest coast.

Jacob was twelve years old then. And insisted he wanted to go to sea as soon as he was old enough.

But most of all, Mother Karen talked about gleaming tables in great banquet halls. About rococo mirrors and fantastic bookcases. About travel chests with removable trays and secret compartments. A disjointed monologue.

She returned constantly to the subject of the furniture she brought to Reinsnes.

The oval table and the plush chairs, which had been reupholstered at the time of Dina and Jacob's wedding.

Jacob had decided to move the furniture from the sitting room to the master bedroom. Because he wanted Dina to be able to sit in the middle of the room and look across the sound in good weather. He wanted her to be able to see the glorious Reinsnes beaches!

Dina listened, expressionless. The clock in the downstairs parlor suddenly struck three. It awakened the old woman. She gave Dina a mild look and seemed to have forgotten she had been telling stories. Once again she was lonely and worried about the future.

"You've got to do something useful! You can't just grieve day and night. The whole estate is neglected. Our people don't know how to run things on their own. Time is passing."

Dina gazed at the beams in the ceiling. It was as though someone had painted a smile on her face but could not do it correctly and abandoned the task.

"You want me to take charge?" she wrote on the black slate.

Mother Karen looked at her in bewilderment and desperation.

"This is yours, after all. Everything!"

"Where is that written?" wrote Dina.

Her fingers whitened around the slate pencil.

One afternoon Dina put on her riding clothes. Then she slid down the banister like a little girl. And went to the stable, without anyone seeing her.

Blackie stood with lowered head, listening to her steps. When she entered the stall, the animal tossed its mane, stamped its forelegs, nipped her shoulder, and snapped its teeth at her good-naturedly.

The horse and the woman. Soon they were one body.

No one noticed them until they flew down the road toward the beach and disappeared.

Those who saw it clasped their hands. Asked the nearest person: Did you see that? Dina was outdoors again! Dina rode away on Blackie!

At first they found it a hopeful sign. Then they became uneasy. By now it seemed unnatural for Dina to be anywhere but in her bedroom.

Tomas was sent to keep an eye on her. He saddled a horse faster than ever before in his life. Fortunately, he did not choose the road across the mountains, but rode along the dark shore. When he overtook her, he acted invisible. Did not make the mistake of shouting a warning when she spurred her horse to a gallop. Just followed at a good distance.

They continued like this for a while.

But suddenly she had enough. The horse was lathered in sweat. At the stable, she reined in Blackie so abruptly that clumps of ice spattered from his hooves and hit Tomas, who let out a yell.

He stabled both horses without a word. Dried them and gave them hay and water.

Dina stood watching Tomas work. It made his movements clumsy and unsure.

Her eyes followed his narrow hips. His strong hands. His long red hair. His wide mouth.

Then she met his gaze. One brown and one blue eye.

She faced him confidently. Gathered her hair above her head with both hands. Then let it cascade over her shoulders. Turned and walked quickly out of the stable.

Jacob Grønelv had written a will. But since he never imagined it would be needed so soon, the document had no validating stamps, or signature, or witnesses. And no copy had been filed with the authorities.

But he had told the sheriff about the document. Because he was not only the sheriff's son-in-law but also his hunting companion and friend.

The thought that a will existed somewhere, no matter how invalid, made the sheriff uneasy. For Jacob had a grown son and two foster sons.

Though he was Dina's father, he was also the sheriff. It was his duty to make everything look right.

When the weather improved, the sheriff went to Reinsnes. To have a private conversation with Dina. About Jacob's last will and testament, which must be somewhere on the estate. Probably in the office at the warehouse.

Dina listened with a blank expression. She did not know anything about Jacob's will and had not seen any such paper. Jacob and she had not talked about such things, she wrote on the black slate.

The sheriff nodded and said they should act quickly. Reach

an agreement. Before anything else got decided. Otherwise there
would be nothing but trouble. He had seen enough of that in his
life.

When the sheriff left, Dina went to the warehouse office.

Niels was completely taken aback. He remained seated behind
the solid oak desk. The corners of his mouth showed both astonishment and displeasure. His face, with its dark stubble of beard and
its bristly mustache, was an open book.

Dina stood looking at him across the desk for a while. When he
gave no sign of wanting to help her, she wrote on her black slate:
Give me the key to the large iron chest.

He rose grudgingly and walked to the key cabinet between the
two windows.

When he turned around, she had taken his place in the old swivel
chair. He instantly realized he was superfluous.

And when he kept staring after laying the key on the counter,
she nodded gently toward the door.

He left reluctantly. Strode past all the bins in the store and looked
straight through the sales clerk when he passed him. As if the man
were air.

Then he busied himself around the estate. Was a black cloud and
a nuisance. Dropped comments about how even live young women
had begun to haunt the estate. And they thought they understood
business and ledgers! The fine madam could just sit there and make
herself important! He certainly would not disturb her! People would
soon see what happened. She could have asked him about the accounts, told him in advance that she wanted to examine the papers
and business contracts. He would have found everything and laid it
out neatly for her. Of course he would have!

Niels's nature was as dark and constrained as his brother Anders's
temperament was lighthearted and open. Had Anders not been in the
Lofoten Islands, he would surely have given his brother good advice.
Anders had so many ideas.

Dina searched systematically, with stifled anger. In the old bookkeeping cabinet, in the iron chest, in drawers and on shelves. Hour
after hour.

Eventually everyone left the store, and the building grew quiet.
The clerk came and asked if he should extinguish the lamp in the
store. Dina nodded without looking at him. And continued searching

among papers and folders. Now and then she straightened her shoulders and rubbed the small of her back with her fists.

Just as she was ready to stop for the evening, she happened to see an old lacquered-birch writing box on one of the crowded shelves. Half buried among order forms and a stack of snuff containers.

She rose quickly and walked across the room purposefully, as if Jacob were there giving her instructions. The wooden box was locked. But Dina was able to pick it open with a penknife.

On top lay drawings of the *Mother Karen* cargo boat and a bundle of old letters from Johan. When she lifted the bundle, a yellow envelope slid out and stubbornly stood on end for an instant. Then it lay down nicely on the table.

She had never seen the envelope before, but nonetheless, she was certain. This was Jacob's will!

She cleared up after herself. Locked the writing box again and put it back in its original place. Then she hid the envelope under her shawl, extinguished the lamp, and fumbled her way through the dark warehouse.

Outside, the moon and an army of stars had overtaken the sky. The northern lights waved a luminous tatter, as if celebrating her discovery with her.

She walked lightly across the snow-covered courtyard. Into the hall and upstairs to her room. Without meeting anyone.

But the entire house seethed with whispers. Dina had left her room! The young wife had inspected the store! Niels thought she had examined the accounts and everything!

"God is good!" Mother Karen said jubilantly to Oline. Oline nodded and listened toward the door as Dina walked past.

Dina climbed into the large canopy bed. Closed all the bedcurtains and smoothed out Jacob's will between her thighs with stiff fingers.

His voice came slowly from the walls and intruded on everything. She had forgotten that he had a fine voice. A friendly tenor that did not sing in tune.

She smiled as he read for her.

No witnesses' signatures. No official stamps. Just a man's last will and testament. Written late one lonely evening. As if in a sudden flash of intuitive understanding. The thirteenth of December, 1842.

Still, the document would be difficult to circumvent if the right people saw it. For in part, Jacob's will was this:

His wife, Dina, and Johan, his son from his first marriage, should lawfully administer the inheritance as long as they retained the estate without dividing it among other heirs.

Jacob Grønelv desired that his wife manage his household and business to the best of her ability until Johan finished his studies, and that she secure whatever services she needed to maintain her status. His son, Johan, was to continue his theological education and receive financial support as an advance against his inheritance. He was to live at Reinsnes as long as he was unmarried and wanted to remain there. He could take over the estate with freeholder's rights whenever he wished.

His wife, Dina, together with Mother Karen Grønelv, were to be responsible for daily tasks related to the house and animals and servants.

Mother Karen was to have not only a pension but all rights, privileges, and comforts until her death.

His foster son Niels was to manage the store and keep the accounts as long as that was appropriate for both him and Reinsnes.

His foster son Anders was to supervise the cargo boats and be responsible for everything pertaining to them.

Both foster sons were to receive one tenth of any profits they earned for the estate.

No one who owed Jacob Grønelv money should be forced to hold an auction to repay the debt.

A large specific sum for the poor was mentioned.

Dina spent the rest of the evening doing justice to Jacob's will. She wrote a new "testament."

She did not try to falsify the genuine will or to pretend that what she wrote was anything other than "my best recollection" of the wishes her "beloved departed husband" had verbally expressed.

It was confusingly similar to Jacob's will, except on a few points: There was no mention of one tenth for the foster sons. And they were to retain their positions as long as it profited Reinsnes and suited his wife, Dina.

Nor did she write that Johan could take over the estate whenever he wished.

Everything else she wrote down neatly and beautifully, point by point. Took care to include the sum for the poor.

Then she stoked the stove well. And lit the seven-candle candelabra on the game table.

* * *

The entire time that Jacob's last will and testament was burning in the black iron belly, Dina smiled.

She placed the page she had written on the polished walnut writing table. Open, so everyone who entered could see it.

Then she lay down on the large canopy bed, fully dressed.

Suddenly she felt Jacob's weight on top of her. He thrust himself into her. His breath was unfamiliar. His hands were hard. She repulsed him angrily. And Jacob gathered his trousers and silk vest and disappeared through the wall.

I am Dina who feels a fishtail beating under my ribs. It has played a trick on me. It still belongs to the sea and the stars. It is swimming inside me and is separate while it eats me. I will carry it with me as long as necessary. After all, it is not as heavy, or as light, as Hjertrud.

What mattered was not how it all happened but how people thought it happened.

She rose and looked in the stove. Added more wood. Watched to make sure the fire destroyed the charred remains of Jacob's will.

That night no one heard Dina pacing the floor in travel boots with iron cleats on the heels.

The sheriff brought a court clerk and two witnesses the next time he came.

The old and the young widow sat erect at the oval table in the master bedroom, along with the men.

Dina's page with her recollections of Jacob's last wishes was presented to those whom it concerned in the presence of witnesses.

Johan was in Copenhagen, but Mother Karen was his guardian.

Dina was dressed appropriately. In the black clothes that had been sewn for the funeral. Everyone in the house was summoned.

They all stood around the table with bowed heads and heard Jacob's words read in the sheriff's booming bass voice. It was very dignified. Solemn.

No one thought of a missing will. After all, there had been an accident. And it happened so quickly. God bless the master of the house! Their benefactor.

Each person received some small remembrance. Everyone praised Jacob for thinking of them all.

*   *   *

The sheriff thought it unnecessary to state that Johan was to receive part of his inheritance to live on while he completed his studies. Parents had a duty to support their children in accordance with their status, without regarding it as an advance against their inheritance.

But Dina smiled and shook her head.

"We have no right to ignore that his father is dead," she wrote on the slate.

The sheriff looked at his daughter with bewildered respect. Then he dictated Dina's wishes to the clerk. And Mother Karen nodded. The stamp was affixed.

The sheriff gave a speech about his dead son-in-law and friend, and about his daughter, and urged everyone to show goodwill toward her. The estate needed a firm hand.

Mother Karen sighed with relief. Life was continuing. Dina had come down from her room.

The sun shone higher and higher. Soon it colored the northern skies at midnight.

The seagulls shrieked, the ptarmigans laid eggs, and the choke-cherry blossomed.

Mother Karen received a letter from Johan.

He offered his condolences and was politely sad. He did not want to make the trip home until after he had taken an important examination. And after all, his father's funeral had already occurred.

Between the lines, Mother Karen read what she already knew. He had no understanding of how to run the business or the farm. He did not want to be stowed away in a warehouse and knew little about bookkeeping. But he would like an advance on his inheritance while he was studying to be a clergyman.

If he felt sorrow, he did not show it by a desire to carry on his father's business.

Mother Karen read the letter aloud to Dina.

"My greetings and deepest sympathy to Dina in this difficult time," were Johan's closing words.

Chapter 2

And Jacob set up a pillar in the place where he had spoken with him, a
pillar of stone; and he poured out a drink offering on it, and poured oil on
it. So Jacob called the name of the place where God had spoken with
him, Bethel.
Then they journeyed from Bethel; and when they were still some
distance from Ephrath, Rachel travailed, and she had hard labor.
And when she was in her hard labor, the midwife said to her, "Fear not;
for now you will have another son."
And as her soul was departing (for she died) she called his name Bennoni
[Son of My Pain]; but his father called his name Benjamin [Son of
Happiness].

— Genesis 35 : 14–18

*O*ne day Mother Karen entered the master bedroom unexpectedly,
without knocking. Dina was standing in the middle of the room,
getting dressed.

It was obvious that she was pregnant. The sun shone through the
tall windows and revealed everything to Mother Karen's wise eyes.
Dina had been a widow for five months.

The older woman was small and frail. Standing beside Dina's
large figure, she seemed more like a rare porcelain doll that always
stood in a glass case with unrumpled hair than like a real human being
of flesh and blood.

The wrinkles in her face were a delicate spiderweb that trembled
in the sunshine when she went to the window to be closer to Our
Lord as she gave thanks.

She stretched both hands toward the young woman. But Dina's
eyes were two columns of icy glacial water.

"Bless you, Dina, you're going to have a little one!" she whispered, deeply moved.

Dina quickly drew on her skirt and held her blouse in front of
herself protectively.

When the old woman showed no sign of leaving, Dina threateningly set one foot in front of the other. Small, determined steps.

And before Mother Karen knew it, she was standing in the dark hallway, facing a closed door.

Dina's eyes haunted the old woman. Not only during the day but even in her sleep and her dreams. She did not know how to approach this self-isolated creature.

On the third day she tried, vainly, to make contact with Dina, she went to Oline in the kitchen. To get comfort and advice.

Oline was standing at the end of the table. Wearing two aprons. One over the other.

The plump body with the firm breasts had never nursed so much as a cat. Nonetheless, Oline spoke as if she were the primeval mother.

She unconsciously knew that she directed most things with her mere presence. With the drawn corners of her mouth and her pink, wrinkled forehead, brimming with kindness.

Oline thought the young wife needed to be left in peace. She needed good food! And warm lined slippers, instead of those terrible shoes in which she paced the drafty floor.

In Oline's opinion, it was quite natural that Dina was angry at having a child when she did not have a husband at her side.

"Women get upset about less important things," she said, rolling her eyes toward the ceiling. As though she could tell scores of similar stories.

You could not expect such a young wife to see either glory or blessings in perpetuating the family line, after what she had experienced.

So Oline reduced everything to a matter of time and loving care.

Those who thought Dina had left her room for good the day she searched the office were mistaken.

She went to the stable. And, to Mother Karen's despair, she went riding. In her condition! But otherwise Dina stayed in her room. She ate in her room. Lived in her room.

When Mother Karen occasionally urged her to come down to the dining room, especially when they had guests, she just smiled and shook her head. Or she pretended not to hear.

Dina had resumed a childhood habit. She had eaten alone then too. Because her father could not stand to see her. Especially not while he was eating.

*   *   *

Tomas tried to catch Dina's eye when she came to get Blackie to go riding. He helped her mount by linking his hands so she could use them as a stirrup. He had begun doing this when it was rumored she was pregnant.

"You should use a saddle . . . until everything is over," he once said, with a shy glance at her abdomen.

She did not need to answer. Since she was mute.

People openly discussed that Mistress Dina was pregnant, mute, and distant from everyone.

They felt sorry for old Mother Karen, who was trying to run the large estate. Even though she was over seventy and had trouble with her legs.

People said that when a doctor was summoned to cure her depression, Dina threw a chair at him because he had walked into her room without knocking.

He reportedly threatened Dina with the insane asylum if she did not behave herself. But she did not pay the least attention. She just gave the doctor such a terrible look that he found it safest to withdraw, without attempting to cure her.

Afterward, Mother Karen offered the doctor a glass of liqueur, and a wild-grouse dinner with wine and cigars, to compensate for the young wife's conduct.

Alone in her room, Dina raged and slammed bureau drawers. Because her clothes no longer fit.

Her stomach and breasts had grown, giving the young body dimensions that would have attracted the attention and envy of those less well endowed. Had she appeared in public.

But she paced back and forth across the bedroom floor and had nothing to do with anyone or anything.

Finally, she allowed Mother Karen to come in for a while. And they sent for a seamstress from Strandsted.

The days flowed into one another. Forged together by dark nights. Heavy. Like sour smoke from an ill-tended hearth.

I am Dina, who reads in Hjertrud's book. Through Hjertrud's magnifying glass. Because Christ is an unhappy creature who needs my help. He will never manage to save himself. Has twelve devoted men who clumsily try to assist him. Without success. They all are cowardly, afraid and helpless. Judas at least can count. . . . And he dares to be truly evil. But he seems

135

to let himself be forced into a role. As if he does not have the sense to say he refuses to be the traitor just so the others do not have to be. . . .

Because Dina was unable to speak, people thought of her as being deaf too.

They chattered in the halls and behind her back. And since she made no sound to indicate that she heard what they said, it became a habit. As a result, Dina always knew what happened and what people thought.

She wrote down her brief orders and wishes. Using a slate pencil on her black slate. She sent purchase orders to the bookstore in Tromsø.

The steamboat brought her crates of books. Which she opened herself with the crowbar lying near the stove.

The maid who emptied the ashes and brought firewood felt uneasy about having such a tool there.

But it was worse when the heavy, sinister-looking object was not in its accustomed place.

The books were about accounting and farm management. Sometimes Dina's reading made her so furious that Oline thought the young wife had completely smashed the stove with the crowbar.

Dina sent for an accounting expert. For several hours a day, she sat in the warehouse office, getting a thorough explanation of the entire bookkeeping system.

It caused great tension between her and Niels. The young accountant stayed for a month. Moved between the main house and the office like a watchdog.

"The next thing you know, Madam will probably start purchasing merchandise for the store," Niels muttered to the young accountant, Petter Olesen, who was not the least tempted to participate in the sarcasm.

He had never had things as good as at Reinsnes. In fact, he would gladly have continued working there forever.

In the evenings he sat in the smoking parlor, puffing Jacob's best meerschaum pipe as if he owned it.

But he had to do without Dina's company. Except while he was teaching her bookkeeping. She stayed in her room. When she was not riding or writing orders and questions. Which were always absolutely clear.

No one could call her friendly. But since she did not speak, she never said a harsh word either.

Mother Karen sparkled with pleasure because Dina showed such energy. But she also had the misfortune to reproach the young woman for not paying enough attention to her "condition."

Dina responded with terrible cries that rattled the mirror and the windowpanes in the drawing room.

If there was one thing everyone at Reinsnes feared, it was when Dina leaned over the banister and emitted sounds that went straight to the marrow of all who were forced to listen.

There was no question whom Dina resembled, Oline said.

But for the most part, things were peaceful. Mother Karen often dozed under her woolen lap robe in the sitting room. She read, and reread, the dry letters that arrived regularly from Johan. Sometimes she read them aloud to Dina. She permitted herself an old age, because she saw the estate was operating somewhat.

For several months the guest rooms stood empty. The sorrow and strange behavior at Reinsnes was not exactly appealing. A lethargic mood settled on the large innkeeping and trading establishment.

However, the *Mother Karen* returned from the Lofoten Islands with good profits. Thanks to Anders. It became evident that many things for which Jacob had taken credit were due to Anders's skills.

Everyone awaited, and talked about, the baby.

Of course, Dina could not talk about it. But she did not write about it on her slate either.

The maids, Thea and Annette, sewed tiny garments in their spare time, and Oline worried because the midwife lived so far away.

One damp day when thunder was in the air, it happened. The thing Mother Karen had feared.

Dina got thrown from her horse.

Fortunately, Tomas was watching from the fields. He ran so fast his lungs hurt and he tasted lead. Found her lying in a patch of budding lingonberry blossoms. Arms and legs outstretched. Crucified to the earth. Her face toward heaven, her eyes wide open.

The only injuries Tomas found were a cut on her forehead and a gash on her leg from a dry pine branch.

He headed for the summer barn because it was closest. And because Our Lord sent a sudden, malicious attack of thunder and pounding rain.

Blackie had been terrified by the first thunderclaps and had thrown Dina when she tried to calm him.

Tomas half carried her into the leaky barn. Helped her lie down on the old, dusty hay. For the time being. Because her labor pains had started, and he had an imminent birth on his hands.

But Tomas had once assisted his mother when she was in similar condition on their remote cotter's farm. He knew what needed to be done.

Blackie was impossible to ride. So Tomas ran to the main house for help.

There they immediately got busy with firewood, hot water, and sheets. The maids scrubbed their hands and followed Oline's quick orders.

Dina should not be moved now, Tomas told them, turning his hat in his hands like a wheel.

Oline waddled up the hill toward the summer barn at an amazing pace. Tomas ran after her, pushing a loaded wheelbarrow.

The sky opened and dumped torrents of rain. Which threatened to inundate everything under the oilskin in the wheelbarrow.

"That's enough!" Oline shouted into the air breathlessly. "We will not have a flood and a birth at the same time!"

She wanted to convince the forces of nature that now she was in command.

Everything was over within scarcely an hour.

Dina's son was a sturdy, but small, baby. Born in a summer barn while the heavens descended and nourished all growing things.

Blackie stood by the barn door, his large head and stained teeth moving restlessly.

Had it not been that the whole thing was a miracle, and that Jacob died in November, Oline would have said this child was born prematurely.

But she laid the blame on the mother, who acted like a young girl when she was "in that condition."

Dina did not scream while giving birth. Just lay with wide, staring eyes and moaned.

But when the baby was out and they were waiting for the afterbirth, she gave the most terrible scream they had ever heard.

Dina flailed her arms in the air, opened her mouth, and howled without restraint.

I am Dina who hears a scream build a nest in my head. It caulks my ears. In the washhouse at Fagerness, the steam seeps out of Hjertrud while she drains herself onto the floor. Then she collapses. Her face splits. Again and again. We drift away together. Far away . . .

Dina lay inert and silent.

Mother Karen, who was in the barn too, whimpered in despair.

But Oline slapped Dina's cheeks so hard that the marks of her fingers remained like a scar.

And the scream poured from her again. As if it had been blocked for a thousand years. It mingled with the thin sound of a newborn baby's cry.

They laid him at her breast. His name was Benjamin. He had dark hair. His eyes were old and black, like coal in the mountains.

The world held its breath. A sudden silence. A liberation.

Some minutes later, from the bloody sheets they heard an unexpected command:

"Shut the door! It's cold!"

Dina said the words. Oline wiped her wrinkled forehead. Mother Karen folded her hands. The rain made its way through the sod roof. A wet, wary guest.

Tomas got the news as he sat on a box under a tree. Soaked to the skin without knowing it. At a respectful distance from the summer barn.

An amazed smile spread over his entire body. Reached his arms. They spread wide, and the rain filled his palms in an instant.

"What did you say?" he cried happily, when Oline gave him the news.

"Shut the door! It's cold!" She laughed, hugging herself with rosy bare arms.

Laughter echoed between them. The old woman smiled in astonishment.

"Shut the door! It's cold!" she muttered, and shook her head.

Dina was carried to the house in a heavy sail. Its four corners borne by Niels, a cowherd, a customer in the store, and Tomas. Anders was in Bergen.

Down the path to the courtyard, through the double doors, upstairs to the canopy bed in the master bedroom.

Only then did the midwife arrive, to make sure that everything had been done properly. She was extremely satisfied, and the midwife's dram was served on silver trays in both the kitchen and the master bedroom.

Dina drank greedily, while the others sipped. Then she asked a maid to get the soaps in the chest of drawers. Her voice was the whine of unused block and tackle.

She placed the soaps in a circle around the child at her breast. Thirteen lavender- and violet-scented soaps. A magic circle of fragrance.

Soon they both were asleep.

Her milk would not come.

At first they fed the baby sugar water. But that would not do for long.

All the women's backs perspired from the constant crying. After four days it became a continuous wheezing, interrupted by brief pauses when the exhausted infant dozed.

Dina was pale but remained aloof from the women's fretting.

Finally, Tomas mentioned that a Lapp girl in the southern part of the parish had just given birth to a child that died.

Her name was Stine. She had large eyes and a slim body, beautiful golden skin and high cheekbones.

Oline openly complained about having such a thin wet nurse. That Stine was Lapp made it even worse.

But her small breasts soon proved to be a source of the elixir of life. And her lean, sinewy body exuded tranquillity, as if created to lull a child.

She had lost her baby boy a few days before. But did not say a word about that. At first she was wary, wretched, and bursting with milk.

They knew she was unmarried, but nobody mentioned it.

In the heavy, fragrant July nights, Stine brought peace and equilibrium. Everything grew calmer.

A sweet smell of infant and milk emanated from Stine's small room. Seeped through the hall and into the most hidden corners. Even in the servants' quarters one caught the scent of woman and child, strange as that might seem.

Dina stayed in bed for seven days. Then she began pacing again. As actively as a goat climbing a mountainside.

"If it's not the baby, then it's the mistress herself," sighed Oline.

It was a hot summer. In the buildings and in the courtyard. People on the estate began to believe everything could be as before, when Master Jacob was alive and a dram was offered to family and friends and cultured travelers from far and near.

Stine nursed the baby. And slipped to and fro like a shadow. Silently. Akin to the groundwater and the summer wind.

Oline told everyone not to mention that the baby was born in the summer barn.

Mother Karen remarked that the Lord Himself was born in a stable, and this might be a sign.

But Oline did not change her mind. She did not want anyone to hear about the barn. Nonetheless, people heard. Dina of Reinsnes had paraded among the guests wearing only pantalets on her wedding day, and now she had given birth in a haymow!

During the summer, Dina began wandering about the house.

Once when she was in the kitchen, she commented that Oline had dandruff on her shoulders.

Oline was deeply hurt. Hadn't she delivered this depraved woman's child in a barn? She glared at the beamed ceiling after Dina left, looking like a fierce dog chained at the doorstep.

Stine and Dina had a silent mutual understanding.

Now and then they leaned over the cradle together, without saying much. This Lapp girl was hardly a chatterbox.

One day Dina asked:

"Who was the father of your child?"

"He's not from around here."

"Is it true that he has a wife and children?"

"Who said that?"

"The fellows at the store."

"They're liars!"

"Then why can't you say who he is?"

"It doesn't matter. The baby died. . . ."

This harsh philosophy of life seemed to please Dina. She looked Stine in the eye, and said:

"You're right. It doesn't matter. It's nobody's business who the father is."

Stine swallowed hard and met the other woman's gaze gratefully.

"Our baby will be named Benjamin, and you're going to carry him at the baptism!" Dina continued, as she grasped the bare little foot kicking in the air.

He was not wearing a diaper. Here on the upper floor, the summer heat was suffocating. The house smelled sun-scorched, day and night.

"Would that be right?" asked Stine, aghast.

"Of course it's right! You saved the little fellow's life."

"You could have given him cow's milk. . . ."

"Nonsense! You'll need a new skirt, a new shift, and a new bodice. And the pastor will perform the baptism."

The sheriff flew into a rage when he was told he would not carry his first grandchild to the baptismal font and the child would not be named after its father.

"His name should be Jacob!" he thundered. "Benjamin is just a strange female notion you got from the Bible!"

"Benjamin is Jacob's son in that same Bible," Dina said stubbornly.

"But nobody in the two families has had the name Benjamin!" shouted the sheriff.

"After next Sunday, somebody will! Now please go to the smoking parlor, so we can have some peace."

The sheriff did not move. His face was flaming. Those in the kitchen and the parlors heard the entire scene. He had come to Reinsnes to put things in order. And this was the thanks he got!

He was supposed to stand in church side by side with this Stine, a Lapp servant girl who had borne an illegitimate child.

The sheriff could feel so offended that his rage got blocked on its way out of his body. When the anger eventually emerged, no one could interpret the sounds.

Finally, he turned on his heels and announced that he was leaving this madhouse. And that Benjamin was no more a man's name than Virgin Mary.

"In Italy men are named Maria," Dina noted dryly. "If you're going home, don't forget your pipe. It's lying in the other room. And his name is, and will remain, Benjamin!"

In the upstairs hallway, Stine wept silently for a long time. She had overheard every word.

Oline muttered something, but nobody paid any attention. The seasonal farmhands eating their evening porridge in the kitchen felt uncomfortable.

But as soon as they got to the servants' quarters, the laughter exploded. This young mistress was certainly a stubborn one! They could not help liking that. Nobody in the parish had a mistress who allowed a servant to carry her child before God the Father Almighty, just because the girl had nursed the baby!

Sheriff Holm tramped toward the outrigger with a heavy, furious stride.

But as he left the gravel road behind, he seemed to collect himself somewhat. His steps slowed until, with a sigh, he stopped completely at the boathouse.

Then he turned on his heels, for the second time that day, and retraced his steps. Clattered unnecessarily on the stairway, and shouted through the open door:

"All right, let him live in sin and be named Benjamin! For God's sake!"

It was a hard blow for Dagny. She had not even been asked to stand at the baptismal font. This obvious, public humiliation tortured her day and night.

The day of the baptism, she was ill with a cold. Had a miserable headache and red eyes.

The boys could not go either, without her supervision. There were two of them by now.

Under her accusing gaze, the sheriff felt guilty for a moment. But he pulled himself together, sighed, and declared that this was his first grandchild, after all. It was his duty to be at the church!

He left with a baptism gift in his pocket and played the role of an important man. Immensely relieved to escape Dagny's accusations and disapproving looks, which constantly said:

"See the kind of daughter you have, my good man! It's a shame."

As if he did not know!

His harshest judges were Dagny's expressive eyes and her comments about her own excellent behavior as a young girl "down south." They made him so angry that on several occasions he had to restrain himself from placing his large hands around her neck.

But the sheriff neither choked nor hit people. He fastened two dark-blue eyes on them. And was deeply offended and unhappy when something was wrong.

Still, he always achieved his wishes, noisily and good-naturedly, both in court and otherwise. At least after Dina was safely at Reinsnes.

More than once he felt grateful to his dead friend and to Mother Karen. But he was afraid to pursue his thoughts about the situation at Reinsnes.

Few people dared to pass on rumors. So it was only when Dagny wanted to punish him for some reason that he heard how bad conditions could be at Reinsnes. With a mistress who was not in her own parlors, but would go riding at night. Who associated with boys and servant girls.

Sometimes he thought about Dina's upbringing. She had no contact with good manners for so long. Until that strange fellow Lorch arrived. He was neither fish nor fowl, as Dagny put it.

An unformulated twinge of conscience flashed through the sheriff's brain. But he thought it an insult, sent only to harm him. And felt he had a perfect right to reject it.

Chapter 3

Now when your words come true, what is to be the boy's manner of life,
and what is he to do?

— Judges 13 : 12

*T*he sweet-sour smell of baby and breast milk had a remarkable
effect on everyone. Especially since it had been twenty-three years
since they last had that smell at Reinsnes.

Sometimes Oline made comparisons.

"He looks like Johan!" Or: "It's like seeing little Johan! He had
the same expression when he dirtied his diapers!"

She was very enthusiastic about the family's progress. And showed
great interest in how little Benjamin's ears were placed on his head.
She loved the way they protruded slightly. This was not a family trait.
She looked at Dina, whose ears were always hidden in her hair.

Oline had to restrain herself from investigating whether the boy's
pointed faun ears were inherited from his mother.

But since one did not just march over and touch Dina, she had
be content with remarking that she had forgotten to note whether the
sheriff had ears like that.

"The sheriff's ears were chopped off when he was small, because
they were so ugly," Dina said disrespectfully.

Oline was offended. But she understood the hint. From then on,
she did not mention the boy's appearance when Dina was present.

But she told Stine one thing and another. First, the baby did not
have a hair on his head, which worried Oline most. Also, he had a
large birthmark on his left shoulder.

The older woman pestered Stine with questions about whether
her milk did not have enough nourishment to make his hair grow.

It made little difference that both Mother Karen and Stine re-
assured her. Told her about children they knew who had been bald even
as toddlers. And said this was often nature's way with human babies.

*   *   *

Benjamin's first summer was unbearably hot.

Stine's breast cloths soured quickly, and a dozen always hung drying on the clothesline behind the washhouse.

The lilacs finished blooming so quickly one scarcely noticed the fragrance. Crops suffered from drought. The heat made people sluggish and irritable.

Meanwhile, young Benjamin ate, cried, and slept like a puppy from a good brood. Everything grew visibly, except his hair.

He veritably devoured the small, lean wet nurse. She developed a toothache in a molar. And became thinner and thinner, despite the cream and butter Oline fed her to make her milk flow profusely.

Dina's triumph in having Stine carry Benjamin at the baptism gave the Lapp girl an unwritten and unspoken status far beyond Reinsnes.

Dina seemed to forget the whole thing as soon as the baptism was over.

And Stine took on the nighttime care, the breast-feeding, the diapering, and all the stories. She enjoyed her new esteem. Straightened her narrow back against the gossip and allowed herself the privileges of breakfast in bed and cloudberries with thick cream on weekdays. As well as newly churned butter and milk sweetened with honey to strengthen and sharpen her appetite.

She fearfully pushed out of her mind the question of what would happen when the boy was weaned. That was still several months away, and nobody talked about it.

Each time Stine placed the baby in Dina's arms, a magic circle was drawn. In the end, Dina never held the child except when Stine put him in her arms. Stine was the first and the last to hold him.

One day when Mother Karen and Oline were bending over Stine as she nursed the baby, Dina announced:

"Stine will stay here at Reinsnes as long as she wishes. We need her for more than breast feeding!"

Mother Karen quickly recovered from her disappointment at not being asked for advice.

So it was decided that Stine would have a secure position at Reinsnes, even with dry breasts.

From that day on, she began to smile. Her toothache stopped once she found courage to let the blacksmith pull the molar.

* * *

146

Tomas remembered the day of Jacob's funeral. As a time of pure madness.

He saw Dina sliding down the banister. Large and naked, with her shift between her and the polished wood to help her glide.

Sometimes he thought he had dreamed it. Other times he was not sure.

Then all at once the realization overpowered him. He, Tomas, had lain on the sheepskin in the master bedroom.

He secretly became both dignified and doomed. He no longer belonged to his own class. It did not matter that only he knew this.

He stood more erect and had an arrogant, introspective look unsuited to a cotter's son and a stableboy.

Many saw this, but no one knew its genesis. He was a stranger at Reinsnes. Someone whom Dina had brought.

None of the farmhands would think of teasing Tomas, however. Because nobody could match his pace in the fields. So they all avoided mowing beside him.

They asked him to slow down a little, but he seemed not to hear them. He always put several meters between him and his mowing partner.

In the end, they found ways to hold him in check. They let him stand all day with a pitchfork, tossing hay onto the wagon. Then they let him mow the most difficult parts of the field in the evenings, alone. They let him bring whetstones and pails of sour milk during rest periods.

Tomas never protested. For his head was filled with images and experiences. Smells. While he lifted his arms over his head with heavy loads of hay for hours. Or ran between the fields and the courtyard. Found new whetstones, turned the grindstone, or filled pails of sour milk in Oline's kitchen.

The summer that Dina gave birth, his body was oily and dark from sweat and sun.

Each evening, he plunged his head and chest into the watering trough near the stable and shook himself along with the horses.

Still, the fire within him blazed. Riding with her was the closest he came to quenching it. His heavy stirrup was always between them.

Tomas would have sold himself to the devil to remove that iron.

*   *   *

Dina often floated in the small, deep bay behind the flag knoll. It was well hidden among mountain peaks and birch forests. And at a good distance from the fields and the shipping channel.

She lay with the cool water up to her chin, while her breasts floated above, like animals trying to learn to swim on their own.

Sometimes when she came ashore, Hjertrud stood at the edge of the woods, waving with her arm half raised.

Then Dina stopped and stood with her shift or towel wrapped around her. Until Hjertrud spoke to her or disappeared.

When Dina was on her feet again after childbirth, Tomas used all his powers to discover when she bathed. It was at the strangest hours.

He had his own alerting system. Which was successful whenever he was not in the fields.

He awoke at night, ready to steal outside. Had a keen sensitivity to rustling in the grass past the servants' quarters and down to the cove. A fox could envy it.

One day he suddenly stood before Dina. After respectfully having spied on her until she was dressed and heading up the path.

Small birds flitted in the shadows among the trees.

They could hear the dinner bell from a farm across the sound.

Blåflag Peak stood newly clad in deep-blue evening shadows, and the air hummed with insects. The fragrance of heather and sunbaked seaweed permeated everything.

Dina stopped and regarded the person facing her. Questioningly. As if wondering who he was. She had a deep furrow between her brows. That made him uncertain. Still, he had to take the risk.

"You said you'd send me word. . . ."

"Word? About what?"

"Wanting to see me."

"And why would I want to see you?"

He felt her voice crush every bone in his body. Nonetheless, he stood upright.

"To . . . because . . . the day Jacob . . . Because that day in your room . . ."

He whispered it. Wailed it. Offered it to her like a sacrificial lamb.

"That was a time for other things!"

She said it definitively, as if she were underlining twice a final sum in the account books. So-and-so much profit. So-and-so many debts to collect. So-and-so much lost due to poor fishing.

148

"Yes . . . but . . ."

She used her smile. Which everyone misunderstood. Except Tomas.

Because he had experienced another Dina. In the master bedroom. Since then, he did not like her to smile.

"Things are different now. People do what they have to do," she said, looking him straight in the eye.

Her pupils grew larger. He saw the amber flecks in the left iris. Felt the coldness of the lead-gray eyes as physical pain. It paralyzed him. He did not move. Although she clearly indicated she wanted to get past him. He did not dare to try to touch her, even though she was so close that only skin and clothing separated them.

Then suddenly she seemed to think of something. She reached up and laid her hand on his downy cheek. It was damp with heat, excitement, and shame.

"It's time to heave to and not do hotheaded things," she said absentmindedly. "But you can still ride with me."

They rode across Skar Pass the same evening, before Dina's hair was even completely dry.

Several times she guided Blackie so close to him that her boot hit his leg.

Autumn had come. Leaves were turning yellow, and from a distance the aspen seemed to be ablaze.

He was afraid to bother her or ask for anything. He could not bear further rejections that day.

But the fire consuming his body was not quenched. Tomas slept fitfully, with many confusing dreams that could not be told in the servants' quarters.

He would stop in the midst of his work and sense her smell. He would think she was standing behind him and turn quickly. But she was never there.

Meanwhile, the willow herb spread its magenta flowers across the meadows and along the roadside.

The baby birds had learned to fly long before. Terns and seagulls subdued their cries to a listless cooing when someone came ashore with coalfish. And the well was beginning to go dry.

149

Chapter 4

Whoever steals a man, whether he sells him or is found in possession of him, shall be put to death.

— Exodus 21 : 16

Mother Karen saw with growing concern that ever since Dina had shunned people completely, her behavior had become whimsical and inappropriate again.

Dina attracted attention among strangers. She had the air of a wealthy man with a high reputation. Calmly smoked cigars after dinner at every opportunity. Seemed determined to shock and upset people.

When the gentlemen withdrew to the smoking parlor, Dina accompanied them as a matter of course.

She stretched out on the chaise lounge with her legs crossed. The hand holding the cigar was flung lazily on the plush upholstery.

She might even kick off her shoes.

She did not say much. Rarely took part in the discussions but briefly corrected anything she thought was an error.

The men felt scrutinized and uncomfortable. Relaxing with a cigar and a glass of *punsj* was not what it used to be.

Dina's presence, and the expressions on her face, unnerved the men. Since she was the mistress of the house, you could not even hint politely that she was not welcome. And she refused to be coldly ignored.

It was like having the pastor there. Somehow you could not stand tall or tell real stories.

For Dina sat there with her smile, listening. Gave them the uneasy feeling they were acting like fools.

It was particularly shameful when she interrupted the conversation to correct them about numbers, dates, potential profits, or items in the newspaper.

At first they thought she would leave when there was a sound from Benjamin somewhere in the house. But she did not even raise an eyebrow.

After a while it became too much for Niels. He moved the after-dinner *punsj* to the office. Eventually created a small sitting room in one corner.

But Dina refused to be banished. She examined the accounts vigilantly. And drank *punsj* in the office.

When Benjamin was about a year old, Dina found Stine weeping over the boy at her breast.

The tears flowed and flowed. Without a sound. The boy stared at his nurse as he sucked. Now and then he closed one eye because he instinctively knew that a tear might hit him in the face.

He was actually sucking just for comfort and closeness, because Stine's milk had begun to dry up. And it was about time, in Mother Karen's opinion.

After much hesitation, Stine told Dina her story.

She had let herself be tempted and taken. Thought she could not get pregnant while she was nursing. But that old rule obviously did not apply to someone like her.

At first she refused to identify the father. But Dina insisted.

"If you don't tell me who he is, so he can make amends, I won't allow you at Reinsnes any longer."

"But I can't tell you," wept Stine.

"Why not?"

"Because he's a gentleman."

"So he's not here at Reinsnes?"

Stine wept.

"Is he from Strandsted?"

Stine blew her nose and shook her head.

"Is he from Sandtorg?"

Dina continued this way until she discovered what she really had known already. Niels was the father of the child.

When the warehouse was closed at night, Niels used the sitting room there for more than drinking *punsj*.

"I hear you're going to be a father!"

Dina closed the office door behind her and put her hands on her hips. Niels was sitting behind the big oak desk.

He looked up. But only for a moment. He had difficulty meeting her eyes at first.

Then he made an about-face and pretended it was the first time he heard this.

Breathless excuses poured out, as if a hole had been punctured in a sugar sack.

"That's ridiculous!" he declared.

"You're old enough to know what you do, so I don't have to tell you. But a baby isn't planted by the Holy Spirit. Not around here! That was in Palestine. And it was a special case. So, this is where you lay with Stine? Here in this room?"

Niels began arguing before she finished speaking. For a few moments, they both talked at the same time.

Then Dina's eyes flashed. Rage and disdain mingled with a certain joy.

She walked slowly across the room to the desk, holding his gaze. Then she leaned over him and put her arm lightly on his shoulder. Her voice was like a cat purring on a sunny windowsill.

"Niels is old enough to choose. Today he can choose between two things. He can go to the altar with Stine immediately, or he can leave Reinsnes for good. With half a year's pay."

Niels turned white as hoarfrost. Perhaps he had suspected that Dina was just waiting for an opportunity to get rid of him. Had understood it from the first time she rummaged through the ledgers.

"You want to drive me away from Mother Ingeborg's estate!" he said, utterly distraught.

"It's a long time since Ingeborg owned this estate," replied Dina contemptuously.

"Johan will hear about this. Today!"

"Don't forget to tell him you're going to be a father in six months and you want Stine to bear the shame alone! I'm sure Johan, who's studying to be a pastor, will find that noble and worthy of a gentleman!"

She calmly turned to leave.

"You can let me know this evening what you've decided," she said, with her back to him. She closed the door carefully and nodded affably to a store worker who stood with her ears cocked toward the door.

At dusk Niels came to the master bedroom, where Dina sat playing the cello. They were well prepared. Both of them.

152

He could not marry a Lapp girl! Who had also borne a child by someone else, even though the child died. Dina must surely understand that.

To tell the truth, he had something else in mind. He had his eye on a girl from a good family. He mentioned her name and other particulars. And gave Dina a tentative smile.

"But you could ignore your refined, sensitive feelings, and the fact that she's a Lapp, when you got her down on the office floor!"

"She went along with it!"

"Yes, of course. And she's still going along with it. It's growing in her womb. You're the only one who isn't going along with it, Niels."

"Jacob wouldn't like it if I had to leave."

"You don't know anything about Jacob's wishes. But I do!"

"You're threatening me out of my home!"

He sank onto a chair.

Dina went to him and stroked his arm. Leaned her firm body over him.

"We only need you on your wedding day. Later you can leave. Or stay," she said softly. "If you stay, your yearly pay will be doubled, for Stine's sake."

Niels nodded and wiped his forehead. The battle was lost.

A tragic figure wandered the gravel paths at Reinsnes that evening. And he did not want any supper. Niels had learned that you must protect yourself when your position is insecure. Different masters have different laws.

Dina's laws were unlike most.

Niels had operated very cleverly for many years. He possessed a shrewd business sense, when it came to procuring his own income. These earnings did not appear in any account book.

Sometimes fishermen and farmers came to Mother Karen or to Anders and complained about the harsh treatment Niels accorded them when they could not pay their debts.

And sometimes Mother Karen settled the account for a poor soul, so Niels would leave him in peace.

Niels insisted he could not allow it to be said that debts were forgiven at Reinsnes. For then everyone would come running to complain about his troubles in order to get the same treatment.

But Mother Karen paid.

Dina stayed out of such matters, as long as the debt was properly recorded.

But sometimes Niels had collected sums that were not in the books. That were just verbal agreements, as Niels put it.

Dina pressed her lips tightly together and said:

"A number that's not written in the account books isn't a number! It can't be collected!"

And Niels gave in.

He simply made sure that people had no reason to complain the next time.

The payment was not laid away like treasure in heaven.

All who saw it promptly forgot that Niels himself had repaired some old rot in the office floor. Under the ponderous washstand with a heavy marble top, which dominated the corner behind the door.

The maids did not move the washstand. It was so heavy. They just neatly washed around it. Let their rags lick its painted blue base.

Over the years, a reassuring scrubbed stripe appeared around the bottom, where the wood had come through the paint. The cash lay safely under the loose, inlaid floorboard. In a fine tin box. The fortune grew nicely.

Niels never differentiated between Sundays and weekdays when it was a question of buying or selling at a profit.

Stine was not there when Benjamin needed to be put to bed. He had played with balls of brightly colored yarn in the servants' quarters all day while the maids took weaving off the loom.

They were annoyed when the boy became tired and fussy. Stine should have come to get him long ago.

So they told Oline. And began looking for Stine.

Even Dina joined the search. All to no avail. There was no trace of the young Lapp woman anywhere.

The third day, Dina found her in the fisherman's hut where her family lived.

Tomas and Dina came in a *faering* boat to bring her back to Reinsnes.

Stine was standing by the stove stirring the evening porridge when Dina entered the hut. Her face was grimy with soot and tears.

At first she would not speak. Just peered shyly at her family sitting nearby. The small hut had only one room. No place for a private conversation.

But when her bony, arthritic father cleared his throat and looked at her gently, she finally responded.

"I don't want to marry Niels!"

She would rather bear the shame and punishment for fornication. Refused to be plagued all her life with someone who had been forced to marry her in order to remain at Reinsnes.

"He's been there since he became an orphan, at the age of fourteen!" she added. There lay an accusation in her words.

I am Dina. I do not need to cry, because everything must be as it is. Stine cries. I carry her with me. Heavy or light. As I carry Hjertrud.

Those in the room heard Mistress Dina of Reinsnes apologize. Again and again.

Stine's old father sat in a corner. Stine's younger sister finished the food preparation. A half-grown boy went in and out and brought firewood.

No one tried to interrupt. Finally, everyone was invited to the table. For herring soup and crisp unleavened bread. The table was made of rough wood. Scoured white as a wind-washed whalebone. The steam rising from the soup bowls was weighted with emotions.

The news spread. Like sparks around ignited dry pine. Niels should have been glad he did not need to be in the servants' quarters. For they had no mercy on him there.

Stine had rejected Niels! What a story! Niels crept around, trying to find respect. The servant girls shunned him. The farmworkers avoided him. He was treated like a leper. The justice of the oppressed was devastating.

But Stine returned to Reinsnes. She gained weight. Had pink cheeks and looked fresh as a rose once the first morning sickness subsided.

She sang for Benjamin and ate well.

Mother Karen conversed with guests from far and near and told about her travels in Europe. It did not matter that she repeated the same stories.

The truly celebrated guests were always hearing them for the first time. And the regular guests grew accustomed to the dignified narratives as one becomes accustomed to the seasons.

Mother Karen had stories suited to the education and temperament of each guest. And she always knew when to stop.

She often withdrew with a gracious sigh as early as the after-dinner *punsj*, saying she wished she were younger and more spry.

Then Dina took charge, with merciless fingers. The music began. Liberation! Fever! It spread through the courtyard, across the fields. Along the shore. Reached Tomas on his hard cot in the servants' quarters. Created sorrow and joy. Depending where the tones fell.

Chapter 5

We must all die, we are like water spilt on the ground, which cannot be gathered up again; but God will not take away the life of him who devises means not to keep his banished one an outcast.

— 2 Samuel 14 : 14

One day Stine's brother appeared in the kitchen at Reinsnes. Dressed in a Lapp fisherman's simple reindeer-hide clothing and a blue calotte with an embroidered band. His well-worn moccasins were soaking wet.

They had no more flour at home. He had lost his way coming across the mountain to ask for charity at Reinsnes. And had been surprised by a bear on Eid Mountain.

It had frightened him so much that one ski slid off his foot and sped down the mountain. He had been forced to wade through deep snow the rest of the trip.

The boy held out his hands as if they were not part of him. He was short and slight, like his sister. Though confirmed the year before, he still did not have a beard. Just some downy fuzz here and there. And a coal-black shock of hair above intelligent eyes.

Oline immediately realized his hands were frostbitten. Without a word, Stine began to move about the kitchen, preparing something. Woolen rags smeared with cod-liver oil.

Stine was wrapping her brother's poor fingers in bandages when Dina entered. The air stank of cod-liver oil, sweat, and wet clothes. The boy sat on a stool in the middle of the kitchen. Helplessly let himself be tended.

"What's going on?" Dina asked. As they were explaining, Jacob entered from the hall with a stench of rotten meat. It was unlike any other smell.

Dina grasped the doorframe and leaned heavily against it, until she felt steady on her feet. Then she walked over to the boy and looked at his poor hands. And Jacob's odor disappeared.

157

She watched while Stine smeared and bandaged. The boy whimpered. The blue-wainscoted kitchen was silent. Except for the creaking floorboards as Stine moved about.

The boy recovered, thanks to Stine's treatment. He stayed at Reinsnes until his hands were completely healed. Slept in Tomas's room.

He could not make himself useful, of course. But after a few days he began to talk.

This unexpected friendship did not please Tomas particularly. Until he discovered that if he looked after the boy it would bring him closer to Dina.

She asked Tomas how things were with Stine's brother. She sent get-well wishes through him.

Tomas had taught Dina to shoot with a Lapp rifle even before she moved to Reinsnes. They did this in great secrecy on the mountain above Fagerness when checking ptarmigan snares. People below would think it was only Tomas who was practicing marksmanship.

The sheriff had confidence in the boy and trusted him not to waste gunpowder.

Later the sheriff gave the rifle to Tomas as a gift. Because he had helped in a successful bear hunt. The beast had taken several of the sheriff's sheep.

Tomas regarded the gift as a consecration. He was to be a bear-killer.

The rifle was made in Salanger. By a Lapp who knew his trade. It was the most precious thing Tomas owned.

And each time there was a bear hunt, Tomas managed to be in the party. He had not yet killed a bear alone.

Dina had been initiated into the art of marksmanship but had no hunting experience.

The sheriff accepted that he had a daughter who could handle a Lapp rifle, as long as she did not mention it when guests were present.

Jacob, on the other hand, thought it was unwomanly to shoot with gunpowder. Gunpowder was as expensive as gold!

But just as he was forced to accept Dina's habit of smoking cigars, he also had to accept that she practiced shooting a Lapp rifle after she came to Reinsnes.

It was a short rifle, with a fine barrel. Its simple breech bolt was defective, which demanded all the more of the marksman.

The flashpan had no cover, so gunpowder flew around one's ears when the weapon was fired.

But Dina learned the knack of it. Her eye and her inborn skill were attuned to the weapon. She appeared to be as quick and sure with gunpowder as she was with numbers.

The story that Stine's brother told about the bear must have been true. Several people had seen the beast. Apparently it was wandering in the mountains. At any rate, it did not plan to hibernate right now. A killer bear. Not too big. But its paw was strong enough to kill two sheep that had not come down from mountain pasturing in the fall.

One evening Dina went to see Tomas in the servants' quarters. She found him alone in his room.

"We're going hunting tomorrow, Tomas. We've got to get that bear that's wandering around," she announced.

"I've been thinking about the bear too. But you can't go along, Dina!" he said. "I'll get some men from . . ."

"Quiet!" she interrupted him. "Nobody knows what we're going to do. Just you and I will get that bear! Do you hear me, Tomas? We'll say we're going to set snares."

The room grew silent.

Then he made his decision. He nodded. He would gladly shoot a bear single-handed in order to have her to himself for hours. From dawn until dark.

The snares were ready. Tomas had the rifle hidden in his sack.

They set the snares not far from the estate. Ptarmigan were plentiful this year. The birds had stayed at the edge of the forest and appeared in no hurry to go to the mountains.

Snow had come early and covered the landscape. But not enough to require skis. The terrain was too rocky. Trudging in the snow for hours would be difficult. But they did not mention that.

The ptarmigan had not yet changed color and were clearly visible against all the whiteness.

Then they set out to hunt the bear.

Dina leaned forward slightly as she walked, her gaze focused among the trees. Tomas walked ahead with the loaded gun.

Hour after hour they searched the area where the bear had last been seen. But they saw no tracks. Did not hear the creature. Finally, they had to turn around because dusk began to fall. They were

159

exhausted. Tomas could not get over his disappointment at finding no sign of the bear.

They went to the ptarmigan snares in order to bring home at least that game.

Tomas removed the birds from the snares and hung them in his belt.

One ptarmigan had partially severed its wing while struggling to escape. Deep-red drops had eaten into the crusted snow. Another was still alive when Tomas retrieved it. Two round, glowing bits of coal blinked twice at them before Tomas grasped the neck and twisted the small head, and everything was over.

Rime covered the moors. They could see their breath in the frosty air.

They did not stop hunting the bear, even though they had come far down the mountain. They walked at the same horizontal line in the terrain. With a good distance between them.

When they came to the fox trap, they found a hare instead. Its hind leg was badly injured. Nevertheless, it managed to hop away when Dina removed it from the trap. It darted uncertainly among the birch trunks and slipped behind some tufts of snow-covered grass. They both ran after it. Dina found it.

She picked up a stick and tried to hit the hare's head. But the blow struck its back instead.

The animal gave a violent shudder and fled across the snow on three legs. But a moment later, it turned around. Whimpered like a year-old child. Then, dragging the helpless rear part of its body, it crept toward her on its front legs. Cried out in the white air, as the snow slowly turned red.

"Fire!" said Tomas, when the hare lay down at Dina's feet.

She stood there pointing at it. Death was already in the hare's eyes.

I am Dina, who stands in the washhouse at Fagerness while the steam cannot choke Hjertrud's scream. It spreads outward. Echoes in the windows. Trembles in all the faces. Clinks in the chunks of ice in the water barrel. The whole world is pink and white with steam and shrieking. Hjertrud is slowly peeled out of herself. In waves. And with tremendous force.

"Fire!" said Tomas again.

She turned her head and stared at him as if he did not belong

160

there. Tomas looked at her in amazement. His mouth curled into a slight smile.

At last he had the upper hand. For the first time. He aimed and fired. The shot was so powerful it lifted the whole hare from the ground. Its small body twisted before their eyes. And fell with a gentle thud.

Then everything was silent. Powder smoke settled on them. Dina turned away. Bits of white fur lay among all the scattered red pieces of flesh. Tomas put the rifle on his shoulder. The smell of blood was pungent and inescapable.

When she turned around, the man stood looking at her. With a knowing smile.

She was a lynx that sprang at the throat of a large prey.

The mountain pass thundered when the man's solid body hit the ground with the large woman on top of it.

As they rolled over and over, she tore at his clothes and bit his neck. Only after he gathered his wits did Tomas begin to protect himself. They were both breathing hard.

In the end, he lay quietly beneath her, and submitted to her handling. She uncovered his organ and rubbed it with cold hands as she murmured disconnected words he did not understand. At first he doubled up, grimacing with pain. Then he closed his eyes and accepted it.

Soon his organ stood erect and greeted her with an eager, glowing head. She had trouble finding herself in all her clothing. Finally, she took his knife from its sheath and slashed her clothes.

The flashing blade gave Tomas a sudden start. But she just sat on him heavily and opened herself for his spear. Then she rode him. Wildly.

She raised herself on her knees and then relaxed her legs with a snarl, putting all her weight on him.

He felt her warm groin embracing him. Frosty air entered now and then as she raised herself. Nails of ice pierced holes in him.

He grasped her hips with bloody hands and held her tight. Tight.

Her hair fell over her face like a dark forest. The evening sky blinded him the one time he tried to look at her. The shattered hare was the witness. Red and white.

When everything was over, she collapsed. Lay on top of him heavily.

Warm wet drops fell slowly onto his face. They trickled down his neck. He did not move. Not until her weeping became audible. Then he fumbled through her hair and found one eye. An open channel in the ice.

He raised himself on his elbow, and his mouth sought her forehead. Then he broke down too.

The snow had melted under him, and his clothes were wet. Suddenly the cold struck him from every direction.

The trembling in his body spread to hers in long, cold shudders. It was hours since the sun had plunged into the mountains. The crusted snow formed icy nails in their gloves.

They wandered home hand in hand, until they were so near the house that they might meet someone unexpectedly. Then their hands separated. Nothing had been said.

He carried the ptarmigan. She carried the rifle. The barrel, pointed calmly to the ground, moved in rhythm to her steps.

When they entered the courtyard, Tomas cleared his throat and said he would prefer to say it had been a fox. He had trapped a black fox the year before. Which he had sold to some Russian traders for a fine price. Ten *speciedaler* was good extra income.

She did not respond.

The moon had risen. It was late.

Hjertrud was not there. Could not be conjured from the corners for even the slightest instant.

But Jacob was gnawing and grinding like a mill. About five o'clock in the morning, she took the hare, which was hanging beneath the eaves outside the servants' quarters, sharpened a knife, and skinned what remained of the animal. There was no other solution.

She made a slit so the membrane broke and the skin slid off. Albeit unwillingly. The dead body curled up its bluish limbs when she let go. As if still trying to protect itself from the inevitable.

She cut off the legs and began to dismember the carcass. Unaccustomed to this work, she did not proceed quickly. As each piece was removed and the object in her hands looked more and more like an ordinary piece of meat from any animal, the ear-splitting scream diminished.

The wind whistled around the corners of the building. The knife crunched against cartilage and bone. The scream got weaker and weaker. Until at last, Hjertrud stood beside her and her head was normal and everything became blessedly quiet.

Finally, she put the hare in cold water. It was encased in a bluish membrane that sent rainbows into her eyes. Right through the water.

She put a lid on the kettle containing the hare and set it on the wooden table in the entryway. Cleaned the tabletop. Covered the blood and skin so that animals and birds could not reach it.

Her hands had suffered from the work and the icy water. She dried them warm and wandered around the house for a while as daybreak came. Then she undressed slowly and went to sleep as the estate awakened.

Chapter 6

Love the sojourner therefore; for you were sojourners in the land of Egypt.

— Deuteronomy 10 : 19

*R*einsnes had overcome its lethargy. You could not put your finger on anything specific. But Mother Karen thought it started when Dina finally got caught in the net called responsibility. And she took care to praise her.

"You're such a capable merchant's widow, Dina!" she might say. Without mentioning that an estate also needed a housewife.

Mother Karen was getting old. She had moved to a bedroom behind the main parlor. Could no longer manage the stairs.

They hired a good carpenter, who knocked down a wall between two small rooms. Which gave Mother Karen space for both her bed and her bookcases.

She needed these pieces of furniture, as well as an old high-backed baroque-style chair.

The key to the bookcases was always in the lock, but no one other than Mother Karen ever touched it.

The room was papered and painted in light colors. Dina gave Mother Karen good help with the redecorating. In fact, for a while there was actually some closeness between the two women.

Dina's practical manner, and her ability to get the work done quickly, delighted Mother Karen. And she thought, as so often before:

If only Dina were as strong and practical about everything at Reinsnes!

Or she murmured to herself:

"If only Dina would marry a proper fellow!"

Benjamin grew and began to explore Reinsnes. Extended his paths to reach all the way down to the warehouses and the store and up to the summer barn on the heath. Stubborn as a willow bough, he trudged off with Stine's little Hanna. To explore the world outside the white courtyard. A deep furrow constantly between his eyebrows.

He had never learned to say Mama or Mother. And he had no one to call Father. But there were many laps that welcomed him.

Each had a name. And its own smell.

He could sit with his eyes closed and still know whose smell he was inhaling. Everyone existed just for him. That people also had other tasks did not worry him. Someone was always there when he needed anything.

Stine was best. She smelled like salty seaweed and ripe blueberries. Had the aroma of clothes that have hung outside at night. Her hands were calm, gentle animals. Brown, with well-clipped nails.

Her dark, wiry hair lay flat on her temples. Did not curl on her forehead when she perspired, as Dina's hair did. Stine's sweat was the best of all. It was open spice drawers. Better than the wild strawberries behind the garden.

Mother Karen had kind eyes and many stories. Her words came like a mild wind. She resembled her flowers. They grew in pots on the windowsill and drooped a little in the winter.

Dina was as distant as a storm far out at sea. Benjamin rarely looked for her. But her eyes told him to whom he belonged.

She did not tell stories. But sometimes she held his neck. Tightly. Still, it felt good.

She set him on the horse, but only when she had time to walk alongside and hold the bridle. She spoke calmly to Blackie. But her eyes were on Benjamin.

They said Hanna was Stine's child, but she really belonged only to Benjamin. She had plump fingers and eyes like scalded almonds. When she blinked, long straight eyelashes trembled on her cheek.

Now and then Benjamin's chest ached when he looked at Hanna. It felt as though someone had ripped him inside. He could not decide whether it was good or bad. But he felt it.

One day a painter came ashore with his easel, a wicker trunk, and a canvas bag filled with tubes and brushes.

He wanted to greet the mistress of Reinsnes, whom he had met at Helgeland some years ago. Asked the captain to wait while he was rowed back and forth. It would take only a few minutes. . . .

An hour after departure time, when everyone was impatient to sail, the captain sent word to the artist.

He was requested to send the man's baggage ashore. And *Prince Gustav* steamed north without the painter. For he sat transfixed in the smoking parlor, listening to Dina's cello.

Dina had played her cello in the parlor for guests several times during the last year.

The ice-colored summer evening made the islands in the sound hang suspended in midair.

The painter called it a shimmering wonder. An optical illusion. He must stay until the next steamer, because the light at Reinsnes was like silk and alabaster!

But many steamers would pass before he made the final brush stroke.

This remarkable man became the new Lorch. Although he was Lorch's complete opposite.

He arrived like a thundering volcano one day in June. Spoke Swedish with a foreign accent and brought his own rum in an earthen jug with a tap.

His chalk-white hair and beard framed a tanned face with innumerable wrinkles. His nose protruded into the world like an impressive mountain range.

His dark, close-set eyes gazed from deep in his head. As if he were withdrawing them from the evil and stupidity of this earth in order to save them for a better existence.

His mouth was as red as a young girl's and had large, sensual lips. The corners constantly turned upward.

His hands looked as though they had been tarred. Dark brown. At once strong and sensitive.

He walked in the blazing sun wearing a black felt hat and a leather vest. In lieu of pockets, the vest had a slash on the upper right side, in which to put paintbrushes or a pipe as needed.

Pedro's laughter echoed throughout the house and beyond. And he spoke six languages. At least that was what he claimed.

Mother Karen discovered that his proficiency in German and French was quite limited. But she did not expose him.

He introduced himself as Pedro Pagelli. No one had the least faith in what he said about his origins. For his tales and his family tragedies shifted characters and content depending on the moon's phase or

166

which people were sitting around the table. But what a storyteller!

Sometimes he descended from gypsies in Romania, other times from noble Italian military men. Sometimes he was a Serbian whose family had been split by war and treachery.

Dina tried to make him drunk to discover the truth. But it appeared the man had learned these incredible stories so thoroughly he believed them himself.

They drank many bottles of wine, both in the smoking parlor and in the summerhouse at night. But nobody got the true story.

They did get paintings, however. Pedro painted them all. And he made a portrait of Jacob from another picture. It was so lifelike that Mother Karen clasped her hands in delight and offered a good Madeira.

One day when Pedro and Dina were at Andreas Wharf to get some canvas that had arrived with the steamer, he became lost in wonder at the cones of light that poured through the open loading doors on the top floor.

"Hjertrud comes in there," said Dina all of a sudden.

"Who is Hjertrud?"

"My mother."

"Is she dead?" he asked.

Dina looked at him in astonishment. Then her face brightened. She took a breath and continued:

"For a long time she walked on the beach. But now she's here! She comes in the cranehouse door and leaves through the herring nets hanging on the first floor. We walk down the stairs together before she disappears. . . ."

Pedro nodded eagerly. Wanted to hear more.

"What did she look like? Was she tall? As tall as you? What colors was she?"

That evening Dina showed him sketches of Hjertrud. She told him about the folds in her skirt. About the cowlick on the right side of her head . . .

He became so fascinated with Hjertrud that he moved to the warehouse and painted her among the fishing nets, large as life. Captured her facial features on the canvas.

While he painted her, he talked with her.

The day Pedro was completing the portrait of Hjertrud, Dina appeared unexpectedly.

"You have the eyes of a woman who's guarding her soul," he murmured to the picture with satisfaction.

At first Dina stood behind him like a pillar. He did not hear her breathing and took that as a good sign.

All of a sudden, there was a thundering sound behind him and the floorboards shook. He turned in alarm.

Dina sat on the battered floor, howling.

A forlorn and furious wolf. With no inhibitions or shyness. The wolf sat on its haunches in bright sunlight and wept its terrifying song.

At last, she seemed to realize she had gone utterly beyond civilized behavior. She stopped crying and laughed.

Pedro knew what every true clown knows. Humor is the most faithful supporting actor in a tragedy. So he let her complete both phases. Just threw her a paint-stained rag so she could wipe most of the tears from her face.

He calmly continued painting until he had made the final brush stroke. By then the blue dusk had turned misty white and the sounds in the courtyard were a faint hum. Shadows transformed the corners into sketches on old parchment. They were filled with smells.

Hjertrud's perfume clung to everything. She had a whole face again.

Hjertrud was hung on the wall in the main parlor. Everyone who came to Reinsnes remarked on it. Even Dagny.

"A brilliant work of art!" she said graciously, and asked Pedro to do a portrait of the sheriff's family.

Pedro bowed and thanked her. He would be delighted to paint the sheriff's wife. As soon as he had time . . .

He painted Dina with her cello. She had a greenish body and was not wearing clothes. The cello was white. . . .

"It's the light," Pedro explained.

Dina looked at the painting in surprise. Then she nodded.

"Someday I'll exhibit this work in large galleries in Paris," he said dreamily. "It's called: 'Child Who Tones Down Her Sorrow.' "

"What's sorrow?" she asked.

The man gave her a quick glance and then replied:

"To me, it's all the pictures I can't see clearly . . . but must carry with me anyway."

"Yes." She nodded. "It's the pictures one carries."

I am Dina. Jacob always walks beside me. He is large and silent and drags the foot they had no chance to remove. The smell is gone. Jacob does not disappear, as Hjertrud sometimes does. He is a steamboat without steam. He drifts with me. Calmly. Heavily.

Hjertrud is a crescent moon, sometimes waxing, sometimes waning. She floats outside me.

Pedro and Dina did not tell anyone about "Child Who Tones Down Her Sorrow." They suspected it was inappropriate for good people's eyes.

They wrapped the painting in old sheets and put it in the alcove where Jacob used to sleep. Behind the old chaise lounge.

Pedro could not tolerate the winter cold and snow. He shriveled up. Became old and feeble, like a sick horse.

When spring came, they feared he would die from his fever and coughing. Stine and Oline practically force-fed him with nourishing food.

The food alone almost killed him at first. But little by little, he revived and was able to sit in bed, painting. Then they knew the worst was over.

Mother Karen read to him from the newspapers, from Johan's letters and whatever else she could find.

But he did not want to hear anything from the Bible.

"The Bible is holy," he growled somberly. "Leave it alone when heathens are in the room!"

He did not specify who was a heathen. Mother Karen chose not to take it personally.

Benjamin often stood in the doorway of the guest room and stared at the old man with many colors on a board in front of him. Watched the pipe smoke, entranced. It curled toward the ceiling between the man's coughing spells.

The boy kept staring until he was beckoned to the bed, where a heavy hand patted his head.

Two lively eyes met his. Benjamin smiled expectantly.

The man coughed, knocked ashes from his pipe, made a few brush strokes, and began to tell stories.

Benjamin liked it best when Pedro stayed in bed. Then he knew he had him.

And Dina could not steal him. Because Dina avoided sickrooms.

Pedro stayed through September of the second year. Then the steamboat took him away.

One whistle blast, and he was gone. With his felt hat and leather vest, with his paints and his wicker trunk. And the rum jug with a tap. Which had been filled to the brim in the cellar at Reinsnes. They did not begrudge him that travel provisioning.

I am Dina. Everyone has gone. "Child Who Tones Down Her Sorrow" is gone. I have taken down Hjertrud from the wall. Her eyes have gone away. I can't look at a picture without eyes. Sorrow is the pictures one can't see but must carry anyway.

Chapter 7

Can papyrus grow where there is no marsh?
Can reeds flourish where there is no water?
While yet in flower and not cut down,
they wither before any other plant.

— Job 8 : 11–12

A childish secrecy about resting in a haybarn like two runaway children.

Tomas gathered crumbs and never threw any away. Lived his lonely life in the servants' quarters, among men with whom he had nothing in common.

He got his pay. And did the work of two men during the busy seasons. As if he needed to show her that he was a man. Never finished showing her. Spring after spring. Ride after ride. Harvest after harvest.

As time went on, Tomas assumed most of the responsibility for the fields, animals, barn, and stable. The old cattle tender was no longer needed. His position was eliminated, with Dina's blessing.

And Tomas dreamed. About Dina and the horse with empty shafts and no sleigh or master. He dreamed his conscience.

Afterward, Blackie had Jacob's eyes for days. His eyes asked about Benjamin. It seemed that Tomas had to bear everything.

When Dina did not look in his direction for a long time, he seemed to catch a witch's scent when she brushed past. He compared her with more slender girls he had seen. Girls with slim wrists and shy eyes.

But the dreams came and destroyed all his defenses. Laid her large, firm body close to his. So he could hide his face between her breasts.

Each time he heard her pacing back and forth in the warehouse for hours, he felt something akin to tenderness.

Once, he slipped into Andreas Wharf and called to her. But she turned him away furiously. The way one repels an impertinent stableboy.

Tomas could not look at Benjamin without examining the boy's features. His coloring. His gestures. Was this Jacob's son?

It became an obsession. A thought constantly in the forefront of his mind. He saw the boy's pale eyes and dark hair. Dina's characteristics. But what about his other traits?

One thing was certain. The boy would never have a large build like Jacob or Dina.

But Johan was not large either. And Johan was Jacob's son . . .

Tomas drew the boy to him. Won his trust. Became indispensable. Told him he should not fear Blackie, because that horse had stood watch while he was born.

Benjamin came often to see the horses. Because Tomas was in the stable.

Dina worked systematically to find all the missing numbers. Numbers did not disappear by themselves, she said. They always existed somewhere, even if apparently no one discovered them.

Numbers could be like lambs lost in the mountains. But they were always there. In one form or another. And Niels would reveal them. Sooner or later. He knew the answer to the homeless numbers.

But she stopped nagging about it. Just searched with her falcon eyes. Worked backward through old ledgers and papers.

She kept a close watch on Niels's financial transactions. What he paid for and what appeared to be free.

Until now, she had not found a single entry missing. Niels had ridiculously modest expenditures for clothing. Was as Spartan as a monk. He owned a silver snuffbox and a walking stick with a silver handle. Both were gifts from Ingeborg, long before Dina's time.

Still, Dina did not give up.

As if the numbers and the search were what really mattered. Not the money.

The accountant from Tromsø whom Dina hired after Jacob's death had taught her the essentials of simple bookkeeping.

The rest came gradually as she grew accustomed to the work.

172

Niels made the daily entries, but she always checked the accounts.

This worked to an extent, until she began to be interested in their stocks of merchandise. Not just what the cargo boats needed for fishing trips and voyages to Bergen, but also daily trade at the store.

In the end, it was Dina's neat figures that appeared in the various ledgers. Her writing was large and slanted left, with simple curls and loops. It could not be imitated.

Exact quantities of salt and flour, syrup and liquor, must be determined. Small items for household use. Sufficient supplies of rope and fishing equipment must be calculated, both for their own use and for the tenant farmers.

Eventually Anders came to Dina with his figures for boats and gear. And this became a sore spot between the two brothers.

Niels made sure he was not in the office on the days when Dina was there.

One day he arrived expecting to be alone and found her sitting behind the desk.

"You could just as well do all the bookkeeping," he said darkly.

"And what would our good Niels do then?" she asked.

"Supervise the store and lend the clerk a hand," he replied quickly. As if he had practiced the sentence for a while.

"Niels doesn't lend a hand to anyone," she declared, slamming the ledger shut. Then she changed her mind and opened it again, with a sigh.

"You're angry. You've been angry for a long time. I think there's something wrong. . . ."

"Oh? What could that be?"

"The new maid hinted that you've been pinching her . . . and bothering her . . . while she makes the bed and cleans your room."

Niels looked away. Fuming.

"You should get married," she said slowly.

The words awakened a devil inside him. His face darkened. He showed courage he rarely exhibited.

"Is that a proposal?"

He even managed to look her scornfully in the eye.

She was taken aback for a moment. Then a faint smile crossed her face.

"The day I propose, the man concerned won't need to ask about anything. He'll answer!"

Dina signed something, biting her tongue in the right corner of her mouth. Then she held the silver knob of the heavy ink blotter that was always on the desk. Pressed it over "Dina Grønelv." Her signature was absorbed. A mirror image but clear enough.

I am Dina. Niels and I count everything at Reinsnes. I own the numbers, wherever they are. Niels is doomed to them. "The slave counts. The master sees." Niels does not give anything to anyone. Not even to himself. He is like Judas Iscariot. Doomed to be who he is. Judas went out and hanged himself.

Niels kept his hands off the servant girls. Lived his lonely existence in the midst of them all.

Sometimes he looked at little Hanna as she trudged past. He did not touch her. Did not call to her. But gave her brown sugar from the drawer. Hastily. As if he were afraid someone would see it.

Or he mumbled a quick order to the store clerk, who cut a large piece of sugar and placed it in the small hand.

Hanna had Stine's golden skin and dark eyes. But when she felt hurt, anyone who knew the situation could see that she withdrew with the same gestures as Niels. Like a wolf cub frightened by its own pack.

The sheriff heard stories about Dina.

Usually it was old news, which he received calmly. But one day it was whispered in his ear that people said the women at Reinsnes, Stine and Dina, lived like a married couple.

The sheriff became so furious he went to Reinsnes.

Dina heard him raging, like a powerful northwest wind on Blåflag Peak in wintertime.

When he entered the parlor and demanded to speak with her alone, his blustering subsided. He forgot what to say.

The subject was extremely delicate. He was at a loss for words. Finally, he spit it out in crude language, pounding his fist on the table.

Dina's gleaming eyes stabbed him like knives. The sheriff knew that gaze well. And looked away.

He could see her mind was working, even before he had finished. She did not comment on anything he had said. Just opened the

174

pantry door and asked the maid to fetch Niels. And she sent for Stine, Oline, Mother Karen, and Anders.

Niels came, out of respect for the sheriff.

Entered calmly and put his well-behaved hands behind his back after shaking hands with the guest.

His sleeve protectors constantly slid over his wrists, and he flushed with uncertainty.

Dina regarded him almost tenderly as she said:

"I hear you know a great deal about Stine and me. That we live like a married couple!"

Niels gasped. But stood remarkably steady. Still, his tight collar bothered him enough so that he swallowed. Just for the sake of doing it.

The sheriff was more than embarrassed. The others in the room lowered their eyes, and the doors to the pantry and kitchen were open.

It was not a short conversation. Niels denied everything. Dina was certain she was right. Nevertheless, she listened to him calmly when he called the whole thing wicked gossip designed to cause trouble between Dina and him.

Suddenly Dina leaned toward him with glassy eyes. And spit on the tips of his shoes.

"That's where the wickedness lies!"

The man was pale. Took a step backward. Was about to say something. But changed his mind. The whole time he looked helplessly from Dina to the sheriff.

Niels had sat in taverns here and there, making comments. And people had interpreted them as if the meaning were unmistakable.

The sheriff set all his powerful machinery in motion against Niels. Made sure the man's sins came to light. His incompetence as a store manager and his cowardice in paternity matters. His greediness. His dream of acquiring Reinsnes and all its manorial rights by marrying Dina. And her humiliating rejection.

In the end, Niels was a broken man. Nobody could understand that he remained at Reinsnes.

But there was peace between Dina and him. He was no longer a worthy opponent.

Dina asked Oline to make a lamb roast. Pink meat inside a crisp, browned exterior. She had fine wines brought from the cellar and

invited the entire household and the relatives at Fagerness for a rec-
onciliation dinner.

Niels declined without a word. He simply failed to appear. Sat in
the office smoking his pipe and refused to join the festivities.

His empty place at the table showed everyone that Dina was not
to blame.

Stine secretly brought him a basket filled with samples of the
feast. Niels refused to let her in, but she left everything outside the
door.

When she returned to get the basket before going to bed, the
food and drink were gone. Only some gravy and bits of dry garnish
remained. And the dregs of a wine bottle. She stole back to the kitchen
with the empty plates. Oline asked no questions, merely gave her a
sidelong glance and sighed as she continued her work.

Piano music could be heard from the parlor. The notes drifted
out to them triumphantly.

One day Dina and Benjamin sat helping Mother Karen straighten a
skein of yarn that Hanna had tangled. They were in Mother Karen's
bedroom.

Benjamin pointed to the pictures on the wall and asked about the
man who had been at Reinsnes and painted pictures of people.

"He's sent two letters," Dina replied. "He exhibits his paintings,
and he's just fine."

"Where is he now?"

"In Paris."

"What's he doing there?"

"He's trying to become famous," Dina said.

Mother Karen took Jacob's portrait from the wall and let Benjamin
hold it.

"That's Jacob," she said solemnly.

"The man who died before I was alive?"

"He's your father," whispered Mother Karen with emotion. "I've
showed you this picture before. . . ."

"What was he like, Dina?" asked Benjamin. Mother Karen became too threatening when she was emotional, so it was best to turn
to Dina.

"He was the handsomest man around here. He was Mother Kar-
en's little boy, even if he was big and grown up. We were married.
He fell in the rapids before you were born."

Benjamin had heard the same words before. He had seen some of his father's shirts and vests. They smelled of tobacco and the sea. Almost like Anders.

"He was an unfortunate man to die so young," said Mother Karen, and blew her nose in a tiny handkerchief edged with lace.

Benjamin followed her with his eyes. When she was like this, like a little bird, he felt like crying too.

"Nobody is unfortunate to die. It's the living who are unfortunate," said Dina.

Mother Karen said no more about the misfortunes of the dead.

But Benjamin realized there was more to say, and he crept into his grandmother's lap. To comfort her.

He thought Dina was like a very dark attic and stayed away from her the rest of the day.

Dina never talked to him while he played with his things on the floor, and she did not bring him inside when he was in the garden. She never called and shouted if he was on the beach without permission.

One summer night shortly after Mother Karen had talked about Jacob's misfortune, Benjamin saw Dina sitting in the big rowan tree in the garden.

He had awakened and decided to go and see if the hens had laid eggs, because he thought it was morning.

She sat absolutely still and did not see him.

He forgot the eggs and stood by the picket fence, staring at her.

Then she waved. But he saw that she was not completely herself.

"Why did you climb the tree, Dina?" he asked when she came down.

"I've always climbed trees."

"Why?"

"It's good . . . to get a little higher . . . toward heaven."

Benjamin heard that Dina's voice was different. A night voice.

"Is it true what Mother Karen says, that Jacob lives in heaven?"

Dina finally looked straight at him. And he realized he had been longing for this.

She took him by the hand and led him toward the house. The dew was heavy at the bottom of her skirt. Drew her down to the earth.

"Jacob is here. Everywhere. He needs us."

"Why don't we see him?"

177

"If you sit on the steps . . . Yes, right there! Then you feel him a tiny bit. Don't you?"

Benjamin sat with his small brown hands on his knees and tried to feel Jacob. Then he nodded energetically.

Dina stood beside him for a moment, deeply serious.

A frightened wind slipped between them. Like a breath.

"Is it only here on the steps, Dina? Is he only here?"

"No. He's everywhere. He needs you, Benjamin," she said. As though the thought surprised her.

Then she let go of his hand and walked slowly into the house. Without saying he must come with her or go to bed.

Benjamin had a deep, reassuring feeling that he missed her.

Then he trudged barefoot across the courtyard and into the henhouse. It smelled of hayseed and chicken droppings. He saw the hens sitting on their roost and understood that it was still night.

That afternoon as he stood by the kitchen window, looking across the fields, he suddenly said to Oline in a loud, proud voice:

"There's Dina riding! Dina rides damn fast!"

"Little boys don't say damn at Reinsnes," Oline told him.

"Didn't Jacob say damn?"

"Jacob was a man."

"Was he always a man?"

"No."

"Did he say damn when he wasn't a man?"

"Oh, dear!" said Oline in bewilderment, as she wiped the backs of her plump hands alternately on her apron. "Too many people are raising you. You'll be a heathen all your life!"

"What's a heathen?"

"Someone who says damn!"

Benjamin slid off the stool and padded calmly across the floor. He wandered through the house until he found Mother Karen. There he solemnly announced that he was a heathen.

The matter caused quite an uproar.

Oline did not change her opinion, however. The boy was getting too little proper upbringing. He was becoming wild! Just like his mother.

She squinted at him. It transformed her face into a shriveled potato with old, white sprouts dangling on each side. Tufts of hair always escaped from under her kerchief.

*　　*　　*

On nights when the moon was full and sleep would not come, Dina sat in the summerhouse until everything grew calm and the world floated away in the stripe between sky and sea.

Sat stroking Jacob's unruly hair. As though nothing had ever come between them. She talked with him about taking a trip. Across the ocean. There was a deep fury in her, which he understood.

Chapter 8

Behold, God is great, and we know him not;
the number of his years is unsearchable.
For he draws up the drops of water,
he distils his mist in rain
which the skies pour down,
and drop upon man abundantly. . . .
Behold, he scatters his lightning about him,
and covers the roots of the sea.

— Job 36 : 26–28 & 30

Mother Karen dated letters 1853. Now and then the world came a little closer. Whenever newspapers arrived with the steamboat. Ludvig Napoleon Bonaparte had become emperor in France. The papers reported that the monarchists had joined the liberal and conservative Bonapartists under a strong leader, to fight "the Red ghost." The wave of revolution spread from country to country.

Mother Karen feared the world would be in flames before Johan came home. She had worried a great deal about Johan in the past years. He had been away so terribly long. She did not know what he was doing. If he was taking his examinations. If he would ever return.

His letters did not tell her what she longed to hear. She read them aloud to Dina to get comfort and comments.

Dina stated her opinion bluntly.

"He writes when he needs money! He spends twice as much as he receives from his inheritance. You're too kind about sending him your own money, Mother Karen."

She did not mention that Johan had once promised to write her from Copenhagen. That was almost nine years ago. Johan was no longer anything to take into account. Except in the loss column.

*   *   *

In late April, when winter had lost its grip and the snow had begun to melt, they suffered a new assault. A meter of snow within just a few days, with a wind so strong it sent every loose object into the sea.

The storm left many widows in the homes along the channel. Since the ground stayed frozen and the heavy snow was like a wall between each farm and the next, the corpses were not laid in their graves until well into June.

The earth clutched the deep frost. The rain would not come and end the longest winter in anyone's memory.

Hjertrud did not appear all spring. Dina paced back and forth in the warehouses. For hours. Until the cold crept under her wolfskin coat and caught her feet in an icy grasp. They turned numb and wanted to go their own way, inside to the stove.

Spring was harder than the winter had been, for people and animals. One even heard prayers for mild weather from the pulpit, and pleas for rain and melting snow were added to the sermons read at home.

Rarely had prayers been so sincere and well formulated and contained so few barbs against one's neighbor.

Summer arrived in mid-June. Suddenly, a hot sun blazed on every living thing. The birch tree stood with its erect trunk half hidden in snow. New leaves formed an immodest veil over the slender branches.

The snowbanks in the mountains rocked gently at first, the night the southwest wind came. Then they let go. One after the other, they swayed and shook loose. And joined the great, exuberant rush down the mountainside. Everything happened so fast, so fast.

Then came the melting snow and the floods. Water covered the fields, rushed through the gorge. Took with it the road through the mountain pass and thundered the same route that Jacob had taken with the sleigh.

Then everything abated. Little by little. The late spring planting sprouted apprehensively.

People and animals emerged from the buildings. Reassuring

summer sounds dared to prevail. The days were finally sated with sun and tar and the scent of lilacs. Late, but extraordinarily good.

I am Dina. The sounds drift in to me like distant shouts or annoying whispers. Or a thundering din that devours my eardrums.

I stand at the dining room window and see Benjamin playing with a ball in the garden. I am drawn into Hjertrud's realm. Like a whirlwind. Cannot resist.

It is Lorch's face! So large it fills the entire window, as far as the fjord stretches, and even farther. Benjamin is a tiny shadow in the pupil of Lorch's eye, whirling very fast.

Lorch is afraid! I let him come inside. It is the seventh of July.

While the late lilacs were still blooming, a letter arrived from Copenhagen. Addressed to Dina at the sheriff's estate. In neat, slanted handwriting.

The sheriff sent a farmhand to deliver it. It was short. As though each sentence were chiseled into a mountain with great difficulty:

Dearest Dina!

I lie ill in the royal city. Will finally die. My lungs are eaten away. I have nothing to leave behind. Except good wishes for you. Each day I regret leaving Fagerness.

Have neither health nor means to return. But the cello is alive. Dina, will you ship it home? Do it carefully! It is a noble instrument.

Your Lorch

Dina paced and paced. In all three warehouses, one after another. On every floor.

She paid no attention to Hjertrud the whole day. Jacob was merely a curl of dust.

She howled softly to herself. Her shoes chopped the hours to pieces. The daylight was unending. Shone through the small leaded windows and across the floor.

She entered the realm of the dead. In and out of the cones of light. It was a nightmare, and a beautiful dream.

Then at last, Lorch leaned against her forehead.

*   *   *

Afterward, she always met Lorch when she needed to find peace.

In death, as in life, he was shy and awkward.

Each year during lilac season, he wandered the garden paths, which were newly strewn with crushed shells. Among flower beds edged with pebbles. The sea had ground and formed them, licked them and left them behind.

Lorch was there. She had brought them to Reinsnes, all of them. Including Lorch. He belonged to her. The discovery was a loud boom from the ocean. The melancholy notes of a cello. Deep bass tones from taluses and mountains. It was uninhibited desire and necessity.

Chapter 9

Now at the feast the governor was accustomed to release for the crowd
any one prisoner whom they wanted. . . . The governor again said to
them, "Which of the two do you want me to release for you?" And they
said, "Barabbas."

— Matthew 27 : 15, 21

*T*he passenger list in the Tromsø *Stiftstidende* said the *Prince Gustav*
sailed from Trondheim carrying theology graduate Johan Grønelv in
first class.

Mother Karen was beside herself with joy and wiped happy tears
from her eyes. Few letters had arrived recently. But they knew he
had taken his final examinations at last.

He had not been home during all these years. But he wrote to
Mother Karen that he was returning to Reinsnes to think simple,
sensible thoughts and to get rested, after years of keeping his nose
in the books.

If the thought of Johan's return made Dina uneasy, she hid it
well.

In his last letter the young theologian mentioned in passing that,
with great misgivings and an admitted lack of modesty, he had applied
for a parish in the Helgeland region. But he did not mention the
specific place.

Dina thought he should seek a parish in the south. They were
wealthier, she added, looking Mother Karen straight in the eye.

But Mother Karen was not concerned about rich parishes. She
tried to remember what he looked like, how he acted the last time
she had seen him. But her thoughts became paralyzed. Jacob's death
was so much greater. She sighed and paged through Johan's letters.
Thoroughly prepared herself to welcome him as he was now. A grown
man and a theologian.

* * *

184

I am Dina, who knows a boy with frightened eyes. He has "Duty" written on his forehead. He does not look like Jacob. He has salt water in his unruly dark hair, and thin wrists. I like his chin. It is cleft and knows nothing about the duty on the forehead. When he comes, he will wear a stranger's unfamiliar face to hide himself from me.

Mother Karen and Oline planned an elaborate homecoming. The pastor's family would be invited. The sheriff's family. All the important people!

They would slaughter a calf and serve a good Madeira. They polished the silver. Washed the tablecloths and stoneware.

Oline happily gave orders and laid plans. Jacob's son would be welcomed like a king!

She took Benjamin in hand and taught him how to bow politely to his older brother.

"Like this!" she told him, clicking her heels together like a general.

And Benjamin mimicked her, very seriously and precisely.

Mother Karen supervised preparation of Johan's room, the south dormer room that she had vacated earlier. There was not time for all the improvements she wanted to make.

But she insisted, despite Dina's furrowed brow, that the two gold leather chairs in the master bedroom must go into Johan's room. And the mahogany bookcase with ivory rosettes on the door handles would be moved from her room to the young theologian's.

Several young men, with Tomas at the fore, strained under the heavy furniture while Mother Karen sat on a chair in the hall, cheerfully giving orders.

Her presence acted as a gentle whiplash on the panting, perspiring men.

"Careful now, dear Tomas! No, no, keep an eye on the wainscoting! Turn slowly there! Watch that the glass doors don't slide open!"

But at last everything was done according to her instructions, and Dina helped her climb the stairs so she could inspect the room.

Either her age was playing a trick on her, or else the room had shrunk, both in length and in width, she said.

Dina bluntly replied that such elegant furniture as Mother Karen deemed fitting for a pastor did not fit in the south dormer room at Reinsnes. They would have to enlarge the house.

Mother Karen held back her words and sat down on a chair near the door. Then she said quietly:

"He should have been given the master bedroom. . . ."

Dina did not answer. She put her hands on her hips, looked around the room, and thought for awhile.

"We'll give him the desk from the master bedroom and the chair that goes with it. They match the bookcase. And we'll move these big chairs back where they were before. . . ."

Mother Karen's eyes looked helplessly from wall to wall.

"The room is obviously too small. . . ."

"He won't be in this room all the time. He's going to live in the whole house, isn't he, Mother Karen? He needs a bookcase, a chair, a desk, and a bed. When he wants to be alone, I mean."

Things were done as Dina had said. But Mother Karen knew that a theology graduate should be given the master bedroom when he came home.

Rain came from the southwest.

The four larch trees, with the old dovecote in their midst, stood with their soft clusters of branches horizontal to the wind.

Ingeborg's rosebushes suffered terrible punishment near the walls and around the summerhouse. And Mother Karen's great pride, the lily bed, looked as though someone had soaked it in lye for hours.

Oline had slammed the oven door three times. She was a veritable Doomsday of brimstone and beseeching, weeping and wailing.

The maids ran back and forth and forgot from minute to minute what they were supposed do. For when Oline occasionally went crazy, it was always worse than the last time.

Anders stopped briefly in the kitchen for some coffee, after supervising the men who were securing the boats at the wharf.

When he saw how bad things were, he remarked good-naturedly:

"Someday Oline will get so angry she'll split right in two. But that won't matter, because there's plenty of her on both sides!"

"Yes, but only one foot and one hand on each side to serve you. Get out of here, my fine fellow!" she retorted, kicking her wooden shoe at him.

But he got his coffee. That was the law. Two loads of birch twigs were the payment.

*   *   *

The men had secured the boats and were lashing down everything on the wharf.

A tattered flag still hung on the flagpole. Most of the blue part was gone. It looked as though someone had disdainfully raised a pirate flag.

The worst thing was the rain. It was so heavy, and its constant racket on the roof and in the gutters wore on Mother's Karen's nerves.

A leak was discovered in the servants' quarters. Maids and farm-hands ran with tubs and buckets to save the bedding and chests.

Tomas rushed to the roof. Tried to fasten new slates over the sorry mess, but soon had to give up.

Out in the sound, the *Prince Gustav* had maneuvered with difficulty for hours, without getting much closer to shore.

People peered toward the steamboat in the midst of all their duties. Was it making headway now? Yes, indeed, it seemed to be doing a little better.

They discussed whether they should take down the tattered flag. It was the only one they owned. Mother Karen said absolutely not! If the weather took half the flag, they could not help that. But a naked flagpole was an insult.

Niels wanted to send Tomas inland to borrow a flag from a tenant farmer.

But Dina said no. Before Tomas returned, Johan would be inside the house and nobody would need a flag.

Twice, Benjamin had run outside to look for the steamboat without wearing a raincoat and had needed a complete change of clothes.

The second time, Oline shouted through the house that the youngster was completely wild and Stine should take better care of him.

But Benjamin shouted back in a loud, cheerful voice:

"No, Oline. Benjamin's a heathen!"

Hanna nodded gravely as she helped him with his many buttons. Their love was unassailable. Hanna trudged after him wherever he led. If he fell in the stream, Hanna fell in the stream. If he scraped his knee, Hanna cried. If Oline thought Benjamin was a heathen, then she cried loud and furiously until Oline had to grant that Hanna was an equally good heathen.

*　　*　　*

187

Cello music poured through the doors and windows and cracks. Mingled with the gusts of wind.

The rain was a water harp that played its own melody.

Dina sat in the midst of it, while the household turned topsy-turvy and the whole estate was as agitated as cream in a churn. She was not involved in the commotion. The chaos did not seem to disturb her.

Intense feelings were necessary now and then. When the steamboat anchored, they would call her. Tramp down the stairs, crunch on the coarse gravel, clatter in the kitchen and pantry, and slam doors.

Then the house would be completely quiet while they greeted Jacob's son on the beach. Even if the ship's whistle and the welcoming shouts of "Hurrah!" were only distant sounds riding on the storm, she would still hear them clearly enough.

It appeared she wanted to wait until that point. And then walk down the broad tree-lined path to wave a welcome. Away from all the people. Perhaps she wanted to meet him alone in order to see who he was.

But nothing happened the way they expected, even though they had accepted both the storm and the delays.

The *Prince Gustav* had sounded the familiar whistle blast and was ready to continue its voyage. Anders and Niels had rowed out to get the returning son themselves. As their boat neared shore, a young farmhand waded out to meet it, grasped the bow, and towed it in among the rocks.

The rain had stopped. Dina stood at the front door, looking down the path.

From behind his trunks, Johan smilingly raised his hat to the people clinging to each other among the rocks and warehouses. Beside him stood a tall, dark-haired man in leather clothing.

On the beach, the kerchiefs, shawls, and fluttering skirts strained toward the northeast. In the furious sky overhead, clouds rushed by at a dizzying pace.

Then the lightning struck. Flames. Large, red, and vicious.

"The haybarn's on fire!" screamed the farmhand.

In the resulting chaos, nobody knew what to do.

Theologian or no theologian, *Prince Gustav* or no *Prince Gustav* — it did not matter!

People rushed to the barn. An irresolute knot of arms and legs.

Tomas was on the roof with a raised axe immediately. Black with soot, he furiously chopped loose the burning timber. And threw it to the ground with a shower of sparks. Nobody knew where he got the strength and resourcefulness. Nobody had told him what to do.

Suddenly Dina was in the midst of the crowd, giving quick orders.

"Anders: The animals! The horses first! Niels: Wet sails on the hay! Evert: Find more axes! Gudmund: Open the fence! Girls: Each find a bucket!"

The orders snapped through the wind and the crackling fire. She stood with her legs apart, her hair a black tangle.

Six breadths wide, her blue muslin skirt was a sail that pressed her body against the wind.

Dina's eyes were cold and concentrated. They never left Tomas, as if her gaze alone could hold him upright.

She spoke with the voice of a raven. Dark and aggressive.

Later several men climbed the ladder that Tomas had leaned against the barn and helped him.

The rain, which had raged like an epidemic over land and sea the past day, had disappeared now. But the wind was treacherous.

They constantly had to run with wet sails and sacks to smother flames where sparks had found something dry and begun devouring it.

Several times, burning beams and boards crashed into the tinder-dry haymow and threatened to ignite the entire mound.

"Anders! Watch inside the haymow! Get wet sails!" shrieked Dina.

People rapidly gathered where they could be most useful. They brought the buckets that had collected water from the leaking roof in the servants' quarters that morning. More buckets arrived from the kitchen and cellar.

It was fortunate that everything outside was so wet. The grass and the outer walls of the barn were completely soaked. Repelled the sparks with spitting and sputtering.

"Our Lord doesn't seem to be guarding the roofs very well today," Anders panted, as he passed Dina, carrying a roll of wet sail on his shoulder. But she paid no attention.

The *Prince Gustav* quickly dropped anchor and lowered small boats into the sea. Soon the crew and male passengers were streaming up the main path to help fight the fire.

The barn stood some distance from the beach. Beyond the main cluster of farm buildings. It was a long way to carry seawater for fighting the flames.

Some men ran to the well between the barn and the main court-yard. But that went slowly, only one bucket at a time, and did not help much.

They formed a relay line, both men and women. From the beach to the barn. They were too few to make a tight chain, so each person had to run several meters to the next link.

But soon the buckets flew from hand to hand through the fields to the hay barn.

The sailors were a good help. Coarse shouts were heard. Curses and cries of "Bravo!"

Both the captain and the first mate were among the firefighters. Tearing off their pea coats and throwing down their caps, they joined the undulating mass along with others from the ship.

The machinist was British and spoke in a booming voice, although nobody understood much of his gibberish. But he had a neck and shoulders like a walrus and was used to working hard.

Three men worked with Tomas. They had a rope around their waists and moved across the roof like a strange wave, at the mercy of the shifting winds and their own ability to stay on their feet. Two chopped with axes, two managed the water buckets.

The axes proved to be the most useful. Soon a quarter of the roof toward the east had been cut away and lay smoldering on the ground.

Eventually the wind reached the hay that was under the un-damaged part of the roof and not protected with wet sails.

Suddenly the hay began to rise in a funnel shape, as if touched by a magic wand. A constant movement where each and every straw seemed to have received a message simultaneously. Up from the roofless barn, straight into the air. It made a slight curve above the people in the barnyard and fitfully continued south across the fields toward the sea.

"Niels! The hay! More sails!"

Dina's orders carried so well against the wind that the captain raised his head for a moment in amazement.

Niels was busy somewhere else and did not hear the order. But others heard it. The sails arrived, and the hay was forced to subside.

*   *   *

Hours went by, but no one noticed. The *Prince Gustav* lay lonely and forsaken in the sound.

Hanna and Benjamin ran around absorbing everything with open minds and wondering eyes. Their legs were caked with mud and their best clothes were filthy. But nobody noticed that.

When everything seemed under control and only an occasional thin column of smoke from the timbers on the ground reminded one that this could have been a catastrophe, Dina let her eyes leave the barn roof. She turned her sore, battered body and set down her bucket.

Her shoulders sank, as if someone had knocked her breath away. Her back curved.

She tossed her hair from her face, like a horse that wants to see the sun. Above she found a wide break in the clouds, and saw blue sky.

Then she met an unfamiliar gaze.

I am Dina. My feet are stakes in the ground. My head is weightless and receives everything. The sounds, the smells, the colors.

The pictures around me are moving. The people. The wind. A stinging smell of soot and burned trees. At first it is only the eyes, without a head or body. Like part of my weariness. A place to rest.

I have never seen such a person. A pirate? No! He comes from Hjertrud's book! He is Barabbas!

Where have I been all this time?

Chapter 10

O that you were like a brother to me,
that nursed at my mother's breast!
If I met you outside, I would kiss you,
and none would despise me.
I would lead you and bring you
into the house of my mother, and into the chamber
of her that conceived me.
I would give you spiced wine to drink,
the juice of my pomegranates.
— The Song of Solomon 8 : 1–2

*H*is eyes were very green. In a face with strong features and a day-old beard. His nose thrust into the world confidently, using wide nostrils as a plow.

She did not need to lower her head to meet his gaze. His tanned face had a long white scar across the left cheek. One might well say it was both ugly and frightening.

His mouth was large and serious. The bow curved up and outward beautifully. As if its creator had wanted a gentle overall expression.

His brown shoulder-length hair was greasy, and wet with per-spiration. His shirt had surely once been white but was soaked through and spotted with soot. One sleeve was ripped in the seam and hung on his arm as if it belonged to a beggar.

A broad belt around his waist held up his wide leather pants. The man was thin and bony like a convict. His left hand was gripping an axe.

This was Barabbas who had been set free. Now he looked at her. As if he were about to chop . . .

Tomas and the stranger had swung their axes together. The one because he knew much was at stake. For Reinsnes. For Dina.

The other because he happened to be stranded on this headland and found a fire he enjoyed battling.

"We did it!" he said. He was still breathing heavily after the combat. His large chest heaved like a blacksmith's bellows.

Dina stared at him.

"Are you Barabbas?" she asked gravely.

"How do you mean?" he asked, equally grave. She could hear he was not Norwegian.

"I see you've been released."

"Then I must be Barabbas," he said, and extended his hand.

She did not take it at first. He did not move.

"I'm Dina Grønelv," she said, finally shaking his hand. It was sweaty and dirty after the work. Wide knuckles and long fingers. But the palms were as soft as hers.

He nodded, as if he already knew who she was.

"You're not exactly a blacksmith," she said, nodding toward his hand.

"No, Barabbas is no blacksmith."

The murmuring and talking around them had become more cheerful, and it concerned just one thing. The fire!

Dina tore herself from his gaze and slowly turned to the people. There were about thirty in all. In a voice filled with amazement, she shouted:

"Thank you! Thank you one and all! Now it's time for food and drink! Tables will be laid in the servants' hall and the dining room. Everyone is invited. Make yourselves at home!"

At that point, Johan came over to Dina. He was smiling broadly.

"This is quite a homecoming!" he said, and pressed her close for a moment.

"That it is! Welcome, Johan! As you see, we're still alive."

"This is Mr. Zjukovski. We met on the boat," he added, gesturing toward the man.

The stranger offered his hand again, as though he had forgotten they had already shaken hands. This time he smiled.

No, Barabbas was no blacksmith.

Later that evening the wind died down. People went indoors. But the *Prince Gustav* still lay at anchor. Already many hours delayed.

A fire watch was organized. To play it safe. They hoped it would not rain, for the hay's sake.

Anders and Tomas would go to Strandsted the following day to buy building materials and hire extra workers. The barn would soon have a new roof.

The sheriff and Dagny did not arrive until after the fire was under control. He scolded good-naturedly because they had not bought insurance on the buildings and equipment. Dina calmly replied that she would consider it for the future. They did not quarrel, because the pastor and the theologian were present.

Mother Karen tripped about like a ptarmigan. Remarkably, her hips and legs were much better than they had been for a long time.

Oline suddenly had been left alone with everything, because the kitchen maids were busy passing buckets of water outside. On the other hand, she got several extra hours to do the work.

And Oline was used to managing by herself.

The meat turned out perfectly. Although she had often rushed nervously between the kitchen and the huge baking oven in the cookhouse where the calf was roasting.

It had been carried into the main house in a barrel during the worst rain, just before the *Prince Gustav* whistled.

And while the fire raged, only arthritic Mother Karen had time to help Oline bring the meat back to the cookhouse.

They both had realized immediately that there would be no festive dinner for a while.

Oline had basted the calf with fat and drippings, so it would not become dry. Then she stoked the oven carefully and lovingly.

She could not make the gravy until the last minute. And first she needed to calm down. You could not make smooth gravy with a racing heart.

Before roasting the calf, she had cracked the ribs and tied the slit belly securely closed around the kidneys. The kidneys were her pride. They would be served too. Cut with a very sharp knife and offered as a delicacy.

The crushed juniper berries lay on a thin board, adding their fragrance to the room. Juniper berries should actually be served with game. But Oline's roast was more than meat from a calf. Juniper berries and miraculous spices went with it.

In the pantry, stemmed crystal bowls filled with cloudberries and currant jelly stood waiting, covered with cloths. The prunes lay in water on the back of the stove. Properly soaked and softened. She had removed each pit with trembling hands, while running between the window and the table.

The new potatoes were still small. They had been scrubbed by the maids the previous evening. Had stood overnight in buckets of fresh water in the cellar. They would be cooked in four large kettles just before dinner.

The maids had taken the buckets to fight the fire long ago. And had hastily dumped the potatoes into a wooden baking trough.

Now that the danger was over, Oline grumbled about the baking trough. It was sacred. It should never be used for anything but dough. If you were careless about how you used a dough trough, trolls might cast a spell on it, or wild yeast or something even worse might get into it.

"But there's been a fire, after all!" she sighed in resignation, and plumped the new potatoes into the kettles where they belonged.

When the blaze was finally under control and Johan properly welcomed, people dressed for festivities for the second time that day.

Some of the men had only one shirt. And perhaps they had remembered too late to remove it during the fire. But they rubbed out the worst spots and left the rest. As long as they had washed the soot and dirt from their bodies, the stained clothing would be a badge of honor.

Oline put the finishing touches on her masterpiece and ordered that tables be set for the *Prince Gustav* crew and passengers who had helped fight the fire.

Mother Karen decided that the captain, the first mate, the machinist, and Johan's friend from the trip would eat in the dining room. All the others would eat in the cottage. They set several long planks on sawhorses, covered them with snowy sheets, and decorated them with field flowers.

Oline was dripping with perspiration and in the best possible humor. Her hands worked rapidly and meticulously.

Spirits were already high when the food arrived. For rum had been set on the tables. The crew had been exceptionally generous. They had rowed ashore with items one mentioned by name, as well as those one consumed quietly.

Nobody spoke of the steamboat's continuing north sometime.

* * *

The men helped with the serving as though they had never done anything else.

Mother Karen had not ordered wine or other strong drink to be served in the cottage. But the rum went a long way, apparently. It was like the widow of Sarepta's pitcher. It flowed hospitably, and you could never drink it dry.

Many trips were made to the blessed steamboat, however. And the men all returned from their errands with lumps in their work blouses or jackets.

After a while, the mood became extremely lively. The stories flew back and forth across the table. Ending with grunts and laughter.

The pastor, who regretted that his wife was not well enough to accompany him, sat at one end of the table.

Despite the summer heat, Dagny wore a velvet suit with a narrow waist and high lace collar. The latest fashion, just arrived from Bergen.

Dina looked several times at the brooch in the collar. It had been Hjertrud's.

Mother Karen sat at the other end of the table, with Johan between her and Dina.

A Swedish couple of noble birth were on a pleasure trip in Nordland. They had to be brought from the ship and entertained, even though they had not helped to put out the fire. The husband sat next to Mother Karen. Due to the seating changes when the officers and others from the ship arrived, the stranger Zjukovski came to sit across from Dina.

Silver and crystal gleamed under the chandelier.

It was twilight in August. Daisies, bluebells, and ivy and rowan leaves were spread on the white tablecloth. Tall glasses enthroned their noble contents. The food and the aromas made people friendly, almost inviting, toward each other. They were not all acquainted, but they had two things in common. The food and the fire!

Mother Karen set her face in an amiable net of wrinkles. Smiled and conversed. This was Reinsnes as it once had been! When there were parties! When there were festive tables and the smell of veal or game. Mother Karen realized how content she was to have things like this again. She was glad she had taught Stine to be a hostess at Reinsnes. You could not instruct Dina in household tasks. And Reinsnes needed a hostess who could do more than play music and smoke cigars. This evening Mother Karen saw that Stine had done her work well.

You could not deny that the Lapp girl was clever and intelligent. She had a winning way about her, whereas Dina repelled people.

Dina looked at Barabbas. He had put on a clean shirt. His hair was still damp. His eyes were greener in the lamplight.

Dina had invited Zjukovski to use one of the guest rooms. He accepted with a bow.

When she heard him go downstairs again with Johan, she stole into his room. It smelled of shaving soap and leather.

His roomy cowhide travel bag had been left half open. At first she just looked inside it. Then she began lifting the clothes and small items. Suddenly her hand found a book. With a thick, well-worn leather binding. She opened it. It appeared to be Russian. On the title page was a slanting, angular signature:

Leo Zjukovski

ALEXANDER PUSHKIN was printed in large, ornate type. That was probably the author of the book. The title of the book was incomprehensible as well.

It was the same strange backward writing as on boxes and crates containing Russian merchandise.

"I don't understand," she said aloud. As if she were angry that she could not tell what kind of book it was.

She held the book to her nose and sniffed it. The smell of damp paper that has traveled a long time. The strange smell of a man. Slightly sweet, but acrid at the same time. Tobacco, dust. Sea!

Jacob emerged from the wall. He needed her this evening. She muttered a few curses, to make him go away. But he did not leave. Ran around her. Begged for mercy. His odor filled the room. She held her hand in front of her, wanting him to disappear.

Then she replaced the book exactly where she had found it. Straightened up. Panting. As if she were doing heavy work.

Listened for steps on the stairs. Had an alibi if he should return. She wanted to put new candles in the candlesticks for the evening. He would not know this was not usually her task. She had set the basket of candles on the floor.

Jacob stayed close to her until she lifted the basket and left the room. In the circle of light from the hall lamp he let go of her bare arm. Dragging his useless foot, he withdrew to the dark corner by the linen cupboards.

"We saved the barn roof! Without your help!" she snarled savagely, and went downstairs to the dining room.

I am Dina, who is floating. My head moves by itself in the room. The walls and ceiling open. The sky is an immense dark picture of velvet and broken glass. In which I am floating. I want to! And I do not want to!

During the first course, the Swedish countess remarked that it was strange to see such a beautiful garden this close to the North Pole. And the lovely paths among the flower beds, strewn with crushed shells! She had noticed them before dinner too. It must be strenuous, time-consuming work to create a garden like that in such a harsh environment.

Mother Karen's mouth tightened, but she politely replied that it could be difficult and sometimes the rosebushes froze in severe winters. She would like to show the countess the herb garden the next day. That was a specialty at Reinsnes.

Then they drank a toast to the young theologian. And one to the barn and the hay. Which, by God's mercy, they had saved from the flames.

"And the animals! God bless the animals!" Mother Karen added.

So they drank to the crops and the animals. And they were still on the first course!

The Swedish nobleman praised Oline's fish soup. And insisted that Oline come to the dining room to receive his tribute. The fish soup was the best he had ever tasted. And he had eaten fish soup all over the world on his travels.

French fish soup! Had anyone tasted French fish soup?

Mother Karen had tasted it. And with that, she was able to tell about her three years in Paris. She jingled her filigree bracelet and gestured mildly with both hands.

Suddenly she quoted poetry in French, as a youthful rosiness came to her cheeks.

Her white, well-groomed hair, which had been rinsed in juniper water and primped with a curling iron for the occasion, gleamed like the silverware and the candelabrum.

When Oline finally came, after having tidied herself a little and removed her outer apron, everyone was far beyond the fish soup.

The nobleman repeated his speech about the soup, albeit somewhat uninspired now. And since he had the floor, he spoke about the main course too. He waxed so loquacious that Oline curtseyed and declared she needed to leave.

There was an uncomfortable pause.

Zjukovski loosened his bow tie. It was warm in the room, even though the windows to the garden were open.

Night moths went astray and entered behind the delicate lace curtains. Captured by the light. One flew into the flame in front of Dina. A tiny puff. And it was over. A charred remainder, like dust on the tablecloth.

She raised her glass. The voices around them disappeared. He raised his glass, too, and nodded. Nothing was said. Then they picked up their knives and forks simultaneously and began to eat.

The roast veal was pink and juicy. The cream gravy lay like velvet on the white porcelain. The currant jelly trembled at the edge of the plate.

Dina placed the jelly firmly on the meat. The new potatoes were so well scrubbed that no skin remained. Just the soft, mealy roundness. She inserted her silver fork and cut a small piece of a potato. Let it glide slowly through the gravy. Combined it with some jelly and raised it to her mouth. She met his eyes as he did the same.

For a moment, a piece of pink meat was between his lips. It shone in his teeth. Then he closed his mouth and began to chew. His eyes were a dead-calm sea across the table.

She gathered both his irises on her fork and put them in her mouth. Let her tongue slide over them. Carefully. The eyeballs tasted salty. They were not to be chewed or swallowed. She just let them calmly roll toward her palate and stroked them with tip of her tongue. Then she brought them to the front of her mouth, opened her lips, and let them go.

He chewed with quiet enjoyment while his eyes resumed their proper places. His face had an intense radiance. As if their mutual enjoyment were pouring through his skin. His eyes settled in their sockets. And winked at her!

She winked back. Gravely. Then they continued eating. Tasted each other. Chewed. Not too greedily. The one who lost self-control was the loser.

A sigh escaped her. For a moment she forgot to chew. Then she smiled without knowing it. It was not her usual smile. It must have survived for years. Since the days when she sat on Hjertrud's lap and felt her hair being caressed.

He was handsome on one side, ugly on the other. The scar divided him in two. Its curve split his cheek with a deep furrow.

Dina's nostrils twitched, as if someone had tickled her with a straw. She put down her knife and fork. Raised her hand to her face and brushed one finger across her upper lip.

The sheriff's voice interposed. He asked Johan if he had applied for a parish.

Johan looked down at his plate in embarrassment and said his life would scarcely be of any interest to the travelers. But the sheriff thoroughly disagreed.

Fortunately, the dessert arrived. The cloudberries were topped with swirls of whipped cream. They were the year's best. Tomas had picked them on nearby marshes for this dinner.

The party preened itself with enjoyment. The first mate told how he was once forced to attend a wedding in Bardu. They had not been served even a bite of meat. And no dessert at all. Each meal had consisted of milk and bread in a dish and cream pudding. And dried mutton. So salty that only the host could cut it. They were afraid someone would ruin the knife!

Mother Karen's face stiffened, and she said it was unlike people in Bardu to scrimp so on food.

But that did not help. Even the pastor laughed.

Tomas had not sampled the seamen's keg.

He was one of the few who did not have time to change into clean clothes before dinner. Needed to get the animals back in the barn, and to organize a fire watch and make sure the guards stayed somewhat sober.

Anders and Niels had quickly disappeared into the main house. And he had not seen them since. So all the responsibility fell on him.

*   *   *

By the time he arrived at the cottage, the meal had already been cleared away and people sat companionably with pipes, coffee, and rum.

Suddenly it was too much for him. He felt exhausted and exploited.

Dina had come over to him after the fire was out. Just briefly. Had given him an amiable thump on the back as usual. "Tomas!" she said. That was all.

That had been enough for him at the moment. But when she did not appear again, did not speak to him, did not thank him in the presence of others, then everything got complicated. Everything.

He knew he had done more than anyone else to save the barn. Had been the first on the roof with an axe. Were it not for him, things could have been much worse.

He suddenly felt something like hate toward her. And toward the tall stranger who had helped him chop down the burning roof.

Tomas asked the sailors about him. But all they knew was that he spoke with an accent and appeared on the passenger list with an un-Christian name. Like a Chinese! He had boarded in Trondheim. Always sat reading and smoking, or talking with Johan Grønelv. He was headed far north and east. Maybe he was a Lapp or from even farther east? But he spoke good Norwegian.

Tomas had seen how the man stood behind Dina when he came down from the roof. It hurt him that she shook his hand twice. It hurt him even more when he learned that the stranger was invited to eat in the main house with the fine folk. He was dressed like a seaman, after all.

Tomas did his tasks with a clenched jaw. Then he went and asked Oline if she needed any help. Carried extra wood and water into the kitchen and stayed.

Sat at the end of the table and let her serve him food. Blamed it on being too tired to take part in things at the cottage.

He ate slowly and thoroughly. As though his thoughts controlled each mouthful as it was chewed and went into his stomach.

"There's no soup left," Oline grumbled. "The Swedish count ate a whole firkin!"

She had never heard of fine folk with such poor manners that they asked for extra servings of the first course. It could not be much of an estate that Swedish fellow owned.

Tomas nodded listlessly. Sat hunched over the table.

Oline gave him a sidelong glance as she squirted whipped cream on the guests' cloudberries. When the last dessert was readied, she dried her hands meticulously with a towel. One finger at a time. As if the cream were dangerous.

Then she made a quick trip into the pantry and returned with a glass of the finest red wine.

"Here!" she said abruptly. Set the glass roughly in front of Tomas and went back to her work.

Tomas tasted the wine. And to hide that he was touched by her thoughtfulness, he burst out:

"Damn!"

Oline muttered brusquely that she had known for a long time where Benjamin learned his ungodly expressions.

Tomas gave her a weak smile.

The kitchen was warm and safe. The steam, the food smells, and the hum from the parlors made him drowsy.

But one spot inside his head was wide awake and watchful.

Dina did not appear in the kitchen. . . .

Stine left with the children. Boys' stubborn voices mingled with Hanna's ill-tempered sounds for awhile. But gradually it grew quiet upstairs.

Dagny, Mother Karen, and the countess drank their coffee in the parlor.

Dina stretched out on the chaise lounge in the smoking parlor, smoked a cigar, and filled her wineglass herself. The count looked at her in amazement at first, then continued his conversation with the men.

After a while the pastor gave Dina a mild look and said:

"Mistress Dina must come and help us tune the organ!"

He had a great ability to overlook things about Dina that did not seem entirely proper. As if he knew she had more important qualities.

He often said that you had to accept people in Nordland the way you accepted the seasons. If you could not stand them, you should stay inside awhile and compose yourself.

The pastor's wife lived according to that rule. So she did not have the strength to come to Reinsnes for Johan's homecoming party.

"The pastor knows I'm no organ expert, but I'll try," Dina replied.

"You did well the last time," said the pastor.

"It depends on one's ear," said Dina dryly.

"That's true. And you are exceptionally musical! You have much to thank . . . What was his name? The tutor who taught you to love music?"

"Lorch," said Dina.

"Yes, of course. Where is he now?"

"On his way to Reinsnes. With his cello," she said. Barely audibly.

"That's interesting news! Very good news!" said the pastor. "When is he expected?"

Dina did not answer, because the count diverted the pastor's attention.

Sitting in a circle of the older men, Johan was the natural focal point. But he did nothing to foster this himself. His quiet voice was interested and attentive. Unconsciously, he kept brushing back his unruly dark hair with his right hand. A moment later, it was on his forehead again.

He had changed during these years. Not just outwardly. His speech had a foreign flavor. He used Danish words and intonations. And he acted as though he were a guest in some unknown merchant's house. Did not seem to recognize anything. Did not run his hand across anything. Did not rush from room to room to see everything again. Aside from helping to fight the fire, he had not yet been anywhere except the main house.

Anders asked Johan about the situation in Denmark. Had he been involved in the political and nationalistic student gatherings in Copenhagen?

Johan seemed ashamed to say no.

"The Danes must be overjoyed since the battle at Isted. The sweet taste of victory over the Germans!" said Zjukovski.

"Yes," said Johan. "But adding Slesvig to Denmark is unnatural. They're two different languages and cultures."

"But this was King Frederick's dream, wasn't it?" said the Russian.

"Yes, and the nationalists' too," Johan replied.

"I heard it was Czar Nicholas who decided the outcome," said Dina.

"Yes, he threatened to fight the Prussians if they didn't leave Jutland," said Zjukovski. "But the new military draft in Denmark also had an effect."

They continued to discuss Denmark's flourishing political development.

"You're very informed about politics," the sheriff said to Zjukovski.

"One hears a little here and there." The Russian smiled.

"Most people in Denmark aren't as knowledgeable as you are," Johan observed admiringly.

"Thank you."

Dina had been watching the men while they talked.

"Mother Karen was afraid Johan would get caught in the war and the demonstrations before he could get home."

"I'm not interested enough in such things," said Johan lightly. "A theologian can't rouse anybody to action."

"Don't say that," said the pastor. "Anyway, now you're here."

"All theologians aren't the same," said Johan, chagrined. "I could hardly be considered a political power. But of course, that's not true of you."

"Well," said the pastor good-naturedly. "I don't want worldly power either."

"But in fact, you do. If I may say so?" Dina interjected.

"What do you mean?" asked the pastor.

"When the authorities do something you think is unfair, you say so. Even if you have nothing to do with it."

"Yes, that certainly happens. . . ."

"And you often get what you want?" continued Dina gently.

"That also happens," the pastor replied with a satisfied smile.

The conversation moved to safe ground again. And the sheriff talked at great length about disputes and legal action at the last Assembly.

Anders was the one most surprised about Johan. He found no trace of the boy he had known at Reinsnes. Excused him because he had been so young when he left. And because so many people were present.

At the table, Anders noticed that Mother Karen found it somewhat difficult to have her cleric progeny home again. She struggled to find topics of conversation with him.

Johan was polite and friendly enough. But he had become a stranger.

The pastor smoked a short pipe and then left for home, with many apologies and blessings. He would save the music until next time, he said.

Dina accompanied the pastor to the door. As she returned through the main parlor, she struck several chords on the piano. Tentatively.

The stranger was there immediately. He leaned against the instrument and listened.

Dina stopped playing and gave him an inquiring look.

Suddenly he began to sing a melancholy folk song in Russian.

Dina quickly grasped the melody and accompanied him by ear. When she made a mistake, he repeated the notes for her.

The strange, exotic song was filled with sorrow. All of a sudden, the tall man began to dance. As Russian seamen often did when slightly drunk. With arms outstretched to each side. Lithe hips and bent knees.

The rhythm grew wilder and happier. The man danced so close to the floor it should have been impossible to stay on his feet. Stretched his long legs to the side and bent them beneath him again. Faster and faster.

He exuded immense vitality. He was serious and concentrated. But at the same time playful.

A grown man who was playful! The scar shone exceptionally white on his flushed skin. He was Janus, with two faces. Whirled round and round, revealing a marred and an unmarred cheek.

Dina watched the man's movements as her fingers danced. Firmly and lightly.

Mother Karen, Dagny, and the countess interrupted their cultured conversation. One after another, the men in the smoking parlor rose to see and hear. Stine stood by the door with four children behind her.

Benjamin's eyes and mouth were wide open. He went into the parlor, without permission.

Hanna and the sheriff's two sons stood shyly in the doorway.

A broad smile filled the room. It leaped like a shaggy little animal from person to person. To have a lighthearted mood in the parlors at Reinsnes was amazing. There had been such long intervals between happy times in the past years.

The music could be heard in the kitchen and throughout the house.

A deep male voice singing a strange, flowing melody and words they did not understand.

Tomas shifted uneasily. Oline listened with her mouth open. The parlormaid came to the kitchen. Giggling and excited.

"They want more *punsj!* The foreign fellow is singing Russian

songs and leaping up and down like a madman, with his knees bent!
He yodels and slaps his heels! I never saw such a thing! And he's
going to sleep in the south guest room. Dina gave orders. To fill the
carafe and the pitcher on the washstand. And lay out clean towels."

Tomas felt a fist knock the breath out of him with a single blow.

Zjukovski stopped dancing as abruptly as he had begun. Bowed gal-
lantly when everyone applauded, took a few deep breaths, and returned to the smoking parlor to relight his cigar.

His forehead was covered with beads of sweat. But he did not
wipe them away. Just raised his eyebrows slightly and loosened his
neckband.

Jacob brushed against Dina's arm. He was not in good humor.

Dina pushed him away. But he kept a firm grasp on her as she
walked over to Zjukovski. He had seated himself in the empty chair
beside the chaise lounge.

She shook his hand and thanked him for the entertainment. The
air was phosphorescent between them. It drove Jacob wild.

Later, when everything had returned to normal and the travelers were
talking about the wonderful light in Nordland, Zjukovski boldly
leaned forward and placed his hand lightly on Dina's.

"Dina Grønelv plays well," he said simply.

Jacob's aversion to the man hit Dina between the eyes. She pulled
her hand away.

"Thank you," she said.

"She's also very good at organizing a fire brigade. . . . And she
has such beautiful hair!"

He spoke very softly. But in a tone that blended with the travelers'
conversation about Nordland weather.

"People complain because I don't pin up my hair," she replied.

"Yes, I can believe that," was all he said.

The children and Stine had gone upstairs again.

It began to get late. But light still filtered through the lace curtains
and potted plants.

"You said your stepmother was musical, and she's shown that this
evening. But you mentioned she played the cello," Zjukovski said to
Johan.

It was the first time anyone had called Dina a stepmother. She
opened her mouth as if to say something. But closed it again.

"Yes," said Johan eagerly. "Play the cello for us, Dina!"

"No, not now."

She lit a new cigar.

Jacob was extremely satisfied with her.

"When did you tell him I played the cello?" she asked.

"On the ship. That's what I remembered about you," replied Johan.

"Yes, you probably don't remember much," she murmured.

Leo Zjukovski looked from one to the other. Niels raised his head. Not a sound had come from him all evening. But at least he was present.

"What do you mean?" asked Johan uncertainly.

"Oh, nothing. Just that you've been away for a long time. . . ." She straightened her shoulders and asked if anyone wanted to take a stroll before bedtime, now that the weather had cleared.

They stared at her in bewilderment. Leo Zjukovski was the only one who rose from his chair. Johan looked at them. As if this were an interesting detail. Then he reached toward the cigar box that Anders had opened and was passing around.

It was his first cigar that evening.

Tomas took more fire watches than were originally scheduled.

Once, as he went from the cottage to the barn, he saw Dina and the stranger strolling on the white crushed shells near the summerhouse.

True, the stranger walked with both thumbs hooked in the armholes of his vest and at a good distance. But they disappeared into the summerhouse after a while.

Tomas seriously considered going to sea. But there were so many things to take into account. For one thing, the fire watch was his responsibility. Then there were his aged parents. And his young sisters.

In the end, he sat on his knees in the haymow, with straw sticking to his clothes. He had made a decision. He would talk to her. Force her to see him. He would get her to go hunting with him!

The pastor's outrigger had sailed far enough away for the dancing to begin on the wharf.

Tomas went to Andreas Wharf to send the next man on fire watch.

Then he returned to the kitchen. Helped Oline store leftover food in the cellar. Brought up more wine. Carried in water and firewood.

Oline turned from her work a few times and looked at him.

"Thea and Annette are down at the wharf . . . dancing," she said tentatively.

He did not reply.

"You don't dance much, Tomas?"

"No."

"Is something bothering you?"

"Oh, one gets so tired," he said easily.

"Do you feel like talking, now that we're finished for the day?"

"Aww," he said, embarrassed.

He cleared his throat all the way to the water barrel with an empty bucket. Filled the bucket to the rim and then the container at the back of the stove. The logs lay neatly stacked in their corner. The kindling box was filled with brushwood.

"Come and sit down," said Oline.

"Aren't you going to bed?"

"There's no rush tonight."

"I guess not."

"Let's see, do you like coffee with brandy?"

"Yes."

They sat at the big kitchen table, lost in their separate thoughts.

The weather had cleared. Now the wind was only a memory and a soft whisper. The August night was full of spices and blue light. They filtered through the open window.

Tomas stirred the sugar thoroughly in his cup.

Chapter 11

Set me as a seal upon your heart,
as a seal upon your arm;
for love is strong as death,
jealousy is cruel as the grave.

— The Song of Solomon 8 : 6

*H*e looked better in the evening light than in lamplight. Dina examined him without shyness. They walked along the crunching shell path. He in shirtsleeves and vest. She with a red silk shawl around her shoulders.

"You weren't born in this country?"

"No."

There was a pause.

"Would you rather not talk about your country?"

"It's not that. But it's a long story. I have two countries and two languages. Russian and Norwegian."

He seemed embarrassed.

"Mother was Norwegian," he said curtly. Almost insolently.

"What do you do when you're not traveling?"

"I sing and dance."

"Can you live on that?"

"Sometimes."

"Where are you from?"

"Saint Petersburg."

"That's a very big city, isn't it?"

"Very big and very beautiful," he said, and began talking about the churches and city squares in Saint Petersburg.

"Why do you travel so much?" she asked after a while.

"Why? Because I like to travel. And besides, I'm searching."

"For what?"

"The same thing everyone searches for."

"What's that?"

"The truth."

"About what?"

He looked at her in surprise that bordered on mild disdain. "Don't you ever look for truth?"

"No," she said crisply.

"How can you live without looking for it?"

He withdrew a little. Jacob was there between them. Quite content.

"There'll be time for such things, I'm sure," the tall man said softly. He grasped her elbow firmly and pressed Jacob outside time and space.

They walked past the damaged barn. Met only an odor of scorched hay and timber. The cattle were lowing loudly inside. But otherwise everything was quiet.

Then they strolled through the white gate and into the garden. She wanted to show him the summerhouse. Set like lace amid all the greenery. White with ornate blue carving. An octagonal building with dragon spires at each angle. Well maintained. But the winter had taken a few stained-glass panes.

He had to duck his head to get through the door. She laughed. Because she needed to do the same.

The light was dim inside. They sat beside each other on the bench. He asked her about Reinsnes. She replied. Their bodies were very close. His hands lay on his knees. Calmly. Like sleeping animals.

He behaved very properly, despite sitting so close. Jacob watched every movement. As if sensing this, the Russian said it was getting late.

"It's been a long day," said Dina.

"It's been a wonderful day," he said.

He rose, took her hand, and kissed it. His lips were warm and wet.

The next morning, they stood in the upstairs hallway. At the top of the stairs.

There was not much light, and the air still smelled of sleep, chamber pots, and soap.

He was the last traveler to leave the house. The others were already on their way to the steamboat.

"I'm coming south before winter," he said, giving her an inquiring look.

"You'll be welcome," she replied, as if he were just anyone.

"May I hear you play the cello then?"

"Probably. I play almost every day," she said.

"But not yesterday?"

"No, not yesterday."

"Maybe you weren't quite in the mood? There was a fire. . . ."

"There was a fire."

"And now you'll make sure the roof gets repaired properly?"

"That needs to be done."

"Do you have many responsibilities? Many servants?"

"Why do you ask about such things . . . now?"

His scar turned upward. His smile was a revelation.

"I'm playing for time. It's not so easy. I'm courting you, Dina Grønelv."

"An unfamiliar situation for Barabbas"

"Not completely . . . So I *am* Barabbas?"

They laughed toward each other, exposing their teeth and throats. Two dogs playing, and measuring their strength, in the shadows.

"You're Barabbas!"

"He was a thief," he whispered, as he came nearer.

"He was set free!" she said, drawing a quick breath.

"But Christ had to die instead."

"Christ always has to die. . . ."

"Wave good-bye to me," he said softly, and kept standing there somewhat irresolutely.

She said nothing. But with a lightning gesture, she took his hand in both of hers and bit his middle finger. Hard. He gave a surprised cry of pain.

Everything was thrown into confusion. Enough so that he pulled her close and hid his head against her breast. And drew a deep breath.

They stood like that for a moment. Without moving. Then he straightened up, kissed her hand, and put on his hat.

"I'm coming south before winter," he said hoarsely.

Stair after stair came between them. He turned around completely a few times and looked up at her. The outer door slammed.

He was gone.

The steamboat had been delayed an entire day.

Leo Zjukovski stood on the bridge with his hand raised in farewell. He was in just his shirtsleeves. It made all the dressed-up, buttoned-up people look ridiculous.

She watched everything from her bedroom window. He knew she was standing there.

I am Dina. We drift across the beaches. Close together. The scar is a torch among the seaweed. His eyes are the green ocean. The light above the sandy bottom. That wants to show me something. And to hide something. He drifts away from me. Behind the headlands. The mountains. Because he does not yet know Hjertrud.

Johan stood on a rock on the seaweed-strewn beach. He shouted something to the steamboat. Leo Zjukovski nodded and waved his hat.

Then the whistle blew. The propellers started churning. The voices drowned. She hung the green eyes around her neck.

The sheriff's family had left Reinsnes at dawn. Anders and Niels took them in the *Mother Karen*. The brothers were going to Strandsted anyway, to buy the materials they needed to repair the barn roof. It was no use to think about cutting timber from their own forest. They needed dry lumber of the proper dimensions.

They had decided to use the cargo boat to bring back all the materials. So the sheriff's farmhand had to struggle alone with the horses over the mountain pass in the blazing sun.

Mother Karen tried to have a heart-to-heart talk with Johan. About the true meaning of life. About death. About Johan's future. His vocation.

Dina went riding alone. And did not return until late afternoon.

Tomas regarded that as a bad sign. He decided he should wait to talk with her until another day.

Amid all the confusion of the fire and Johan's homecoming, no one had told Dina that a large, oblong box had been brought ashore from the steamboat.

When the clerk came with the message, she went down to Andreas Wharf. Her strides were long and light.

She unpacked the box on the spot. It had been in the warehouse a whole day!

Lorch felt betrayed. But he did not reproach her. His smell became more and more evident the nearer she got to the cello. The instrument was well packed.

She lifted it from the box carefully. And tried to tune it then and there.

The strings wept at her. They refused to be tuned. She talked to Lorch about it. Became flustered and angry. Tightened the strings and tried again. But got only bewildered weeping.

Small waves sloshed against the rocks beneath her, irritatingly carefree. Glistened between the cracks in the floor.

She howled with rage and disappointment at being unable to tune the instrument.

She would bring it to the master bedroom. It probably had to be all the way home before it could be tuned.

But when she came out into the sunshine, she understood. The cello had given up on the trip. It was dead. The worst had happened. The instrument was cracked!

Mother Karen tried to comfort her. Blamed the temperature and the changing moisture along the long coastline.

Dina put the cello in her bedroom. In the corner. Beside her own. The dead and the living. Together.

Chapter 12

Thus I was, by day the heat consumed me, and the cold by night, and
my sleep fled from my eyes.

— Genesis 31 : 40

*T*here was a breathing space between haying season and potato
digging. So the roof repair had to be completed during this time,
before workers were needed in the fields again.

Also, fishermen began to arrive with dried cod. It had to be carefully sorted, compressed into forty-kilo bundles in the fish press on
the top floor of the warehouse, and stored for shipment to Bergen
and foreign markets.

The livers, brought with the dried fish, were burned to cod-
liver oil during the fall. Everyone reeked of it. The odor hung like
a plague over the whole estate. Clung to hair and clean clothes.
Settled like an evil spirit in the unfortunate workers who burned
the oil.

Everything took time. And required people. But it provided skillings and security for everyone.

Problems arose with the new young milkmaid. She was almost afraid
of the bell cow.

Since the fire, the cow and the milkmaid seemed to get on each
other's nerves. Nearly every day, the milk spilled in the stall and the
milkmaid came to Oline in tears.

Dina overheard the commotion one evening.

She went to the kitchen and heard the unhappy story about how,
once again, the milk had spilled on the barn floor.

"Do you know how to milk properly?" asked Dina.

"Yes." The girl sniffed.

"I mean, do you know how to milk live cows?"

"Yes" said the milkmaid with a curtsy.

"Well, how do you do it?"

214

"I sit on the stool and put the pail between my knees and . . ."

"And the cow? What do you do with the cow?"

"I . . . wipe the teats . . . you know . . ."

"But besides that?"

"Besides that?"

"Yes. Do you think you're milking a stool?"

"No-o-o . . ."

"A cow is a cow and must be treated like a living creature. Do you understand?"

The milkmaid squirmed uncomfortably.

"She's so nasty."

"She gets nasty when you come to milk her."

"She wasn't like that at first."

"Only since the fire?"

"What's that got to do with it?"

"It's because you're impatient, because you want to get to the servants' quarters and see what's happening there. To the cow, you're like a fire."

"But . . ."

"That's the truth. Come! We're going to the barn."

Dina found some suitable clothing in the servants' quarters. Then she and the milkmaid went to the barn.

Dina left the pail and stool outside the stall. She walked over to the lowing animal and laid a hand on its neck. Calmly and firmly.

"Stop that!" she said quietly, and began stroking the cow.

"Be careful, she's nasty!" the milkmaid cautioned anxiously.

"So am I," replied Dina, and continued stroking.

The milkmaid watched, wide-eyed.

Dina went into the stall and beckoned the milkmaid to follow her. The girl hesitantly put one foot in front of the other.

"Now be nice to the cow," Dina ordered.

The milkmaid patted the cow, apprehensively at first. Then more calmly.

"Look her in the eye," Dina commanded.

The milkmaid did her best. Gradually, the cow quieted down and took a few mouthfuls of hay from the manger.

"Talk to her like a person!" Dina ordered. "Talk about the weather and about the past summer."

The girl started a conversation with the cow. At first she was reluctant and uneasy. Then she grew more confident and, in the end, almost sincere.

"Let her see the pail and the rag, and talk the whole time," said Dina, withdrawing from the stall but still watching the girl.

The final result was that the cow turned its large head and gave the milkmaid a look of understanding and interest while she milked.

The girl beamed. Strong white streams of milk squirted into the pail and foamed over the edge.

Dina waited until she was finished.

As they walked back across the courtyard with the milk pails, Dina advised in a serious voice:

"Talk to the cow about your sorrows. About your sweetheart. Cows like stories!"

The milkmaid had been about to thank Dina for her help but stopped short in alarm.

"What if people heard me?" she asked, embarrassed.

"They'd be struck by lightning and disaster," said Dina gravely.

"But if they talked about me in the parish before lightning struck them?"

"That won't happen," said Dina confidently.

"How did you learn all this?" asked the milkmaid.

"Learn? I grew up in the sheriff's barn and stable. But don't bother to tell people that, because the sheriff is nastier than any cow."

"Did you learn to milk there?"

"No, I learned that on a cotter's farm. They had just one cow."

The girl gave her a strange look and swallowed the next question.

The young milkmaid could not stop thinking about what a fine mistress she had. She told everyone who would listen. About the mistress who knew how to handle animals. So friendly and helpful.

She elaborated on the story, and it went from one estate to the next. A triumph for Dina, the milkmaid, and the cow.

Clearly, Dina of Reinsnes knew more than the Lord's Prayer. And she sided with the lower classes. People remembered the story of the stableboy Tomas. Who had grown up with her. He had respect and responsibility at Reinsnes.

And then there was the Lapp girl Stine. Who bore two illegitimate children, one dead and one living. She became part of the family. And carried Benjamin at his baptism!

People added small details that made the stories better and heightened Dina's sensitivity to the common people. Her sense of justice. Her generous heart.

The less flattering stories about Dina eventually lost their negative effect. Rather, they became evidence of a distinctive quality that distinguished her from other mistresses. And made her even stronger and more special.

Autumn heather colored the riding path a reddish purple. Large drops of water fell like rain showers as they rode under the trees. The sun was a mere spot overhead, without strength or warmth. And the bracken slapped apathetically against the horses' hooves.

For months, Tomas had felt that Dina stared right through him, as if he were air. So now he spoke to her:

"Would you like me to find a post somewhere else?"

Dina reined in her horse and turned toward him. Her eyes showed surprise.

"Why do you say that?"

"I don't know, but . . ."

"What are you trying to say, Tomas?"

Her voice was quiet. Not a trace of the rejection he had feared.

"I think . . . I so often think about that day. The bear hunt . . ."

Tomas could go no further.

"Are you sorry?"

"No! No, never think that!"

"You want to go bear hunting again?"

"Yes . . ."

"In the master bedroom?"

"Yes!" he said firmly.

"And how long do you think you'd last at Reinsnes when people started stumbling over you in the upstairs hall?"

"I don't know," he said in a thick voice. "But would you, could you . . . ?"

He reached for her reins and looked desperately her in the eye. Tomas. A horse afraid of large hinds. Still, he jumped.

"Could you?" he repeated.

"No," she said brutally. "I am Reinsnes. I know my place. You're very bold, Tomas! But you know your place too."

"But if it weren't for that, Dina? Then could you . . . ?"

"No," she said, tossing her hair from her face. "Then I'd go to Copenhagen."

"What would you do there?"

"See the rooftops. And the towers! Study. Find out everything about numbers. Where they hide when you can't see them. Numbers are constant, Tomas. But not words. Words lie all the time. When people speak and when they keep still . . . But numbers! They're true."

Her voice. Her words. Were like a whiplash. Beating him. Mercilessly.

But still . . . She talked to him! About her thoughts. If he could not come to her bedroom, he would try at least to learn something about her thoughts.

"What about Benjamin, Dina?"

"Benjamin?"

"Is he mine?" he whispered.

"No," she said harshly. Then she jabbed Blackie with the tip of her shoe and rode away.

I am Dina. The living need someone too. Just like animals. Need someone to stroke their flanks and talk to them. Tomas is an animal like that.
I am Dina. Who strokes my flanks?

The flag knoll was a good place. The wind blew almost constantly there. Nothing was forever, everything was fleeting and incessantly in motion. Grasses and trees, birds and insects. Snowflakes and snowdrifts. The winds lived on that hill.

But the knoll itself stood firm. Windswept, covered with tangled grass. There, many years ago, the owner of Reinsnes had raised a flagpole. It stood more sturdily than most flagpoles along the shipping channel. Despite its dramatic location, which was directly in the path of every wind and squall.

The flag usually could be mended. Still, they often had to order a new one. But nobody criticized that expense. For the flag at Reinsnes was visible from a great distance in the sound, when coming from both the north and the south.

Dina had always felt drawn to the windy knoll. This fall she practically lived there. Or she reached for her cello. The strings shrieked loudly. People held their ears, and Mother Karen hobbled into the hall and called to her to come downstairs.

Or she climbed into the rowan tree. To conjure up Jacob and give her an object for revenge.

But the dead avoided her when she was in such moods. They seemed to understand that they were not in her world. Where only this man Barabbas existed.

*   *   *

218

"I'm coming south before winter." But Dina could not wait for winter. Patience was not part of her nature. She reached for Blackie's muzzle more frequently. Made swings in the trees for Hanna and Benjamin. But first and foremost, she went to the flag knoll at the first sign of a southbound sail.

And she stood there when the steamboat was hailed on its southern voyage.

She tried to coax information from Johan about Leo's destination.

He shook his head but gave her a strange look. She had revealed herself. Then he walked over and put his hand on her shoulder.

"Don't wait for that fellow Leo. He's like the wind. He never returns," Johan said arrogantly.

She rose abruptly to her full height. Before either of them knew what was happening, she knocked him down with a single blow.

For a moment, she stood looking at him. Then she sank to the floor and took his head in her lap. Whimpering like a whipped dog.

"You mustn't forswear anything, being a pastor and all. Don't you understand? Don't you understand anything? Anything . . ."

She wiped his bloody nose and brought him back to reality. Fortunately, nobody came into the room.

Neither of them told anyone about the episode. But Johan developed a reflex that sometimes struck people as strange. If Dina made a quick, unexpected movement, he ducked instantly. Then he would look ashamed and troubled.

Johan's search for a parish took a long time. He had indicated interest in both Nordland and the south. But his existence seemed to have been forgotten.

Dina left Mother Karen and Johan to their own concerns. Jacob remained distant and weak. Hjertrud slipped away between the coils of rope without a word. It happened time and again.

Benjamin let her take him on her lap, a surprised expression in his blue eyes. But he soon tired of her heavy-handed, demanding manner. Slid from her lap and ran out the door.

She was a sleepwalker. Who read in Hjertrud's black book. About justice and injustice.

Which struck hard. Caressed hard, and swore revenge.

*　　*　　*

The season's first night frosts came. Glazed the mud puddles and forgotten currants. One evening they got light snow, like a small loan. Strong, threatening winds followed. It was no longer "before winter."

Dina delayed Oline's customary orders to have the bedclothes and sheepskin coverlets brought from the warehouse loft at the right time.

"It's too early for winter bedding!" she stubbornly insisted.

This was an unforgivable intrusion into Oline's domain. She lost face on the estate.

Dina and Oline were two glaciers. With a deep fjord between them.

One night the cold cut through cotton coverlets and sheets, straight into the soul.

The next morning, Dina went to see Tomas in the stable. Leaned over the horse he was grooming and gave him a thump as usual.

Their eyes met with different messages. His surprised, tense, listening. Hers furious, commanding, hard. She snarled an order for him to clear out the warehouse loft and carry the winter bedding into the house. As if he were in disfavor.

When he asked who would help him, she made it clear that he was to do the work alone.

"But, Dina! That will take the whole day, and the evening too!"

"Do as I say!"

He bit back a reply.

Winter had showed its teeth.

Tomas carried a lamp. He came toward her with his head down, not knowing she was there. Watching every step. People might have put things on the floor that could leave a poor fellow lying with his nose in the dust.

Suddenly she strode from the corner.

The sheepskins hung from the beams like huge, soft walls. Soaked up the sounds. Buried them forever.

Outside, the bare ground was frost-covered, and a full moon hid behind restless scudding clouds. It would be hard for anyone to decipher tracks.

Her rage was strong and deep.

"I'm coming south before winter," the moon chanted through the clouds and the old warehouse roof.

She snapped a hold on Tomas like a starving dog. Barely let him know who she was before they were lying among the sheepskins.

It took him a few moments to realize what was happening. He gave an initial gasp of pain and fright as he felt her teeth in his neck and her arms around him. Then he let himself be dragged down onto two foam-colored wool coverlets that had aired all summer. He just barely managed to protect the lamp. It stood chastely watching.

Dina was pain, or delight. It made no difference to him whether he was in her bedroom by the black stove or in the warehouse loft. If the heavens swooped down on him like a black hawk, it was, still, heaven.

She tore off her shawl and unbuttoned her bodice. Raised her skirt to her stomach. Stretched her large, strong body toward him with no preliminaries.

He knelt on the sheepskin and stared at her in the yellow lamp-light. Then he removed the most essential clothing. So fast that everything got tangled and she had to help him.

Several times he wanted to say something. He felt a need to bless her. Felt he should repeat the Lord's Prayer.

But she shook her head and grew into the darkness with him. Her body was a bare smooth sloping rock in the moonlight. Her aroma filled his brain and drove out everything else. Made every muscle shudder and explode. A desire so enormous it could fill a church! Start an avalanche, a giant wave. Foaming, powerful, and wet.

He was carried away on it. Driven willingly into the tumultuous sea. The waves washed over his head.

Now and then he surfaced, to see if he could tame her.

She let him do so. Then pulled him under again. Down to the kelp forest. To salty seaweed and ocean currents that suddenly grew wild. She drew him across the long beach, where the tide was out and the exciting aroma of bladder wrack filled his nostrils. She rode him into the shallows, among schools of fish swarming side by side. Belly to belly. He smelled them. Felt them spread their odors on his hips. Like this!

Then he was borne into the deeps. And knew nothing more. Air and liquid exploded from him as she finally rode him ashore. He had large fishhooks and fish knives in his groin and chest. His stomach was a cracked rinsing trough. He might as well die. He was where he belonged.

But he did not die. She carefully let him lie there. At the high-water mark. He was a young birch bough. Broken from the trunk in a great storm. Leaves and color still remained. But nothing else. Except this one thing: to have given — and received.

Not a word was said inside. Outside, the air was blue-violet. Gulls scratched on the roof. The rage was lived out. Not beautiful, but strong as the *draug.*

As they lay outstretched, catching their breath, Hjertrud suddenly came from the corner and tried to snuff the lamp.

She leaned over to blow out the flame. Close, close to Dina's arm. The bottom of her skirt brushed the young woman's arm.

"No!" exclaimed Dina. She quickly reached out and drew the lamp to her.

Hjertrud retreated and then disappeared.

Dina was left with burned fingers.

Tomas sat up to see. Held her. And murmured comforting words as he blew on her hand. As if she were Benjamin . . .

She wanted to pull back her hand. He had not seen Hjertrud! Had not understood that she wanted to darken the world for them.

Dina dressed slowly and thoroughly. Without looking at him. When he put his arms around her before they left the loft, she rested her forehead against his for a moment.

"Tomas! Tomas!" was all she said.

The sheepskins and other things got moved into the house that year too.

Tomas carried loads as high as a hayloft, using every ounce of strength in his body. Without a sound of protest. He finished the task before the evening meal. Then broke the thin crust of ice on the water barrel in the courtyard and submerged his head and chest. Several times. Finally, he put on a clean shirt and went to Oline's kitchen for the evening porridge.

It had begun to snow. Cautious white shreds. Our Lord was discreet and good. Often the sin is not as great as the sinner believes. Tomas was the happiest sinner in Nordland.

His body was sore from unaccustomed movements. Lying among sheepskins and carrying sheepskins. Every muscle was a wound. He savored the feeling with immense joy and weariness.

Chapter 13

Until the day breathes
and the shadows flee,
turn, my beloved, be like a gazelle,
or a young stag upon rugged mountains.
— The Song of Solomon 2 : 17

Stine taught Hanna and Benjamin to control their excited anticipation by giving them small, manageable tasks.

Sometimes they grew tired of her motherly hand and came clattering into the master bedroom.

Dina rarely chased them out, but at times she ordered them to be quiet or refused to talk to them. Or she told them to start counting everything in the room.

Benjamin hated this game. He obeyed Dina, hoping that when he had counted for a while she would look at him. But he guessed at the numbers and remembered figures from the previous time. Pictures, chairs, and table legs.

Hanna did not know how to count well and failed miserably.

Since Johan still did not have a parish, they decided he would remain at Reinsnes through the winter as a teacher for Benjamin.

But Hanna was Johan's most faithful follower. Benjamin did not completely trust this grown-up brother who was going to teach him forever.

It was fourteen days before Christmas. The busiest time of the year. Oline gave orders. Anders, Mother Karen, and Johan were in Strandsted, doing errands before the holidays.

Benjamin and Hanna came into Dina's room. They complained that Johan had told Benjamin to study today, even though it had been decided long ago that this was the day they would make Twelfth Night candles.

"There are many hours in the day. Benjamin can both study and make candles," said Dina.

Hanna scampered around the room restlessly. She was a puppy that bumped into everything standing in her way. As she hurried past Lorch's cello, she pulled off the blanket covering it.

Dina stared at the instrument. The crack was gone! The cello was in perfect condition!

Hanna started to cry. She thought she had done something terrible when the blanket fell and Dina gave a loud exclamation.

Stine heard the crying and came running.

"The crack in Lorch's cello is gone!" shouted Dina.

"Is that possible?!"

"Anyway, it's gone!"

Dina carried the cello to the nearest chair. Slowly, oblivious to everything else, she began to tune the instrument.

When the clear tones streamed through the house, people lifted their heads and Hanna stopped crying.

This was the first time Lorch's cello had been heard at Reinsnes. It had a darker effect than Dina's cello. Wilder tones and greater power.

For hours, nothing else was worth hearing. Not even the news that the steamboat had arrived on a southbound voyage.

Only Niels was on hand to welcome the ship as usual. A heavy snowfall had started. The boat was several hours behind schedule.

Not many travelers came so late in the year. Just one tall, dark figure carrying a leather travel bag in his hand and a seaman's sack on his shoulder. He wore a fur coat and a splendid wolfskin hat, and it was hard to recognize him in the Advent darkness.

But Tomas was standing in the stable doorway as the man walked from the beach with Niels. They crossed the courtyard to the main entrance.

Tomas greeted the stranger stiffly when he saw the scar on the man's left cheek. Then he returned to the stable.

Leo Zjukovski politely requested lodging for a few days. He was tired after several days of stormy weather in Finnmark. He did not want to trouble anyone. Heard the mistress playing. . . .

Lorch's cello kept playing upstairs. Deep and resonant, as if a crack had never existed.

Leo Zjukovski was served some simple food in Oline's kitchen, at his request.

He heard about the cello. About how it had been cracked but now, miraculously, was perfect again. And about Dina's happiness with the old instrument she had inherited from her poor tutor, Lorch.

Niels talked with the visitor for a while. But when Stine arrived with the children, he explained he had work to do and left.

Stine wanted to tell Dina that a guest had arrived. But Leo Zjukovski refused to allow that. However, if they would open the doors to the hall, so he could hear the music better . . .

The traveler ate porridge and drank Oline's raspberry juice. He told her he appreciated being able to sit in her kitchen and thanked her for the meal by bowing slightly and kissing her hand.

Oline had not been the object of such gallantry since Jacob died. She became very animated. Talked eagerly about the house and the workers and the farming seasons. An hour passed. Oline did her strictly necessary tasks, moving to and fro.

Leo listened. He kept looking toward the door. His nostrils quivered slightly. But his thoughts were hidden inside the polite, serious skull.

Oline was amazed that he did not think it beneath him to add kindling to the stove of his own accord. Without any fuss. She gave him an admiring nod.

Lorch's cello wept. Tomas did not come to the main house for supper. The Russian was sitting in the kitchen!

Dina started downstairs to get some wine to celebrate Lorch's cello. She did not recognize the wolfskin lying on the chair at the bottom of the stairway.

But she did recognize the leather travel bag. The sight and the smell of it hit her so powerfully she had to grasp something firmly.

Her large body leaned on the banister. Doubled over, as if in extreme pain. The smooth round wood became wet with perspiration instantly. She sat down on a stair and snarled when Jacob appeared.

But he could not do much. Was as surprised as she.

She raised her skirts and sat with her knees apart and her feet on the step below. Firmly. Her head hung between her hands, as if it were chopped off and placed in her safekeeping.

She sat until her eyes became accustomed to the dim hallway and the meager candlelight on the glass table. Then she rose very slowly and walked down the stairs. Reached greedily for the travel bag. As if to make sure it really existed. She opened it and touched what lay inside. Found a book. This time too. Sighed and tucked it under her shawl. Then she closed the bag.

The candle flickered when she left. She had taken a forfeit.

She climbed the stairs again. Quietly. Did not add wood to the stove. Did not want anyone to hear the stove door slam.

She lay down fully clothed, her gaze fastened on the door latch. Sometimes she moved her lips. But no sound came. Nothing happened.

Jacob sat on the edge of the bed, watching her.

Stine showed the guest to the dormer room. He did not want her to light the stove for his sake. He was just fine, and warm as a live coal, he said.

She quietly brought towels and pitchers of warm and cold water.

He bowed and thanked her, while he looked around the room. As if he expected something to leap from the walls.

One of the maids, Thea, was sent upstairs to get something. She hesitated near the linen cupboard and glanced into the room. Wanted her part of the stranger too.

Something about the man made Stine shy. She whispered good night and hurriedly withdrew backward through the open door.

"Dina Grønelv has gone to sleep for the night?" he asked, as she was about to disappear.

Stine became flustered.

"She was playing a while ago. . . . Shall I see?"

Leo shook his head. He took the few steps across the floor and stood in the doorway.

"She sleeps there?" he whispered, nodding into the darkness in the direction of the master bedroom.

Stine was so astonished she did not even become offended by such an improper question. Just nodded, and curtsied her way into the darkness toward the small room where she and the children slept.

The large house grew quiet. The night was not cold. But black, with heavy skies. Inside was a dark hallway and two closed doors.

The lights in Dina's bedroom were watched from the servants' quarters. For Tomas, the night was a hell. Clung to his body like an insatiable leech when daylight came.

Thea came to the master bedroom to light the stove in the morning. She said that the Russian with the scar had arrived on the steamboat the previous evening.

"The man who was here when the barn roof burned!" she added.

"I see," said Dina, from deep in the pillows.

"He brought a seaman's sack and a travel bag. He didn't want to bother the mistress. Asked us to open the door to the hallway, so he could hear the cello. . . . And sat in the kitchen for hours. Oline was dead tired. The fire had gone out in the stove and everything!"

"Wasn't Niels there?"

"Yes, for a while. They smoked a pipe or two. But no *punsj* . . ."

"In the kitchen?"

"Yes."

"Did he say what his plans were?"

"No; he just asked for food and lodging. They had a lot of bad weather up north, it seems. He didn't say much, just asked questions. About everything. And Oline kept jabbering!"

"Hush about Oline! Is he going to stay until the next steamboat?"

"I don't know."

"Was Stine there?"

"Yes. She showed him to his room with the water pitchers, and it . . . I heard him ask if the mistress slept in here, and . . ."

"Hush! Don't rattle the stove so much!"

"I didn't mean . . ."

"I know."

"I just thought he . . . he probably wanted to talk . . ."

"Think what you think. But stop slamming the stove."

"I'm sorry."

Thea finished her task. With scarcely a sound.

The big black belly rumbled and roared. Heat began to spread through the room.

Dina remained lying in bed, still fully dressed, until Thea had disappeared and she heard the girl knock on the guest room door.

Then she got up and turned the strange night inside out on a chair. One garment after another. Poured tepid water over naked skin and forced Jacob to stay at a distance.

She took a long time brushing her hair and dressing. Chose a black cloth skirt and red bodice. No brooch or other decoration. Tied a moss-green knitted shawl around her shoulders and waist, as servant girls did. Then she took a deep breath and slowly went downstairs for breakfast.

Mother Karen had just returned from Strandsted and apologized for not being home the previous evening when their guest arrived.

Oline was offended about something or other and pursed her mouth ominously.

Dina said with a yawn that it did not really matter. After all, he was neither a government official nor a prophet. They could certainly make amends with a proper dinner in the middle of Advent.

Mother Karen began by ordering a fine breakfast.

Oline shot a furious look at the old woman's back and thought about all the things she needed to do that morning. The baking woman would arrive the next day. Everything was behind schedule. An outbreak of measles and other illnesses in the parish had kept people bedridden for days. All the extra help she had ordered was delayed. And the new milkmaid was still inexperienced, although she was a willing worker. Stine had her hands full with the children, and Dina was no help in the house.

What was a poor woman to do? A fine breakfast! Puh!

"So Leo Zjukovski is visiting us before summer?" Dina's voice was icy.

She heard him coming downstairs and went into the hall.

The smile he had sent her stiffened.

"Maybe you don't take guests so close to Christmas here at Reinsnes?" he asked, walking toward her with outstretched hands.

"At Reinsnes we always receive guests, both those who have promised to come and the others. . . ."

"So I haven't arrived at an inconvenient time?"

She stood looking at him, without replying.

"Where did you come from?"

"From the north."

"The north is a big place."

"Yes."

"Are you planning to stay long?"

He held her hand in both of his, as if wanting to warm it.

"Until the next steamboat, if that's all right? I won't be a bother."

"Did you bring some of those good cigars you brought last time?"

"Yes."

"Then we'll have one before breakfast! By the way, a book printed in the unreadable Russian alphabet came to my room. Last night."

His eyes smiled, but he was serious.

"You may keep that for now. . . . Books get so damp, the binding pulls loose with constant sea voyages. But I'd like to translate the poems. They're jewels. In a mad world. I'll write a translation that you can keep with the book. Do you know Pushkin?"

"No."

"I'd like to tell you about him, if you're interested."

She nodded. Her eyes still reflected blind rage.

"Dina . . . ," he said gently.

The frost had created lacework on all the windows. A faint aroma of cigar smoke seeped from the parlor.

"Barabbas is no blacksmith," she whispered, as she rubbed his wrist with her index finger.

Chapter 14

He opened the rock, and water gushed forth;
it flowed through the desert like a river.
— Psalms 105 : 41

*N*iels moved in Leo's shadow, as if seeking the Russian's protection. He even came to the main house for meals and spent evenings in the smoking parlor. The two men held long conversations in low voices.

Anders was busy preparing for a fishing trip to the Lofoten Islands after Christmas. One of his longboats had returned from Andenes with an excellent coalfish catch. In the past year he had become known as the "Coalfish King" far beyond the parish. He had bought new nets, both sink seines and dragnets.

One day when the sheriff and his family were at Reinsnes, Anders came with some sketches just before they all sat down for dinner. Proud as a rooster, he spread out the papers at the end of the table.

The steaming salted meat had to wait while everyone looked at the wonderful drawings.

Anders wanted to build a cabin on a longboat and put in a stove, so they would no longer need to go ashore to cook. Then they could remain at sea day and night, sleeping in shifts under a roof.

The sheriff nodded and stroked his beard. The boat would look rather clumsy, he thought, but the idea would probably work. Had he consulted Dina?

"No," Anders said, glancing at her.

Niels thought it was a crazy plan. A longboat like that would be downright dangerous! High and hard to maneuver, and impossible to tow.

Leo liked the idea. Russian *lodjes* were also bulky but were seaworthy fishing boats nonetheless. He examined Anders's drawings and nodded approvingly.

230

Mother Karen clasped her hands and praised the undertaking, but she urged everyone to the table before the food got cold.

Dina thumped him on the shoulder and said cheerfully:

"You're an excellent fellow, Anders! There'll be a cabin on the longboat, I'm sure."

They looked at each other for a moment. Then Anders folded the drawings and sat down. He had achieved his goal.

I am Dina. Eve and Adam had two sons. Cain and Abel. One killed the other. Out of jealousy.

Anders will not kill anyone. But he is the one I want to keep.

Niels's presence at the table, and his constant turning to Leo, infested Dina's food like insects. At first she watched him with her small smile, then she demanded Anders's and Leo's attention.

Stine was also on guard as long as Niels was present. She spoke to the children in her low, penetrating voice when necessary. Handled them in a gentle, authoritative way. Contrary to usual household decorum, they sat at the table with the grownups. When they finished eating they could leave.

It was hard to get the children to bed. But whipping rods were not used at Reinsnes. Dina made that decision. If you could control a wild horse by simply showing it the whip, you could certainly manage two small children with no whip other than a stern look.

Stine did not always agree, but she kept that to herself. When she felt she needed to pull Benjamin's hair, that was between the two of them.

Benjamin accepted Stine's punishments because they were always fair. Besides, Stine secreted a special smell when she exerted herself. That smell had blessed Benjamin ever since he was a baby.

He accepted her discipline, whether given with anger or with composure, as one accepts shifting weather and seasons. He bore no resentment and cried everything out of his system at once.

Hanna was different. If she was punished without knowing why, it could unloose an avalanche of sounds, anxiety, and revenge. And no one could comfort her, except Benjamin.

The day the sheriff and his family were at Reinsnes for a pre-Christmas visit was a day Benjamin chose to be especially restless at the table.

The sheriff muttered irritably that it was not right to have two youngsters growing up at Reinsnes without a father's discipline.

Stine bowed her head, her face flaming with shame. Niels stared at the wall as if he had caught sight of a rare insect in the middle of winter.

But Dina laughed and told Benjamin and Hanna to finish eating in the kitchen with Oline.

They took their plates and left the table, happy and unabashed.

"My father didn't need to be there in order for me to grow up. We all know that."

It was as if someone had spit tobacco juice in the sheriff's face.

Mother Karen looked desperately from one person to another. But she could not find anything to say. The atmosphere in the room became rancid liver fat when Dina added:

"Little Dina didn't get much of a father's upbringing while she was boarded with the cotter's family at Helle. And now she's mistress of Reinsnes."

The sheriff was on the verge of losing his temper. But Dagny gripped his arm. She had given him an explicit warning. If he could not keep peace with Dina when they visited her, she would never set foot at Reinsnes again.

For Dina's spitefulness and revenge in response to the sheriff's reprimands affected Dagny too. In fact, she was the only one humiliated. Because when it came to scratches and battles, the sheriff was as thick-skinned as a walrus in mating season.

He pulled himself together with effort and chuckled the whole thing off as a joke. Then launched into lively conversation with Anders about the cabin on the longboat.

For the rest of the meal, Leo's eyes were two falcons hovering above the people at the table.

Everyone seemed paralyzed by all that Dina did not say when she hurled her shameless reply.

Stine did not raise her eyes before she was well out of the room a half hour later.

The evening was short, people went to bed early. The next morning, the sheriff and his family returned home.

Mother Karen tried to repair the damage. Sent many gifts with them and spoke kindly to Dagny before they left.

Dina chose to sleep late, so she had to shout good-bye from her bedroom window as they trudged down to the pier.

"Have a blessed Christmas week!" she called unctuously, and waved.

*   *   *

232

The days before Christmas changed pace from pitch-black morning to afternoon's dark mirage above frozen tracks in the snow. Hectic activity slowly merged into evening and heavy repose. Even the animals were affected by this rhythm, although they scarcely saw daylight.

Lorch's cello was heard from the master bedroom late in the evenings, and lighted candles shone from all the windows. They did not ration candles now. The normal quota was six candles in the living room on weekdays during the winter. Two at a time. Plus the four large lamps.

The house smelled of green soap and baking, birch logs and smoke. Oline hired a woman to help with the baking, which left a wonderful aroma in the kitchen and pantry. But some tasks she trusted to no one but herself. The butter dough, for example. Her floury hands created it on the large table in the entryway. With the doors open to the cold December evening.

Wearing a fur coat and a baking kerchief, she held sway like a large bustling animal. Her cheeks turned rosy from the cold.

Stacks of *lefse* filled wooden boxes in the boathouse loft. Cookies were stored in the huge pantry. Pickled meat lay in a press in the cellar. For an entire day, the cookhouse rang with the sound of a chopping knife as Oline prepared meat for sausages. Curdled-milk cheese was placed in bowls, sprinkled with cinnamon, and covered with a linen cloth. Loaves of bread lay ready in boxes and chests, enough for the Lofoten trip as well.

There were many rooms, both large and small, at Reinsnes. Dina could certainly have had Leo Zjukovski to herself if she tried. But there were many doors. And they all opened and closed, without first knocking. So Leo became everyone's guest.

The steamboat was not expected until the week after Christmas. Perhaps not until after New Year!

The visitor discussed politics and religion with Johan. With Mother Karen, he talked about literature and mythology. He paged through her books. But admitted that he read Russian and German better than Norwegian.

Leo Zjukovski became Mr. Leo to everyone. He gave coins to Thea, who stoked his stove each morning. But no one knew where he came from or where he was going. When anyone asked, he replied convincingly, but briefly, and usually without naming dates or places.

People at Reinsnes accepted this calmly and politely, for they were used to strangers. Instead they interpreted everything about the Russian according to their own abilities and interests.

Dina thought he must have been in Russia since his last visit, because there were Russian books lying in his room. Twice, when she knew he was at the warehouse, she stole into his room on some pretext. Inhaled the smell of him. The tobacco, the leather clothing, the travel bag.

She rifled through his books. They contained underlining, but no notes as in Johan's books. Just pale pencil lines.

Shortly after Leo arrived, Anders asked when he had last traveled to Bergen.

Leo merely answered:

"I was there last summer."

Then he began to praise the *Mother Karen*, which lay on the beach waiting to be launched on its Lofoten voyage.

"Nordland vessels are true vessels!" he said.

And Anders's eyes shone, as if he had bought and paid for the cargo boat himself.

Leo removed his jacket and vest, and danced and sang in the evenings. His strong, dark voice filled the whole house. The parlor doors were opened, and people came from the kitchen and the surrounding buildings to watch and listen. Squinting winter-season eyes began to glow toward the warmth and the singing.

Dina learned the melodies and played the piano by ear.

Lorch's cello never came downstairs. She insisted it could not stand changes.

On Christmas Eve the sky was milky with snow. An unexpected thaw had begun. It did not augur well for Christmas visits and festivities. The road could become impassable for sleighs in less than a day, and the sea was already rough. The sound churned with a winter storm that seemed reluctant to reveal itself. One did not know its strength.

Dina rode on the ebb-tide beach, because riding on porous snow with a sharp crust underneath could hurt a horse's hooves.

Blackie trotted with slack reins as she stared at the cloudy horizon.

She had wanted to invite Leo to ride with her, but he had already gone to the warehouse. Wanted to make him reveal his feelings. For he had not repeated anything he had said in the upstairs hall the day after the fire.

She wrinkled her forehead and squinted toward the cluster of buildings around the courtyard.

Shafts of yellow light shone from the many rows of windows. Frozen rowan berries and sheaves of grain were ravaged by small thieves of heaven on quick wings. Amid all the whiteness, traces of animals and humans, rubbish and manure, formed gray and brown patches around the buildings. Icicles hanging from the roof created shadows on the snowdrifts that looked like voracious teeth.

Dina was not a pleasant sight.

But an hour later, when she rode up to the stable, she was smiling.

That made Tomas uneasy. He took the reins and held Blackie as she dismounted and clapped the horse's flank.

"Give him a little extra . . . ," she said.

"What about the other horses?"

"Do as you wish."

"Can I have a few days off, the week after Christmas?" he asked, kicking a clump of ice with horse manure in it.

"Just make sure there's someone in the barn and stable," she replied indifferently, and turned to leave.

"Will he be here long? Mr. Leo, I mean."

The question gave him away. Showed that he demanded an accounting from her. That he assumed the right to wonder.

Dina seemed ready to hurl a devastating reply. But suddenly restrained herself.

"Oh, why do people at Reinsnes put on such acts, Tomas?"

She leaned toward him.

He thought about chewing the first sorrel grass in early summer. Raw summer . . .

"People come and go . . . ," she added.

He was at a loss for an answer. Clapped the horse absentmindedly.

"Merry Christmas, Dina!"

His eyes brushed her mouth. Her hair.

"Be sure to eat Christmas dinner before you go home," she said lightly.

"I'd rather take home something extra, if that's possible."

"You can do both."

"Thank you."

Suddenly she became angry.

"Don't stand there looking so unhappy, Tomas!"

"Unhappy?"

"You're the perfect picture of gloom!" she elaborated. "No matter what happens, you always look like a funeral."

It grew very quiet. Then the man drew in his breath. Deeply. As if preparing to blow out all the tallow candles at one time.

"A funeral, Dina?" he finally said, emphasizing each word.

He looked straight at her. Mockingly?

Then it was over. His firm shoulders sank. He led the horse inside and fed it oats, as she had ordered.

Leo was just leaving his room as she came upstairs.

"Come!"

She said it like an order, with no preliminaries. He looked surprised but followed her. She opened the door to the master bedroom and invited him inside.

It was the first time she had been alone with him since he arrived. She pointed to a chair by the table.

He sat down and gestured for her to sit on the chair nearest him. But Jacob was already sitting there.

She began to take off her riding jacket. He rose and helped her. Laid the jacket carefully on the imposing bed.

She ignored Jacob and sat down by the table. They were figures in a tableau. Jacob watched them.

Not a word had been said.

"You look serious," said Leo, breaking the silence. He placed one thigh over the other and regarded the two cellos. Let his eyes glide to the window, to the mirror, to the bed. And finally back to Dina's face.

"I want to know who you are!" she declared.

"Does it need to be today? Christmas Eve?"

"Yes."

"I keep trying to discover who I am. And whether I belong in Russia or here in Norway."

"Meanwhile, what do you live on?"

For an instant, his green eyes flashed.

"The same as Mistress Dina, my family's property and privileges." He rose, bowed, and sat down again.

"Do you want payment for my lodging immediately?"

"Only if you're leaving tomorrow."

"I owe you more with every passing day. Perhaps you want a security deposit?"

"I already have one. Pushkin's poetry! Besides, it's not our custom to take payment from guests. That's probably why we insist on knowing who they are."

Something was going on in his head. A knot at the jawbone moved on either side of his face.

"You seem unfriendly and unhappy," he said bluntly.

"I don't mean to be. But you're hiding from me."

"It's not exactly easy to communicate with you. . . . Except when you're playing music. And then one doesn't talk to you."

She ignored the irony.

"You said — before you left — that you were courting me. Was that just nonsense?"

"No."

"What did you mean?"

"That's hard to explain under cross-examination like this. You're used to getting answers from people, aren't you? Objective answers about objective things? But courting a woman is not objective. It's an emotional challenge. That requires tact and time."

"Do you use tact and time when you sit talking with Niels in the office?"

Leo laughed, showing all his teeth.

"That's all I wanted," she snarled, and rose from her chair. "You may leave!"

He bowed his head, as if wanting to hide his face. Then suddenly he looked up and said pleadingly:

"Don't be so angry. Play for me instead, Dina!"

She shook her head but walked over to the instruments anyway. She let her hand glide over Lorch's cello, keeping her eyes fastened on the man.

"What do you talk about with Niels?" she asked abruptly.

"You want to know everything? Have complete control?"

She did not answer. Just kept gliding her hand over the instrument in large, slow circles. Followed the lines of the cello's body. It made a soft sound in the room. A whisper from beyond.

"We talk about Reinsnes. About the store. About keeping accounts. Niels is a modest man. Very lonely . . . But you know that, of course. He says Mistress Dina is headstrong and examines everything."

There was a pause. Dina did not reply.

"This morning we discussed the idea of building an addition to the store to make it more modern. With better light. More space for merchandise. And we talked about establishing contacts in Russia, in order to get merchandise not readily available in this country."

"You discussed Reinsnes with one of my people but not with me?"

"I thought you had other interests."

"What kind of interests?"

"Children. Household."

"Then you don't know much about an innkeeper's responsibilities! I prefer that you discuss Reinsnes with me, not with my people! By the way, why are you so interested in Reinsnes?"

"Communities like this interest me. It's a complete world, which is both good and bad."

"Don't you have similar communities where you come from?"

"No, not exactly the same. People who don't own property are less free. The common people have no reason to feel strong loyalty, as they do here. These are hard times in Russia."

"Is that why you came here?"

"Among other reasons. But once I helped put out a fire at Reinsnes. . . ."

He came closer. The scant daylight furrowed his somber face.

They stood with the cello between them. He laid one hand on the instrument too. Heavily, like a sun-warmed stone.

"Why was it so long before you came back?"

"Did it seem like a long time to you?"

"It's not just how it seemed to me. You said you'd come before winter."

He appeared to be enjoying himself.

"You remember my words so precisely?"

"Yes," she snarled.

"Then surely you can be good, now that I've come," he whispered. Close to her face.

They looked each other in the eye. A long time. Probed intently. Measured their strength.

"How good does one have to be, with Barabbas?" she asked.

"It doesn't take much. . . ."

"Like what?"

"A little friendliness."

He took the cello from her and leaned it against the wall. Carefully. Then he grasped both her wrists.

Somewhere in the house, something broke. The sound was followed immediately by Benjamin's crying.

He saw something stir briefly in her eyes. Then they glided together against the wall. He had never imagined she was so strong. Her mouth, her open eyes, her breath, her large generous bosom. She reminded him of the women at home. But she was harder. More determined. Impatient.

They were a knot against the dark wall. A stubborn, moving knot in Jacob's tableau.

Then Leo held her away from him and whispered:

"Play, Dina! So you can save us."

She whimpered softly, like an animal. Burrowed herself in his chest for a moment. Then she reached for the cello, carried it to the chair, and spread her thighs to receive it.

The bow rose toward the gray daylight.

The tones came. Rushing with no particular beauty at first. Then her arm became confident and gentle. She was inside the music. And Jacob retreated.

Leo stood with his arms at his sides and looked at her breasts, which were pressed against the instrument. Her long fingers, which occasionally trembled to give fullness to the tones. Her wrist. Her leather trousers, which revealed firm, generous thighs. Her cheek. Then her hair fell forward and hid her face.

He walked across the room and out the door. But he did not close it. Nor his own door either. An invisible line was drawn on the wide floorboards. Between the guest room and the master bedroom.

Chapter 15

I stretch out my hands to thee;
my soul thirsts for thee like a parched land. *Selah*.
— Psalms 143 : 6

*M*other Karen had packed boxes and baskets to be brought to the three cotters' farms and other needy families.

She had them delivered by horse or boat, or sent word when people came to the Reinsnes store to buy things they needed for the holidays.

Oline served refreshments in the kitchen. It was warm and cozy there, and orderly down to the smallest detail.

Lapp boots made from reindeer hide, overcoats, and heavy snow boots were placed near the large, black iron stove. They had to be thawed, dried, and warmed for the homeward journey. There was always warm water in the newly polished container at the back of the stove. It cast its glow on the kettles and wooden bowls when the stove's iron rings were removed to place the coffeepot directly on the fire.

People had come and gone the entire week. Eaten and drunk. Walked down to the store, sat near the stove on boxes, barrels, and stools, and waited for transport.

Closing hours were out of the question now. The store was open as long as people were there. It was as simple as that.

Niels and the store clerk ran busily back and forth. And they constantly had to remove the rings to put on the coffeepot. The water simmered for a while, then splashed noisily through the spout. With all the sputtering and steam, someone would realize it was time to pull the pot off the fire and add ground coffee.

On the floor near the stove was a flat stone on which to set the pot. As the coffee steeped, its aroma filled the nostrils of those who came in from the cold and darkness and sea spray.

The blue-flowered cups with gold edges, six in number, were

240

rinsed lightly after the previous customer and then refilled. An occasional unground coffee bean might float like a brown bark boat at
the edge of the cup as a poor frozen fellow warmed his hands on the
cup and raised the bitter nectar to his lips. Often, brown sugar and
cookies were served too.

A few customers received a dram behind a closed door. But liquor
was not offered freely at Reinsnes. That was as it should be, Niels
said.

In Oline's blue kitchen, liquor was never served to anyone except
Oline herself. Now and then she allowed herself a stiff shot of brandy
in her coffee, to thin her blood.

Only a few people came to the parlor for Mother Karen's sherry.

Dina rarely received guests herself. When visitors came to
Reinsnes, she let others extend hospitality.

Niels liked the weeks before Christmas. There was maximum turn-
over of their best merchandise. He had a habit of wrinkling his forehead deeper as business got better.

And this Christmas Eve the wrinkles were unusually deep, as he
examined the half-filled shelves and checked the empty storage spaces
in the store and warehouse. He assumed the air of a ruined man.

When Anders came in, whistling and wearing a holiday shirt, Niels
mournfully told him he feared they did not have enough flour left
for the Lofoten trip.

Anders laughed. He regarded his brother's worries about empty
bins and shelves with good humor. But sometimes he wondered why
the profits were not greater. Because their customers were numerous
and reliable. And those whom they equipped for fishing trips were,
almost without exception, dependable people who delivered fish or
money as promised when they returned.

After the last customer had left and everything was closed, Niels went
to lonely Mass. In the warehouse office, behind locked doors and
drawn curtains.

He neatly packed his offerings in two thick envelopes, which he
placed on the table. Then he screwed down the wick on the oil lamp
and moved toward the altar with one of the envelopes.

The washstand was made of solid oak with a heavy marble top.
On it stood an enamel bowl and soap dish.

Solemnly, he applied his whole body weight and shoved the

washstand aside. The loose floorboard lay there faithfully, looking at him with its many knots and dents.

Moments later, he lifted a tin box in the dim light, opened it, and made a new offering.

Then he put everything back in place.

Afterward, Niels took the money he had recorded in the ledger and locked it in the iron chest in the corner.

Finally, he stood in the middle of the room, took a puff on his pipe, and looked around. Everything was very good. It was a holiday.

Just one thing worried him. His map of America had disappeared. It had been lying on the table. And now it was gone!

He had searched everywhere. And asked Peter, the store clerk. Who insisted he had not seen or heard anything.

Niels knew he could never bring a wife to Reinsnes as long as Stine and the child were there. This sad realization had forced him to make a major decision. To get a map of America. And now it had disappeared.

Crisp unleavened bread softened in meat juices and sweetened with syrup was always on the table at five o'clock on Christmas Eve. Along with aquavit and beer. Everyone tried to finish their tasks by then.

Niels was at the table this year. Thanks to the Russian, he could show the courtesy of eating with the others.

Besides, there was the question of the map. Perhaps he could tell by people's expressions who had taken it.

The table was set for everyone in the dining room. Nobody ate in the kitchen on Christmas Eve. A custom that Mother Karen had introduced when she came to Reinsnes.

But people did not feel as comfortable in the dining room. They scarcely dared to talk to each other, for fear of seeming impolite or saying the wrong thing.

Leo and Anders lightened the atmosphere by clowning with the children. People had a reason to laugh. Something in common.

Platters were carried in and out. The steam from the warm food moistened everyone's skin and blended with juices from inside their bodies.

Mother Karen sat by the lighted Christmas tree. A holiday fragrance permeated the entire house. Braided paper baskets held raisins, ginger cookies, and sugar candy. Which could not be touched until Mother Karen gave the word.

After the meal, sitting in the armchair at the head of the table, she had read the Christmas Gospel. First in Norwegian. Then in German, to please Mr. Leo, she said.

Benjamin and Hanna were nearly bursting with eagerness for the packages and sweets. To them, the Christmas Gospel became not only twice as long but an unreasonable punishment from God.

Later they would have a saying between them: "Now she's going to read in German too!"

Dina was a broad river flowing through the room. In her royal-blue velvet dress with a damask breastpiece. She looked directly at people and appeared almost friendly. When she played the Christmas carols she seemed to caress the keys.

Leo led the singing. He wore a black vest and a white linen shirt with full sleeves, lace cuffs, and a silver brooch at the neck.

As always on Christmas Eve, a pair of flickering, tribranched Epiphany candles stood on the piano. The silver platter under the candleholders sparkled. During the evening it became covered with melted wax, which created a small landscape beneath the candles.

The Epiphany candles were Stine's work. One pair for Hanna and one for Benjamin. Although Mother Karen explicitly said they were in honor of Jesus.

Since a shoemaker had been at Reinsnes before Christmas, it was not hard to guess what was in the packages from the Reinsnes owners. Soon all the servants were trying on shoes.

Leo got up and sang a Russian jingle about all the busy shoes in the world.

Benjamin and Hanna sang, too. Russian gibberish. Painfully off key and very serious.

Mother Karen, elegant in starched lace collar and a fine coiffure, grew tired after a while. Suddenly Hjertrud walked through the room and stroked Mother Karen's white, wrinkled cheek. And the old woman half closed her eyes and dozed for a moment.

Oline let others serve her this evening. She had an open sore on her ankle. It had worsened during the busy Christmas preparations. Stine had applied a salve of boiled honey and spices. But it did not help.

Leo had said she should sit down and let others wait on her until she was well again. Since then, Oline's eyes had followed Leo. Just as they had once followed Jacob.

Stine exuded an air of great calm. Now and then she looked at Niels, as if he were a newly scrubbed floor. She seemed reflective and deeply satisfied. Her eyes were darker, her face more golden than usual. Her tight braids were twisted into a bun. But this did not hide the fact that Stine had an exceptionally beautiful neck.

Johan's memories of Christmas Eve were all connected with Reinsnes, except for his years as a theology student. He was filled with these memories. Ingeborg lighting the candles, Mother Karen reading aloud from the Bible. Jacob's face, which was always ruddy from drinking with the workers before the evening festivities.

Tonight he had felt childlike and weak when Mother Karen took Benjamin and Hanna on her lap. He was ashamed of himself and compensated by being particularly friendly toward everyone, especially the two children.

He saw that Dina's spirit had settled upon Reinsnes for good while he was away. She influenced Anders and Niels. Beneath her gaze, they became puppets. Mother Karen was the only person left to him.

Anders was a smiling brother this evening. For the most part, he sat listening to Mother Karen, Johan, and Leo. Now and then he glanced at Dina. Once, he nodded to her, as if they shared a secret. Clearly, this man did not have a guilty conscience about anything.

Niels made a few brief stops in the main parlor. But in between he had other things to do, which nobody asked about. Sometimes he passed around cigars, or filled glasses. But his words were locked up tightly. His eyes were restless shadows over the people in the room.

I am Dina. Hjertrud stands weeping in the sheriff's parlor tonight. She has hung garlands and angels and has read from the black book. But it does not help. Holiday celebrations make some people bad. So Hjertrud weeps and hides her ruined face. I put my arms around her and count shoes.

Now and then Dina's eyes met Leo's. The hardness was gone. As if she had forgotten that he came too late. Forgotten the conversation in the master bedroom earlier that day.

Mother Karen went to bed. The children slept. Fitfully, with perspiring foreheads, after all the cakes and goodies and the fear-tinged delight of being six and eight years old and celebrating Christmas Eve at Reinsnes. All the stories about Christmas elves, all the hands and laps. The voices, the music, the presents.

The servants had finished their work early and gone to bed. The girls in the rooms above the kitchen and the men in the servants' quarters. Oline guarded the kitchen hallway against nighttime suitors. She slept with the kitchen door ajar.

Oline's sleeping sounds were like a nighttime instrument. The day they were silenced, Reinsnes would lose its most important timepiece.

Niels had left the house. Nobody gave a thought to whether he was in the cottage, where he had two rooms, or in the office.

Nobody, that is, except Stine. But she gave no outward sign. Kept her thoughts under her dark, smooth hair without troubling anyone. She undressed slowly before the mirror and examined her body in the dim candlelight. After having first drawn a curtain in front of the sturdy bench bed where the children were sleeping.

The evening had brought nothing new into her life. Except one thing. She had begun to demand her child's inheritance. Slowly, but surely. And so she put a map of America in the bottom drawer of her dresser for safekeeping.

She had learned some things by watching Dina. What you did, you did. Without asking anyone's advice, if you could manage alone.

Anders, Johan, Leo, and Dina remained in the smoking parlor.

Dina leaned back on the chaise lounge and toyed with one of the heavy silk tassels attached to the armrest. She smoked a mild Havana cigar. And blew unfeminine but very expert smoke rings over their heads.

Anders described preparations for the fishing trip to the Lofoten Islands. He planned to send just one boat initially. Then, if fishing was good, he would outfit the other boat. He was sure he could get the necessary crew. According to all predictions, the fishing should be excellent. Would Leo like to join them?

Leo seemed to consider the idea, then replied slowly. He did not think he was suited to that sort of work. Besides, he had to go to Trondheim.

Dina studied him.

"May I ask what you need to do there?"

"I'm going to take a prisoner north to Vardø. He'll serve his sentence at Vardø Fortress."

"You travel with people who are going to prison?" asked Dina.

"Yes," he said simply, took a sip of *punsj*, and gave a teasing look to each of them in turn.

"Is that good work?" asked Anders skeptically.

"It's as good as anything else."

"But those wretched people?"

Dina shuddered and sat erect.

"We all have our prisons," Leo observed.

"That's different," said Anders.

He tried to hide that he was shaken by this Russian's work.

"Do you travel with prisoners often?" asked Dina.

"No," he replied laconically.

"What made you decide to do it?" asked Johan.

He had been sitting quietly, and somewhat shocked, saying nothing.

"Laziness, and a desire for adventure." Leo laughed.

"Wouldn't you prefer some proper trade . . . rather than this prisoner business?" Anders wondered.

"This isn't business. I'm not interested in business. This is being involved with people in difficult circumstances. People interest me. They teach me things about myself."

"I don't understand," said Anders, embarrassed.

"And what have you learned from the prisoners?" Dina interjected.

"That your actions don't always reveal who you are!"

"The Bible says our deeds determine who we are. Isn't that true, Johan?" said Dina.

Her back was very erect now.

"That's true," agreed Johan, clearing his throat. "But of course, there may be much we don't know about a person's unhappy fate."

"Niels, for example, does things he really doesn't want to do, because he's a stranger at Reinsnes. Had he felt at home here, he'd have done things very differently," said Leo.

Anders stared at him, gaping.

Dina leaned forward.

"Niels is surely no more a stranger than I am," Anders protested, with a quick look at Dina.

Dina leaned back in the chaise lounge and said:

"Tell us about it, Leo Zjukovski!"

"I've heard how Niels and Anders came to Reinsnes. Heard their

246

stories. Which are parallel. Nonetheless, something about this house excludes Niels and embraces Anders."

"What do you mean?" Dina asked brightly.

"I think it's the mistress's example, which everyone else must follow."

One could hear the snow swishing past the windows. A slow, warning rustle.

"Why should I exclude Niels?"

"I don't know."

"Perhaps you could ask him, or anybody else, for that matter?"

"I've already asked Niels."

"And what did he say?"

"That he hasn't noticed it."

"And doesn't that tell you that something is haunting Niels's conscience? Like dirty lice in a clean bed."

"You may be right," said Leo.

Anders grew uneasy. He found the conversation disgraceful.

"He made Stine pregnant and denied paternity!" Dina burst out contemptuously.

"Men do shameful things like that all the time. But they don't often go to prison for it nowadays."

"No, but maybe a man ought to go to prison if he deceives someone into believing he wants to get married," said Dina.

"Maybe. But the prisons would be filled. And then what would we do with the murderers?"

"The murderers?"

"Yes. Those we regard as dangerous. Those whom we must isolate from everyone in any case."

Somewhere inside her, she shot out a fumbling hand. Hjertrud was not there! Lorch! He was in pitch darkness.

"It's getting late," she said lightly, and stood up.

Johan pulled his coat lapels. He thought the conversation had little to do with Christmas.

"I can't see that anyone here at Reinsnes has treated Niels improperly. We give him our confidence . . . and work and housing and food. I agree he's a bit strange. But Dina can't be blamed for that," Johan concluded.

He cleared his throat several times.

"I think he feels so excluded that he's considering going to America," Leo said into thin air. As if he had not heard Johan's last words.

"America?" gasped Anders in disbelief.

Dina's face was a mask.

"One day just before Christmas I found him looking at a map of America. I asked if he was thinking about taking a trip. Judging from his response, the thought is there," Leo explained.

"But he's never said a word! And it's so expensive!" muttered Anders.

"Maybe he's been saving money," said Leo.

At that instant, Dina's eyes began to sparkle. She sat down again. And one shoe, which had been only halfway on her foot, soon lay askew under her toes.

The numbers? Columns of numbers rose up the wainscoting. And crept from the shadows along the silk tapestry. They became so clear!

Dina watched and listened with an open expression.

"Saving? How could he possibly save any money?" asked Anders. "I have a larger income, since I get a percentage of the cargo boat profits, and I don't have anything to save! Niels only receives a salary, after all. . . ."

He looked apologetically at Dina and Johan, in case they felt he was talking too freely.

"He doesn't have as many living expenses as you, Anders. He may have been saving for years!" said Dina harshly.

She put on her shoe and tied the laces properly so she would not trip and break a leg. Then she gathered her skirts and got to her feet again.

She was no closer to Leo than to the Big Dipper.

"It's getting late," she repeated, and walked across the room toward the door.

"If you need Niels in the warehouse and store, you must make him feel he's part of Reinsnes. Otherwise you'll lose him," Leo said slowly and clearly to Dina's back.

"You may be right," mumbled Johan. "I've known there was something. He wrote me such strange letters when I was away. . . ."

Dina turned so abruptly that her skirts flared.

"Those who don't behave like decent human beings, and don't accept responsibility, will have no peace, no matter where they go," she said, suddenly breathless.

"But that's not for people to judge," remarked Johan.

"Nobody has judged!" she said firmly.

"That's not completely true," Anders objected. "Niels doesn't

248

know how to make things right again. It's an impossible situation. And he couldn't marry Stine . . . just because of the child."

"Why couldn't he?" she snarled.

"Oh, for God's sake. . . ." Anders hemmed and hawed.

"He did something wrong, obviously. But we all do that, sooner or later," Johan said quietly. "And after all, Stine has a good life here now," he added.

"Stine doesn't have a good life! She's rotting here. While he's making plans to go to America! But I think that's fine! For everyone concerned. Then the air will be clean. And we'll be able to breathe."

"What about the warehouse?"

Johan did not know what objections to raise. Just knew he must say something.

"Don't worry, we'll find someone," said Dina confidently. "But after all, he hasn't left yet!"

"I heard rumors at the warehouse that Niels would prefer Mistress Dina," said Leo.

The man did not give up, apparently. Dina should have been out the door already. Now it was too late. She had to stay longer.

"I see! And does Leo Zjukovski want me to marry Niels so he won't feel excluded?"

The small smile was a barrier around her.

"Forgive me! That was impolite," said Leo. He rose and bowed, then hurried across the room to hold the door for her. He said good night and closed the door behind them.

The hallway was dark. The candle had burned all the way down in the brass candlestick. But through the tall window, the moon created pillars of light and turned the grating of small panes into a latticework over them.

He had crossbars on his face and shoulders. They moved in the same grates.

He put his arm around her as they climbed the stairway. It creaked slightly, as it always did. His hips touched hers. The words he had just spoken, and everything in their wake, disappeared. Simply no longer existed.

He was a solid weight. Deep, deep in her lap.

"Forgive Niels," he whispered, as they reached the second floor.

"That's not up to me," she replied, angry that he had broached the subject.

"It will give you peace."

"I don't need peace!"

"What do you need, then?"

She grasped his hips with both hands and forced him toward her. Then she opened the front of his shirt and put her hands inside.

The brooch in his neckband pressed against her hand, jabbed it again and again.

Suddenly she twisted free and slipped into her bedroom. It happened so fast. Was so dark. Could have been something they had dreamed. Each one separately.

Chapter 16

Make a joyful noise to the Lord, all the lands!
Serve the Lord with gladness!
Come into his presence with singing!
Know that the Lord is God!
It is he that made us, and we are his.

— Psalms 100 : 1–3

*T*hey went to church on Christmas Day. In the longboat. Johan had to give the sermon on short notice, because the pastor was ill.

It was an important occasion, so they bundled up Mother Karen carefully and carried her aboard like a package.

She smiled and nodded to everyone again and again and was bursting with pride over Johan.

The pastor was confined to bed, but his wife attended the service.

Mother Karen sat with her in the first row. Dina and all the others from Reinsnes were seated in the second row.

Leo chose to sit in the back of the church.

The massive stone walls. The candles. The shadows that lived in corners where neither daylight nor firelight ever prevailed. The hymn-singing. Humans grew small under God's immense ceiling. They sat close to one another on the wooden pews and warmed themselves together.

The Gospel of John: "And the light shines in the darkness, and the darkness has not overcome it. . . . He came to his own home, and his own people received him not."

Johan had prepared his sermon carefully during the days just before Christmas. Had practiced it with Mother Karen. His face was extremely pale, and his eyes asked for mercy. But his voice was resonant.

He spoke about the grace that comes from believing in Jesus.

251

About being ready to accept revelation and salvation. About how sin loses its power when a person lets in the light. The two greatest marvels known to mankind were Jesus Christ and Grace.

Mother Karen nodded and smiled. She knew each word by heart. Old as she was, her brain still functioned like a chest of drawers. Once she had put something there, she could find it when needed.

People liked the sermon, and after the service they flocked around Johan in the churchyard.

"It truly gave one peace," said the pastor's wife, pressing Johan's hand.

A constant vapor came from each mouth. It formed a cloud over their heads. Slowly, the congregation made its way to the parsonage for a coffee hour.

Dina took her time. Went to the outhouse first. Alone.

The churchyard grew quiet at last. She walked along a narrow, trampled path to the side of the church that faced the sea. Then she climbed the snowdrifts to the parapet. This was a church in which you could defend yourself. With thick walls and an unobstructed view of the water.

As Dina gazed at the mountain ridges across the fjord, Hjertrud showered them with millions of mother-of-pearl shells. They gleamed so brightly that the sounds from the parsonage disappeared. The boats on the ebb-tide beach were enchanted spirits that lay waiting.

She stood unseen. With the huge stone church between her and the others.

Then his steps broke into Hjertrud's glow.

They walked into the empty church, through the sacristy. The door was not visible from the parsonage. It was quite dark inside, now that there were no candles burning.

Their steps echoed from the stone walls. They walked the entire length of the church, from the choir to the main door. Side by side, without saying a word. Up the steps to the organ loft. There, it was even darker than below. The organ leaned over them, ponderous and silent.

"I think we need a blessing," he said.

"Yes. But we'll provide the light ourselves," she replied, with her mouth against his neck.

There should have been silk sheets and lighted candles in the choir. It should have been summer, with vases of birch leaves lining the center aisle. At the very least, the hard wooden floor should have been swept. But there was no time for preparations.

They did not see much of each other. But blood pumped strongly into all the small veins and vessels. Time was very limited. But it sufficed for a complete initiation.

His scar was her landmark during the wildest storm. There was no way back.

Before Leo appeared at the parapet, he had seen the sexton leave the churchyard. Witnesses could wait until another time. The location was not planned. But since it was to be, there was no better cathedral in all of Nordland.

At the parsonage, the coffee hour proceeded with dignity.

The sheriff and Johan sat on either side of a merchant from Bergen who had settled in the parish and received an innkeeper's license. This had irritated many people, because he threatened existing trade.

The conversation was about glaciers. The man from Bergen wondered why so few glaciers existed here in the north. After all, there were high mountains. And dampness from the sea all year round! In Vestland, and especially in Sogn, where he had lived, the climate was milder, but there were large glaciers nonetheless.

The sheriff spoke knowledgeably. The sea here was not as cold as people might think. And there were warm currents.

Johan agreed with the sheriff. And added that whereas farther south in Norway you had to go far above the tree line to find cloudberries and dwarf birches, here in the north these luxuriantly crowned birches grew all the way down to the sea. And cloudberries ripened even on the islands and beaches!

But no one had a true explanation of such complex natural phenomena.

Mother Karen thought God made people different according to His own wisdom. He probably saw He needed to let the cloudberries and birch thickets grow down to the seashore in the north. And He wanted to spare the Nordlanders from the awful glaciers, because they had enough problems. All the cold weather. All the autumn storms and crop failures! And the inscrutable ways of the fish in the sea. Everything considered, God was wise!

The pastor's wife nodded amiably. At that, less-informed people from surrounding farms nodded too. If the pastor's wife agreed, it must be so.

Johan did not want to discuss Mother Karen's theological explanations of the nature and distribution of glaciers. He just gave her a tender look and kept silent.

The merchant ignored the old woman disrespectfully. He said it was very strange that glaciers were not always found on the highest mountain peaks. They seemed governed by no plan and no law.

Dina entered the room quietly, and a girl in a sheer white apron served her coffee and *lefse*. People made room for her at the table, but she chose to sit on a high-backed chair near the door.

The sheriff said he could not accept the theory that glaciers were formed by damp sea air. For as far as he knew, the Jostedal glacier was in one of the driest districts in Sogn, whereas the Romsdal and Nordland mountains, which rose from the edge of the sea, had scarcely any glaciers!

About this time, something occurred. A general unrest. Which had nothing to do with Norwegian glaciers. It was hard to say where it began. But soon a subtle fragrance spread in the room. Carefully at first. A peculiar earthbound vapor. It made people restless.

Leo arrived a few minutes later, and praised the marvelous church. This did not lessen the distinctive smell of earth and salty sea winds. But by then, the altar candles had already sensed the fragrance for a while.

People were reminded of something they had once felt. In the distant past? In early youth? Something that had long lain fallow within the soul?

Still, some nostrils trembled when the tall Russian came too close. Or when Dina's hair and hands brushed past. Somehow the men could not continue the conversation any longer. They bowed their heads over their coffee cups.

The sheriff absentmindedly inquired about the pastor. The poor man lying upstairs with a cough. The pastor's wife nodded in bewilderment. This was the second time the sheriff had asked the question. She had told him that the pastor was still feverish and coughing. So no one should go upstairs to visit him. But she was to greet everyone.

This time, she replied tersely, "He's fine, thank you!" and brushed a tiny speck of dust from her sleeve.

They passed the cookie plate around, again and again. Poured coffee. A mood of sleepy contentment settled on everyone. And between mouthfuls, their noses sniffed the air.

Even if people's imaginations had been clever enough to identify the smell, they were not bold enough to track down its origin. Simply because it could not exist in good people's thoughts.

But it was present. It affected appetites. Interrupted conversations unexpectedly, as words stopped for a moment and gazes became blissfully distant. Was a stimulating balm that gently dissolved toward the end of the coffee hour. Only to reappear again in memories, long afterward. As people wondered what had created the marvelously good atmosphere at the parsonage on Christmas Day.

The pastor's wife also felt the effect. She sniffed the air lightly after the parish flock was well on its way.

What a blessed coffee hour!

She went upstairs to her sick husband. Brought him great comfort, and peace to his soul.

Dina sat in the boat and let the wind blow freely.

Leo! His skin burned into her, straight through her cape and clothing. Her body was a divining rod, a taut arc over a hidden mountain spring.

She wrapped the sheepskin tightly around her and talked with Johan and Mother Karen. She thanked Johan for the sermon. She praised Mother Karen for going to church even though she had not been feeling well lately.

Her gray eyes were two shining hollows. Leo met her gaze. Stared from one endless horizon to another.

Dina sat between Johan's attentiveness and Leo, who protected her from the sea spray.

Chapter 17

He brought me to the banqueting house,
and his banner over me was love.
                    — The Song of Solomon 2 : 4

*T*hey could not hide that something was happening. No more than one could hide the seasons from people on their daily rounds outdoors.

Johan was the first to understand the glances between Leo and Dina. He recalled Dina's curiosity about Leo's plans when the Russian left Reinsnes after his first visit.

During Johan's student days, the memory of his father's wife had chafed at his thoughts. Like a naughty picture on a page of the Bible. She became like Oline's cookie tins in childhood. High on the shelf and forbidden. The object of sinful thoughts.

Asleep and awake, he dreamed of her. Naked, gleaming white, with moonlight and cool drops of water trickling down her body. Standing hip-deep in the sea, with nubbly skin and bristling nipples. As he had seen her the night they went swimming before he left.

When he returned to Reinsnes, he was nine years older. And thought he was well prepared. Still, each time he saw her, he felt both pain and excitement. But Dina was his father's possession before God and humanity. Even though Jacob was dead and gone. She had given birth to his stepbrother and managed their home like a mother.

Mother Karen was concerned when she saw the looks between Leo and Dina. But she was moved by them. She quickly settled things with the memory of her son. And became content with Dina's having a living man.

True, she doubted this Russian possessed a fortune. She did not think he could manage an inn, or a store either.

But when she thought about it, Jacob had been a sailor before he came to Reinsnes. . . . Yes, she was already beginning to enjoy having someone in the house with whom she could discuss art and literature.

Someone who spoke German and French and who had traveled all the way to the Mediterranean.

Niels was surprised and disconcerted when he saw the obvious attraction. For some reason, which he did not bother to analyze, it made him uneasy. As if love were a personal threat to him.

Anders watched in amazement. But he had difficulty believing the attraction would come to anything.

Stine remained calm and expectant and gave no sign of what she knew or thought. To her, Dina's good humor and glittering restlessness were no cause for worry.

Oline, on the other hand, began loudly to extol the virtues of dear, departed Jacob one day when Leo came to the kitchen. He listened politely and interestedly. Nodded and asked for details about this hero, the former master of Reinsnes.

Oline talked at great length about Jacob's strong points. His handsome face, his stamina that enabled him to dance all night, his concern for the servants and the poor. And, not least, his curly hair and youthful nature.

Without realizing it, Oline let herself be taken in by Leo's willingness to listen. She was finally able to express thirty years of love. In the end, she wept her sorrow and longing against Leo's breast and became inseparable from him.

Tomas returned four days after Christmas and found Leo singing sad Russian folk songs in the kitchen to cheer a distraught Oline. It made Tomas homeless.

He immediately began tormenting himself by spying. Listened for Dina's cooing laughter in the evening when the doors between the kitchen and the parlors were open. Looked for tracks in the snow outside the summerhouse, because it was almost the night of the full moon. And he got heart-wrenching proof. Two large melted spots in the hoarfrost on the summerhouse bench. So close together they blended into one large spot. Two fur-clad bodies on the bench. Furs with openings in the front.

So she had taken the Russian to the summerhouse! Where she made her offering in the moonlight!

He also stole in front of the main house, at a good distance, to see how many figures were shadowed against the curtains in the master bedroom. But the heavy velvet drapes kept all their secrets. When he could not see any shadows, he tormented himself with the fact that there was so little light.

In his mind he saw Dina's white body in the other man's embrace, the stove, the glowing candelabrum on the table by the mirror. And the image of the canopy bed so tormented him, night and day, that he scarcely touched the sumptuous Christmas foods.

Tomas began to avoid the kitchen, except at mealtime, when he was sure the Russian would be in the dining room.

As it happened, there were in fact two shadows in the master bedroom. She brought him there seven days after Christmas. Despite the danger of revealing everything to the whole house. To Johan. To Mother Karen!

The rutting instinct was like the leader of a pack of wolves. It was gray and invisible to others, perhaps, but to Dina, it had red jaws with sharp, pointed teeth and a pungent odor. And led to death and hunger and furious raging.

So she got out of bed and dressed again. Combed her hair and stole into the dark, windowless hallway. She gagged Jacob behind the linen cupboard and located the correct door. Pressed the shrill brass latch and slipped inside.

He sat waiting for her like a faithful bodyguard. True, he was not wearing boots or a shirt, just his trousers. As if he had been reading, with an ear cocked for the slightest signal.

The two could not stay in the guest room. For the thin walls would betray them to Anders and Johan. But the master bedroom had empty rooms on both sides. She snuffed the candle between two fingers. Quickly, without licking her fingers first.

"Come!" she whispered.

As if everything had been planned, the man followed her.

Safely inside her bedroom, she turned the key with a sigh and led the tall man to the bed. He started to say something, but she formed a soundless "shhh" against his mouth.

Green eyes shone with laughter. Smiling seriously like a praying Buddha.

He closed his eyes a few times and bared his throat. She came so close, so close. But he did not reach for her at first.

Jacob's canopy bed proved unsuitable, so they had to use the floor. But they had eiderdown quilts and sheets of the finest damask.

He satisfied his hunger playfully, but greedily. Laughed himself into her. Silently and lasciviously. Like an ancient mountain that strangles its echo so as not to startle the sun. Or like clouds drifting so as not to frighten night dew on the lingonberries or fledgling eagles in a mountain crevice.

She was a river that guided a boat with a strong, plowing hull. With a bow that could force its way through rocks and rapids. Her banks were omnivorous and abraded his sides.

Just before the last rapids, where the waterfalls would overpower him, the riverbed split open and he was carried to the bottom.

The sandbanks were a mere whisper. But the water thundered and roared, and her shores were equally voracious. He forced the boat up again, its keel in the air, its oars gone. But with strength and determination. A large animal leaped from the shore. Its bite was deep, and deadly.

Then he was in the waterfalls.

The canopy bed stood calmly in the middle of the floor, as if it realized its old age and weakened state.

It had never seen anything like this. And seemed to be giving its entire weight to the moment. Quietly and with rare consideration, the four posters and the solid headboard tried to dampen all that echoed in the room.

But the canopy bed did not keep Jacob at a distance. He came between them like a lonesome child. It was useless to chase him away.

Jacob stayed nearby until the animals began to stir noisily in the barn and the morning was a winter wall behind Blåflag Peak.

Days and nights were cold. The sky spilled its intestines. Sharp green northern light edged with red and blue villi. Undulating toward the black starry heavens.

The *Prince Gustav* was an unwanted sea lizard when it arrived.

Dina began to pace upstairs again.

Book Three

Chapter 1

One man gives freely, yet grows all the richer;
another withholds what he should give, and only suffers want.

— Proverbs 11 : 24

*T*he young sewing girl they had hired before Christmas remained at Reinsnes. It turned out she had nowhere to go when she finished her work.

Stine had found her weeping. The girl was wearing her winter wraps and holding her cardboard box tied with a rope. She had cleared away all the fuzz and spools of thread, swept her work space in the servants' quarters, and received her pay. Now it was time to leave.

Stine would not reveal the details of the sad story. But one thing was certain. They could not chase the girl from the estate the night before Christmas Eve. The news would spread throughout the parish and bring no honor to Reinsnes.

She was given the task of cleaning the store and the office. The tobacco-stained floorboards were rough and hard to scrub. But she did not complain.

One day Dina walked past the pantry and heard the sewing girl chattering with Annette. She mentioned Niels.

"He shows up when I'm cleaning the office," said the girl.

"Don't be afraid; just give him a scolding. He's no gentleman," said Annette.

Dina kept standing near the open door.

"Oh, I'm not afraid. But I don't like it. Of course, he's obviously not quite right in the head," she said seriously. "Once he moved that heavy washstand back and forth like a crazy man."

"The washstand!"

"Yes, the one in the office. On Christmas Eve, Oline told me to go and check the stove there. In case nobody had sense enough to realize you could have a fire any day on a farm where lightning struck the barn roof. And that's when I saw him! He'd pulled the curtains,

263

but I saw him. He dragged the washstand, making such a racket! Bent down and looked at something in the corner for a while. Then he dragged the washstand back in place and lit his pipe. No sensible person would act like that!"

The February days had turned blue and sparkling.

She entered the office without knocking. Niels barely looked up from his papers to greet her. The room was warm. The stove gave a crackling sigh from its glowing throne in a corner.

"So you're working on the weekend as usual?" she began.

"Yes; I thought I'd record these figures before Anders comes with new ones. There's a lot to do. . . ."

"I'm sure."

She walked over to the solid desk and stood there with her arms crossed. He began to perspire. The unpleasant stickiness paralyzed his words and thoughts.

"What did I want to say . . . ? Oh, yes . . . I hear you're thinking about America?"

He lowered his head imperceptibly. The graying hair at his temples bristled slightly. He sat in shirtsleeves and an unbuttoned vest. His neck was sinewy and thin, like his hands.

He was not an ugly man. His upper body was surprisingly strong and supple for a store manager. His straight nose and other facial features could have belonged to a nobleman.

"Who told you that?" he asked, and moistened his lips.

"That doesn't matter. But I want to know if it's true."

"Was it you who took the map of America from the desk here?"

He had mustered the courage for an attack. And felt satisfied with that for a moment.

"No. Have you gotten a map? Things have gone that far? Where are you planning to go?"

He gave her a distrustful glance. They were both standing now, one on each side of the desk. He steadied himself, his palms flat on the desk, and looked at her.

Then he straightened his back, so abruptly he almost tipped the inkstand.

"The map has disappeared! Completely! It was still here the night before Christmas Eve."

He paused.

Dina looked at him without a word.

"No; America was just a thought . . . ," he said at last.

"It will be an expensive trip," she replied quietly.

"It's just a thought, after all."

"You've probably arranged a loan from the bank? Maybe you need a guarantor?"

"I haven't thought about that. . . ."

Niels changed color and ran his hand through his hair a few times.

"Maybe you have the money yourself?"

"No, not really. . . ."

Niels cursed himself for not having prepared for the situation. Learned his replies by heart.

It was always like that with Dina. She came like a large halibut, flailing in every direction, where you least expected it.

"There's something I should have discussed with you before, Niels," she said invitingly, seeming to change the subject.

"Yes?" he said, relieved.

"It's the numbers. The ones that are there but I can't find. . . . The extra numbers. That only appear when I count barrels, and goods we've loaded and unloaded. And when I talk with people about their debts and their credit. I've made quite a few notes. They're nothing to show the sheriff and the judge, but I've discovered where the numbers are, Niels."

He swallowed hard. Then he marshaled his anger and looked straight at her.

"This isn't the first time you've accused me of tinkering with the books," he hissed. Precisely three seconds too soon.

"No," she almost whispered, gripping his arm. "But this time, I'm sure!"

"What proof do you have?" he snarled. Vaguely sensing that it was serious.

"I'll keep that to myself for now, Niels."

"Because you don't have any proof. It's nothing but spite. Spite and lies, the whole thing! Ever since that business with Stine's child . . ."

"Niels's child," she corrected him.

"Call it what you wish. Anyway, ever since then, I've had no home at Reinsnes. And now you're going to make the whole world think I'm a scoundrel! Where's your proof?" he shrieked.

His face was pale in the lamplight, and his chin trembled.

"I'm sure you can understand that I don't want to waste my proof by telling you. Before I know if you'll do the right thing."

"What do you mean?"

"Show me where the numbers are, in hard cash! Then we can make an agreement about the rest and about a guarantee for your trip to America."

"I don't have any money!"

"You do! What's more, you've even cheated your own brother out of his rightful ten percent of the Bergen profits. You've used numbers that in no way agree with what Anders took south. That's where you made your biggest mistake. You implicated your brother. So that in the worst case, *he* would appear the swindler. But you forget that I know you. Both of you!"

He raised his fist at her furiously and started around the desk.

"Sit down, Niels!" she said. "Would you rather I'd brought the sheriff and a police officer and laid everything on the table? Answer me!"

"No," he said. Barely audibly. "But there's no truth in what you say . . ."

"You bring those numbers to light, preferably as cash, and do it fast! Have you spent them, or buried them? Because they're certainly not in any bank."

"How can you say all this?" he asked.

She smiled. An ominous expression. Which sent chills through his whole body. He closed all the openings. As if he were afraid she would creep in his pores and destroy him from within.

Niels sat down again behind the desk. Involuntarily, his gaze wandered toward the washstand. His eyes were those of a little boy who reveals where he hid the wooden horse he took from his playmate.

"Have you buried them? Or do you have them under your mattress?"

"I don't have anything!"

Then her eyes dug into him. Like an iron plow.

"I see. Well, you have until tonight. Otherwise I'll send a message to the sheriff!" she said harshly. And turned to leave.

Then, on impulse, she whirled around.

Niels was looking at the washstand!

He realized he was being observed.

"I actually came to examine the books. So you can leave," she said slowly. A cat. That suddenly extends her claws yet one more time.

He rose and was careful to walk erect as he left the room.

*　　*　　*

She locked the door after him and did not mind that he heard her do it. Then she rolled up her sleeves and went to work.

The large washstand with the heavy marble top would scarcely budge. Oak and marble. Solid indeed.

She leaned her weight against it.

Niels paced back and forth in the store while she stood with the tin box open and counted the money under the lamp.

The next morning, Dina set out to cross the mountain. With snowshoes, for both herself and the horse, hanging on the pack saddle over her travel bags.

Just as she was passing the smithy, Niels came from the warehouse.

When he saw the tall woman on the horse heading toward the mountain, everything went black. He knew where she was going.

His insides had refused to function ever since he heard her rummaging in the office. It had come both ways, so suddenly he barely managed to get to the outhouse in time. Had to lean over one hole to vomit as he sat emptying his bowels over the other.

Several times the past evening he had started toward the master bedroom, to ask for mercy. But he could not do it.

The night was an empty hell, filled with dreams of ghosts and shipwrecks.

He got up in the morning, smothered his beard in foam, and shaved the gray stubble, as if that were the most important thing in the world.

He was still contemplating going to the main house to plead with stone-cold Dina Grønelv.

But he could not make the decision. Delayed it minute after minute. Even when he saw her riding out of the courtyard, he could have done it. Rushed after her and grabbed the horse's reins.

He had felt her strength before. Knew she would show no mercy unless he groveled completely.

But he could not do it.

He should have left while there was still time! Should not have waited until after Christmas, just because a man whom one could talk with like a human being came to Reinsnes.

And the map! Why had he naively imagined that in order to travel to America one had to have a map? Now he had neither map nor money.

He found an excuse to go to the kitchen, in time to hear Oline explain that Dina had ridden to Fagerness.

"Oddly enough, she has something to say to the sheriff," Oline remarked with a dry laugh.

A black hood tightened over his head. He could not see clearly. Heard the judge's voice thundering at him already.

He refused the coffee Oline offered him.

The kitchen was bright and much too warm. He had trouble breathing all the way to the cottage.

Nobody saw him the rest of the day. When a maid came to check on him that evening, he said he did not feel well and refused to let anyone enter. The tray of food stood untouched outside the door when the maid returned later.

She shrugged her shoulders. Niels had pretended to be sick before. He was like a child in that respect.

Dina rode across the mountain, carrying an impressive sum of cash to be deposited in the bank.

Both she and the horse needed to use snowshoes at times. The horse set the pace as they climbed the road, which was icy and partially covered with snowdrifts.

She paused at the top, where, during most of the year, a roaring river tumbled over the cliff and ended in a deep pool. Today there was just a thin stream of water. Green icicles hung over the edge in ingenious patterns.

She stood looking down the steep slope where the sleigh had once fallen.

I am Dina. Jacob is not in the deep pool. He is with me. He is not particularly heavy. Just bothersome. He always breathes on me. Hjertrud is not in the raspberry bushes where the old smithy stood at Fagerness. The scream is there. It drips to the ground when I crush the berries in my hand. And Hjertrud's face becomes whole again. Like Lorch's cello. I count and choose for all of them. They need me.

She swung herself onto Blackie's back without preparing the animal as she usually did. The horse was startled and whinnied. Did not like being on the cliff. Had memories of it that would not disappear.

Dina laughed loudly and clapped the horse's neck.

"Ho!" she shouted, tightening the reins.

It was a difficult trip. She did not arrive until late afternoon. Sometimes she had to wade through the drifts ahead of the horse because it sank so deep in the soft snow.

When she reached the first farms, people came out and stared, as they always did in that region.

They immediately recognized Dina of Reinsnes. The black horse without a saddle. A fine lady wearing trousers like a man. The women both envied and disapproved of the sight. But above all, they were curious to know why she came riding to her father's estate in the dead of winter.

They sent children and hired men on errands that crossed her path. But became none the wiser. Dina greeted everyone politely and rode past.

Just opposite the sheriff's estate, she stopped to look for the ptarmigan that she knew was there.

The bird did not flit away when she and Blackie arrived, both breathing hard. It just sat with shining eyes and thought it was invisible.

She rode nearer, until it fluttered across the snow a distance. Laughing like a child, she followed it. Finally, she came so close it began to hiss and coo.

She and Tomas had played this game there in the winter. They had set snares too.

During the winter the ptarmigan in the bushes around Fagerness were as tame as chickens. They did not get frightened when you chased them.

It was another matter in the spring and summer, when the ptarmigan had fledglings. Then their small bodies huddled in the bushes or flew low over people's heads to lure them away and let the fledglings escape.

Shrieking hoarsely all the while. "Ke-beu ke-beu!" It was amazing that such tiny creatures could be so brave!

She knew there were bears on Eid Mountain. So for safety's sake, she rode with Tomas's rifle under her thigh. But it would be unusual if a bear came out of hibernation at this time of year.

The sheriff was alarmed. He peered through the office window with nearsighted eyes when he heard the horse. Dropped what he was doing and ran to the hall stairway with outstretched arms.

His greeting was profuse and filled with reprimands. She had not told them she was coming! She made that long trip, on bad roads, without a saddle! And she, a mother and a widow, did not have the sense to dress like a woman!

He said nothing about their not having parted as the best of friends the last time he was at Reinsnes.

But he created a great fuss about her having ridden alone through the dark and disgraced the whole family. Had she met people on the way? Who were they? Did they recognize her?

Dina took off her fur coat and dropped it on the floor by the stairs. She answered the questions like a calm, everyday oracle. Made no grand gestures. Simply allowed him to release the stream of words.

Finally, to put an end to it, she shouted:

"Have you got a toddy in the house? And make it hot as hell! I'm frozen to the bone!"

Then Dagny and the boys arrived. Oscar, a tall beanstalk of a fellow, showed clear signs of being the eldest, of having been given the most upbringing and responsibility. He already had a cowed expression and did not look directly at people.

Dina held his chin and regarded him. His eyes flickered, and he longed to escape her grasp. But she held fast. She nodded gravely and shifted her gaze to the sheriff:

"You're too hard on the boy," she said. "He'll run away one day. You'll see."

"Come to Reinsnes if things get difficult," she whispered loudly to the boy.

Then she sank onto a chair by the door.

Egil, the sheriff's younger son, came running like a puppy between his brother and Dina.

"Hello, Master Egil Holm. How old are you today?"

"Ten, pretty soon!" he replied, beaming.

"Well, don't just stand there staring! Pull off my boot, and let's see if there's gangrene in this frozen foot!"

Egil tugged like a man. The boot came off, and he tumbled against the wall. He was as short and dark as his brother was tall and blond. And he expressed himself in an entirely different way.

His frank, persistent love for Dina overshadowed his feelings for everyone and everything else. And led to constant quarrels and fist-fights with Benjamin when they were together.

Dina never got involved in these squabbles.

Egil's obvious love for Dina did not please Dagny. But she murmured politely that it was too bad they had not known Dina was coming, so they could have prepared a special dinner.

"I didn't come for a fancy dinner. I came on business!" Dina retorted.

Dagny was hurt by the haughty remark but said nothing. She always had the uncomfortable feeling that Dina was laughing at her and found her stupid.

Her cheeks were flaming with humiliation when Dina took the sheriff and a toddy into the office.

Behind closed doors, Dina explained the reason for her visit. She wanted her father to deposit money in a savings bank.

The sheriff folded his hands, sighed, and stared as she counted out the large bundle of bills.

"May I ask the source of all this cash?" he asked breathlessly, speaking in solemn sheriff language. "A surplus after all payments for merchandise? In the midst of Lofoten fishing? Without sending a cargo boat to Bergen? Does the sheriff's daughter hide cash in her bureau drawers in these modern times?"

Dina laughed. But she refused to say where she had gotten the money. Just that it was extra cash, whose whereabouts she had not known until now.

She did not want to go to the bank herself. It was beneath her dignity to come with an envelope filled with bills. Her father could perform that task. And he could keep the bank receipt until his next trip to Reinsnes. One third was to be deposited in Hanna's name, one third in Benjamin's, and one third in her own name.

The sheriff had been entrusted with a business matter and took the task very seriously. But at first he refused to hear of donating so much money to a Lapp child conceived in sin!

"Isn't it enough that you keep both the child and its Lapp mother at Reinsnes? Give them food and shelter and all the necessities? And now, in addition, you want to squander all this money?"

Dina smiled, while her eyes furiously plucked off his mustache.

The sheriff realized he might as well relent. But he was as curious as a child before Christmas Eve about how she had gotten the money.

As they sat at the supper table, he said:

"Have you, by any chance, sold a cargo boat or a piece of property?"

"No," she said tersely, and gave him a warning look. They had agreed that everything would remain strictly between the two of them.

"Why do you ask?" Dagny wondered.

"Oh, for no reason . . . One has all sorts of thoughts."

"I asked him how much he thought Reinsnes was worth," Dina replied calmly, wiping her mouth with the back of her hand. The latter was to entertain the boys and irritate Dagny.

Dina's presence put the sheriff in high spirits. He talked about one of his current cases before the prefect in Tromsø. The sheriff thought the prefect paid too much attention to sheriffs who had a legal education, those young fellows from the south who knew nothing about life in Nordland. Whereas old hardworking sheriffs, who understood the parish and its people's soul, were no longer regarded as worthwhile.

"Surely there's nothing wrong with having an education?" said Dina in a teasing tone. She knew this was a particularly sore subject with the sheriff.

"No, but why can't they see that others have knowledge too, the kind that comes from experience and wisdom!" said the sheriff, sounding offended.

"Maybe all your talk will make the case disappear," Dina suggested, with a wink at Dagny.

"He's tried hard to mediate it," said Dagny.

"What's it about?" Dina asked.

"A thoroughly un-Christian judgment," growled the sheriff. "A cotter's widow got sentenced to two months' imprisonment in Trondheim because she took a flowered kerchief, three cheeses, and some money from the estate where she had to work! I complained to the chief magistrate at Ibestad. About both the sentence and the witness. But he was already allied with the prefect."

"Be careful, Father. Those are powerful enemies." She laughed.

The sheriff gave her a hurt look.

"They treat common people like animals. And respectable old sheriffs like lice! It's the times, I tell you. The times show no respect."

"True, the times show no respect," Dina agreed, yawning openly. "And what about my father? He has no false judgment on his conscience?"

"No, by God and my king!"

"Except his judgment against Dina?"

"Against Dina?"

"Yes."

"What judgment?"

"Hjertrud!"

Everyone stopped chewing. The serving girl retreated through the kitchen door. The walls and ceiling held each other.

"Dina, Dina . . . ," said the sheriff huskily. "You say the strangest things."

"No; I keep quiet about the strangest things."

Dagny ordered the boys to leave the table and followed them herself. The sheriff and Dina of Reinsnes sat alone under the chandelier. The doors were closed, the past probed infected wounds.

"You can't blame a child," the sheriff said heavily. He did not look at her.

"Then why is she blamed?"

"Nobody blames her."

"You do!"

"Oh, Dina . . ."

"You sent me away. I was nobody. Until you sold me to Jacob. Fortunately, he was a human being. But I'd become a wolf pup."

"What wicked talk! Sold! How can you . . . ?"

"Because it's true. I was in the way. Had no upbringing. If it weren't for the pastor's advice, I'd be milking cows and goats at Helle today! You think I don't know that? And you feel sorry for strangers who steal flowered kerchiefs! Do you know what Hjertrud's black book says about people like you?"

"Dina!"

The sheriff rose ponderously. Silverware clattered, and his glass tipped over.

"Go ahead and be furious! But you don't know what Hjertrud's book says. You're the sheriff, and you don't know anything! You collect common people who don't know you. So you can hang them on your watch chain. So everyone can see that Sheriff Holm of Fagerness is a just man."

"Dina . . ."

All of a sudden, the sheriff doubled over and turned white behind his beard. Then he collapsed nicely on the chair before plopping to the floor. His legs and body were a folding knife that fit too loosely in its handle.

Dagny rushed through the doorway. She wept and embraced the man on the floor. Dina sat him on a chair, gave him a drink of water, and left the room.

* * *

The sheriff recovered quickly. His heart was running wild, he explained, shamefaced.

They all ate dessert together, nearly an hour late, in peace and tolerance.

Clutching the banister and feeling terrible, the sheriff had called Dina, downstairs, in a loud, pleading voice.

The boys stared at Dina in admiration tinged with fear when she seated herself at the table. Little boys were not supposed to hear, or see. But today, once again, they had seen Dina punish their father's fury. They learned it did not kill her. Quite the contrary. It was the sheriff who fell on the floor.

Dagny constantly shifted facial expressions as long as Dina was present. When she looked at the sheriff, she was an early buttercup by the creek. When she turned to Dina, she became rotten seaweed.

I am Dina. My feet grow into the floor as I stand in the mild winter night and watch the moon roll across Hjertrud's heaven. It has a face. Eyes, mouth, and nose. One cheek is slightly hollow. Hjertrud still stands by my bed weeping when she thinks I am asleep. But I do not sleep. I walk across the sky and count stars so she will see me.

Dina entertained herself by moving things when she visited Fagerness. She put them in their old places. Where they had been before Dagny's arrival.

Dagny made no comment. She had known Dina's ways for years. And would not give her the satisfaction of seeing she was annoyed. She just clenched her teeth and waited until Dina left.

This time, she had only to wait until the next morning. Then she hurried through the rooms, snarling and sputtering, and returned everything to its place. The sewing box, from the smoking parlor to the sitting room. The portrait of Hjertrud's family, from the dining room to the upstairs hall.

Dina had exchanged the portrait with a blue porcelain Prince Oscar platter with a gilded edge.

God help anyone who got in Dagny's way or commented on her actions.

Later that day, as the sheriff was puffing his after-dinner cigar and feeling peaceful and secure, she could not contain herself:

"I'm sure it takes great intelligence to be as brazen and tactless as Dina!"

"Now, now . . . What is it this time?"

He was tired of women's ways. He did not understand them. Did not want to know, or to take sides. But still he had to ask.

"She scolds you! Ruins the dinner! She moves things, as if she were still living here. She emphasizes Hjertrud's family to show disdain for me," Dagny said shrilly.

"Dina has a difficult temperament. . . . I'm sure she doesn't intend any harm."

"Then what does she intend?"

He sighed and did not answer.

"I'm glad I've got only one daughter," he mumbled.

"So am I!" she hissed.

"That's enough, Dagny!"

"Yes, until the next time she rides through the parish like a stableboy, astride her horse without a saddle, and acts as if she owns Fagerness! She even makes your heart go crazy!"

"It's not often, after all. . . ."

"Thank God!"

He scratched his head and took his pipe into the office. He no longer had the strength to maintain household discipline. Was ashamed that he did not put his wife in her place so emphatically that there would be peace in the house. Felt he was starting to get old and had become less tolerant. At the same time, he had to admit that Dina's arrival had been like a breath of fresh air. He was doing her a favor! One that nobody else could do. In spite of everything, she was the sheriff's daughter. Of course he would help her! Besides, he enjoyed having someone who could take a little roaring and raging now and then. Most people had such confounded delicate feelings!

He sighed, sat down in the big wing chair, laid his pipe on the table, and chose the snuffbox instead.

A pinch of snuff always helped him think clearly. And right now he had thoughts he wanted to pursue. But he did not know quite where to begin.

Something about poor Hjertrud . . . What had Dina said? What did it say in Hjertrud's book?

Chapter 2

Lo, he passes by me, and I see him not;
he moves on, but I do not perceive him.
Behold, he snatches away; who can hinder him?
Who will say to him, "What doest thou"?
— Job 9 : 11–12

*T*he silence was a wall when Dina rode into the courtyard.

Light flickered restlessly from the cottage. A white gleam across the bluish snow. Sheets hung in the windows. Death had come to Reinsnes. A shadow through the frosted window. Tomas had cut him down. A stump of rope remained. It dangled rhythmically a long time.

Niels had found a crack between the beam and the ceiling. Must have poked and prodded to get the rope through, because the crack was very narrow.

Then he had hanged himself.

He had not bothered to leave the warm cottage to do as people usually did in such weather. Hang themselves in the boathouse. Where it was easy to find beams with enough space.

In his final moments he had chosen to be near the warm stove. It was too lonely and high under the boathouse roof. A generous arch, with room for as many bodies as necessary.

So Niels hung himself near the stove. From a ceiling that was so low a full-grown man could barely dangle from it.

He was not a frightening sight as he hung there, despite the circumstances. Neither his eyes nor his tongue was distended. But his color was not good.

His head did not have much contact with the rest of the man. His chin pointed toward the floor. He swayed gently from side to side. Must have swayed a long time.

276

Tomas had burst in through the door, his heart thumping like a steam engine.

The old building began to be filled with movement, and Niels swayed with it. His dark hair drooped on his forehead. As if he had drunk too many glasses of liqueur. His eyes were closed. His arms hung straight down, slightly irresolute.

Now, for the first time, he revealed who he was. A very lonely store clerk, with many invisible dreams. Who had finally made a decision.

Niels lay on a wooden shutter on the dining room table until they could arrange a fine coffin.

Anders was in Lofoten. But they had already sent word to him.

Johan kept vigil over the corpse with Stine. Tended the wax candles all night long.

Stine threw herself onto Niels's body again and again. Paid no attention to anyone in the room. Not even when Mother Karen hobbled in and laid a thin hand on her shoulder and wept. Or when, at regular intervals, Johan read passages from the Bible.

Stine had turned her dark, eider-duck eyes toward the sea. Her cheeks were less golden than usual. She did not share her thoughts with anyone. The few words she said, on the day they cut down Hanna's father, were to Johan:

"You and I were closest to him and should wash him."

Dina looked reflectively at Niels's face when she entered the room, almost as if appraising an animal she had just decided not to buy. But it was not an unwilling gaze.

People from the estate had gathered. Their faces showed helplessness and disbelief, along with genuine horror and a drop of conscience.

Dina nodded mutely to Niels's last thoughts, which still rushed around the room futilely. In that nod was recognition at last.

Johan needed all his wisdom to convince Mother Karen that Niels should be buried in hallowed ground. Despite the sin he had committed before God and humanity.

"If they won't accept Niels at the churchyard, then we'll bury him in the garden," said Dina brusquely.

Johan shuddered at such words, while Mother Karen wept silently and sincerely.

Niels was buried in hallowed ground for several reasons. First, it took six weeks before one could even think about a burial, no matter whether the ground belonged to God or to humanity. Because the parish was hit by the worst freeze in memory. The earth was like granite everywhere.

Secondly, the official story was that Niels just died. The conversations Johan and the pastor had, with each other and with God, were very useful in the matter.

Moreover, the worst talk had subsided by the time a grave could be dug. Niels got what space he needed behind the church. In silence.

Everyone knew he had hanged himself from a narrow crack in the cottage at Reinsnes. With a brand-new hemp rope that Anders had gotten from Russia, or Trondheim, or wherever it might have been. But they also knew that the people of Reinsnes had their methods and their might.

Stine began to say to Hanna: "It was three weeks before your father died . . ." Or: "It was the winter after your father died."

When Niels was alive, she had never mentioned who Hanna's father was, but now she took every opportunity to emphasize it. This had an amazing effect.

Before long, everyone accepted that, unfortunately, Hanna's father had died and Stine was a woman with a fatherless child.

In death, Niels restored her honor as he could not do in life.

Dina dropped a few words. People on the estate heard them and put the words together to form the truth:

Niels had changed his mind at the end. He had given Dina some money he had saved and asked her to deposit it in the bank as an annuity for Hanna. The news spread faster than a grass fire in May. Once the Lofoten fishing boats returned, everyone in the parish had heard it.

People realized Niels was actually not so bad. He could have his place with the Lord, despite having taken things into his own hands.

*   *   *

The cargo boat returned from the Lofoten Islands with good profits. But Anders was gray and drawn.

He went straight to Dina's room and wanted to hear how it had happened.

"He couldn't just do such a thing, Dina!"

"Yes, he could," said Dina.

"But why? What could I have done for him?"

He put his arms around Dina and hid his face against her. They stood this way a long time. That had never happened before.

"I think he had to do it," said Dina darkly.

"Nobody has to do a thing like that!"

He created a flowing stream between their faces.

"Some do!" said Dina.

She clasped his head. Looked long into his eyes.

"I should have . . . ," he began.

"Hush! *He* should have! Everyone needs to take responsibility for his own life!"

"You're hard, Dina."

"Some people need to hang themselves, and some need to be hard," she replied, as she pulled herself away.

Chapter 3

A liberal man will be enriched,
and one who waters will himself be watered.
— Proverbs 11 : 25

*M*other Karen had a special book in her bookcase. Written by a public official in Drammen, Gustav Peter Blom, who bore the venerable title of Chief Land Tax Commissioner. He described a trip through Nordland and offered instructive information about Nordlanders in general and Lapps in particular.

"Lapps never feel pain or loss," and "Nordlanders are superstitious, probably due to their dependence on the powers of nature," he asserted.

Mother Karen did not understand what was superstitious about people who placed their fate in God's hands and who trusted nature more than the false promises of human beings. But she had no opportunity to discuss the matter, so she accepted it for what it was.

According to Mr. Blom, few creatures there near the North Pole were cultured or enlightened. And he was very dissatisfied with the Lapps' appearance.

He had not seen Stine of Reinsnes, mused Mother Karen. But she kept the thought to herself. And just laid the book lengthwise behind the others. In case Stine ever did the dusting.

For Mother Karen had traveled the world with her husband. To the Mediterranean, to Paris and Bremen. She knew that people stand naked before God with their new sins, no matter what their lineage.

Mother Karen had taken it upon herself to teach Stine to read and write when it became evident that the young woman could do neither. But she learned quickly. It was as if she put a glass to her lips and drank knowledge.

Mother Karen had also waged war with Oline. And, after a long siege, made her see that Stine had a natural talent for running a large house.

In the end, Stine, like Oline and Tomas, held an indispensable position at Reinsnes, for which she was respected.

But beyond the estate, she was the Lapp girl whom Dina had befriended. The fact that Dina let her stand at the font when Benjamin was baptized could not change the general opinion about Lapp girls.

People now said that Niels had died because Stine had cast a spell on him. And while animals and skillings multiplied at Reinsnes, the mistress who had banished Stine from Tjeldsund died. It was the Lapp servant's revenge for the treatment she had received.

Stine seldom went far from Reinsnes. Her sinewy body moved from room to room with silent energy.

It seemed as though she was so filled with grief that she had to work constantly in order that her body would have no chance to break down.

Her Lapp heritage had settled in her muscles. And her calm, gliding movements affected the young girls she trained.

She seldom revealed what she was thinking. Her face and eyes darkly radiated the message: I tolerate being in the same room as you, but I have nothing to say to you.

Her high cheekbones and musical speech clearly bespoke her ancestry. They held mountain plateaus and the rhythm of rivers.

She no longer wore leather jackets in the summer and a fur jacket in the winter. But from her belt still dangled a knife and scissors in tanned leather sheaths and a brass needle box and brass rings, just as on the day she arrived at Reinsnes to nurse Benjamin.

One day Dina asked Stine about her origins. She told her brief story. Her ancestors were Swedish Lapps who had lost all their reindeer in an avalanche. For years, they roamed Swedish Lappland. Herded wild reindeer, hunted, and fished.

But then rumors began about her father and grandfather. It was said they stole reindeer from other herds.

The whole family had to flee south.

Eventually they settled down in a turf hut in Skånland, procured boats, and began earning their livelihood by fishing. But Lapps without reindeer, who had become small fishermen, felt no self-respect.

In Swedish eyes, they were just poor "field Lapps" and were not even counted in the census.

At the age of twelve, Stine had to leave home and begin earning her own keep. She tended the barn on a farm in Tjeldsund. But that ended when she gave birth to a dead child one day. They could not accuse her of infanticide. There was just talk of sinful fornication.

The master defended her. But the mistress could not bear the sight of the Lapp girl. She had to leave the farm. With her breasts bursting with milk and bloody cloths between her thighs.

"Women often tear people into tiny shreds that they scatter to the wind. Then they go to church!" Dina commented.

"Where did you hear that?" Stine asked hesitantly.

"From the sheriff."

"Nobody at Reinsnes acts like that," observed Stine.

"No, but the men here aren't sheriffs either."

"Was your mother like that?"

"No!" said Dina, and left the room quickly.

Each season had its specific rituals for Stine. Weaving birch baskets, making doilies, gathering herbs for medicine and yarn dyes. Her small bedroom smelled of insects and wool and children's healthy bodies.

She had her own shelves in the pantry. Where her decoctions would cool. Or the dregs settle before the liquid was poured into bottles. To be ready when needed.

After Niels was cut down from the cottage ceiling, she became just two hardworking hands. For a long time.

One evening Dina sent for her. Late, after the others had gone to bed, Stine knocked on Dina's door and handed her a map of America.

"I should have brought you his map long ago, but I didn't," she said.

Dina unfolded it on the bed, bent over, and examined it carefully.

"I didn't know you had Niels's map. That's not what I wanted to talk about. . . . Were you going with him?"

"No!" said Stine harshly.

"Then why do you have the map?"

"I took it. He couldn't leave without a map!"

Dina straightened up and held Stine's gaze.

"You didn't want him to leave?"

"No."

"Why did you want him here?"

282

"For Hanna's sake . . . ," she whispered.

"But if he'd asked you, would you have gone to America with him?"

The room grew silent. Sounds from the rest of the house settled on them like a loose lid on a tin pail. They sat inside the pail. Shut in with each other. And themselves.

Stine began to realize that this conversation was more than just questions.

"No," she finally answered.

"Why not?"

"Because I want to stay at Reinsnes."

"But you could have had a good life."

"No."

"Do you think that's why things happened the way they did?" asked Dina.

"No . . ."

"Why do you think he did it? Why did he hang himself?"

"I don't know. . . . That's why I brought you the map."

"I know why he did it, Stine. And it had nothing to do with you!"

"People say I put a spell on him and made him die."

"People talk with their rear end," snarled Dina.

"It could be . . . that people are right."

"No!"

"How can you be sure?"

"There were other reasons, which only I know. He couldn't stay here."

"Was it because he wanted you?" Stine asked suddenly.

"He wanted Reinsnes. That was the only thing we had in common."

Their eyes met. Dina nodded.

"Can you cast spells, Stine?"

"I don't know . . . ," she replied, barely audibly.

"Then maybe there are several of us," said Dina. "But people will have to watch out for themselves, won't they?"

Stine stared.

"Do you mean that?"

"Yes!"

"You understand there may be powers . . . ?"

"There *are* powers! How would we have managed otherwise?"

"I'm afraid of them."

"Afraid? Why?"

"Because it's . . . the devil. . . ."

"The devil doesn't bother much with small things. Ask Mother Karen."

"It's not a small thing that Niels hanged himself."

"Do you care about Niels?" asked Dina.

"I don't know."

"One doesn't stop caring about people, even if they hang themselves."

"No, I guess not."

"I think if you care about Niels it can save him from everything and from himself. Then he didn't hang himself in vain."

"You really believe that?"

"Yes. And Niels did one thing at least. That's why I sent for you. He deposited a small annuity in the bank for Hanna. You're her guardian. There's about enough for a trip to America."

"Good Lord," murmured Stine, studying her checked apron. "I've heard people talk about that, but I thought it was just lies, like everything they say about me."

"What should I do with the money?" she asked in a whisper.

"The two of you won't have to beg for anything, even if the devil should move to Reinsnes," Dina said emphatically.

"The devil has never been at Reinsnes," replied Stine gravely. Then, retreating into herself again, she calmly rose to leave.

"He must have thought about Hanna . . . before he did it."

"I'm sure he thought about you too."

"He shouldn't have done it!" Stine declared with unexpected force.

"Given you money?"

"No; hanged himself."

"Maybe that was the only way he could give anything to the two of you," Dina said dryly.

The other woman swallowed. Then she brightened. The large door with its venerable rococo panels and heavy brass knob was closed carefully between them.

Mother Karen called it the "spring marvel."

It had occurred every year since the first spring after Stine stopped nursing. And it all began when Stine saw the legion of eider ducks that nested on the islands and skerries in the channel. Then she heard that gathering eiderdown had been a profitable source of income in the past.

Stine felt at home in nature. She built a shelter for the ducks with her own hands. Bound clusters of juniper branches into a natural tent. She fed the birds and talked to them.

Most important, she prevented anyone from disturbing them or stealing their eggs.

The birds returned by the hundreds to the beach and the buildings. Spring after spring. They plucked feather after feather from their breasts and lined their nests.

Throughout the parish, people told how the Lapp girl at Reinsnes tended eider ducks. And the sums she earned by collecting down from the deserted nests grew to enormous dimensions.

Now the income was so great that the Lapp girl had put the money in the bank. And apparently she was going to America to get ahead in the world.

Occasionally other women tried to follow Stine's example. But nothing came of it. For the Lapp girl put a spell on the eider ducks in the parish and brought them all to Reinsnes! She certainly knew her art, said those who understood the matter.

Eider ducks appeared in every imaginable and unimaginable place during brooding season. One spring a duck entered the cookhouse through the open door and settled in the large baking oven.

In the following weeks, Oline and Stine waged a tug-of-war to decide what was most important: to use the baking oven or to leave the eider duck in peace.

Oline lost the battle, with few words said.

When she sent a boy to the cookhouse to move the nest and lay the fire, Stine appeared like a bolt of lightning. She grasped the fellow's arm firmly and, with flashing eyes, said some Lapp words.

That was enough. The boy returned to the kitchen, pale, shaking his head.

"I don't want her to cast a spell on me!" he declared.

That was the end of the matter.

And the doors to the cookhouse and the baking oven remained open so the eider duck could go in and out to get food.

There was movement behind each hillock and under each tiny roof.

Stine gathered eiderdown as soon as the birds finished laying eggs and began to brood. Her skirts swept between the nests.

She did not take all the down at once, just plucked a little here and there.

Sometimes two dark glances met. Her deep-brown eyes and the round black eyes of the eider duck. The bird sat calmly as she pulled some downy lining from the nest.

When she left, the bird swayed a little, stretched its wings, and settled onto the eggs again. Then it quickly plucked some down from its breast to replace what Stine had taken.

She had hundreds of birds in her care these weeks in April and May. They returned year after year. Those hatched at Reinsnes returned. And the spring marvel became greater and greater.

As soon as the eggs hatched, Stine carried the tousled balls of fur to the sea in her sackcloth apron. To help the eider ducks protect their young from the crows.

The ducks calmly accepted the escort. They waddled at Stine's heels, chattering loudly. As if asking her advice about rearing the fledglings.

She sat on the sloping rocks and guarded the small families until they were reunited and safely in the water. The males had already flown away. Toward the sea and freedom. The females were alone again. Stine shared their loneliness.

The small, downy balls developed feathers and other colors and learned to find food. In the autumn they disappeared.

The baskets of eiderdown were emptied, and it was cleaned and sewed into cambric bags to be shipped to Bergen.

Eiderdown was a desirable product. Especially if you had contacts with merchants in Hamburg and Copenhagen.

Anders was not strict about his percentage where Stine was concerned. To tell the truth, he did not charge anything for brokering or transport.

Stine's eyes grew more and more like the round, damp eyes of an abandoned female eider duck when the male flies toward the open sea again.

She feared that sneering crows would come and put an end to the young life for which she was responsible.

Stine did not know that Mother Karen's book said, "Lapps never feel pain or loss."

Chapter 4

For lo, the winter is past,
the rain is over and gone.
The flowers appear on the earth,
the time of singing has come,
and the voice of the turtledove
is heard in our land.
— The Song of Solomon 2 : 11–12

*D*ina had the loose floorboard in the office nailed down. And as an added precaution, she told the maid to move the washstand when she cleaned each Wednesday.

Niels troubled her only on rare occasions. Usually when she wondered whether the lists of merchandise were complete or whether she had forgotten something important. Or when she saw Hanna trudge barefoot across the courtyard with Benjamin behind her.

Niels could suddenly stand in front of her and refuse to move. Then she had to review the inventories again. Until she was absolutely sure the details and columns of numbers were correct.

Sometimes he made her take the fatherless little girl on her lap.

Niels had been of some practical use while he sat in the swivel chair in the office. But he was not indispensable.

Dina familiarized herself with order forms and daily bookkeeping. She cleared out all the trash that had accumulated through the years. Created order in the shelves and cupboards. Cleared up unpaid sums.

She sent messages to those who she knew could pay what they owed. And she warned those who felt so ashamed of old debts that they did not come to Reinsnes to purchase their farming and fishing needs, but went to Tjeldsund instead.

Her warning was clear. As long as she saw them at Reinsnes whenever they had purchases to make, she would ensure that they did not starve when they had no money. But the moment they were seen with furs or fish anywhere else, she would take legal action to recover what they owed her.

It had a rapid effect.

The main house abounded with people. There was activity behind each wall and in each chamber.

No matter what the hour of day or night, Dina was sure to meet someone going to the outhouse, to the kitchen, or whatever place it might be.

The worst thing was all the women. They fluttered about constantly. The bustling, knitting, chattering, changing women created utter confusion. At the same time, they were necessary.

It annoyed Dina intensely.

She decided to renovate the cottage and live there.

"Then Johan can move into the master bedroom with all his books," Dina told Anders.

He was the first to know about her plans. And an important ally.

Anders went to Namsos to buy materials for the cabin he planned to build on the longboat.

To everyone's dismay, he returned with an entire raft of materials in tow. He had good business contacts and could buy high-quality lumber at a low price.

Since first only Anders knew about Dina's plans, it shocked everyone to hear that she wanted to renovate the ill-fated cottage where Niels had hanged himself.

Oline began to cry. She thought the place should be torn down and forgotten. But had just not said so. Until now.

"You want a living soul to move into that unlucky place? Not Mother Karen! There's plenty of space for her in the main house!" she scolded.

Dina and Anders gave explanations and showed drawings. Talked at length about the enclosed veranda that would face the sea. Where one could sit leisurely and watch the oyster catcher when it came strutting across the field to hunt earthworms on an early spring morning. They talked about the chimney that would be repaired. About the windows that would be moved to the southwest wall.

Not least, they made clear that it was Dina who would live there.

But Oline was still upset. She wept for Dina. And for little Benjamin, who was to live with his mother in the house of death.

"I wish lightning would strike that house! And make it disappear!" she fervently declared.

At that point, Mother Karen took charge. She would not allow such talk. Oline had to retract her un-Christian wishes and promise to curb her nasty tongue. If Dina wanted to live in the cottage, there was probably a reason for it. Young people needed some time and space for themselves. Dina had heavy responsibilities, after all, and many complicated thoughts. About the estate, the store, and the accounts.

Mother Karen made many excuses.

Oline continued to grumble. Declared that Dina could think about numbers and responsibilities when she was in the warehouse office. *Basta!*

Finally, Dina lost patience and said bluntly that she had no intention of asking the servants for advice about building improvements. The rebuke lodged in Oline's breast like a poison arrow. She bowed her head immediately, but she never forgot it.

Months earlier, Dina had ordered colored glass windows from Trondheim for the veranda and a white-tiled stove from Hamburg.

She used part of Niels's savings, which the sheriff withdrew from the bank as needed.

That way she renovated the cottage for Niels too. So he had no reason to complain.

She had the crack between the ceiling and the beam caulked. On the explicit advice of Mother Karen. Who could not bear to be reminded of poor Niels's final deed each time she entered the cottage.

The servants and farmhands needed food and supervision. That meant much hard work for Oline.

But she took her time with everything. Did not rush. It was better for people to feel hungry for half an hour while waiting for good food than to eat bad cooking or leftovers, she maintained.

Oline decided breakfast would be at five o'clock in the morning.

Anyone not in place when the *stabbur* bell sounded its three short clangs did not get any food.

"When the table is clear, food won't reappear!" she chanted, with a stern look at a poor soul who had to go to work on an empty stomach.

Mother Karen and Dina never interfered with Oline's ironclad discipline. For its result was that most work got done long before evening.

Sometimes they hired workers who were unaccustomed to such a strict system and asked to leave.

Oline had a brusque response:

"It's good the wind blows away rotten hay!"

One day when Dina stood on the flag knoll counting mountaintops with Hanna and Benjamin, the *Prince Gustav* came sailing north. The new store clerk had rowed out to bring mail and merchandise ashore.

It was he! Dressed like a sailor. Carrying his sack and travel bag. His face was not clearly visible.

The rowboat made its way slowly toward the pier, as the steamboat whistled — and continued its journey.

Dina tugged Benjamin's hair and counted the northern mountaintops in a resounding voice. She mentioned them all by name, at breakneck speed, as she pulled the youngsters down the rocky path toward the house. Then she left them, as though they were total strangers.

She went to the master bedroom. Could not find a dress. Or a hairbrush. Or a face. Tripped on the rug.

And the cottage was not ready to receive guests whom she wanted to have to herself!

Meanwhile, he had entered Oline's blue kitchen. His voice rose through the stairwell and open doors. Settled in her auditory canals. Like myrrh from Hjertrud's book.

She welcomed him like a friend of the household, in front of everyone. But Oline and the maids knew better. There were not many people Dina welcomed with a hug. They turned away and busied themselves, but made sure they stayed nearby.

Stine greeted the guest and began setting a large dinner table. Johan and Anders arrived in the hall carrying Leo's sailor sack. They dropped it by the staircase and came to the parlor.

Anders stuck his head into the kitchen and asked for a welcoming drink to be served.

Johan shouted from the hall as he hung his wraps on a hook. Inquired about the weather during the voyage and about the traveler's health.

The children came to the parlor too, and recognized the stranger. They were two small mice scampering near their hole, constantly aware the cat might come hunting for them.

Conversation was lively at the dinner table.

"Where's the prisoner?" Dina asked suddenly.

Two green and two ice-bright eyes met.

"His pardon was rescinded," he said, looking at her intently. As if amazed she remembered about the prisoner.

He sat nearby. Smelled of tar and salt winds.

"Why?" she asked.

"Because he acted like a madman and went after a guard with a chunk of firewood."

"Did he hit the guard?"

"Yes, just barely," Leo replied, and winked at Benjamin, who sat listening openmouthed.

"What kind of prisoner was he?" Benjamin asked boldly, stealing over to the visitor's knee.

"Hush!" said Dina gently.

"Someone I was supposed to take to Vardø Fortress when I went north again," Leo answered.

"What did he do?"

"Terrible things," said Leo.

"Like what?" Benjamin did not give up. Despite Dina's look, which felt like touching a hot stove.

"He killed his wife with an axe."

"With an axe?"

"With an axe."

"Damn!" said Benjamin. "Why did he do that?"

"He must have been angry. Or she stood in his way. Who knows?" Leo was not sure how to take the youthful curiosity.

"Would you have taken him here to our house, if he hadn't smacked the guard with a log?" asked Benjamin.

"No," said Leo gravely. "One doesn't bring people like that here. In that case, I guess I'd need to go right past."

"Then it wasn't so bad that he hit the guard?"

"No, not to my mind. But for him, it was bad."

"Does he look like other people?" the boy wanted to know.

"Yes, when he washes and shaves."

"What did he do before he killed her?"

"I don't know."

"What will happen to him now?" Benjamin wondered.

"He has to stay where he is for a long time."

"Is it worse there than at Vardø Fortress?"

"They say it is," said Leo.

"Do you think he'll do it again? Kill somebody?"

"No," said Leo, still very serious.

"Niels hanged himself!" said Benjamin suddenly, looking into the tall man's face.

The scar shone bluish over ashen brown skin.

"But Tomas says it's almost ten years since the last time somebody died at Reinsnes," Benjamin continued. "That time, it was Jacob," he added knowledgeably.

The boy stood in the middle of the room and looked at the grown-ups one after another. As if seeking explanations. The silence breathed heavily in their ears.

Dina's eyes were ominous. Her skirts rustled threateningly, and she came toward him like a swiftly gliding cargo boat.

"Take Hanna outside and play!" she said in a dreadful, gentle voice.

Benjamin grabbed Hanna's hand. And the two children disappeared.

"Yes, Niels is no longer with us," said Mother Karen, who had entered the room unnoticed. She clutched the silver handle of her cane as she closed the door carefully behind her. Then she turned, walked laboriously across the room, and grasped Leo's hand.

He was a sleepwalker, who rose and gave her his chair.

"But the rest of us must go on living. Welcome back to Reinsnes!"

The story, told in a few simple words, filled the air. It settled like a film of dust on their faces.

Mother Karen assumed the task of telling the story. At one point, a sigh was heard between the sentences. At another time: "My God . . . !"

"But why . . . ?" asked Leo in disbelief. He looked directly at Dina.

Stine slipped quietly into and out of the room. Anders put two tanned hands to his face like overturned boat hulls. Johan sat with lips pressed tightly together and homeless eyes. Mother Karen invoked a blessing on poor Niels.

"Why did he do it?" Leo repeated.

"The Lord's ways are inscrutable," said Mother Karen.

"This wasn't the Lord, Mother Karen. It was Niels's free will. We mustn't forget that," said Johan quietly.

"But not even a sparrow falls to the earth without God knowing it," Mother Karen insisted.

"That's true," said Johan amenably.

"But why did he do it? What was wrong with the man? Why didn't he want to live any longer?" Leo asked.

"Perhaps he didn't have anything to live for," said Anders. His voice was husky.

"One has what one can see, and something must have blocked Niels's view," said Johan.

Leo looked from one to the other. And he did not try to hide his emotion. Suddenly he stood up, held the edge of the table, and cleared his throat, as if he were going to make a speech. Then he began to sing.

A strange foreign melody in a minor key. Sorrow flowed from him as from a child. He threw his head back and gulped noisily, but continued singing. For a long time. One refrain was repeated again and again:

Погасло дневное светило,
The day is ending,
на море синее вечерный пал туман.
a blue pillow of evening falls on the sea.

Шуми, шуми, послушное ветрило,
Sigh, sigh, obedient sail,
волнуйся подо мной, угрюмый океан.
rock beneath me, dark ocean.

They had never seen or heard anything like it. He had been sent to help them face what they had hidden from one another for many weeks. The lonely, cursed question: "Was I to blame?"

After dinner Dina and Leo rode off on horseback, as Tomas watched in helpless resignation.

The spring light was a keen-edged knife above them until late evening.

"Do you and Tomas ride together?" asked Leo.

"Yes, when it's convenient."

Patches of snow still lay here and there. She led the way up the mountain.

"Has Tomas been here long?"

"Yes. Why do you ask?"

"He has eyes like a dog."

"Oh?" she said with a laugh. "They're just a little unusual: one blue and one brown. He's energetic. Dependable."

"I believe that. But when he looks at you, Dina, his eyes are just like Niels's eyes."

"Don't talk about Niels!" she panted, and urged her horse to a gallop up the steep slope.

"You drive men to great lengths!" he shouted after her.

She did not turn around. Did not reply.

He overtook her and grabbed the reins. It frightened Blackie, and the animal reared with a furious whinny.

"Let go! The horse doesn't like that!" she said. Her voice sounded as if it had been imprisoned for hours.

"Do you know why Niels died?" he asked urgently.

"Yes. He hanged himself!" she snarled, as she pulled herself loose.

"You're a hard woman!"

"What do you want me to say? That I drove him to it because I refused to have him? Do you really think that was the reason, Leo Zjukovski?"

He did not answer.

They withdrew silently into themselves.

I am Dina. Why do I bring Hjertrud's messenger here? Is it so he will see time and place? See the sleigh in the deep pool? And when he has seen, will he become mute?

When they came to the spot above the canyon where Jacob and the sleigh had thundered over the edge, Dina reined in her horse and said:

"Have you been in Trondheim the whole time?"

"No."

"Where have you been, then? You never sent a word."

She slid off the horse and let it roam freely. Leo followed her example before he replied.

"I expected to come north long before now."

"From where?"

"Bergen."

"What did you do there, Leo? Do you have a widow there too?"

"No. No widows in Bergen. No widows in Trondheim. No widows in Archangel. Only at Reinsnes. . . ."

She did not respond.

Blackie whinnied nervously and trotted over to Dina. Stuck his muzzle in her hair.

"Why is the horse so uneasy?" Leo asked.

"He doesn't like this place."

"Oh? Why not? Is he frightened by the noise of the waterfalls?"

"Jacob fell over the edge here. The horse and I escaped."

Leo gave her a questioning look.

"And that's almost ten years ago, as Benjamin said?"

"Yes. The horse is getting old. I'll have to get a new one soon."

"It must have been . . . horrible."

"It was no fun," she said tersely, and leaned over the cliff.

"Did you love Jacob?" he asked after a while.

"Love?"

"Yes. I understand he was much older than you."

"Older than my father."

He looked at her with curiosity and amazement, until she asked:

"Whom does one love among those one meets? You must know that, having traveled so much."

"Only a very few. . . ."

"Since you feel so free to ask if I loved Jacob, you can surely tell me whom you love among those you've met."

"I loved my mother. But she's no longer alive. She never adjusted to living in Russia. Always felt homesick for Bergen. For the sea, I think. . . . Also, from age twenty to twenty-three, I had a wife. She died too."

"Do you ever see her now?"

"If you mean do I think about her . . . Yes, sometimes. Like right now . . . Since you ask. But I didn't love her as I should. Our families thought we were a good match. I was just an irresponsible medical student who preferred to be a radical and ingratiate myself with artists and rich charlatans in the czar's court. I studied and drank wine. Gave political speeches and . . ."

"How old are you?"

"Thirty-nine," he said with a smile. "Do you think that's old?"

"It's not a question of age."

He laughed heartily.

"Do you come from an upper-class family? Were you received at court?" she asked.

"I tried."

"Why didn't you succeed?"

"Because Pushkin died."

"The man who wrote poetry?"

"Yes."

"How did he die?"

"He was shot in a duel. Caused by jealousy, they said. But in fact, he was a victim of political intrigue. Russia is rotting from within. It affects all of us. Pushkin was a great artist surrounded by ordinary people."

"He sounds somewhat 'ordinary' too," she said firmly.

"Everyone's ordinary when it comes to love."

She glanced at him quickly and said:

"Could you imagine shooting someone out of jealousy?"

"I don't know. Perhaps."

"Where did the bullet strike?"

"In his stomach."

"A bad spot," she said dryly.

"You don't show much sympathy, do you, Dina?" he said, suddenly irritated.

"What do you mean?"

"For a woman, you certainly take suffering and death very well. When you talk about your dead husband . . . about Niels . . . and now Pushkin. That's unusual."

"I don't know that man Pushkin."

"No, but the others . . ."

"What do you expect?"

"A little sympathy in a woman's voice."

"It's women who care for the dead, after all. Men just lie down and die. You can't cry about a stupid dueling wound in the stomach. Besides, men don't lose their lives that way around here. They drown."

"Or hang themselves. And women weep in Nordland too."

"That's not my concern."

It was not only the words that repelled him.

"Your mother is dead too? A violent death?" he asked, as if he had not heard her last words.

Dina bent over and picked up a suitably large stone. Drew back her arm and threw the stone powerfully over the precipice.

"Masses of boiling lye were dumped on her," she said firmly, without looking at him. "That's why the sheriff tore down the washhouse at Fagerness and prefers that I spend my life at Reinsnes."

She put two fingers between her teeth and whistled for her horse.

Leo stood with his arms hanging limply. Somewhere in his green eyes, unbounded tenderness arose.

"I knew there was something. . . . That scene with your father at Christmas. You aren't very good friends with your father, are you, Dina?"

"He's the one who's not friends with me!"

"That's a childish attitude."

"Well, it's still true."

"Tell me about you."

"Tell about yourself first," she insisted sullenly.

But after a while she said:

"What would you have done if your child had touched the handle and made the lye spill? And what would you have done if your wife disappeared before you had shown her a little love, after plaguing her for years?"

Leo went to her. Put his arms around her. Held her close. And kissed her blindly and hard.

The waterfalls were a church organ. The sky hid the horse. Jacob was only an angel. For Hjertrud's new messenger was there.

"You underline your books. That doesn't look nice," she suddenly remarked as they rode down the steep slope.

He quickly hid his surprise and said:

"You spy on people. You examine books and travel bags."

"Yes, when people won't tell me who they are themselves."

"I've told you . . ."

"About that man Pushkin, whom you admire like a god. You promised me a translation."

"You'll get one."

"It has to be from the book you gave me."

"I didn't give it to you. You took it! I gave you the other book."

"You had two identical books. One with underlining and one without. I liked the one with underlining best."

"She's wise," he said, as if talking to himself.

She turned on her horse's back and gave him a teasing look.

"You need to be more careful!"

"Yes, after this. That book was important, in fact . . . ," he said, but stopped abruptly.

"Who gives you Russian books here in Norway?"

"You, for example."

"I had to take the book I wanted."

"You're shameless," he said dryly.

"That's true."

"Why did you take the underlined book?"

"Because it meant the most to you."

He said no more. She had exhausted him.

"Do you have the other book with you now?"

"No."

"Where did you leave it?"

"A widow stole it."

"In Bergen?"

"In Bergen."

"You're angry."

"Yes, I'm angry."

"Are you going to come to my room tonight and translate what you like best in Pushkin's book?"

"Would that be appropriate?"

She laughed, as her body moved up and down on the horse's back. She sat astride Blackie. Her thighs held the horse's flanks firmly and gently, and her hips swayed in rhythm with the animal.

The man wished it were summer. With warm weather. Then he would have tied the horse to the tree.

The third day, he left. Dina began to pace at night. And springtime struggled with its tasks.

Chapter 5

You shall not uncover the nakedness of your father's wife.
— Leviticus 18 : 8

The women at Reinsnes were like the cargo boats at Reinsnes. Beached on the same shores. But with different destinations when they set sail. Different cargoes. Different sailing characteristics.

But whereas the cargo boats had a skipper, the women raised their sails into the wind themselves. They were headstrong and obstinate and had great individual power.

Some people believed Stine could bewitch the wind. Others thought Dina was in league with the devil. Otherwise why would she sit, bundled in wolfskin, drinking wine in a snow-covered summerhouse on moonlit winter nights?

Still others felt there was a balance between good and evil powers at Reinsnes. But Mother Karen's death would be a catastrophe.

The old woman held to life tenaciously. Her skin looked like soft, shining birch bark. White, with dark spots. Her hair was carefully combed each day by Stine. After its weekly juniper rinse it had a golden sheen. And was soft as silk.

Her prominent hooked nose held her monocle in place. She read for three hours every day. Newspapers, books, old and new letters. It was important to remain alert in old age, she said.

She took her afternoon nap in the wing chair, with a woolen lap robe over her knees. She went to bed with the farmworkers and got up with the rooster. Her legs gave her considerable trouble, but she did not complain, now that she had moved into the bedroom behind the dining room and no longer needed to climb stairs.

Mother Karen had been opposed to Dina's plans for renovating the cottage. But she changed her mind when Dina did not relent and carpenters arrived at the estate.

The cottage was patched and repaired until it was like a polished jewel.

When the work was finished and Dina's things had been moved in, Mother Karen crossed the courtyard to see it all.

She had decided the building should be painted ocher, with white trim.

Dina agreed. The cottage would be ocher! One white house on the estate was enough. And yet the cottage must not look like a red barn.

The best thing about the building was the new, enclosed veranda that faced the sea. It had dragon spires and stained-glass windows. Double doors and broad steps. One could sit there, or go in and out, without being observed from the other buildings.

"An enclosed veranda, with double doors, facing southwest! That means a lot of firewood and drafts," Oline said firmly. "And the indoor ferns and rosebushes won't survive even one winter day!"

"Megalomania," declared the sheriff when he saw the veranda. "It's not fitting for a sod-roofed house." But he smiled.

Anders supported Dina. Said it was a comfortable place.

"In wintertime it's certainly better to sit in an enclosed veranda than in a summerhouse," he said, and winked at Dina. Boldly acknowledging her vices.

Mother Karen contributed sturdy geranium cuttings for the new sitting room windows.

She sat in the rocking chair on moving day and smilingly observed all the wonderful things. She never mentioned that Niels had died in the cottage.

"My goodness! Jacob should have seen this, Dina!" she exclaimed, clasping her hands in delight.

"Jacob sees what he sees," said Dina, as she poured sherry into two small glasses.

The moving was finished and the men had gone, leaving the women alone in the cottage. Annette had stoked the stove. The smoke rose from the chimney and drifted delicately over the sound. Like a small wisp of reindeer lichen on the huge expanse of sky.

"We must call Oline and Stine!" said the old woman.

Dina opened the new window and shouted across the courtyard. Soon they were there. Four women under the cottage beams.

Oline stole furtive glances at the beam from which Niels had hung himself.

"Doesn't the place smell different now?" she asked, twisting the small glass between strong fingers.

"Like lumber that's just been cut. And slightly bitter, from the new stove," Stine said.

"It's just wonderful! A white stove! Nobody else in the parish has a white stove!" said Oline proudly.

Dina had not taken much furniture from the master bedroom. Had declined the canopy bed with thanks. Johan would get that. But she had taken the mirror and the silver candelabra. And the oval table and matching chairs Mother Karen had brought to Reinsnes now held the place of honor in Dina's parlor. They fit with the pale linen wallcovering and the soft-green wainscoting.

She would order new furniture from Bergen this summer.

Dina had told Hanna and Benjamin she was going to buy a desk with secret drawers for gold and silver and precious stones.

And she had decided to get a good, wide widow's bed.

The kitchen was equipped with the essentials. No one thought Dina would do any work there, but they did not say so.

The cellos stood in the parlor. Both of them. She had carried them across the courtyard herself with a grim expression that sunny day.

When her glass was empty, she opened the door to the veranda and sat down with Lorch's cello between her thighs.

Her back to the others and her face toward the sea, she played polonaises. Behind stained-glass windows on the new veranda. While the sea lay crimson or gold, pale blue or green, depending on which pane she looked through. The world continually changed color.

Behind her in the parlor, the women of Reinsnes sat listening with folded hands. It was the first time they had all stopped working simply to be together.

I am Dina. He walks through my freshly painted rooms. He bows his head over the table and listens to Lorch's cello. The cowlick on the left side of his head is so large that it looks as if all his hairs are spurting from a single point and falling in a brown waterfall over his head. His hair is glacial water that becomes silk threads as it flows to the sea. It splashes my face.

Leo!

He is like the old thoughts that constantly recur. Like standing outside the sod-roofed barn at Helle, warming my bare feet in fresh cowpies in late

301

autumn. When he walks through the room I am amazed that I can move, make sounds, feel the wind in my hair. Or set one foot in front of the other. Where does the strength come from? All the sap, all the moisture? All that is fresh at first but changes to disgusting, sticky, stinking shells. And the stone? Who gives the stone such unwieldy power? To lie there forever! And the repetitions. Who determines all these repetitions? Notes continually repeated in the same pattern. Endless numbers following their own law. And northern lights that chase across the sky! In paths I never understand. But that have their system. Which are a mystery. The questions become easier to bear when the man with the large cowlick walks through my rooms. He chases them all away. Because he saw the cliff. He heard about Hjertrud. And did not become mute.

Will he return?

Who am I? Who thinks these thoughts? Am I Dina? Who does what she wishes?

They heard Lorch's cello from the cottage at night. Dina began to shrivel like a frostbitten winter potato.

Oline's hawk eyes saw it first. And she put it bluntly: This was the curse of that house of death. No one could go unpunished under those heavy beams. You could not hide such scandalous sin with buckram, wallcoverings, and paint. It lasted for all eternity. Amen.

Everyone noticed that the curse had an additional effect on Dina. She worked like a field hand. She rose before dawn. And long after midnight you could see shadows behind her windows and hear music from the veranda.

Tomas was tied to the weekdays at Reinsnes. He sensed Dina's aroma even through the odors of herring barrels, boiling cod-liver oil, and Oline's bread. He blessed the day the Russian left and Dina began working like a horse.

Tomas smelled her, saw her hips, was surprised that her wrists had gotten thinner. That her hair was losing its vitality.

She refused to have him along when she went riding. Had stopped acting playful. Her look had become as sharp as a master seiner's, her voice as rare, but as inescapable, as a thunderstorm.

When she moved to the cottage he expected she would send for him.

The door to her veranda could be seen only from the side facing the sea.

*   *   *

One day a letter with a heavy wax seal arrived. For Johan.

It was a spring day filled with sea gulls' cries and bustling activity as people prepared to launch the cargo boat on a voyage to Bergen.

Amid all the din, Johan stood in the warehouse with the letter in his hand. He was alone for the moment. So he opened the seal. And read that he had finally received a parish. In a tiny community on the Helgeland coast.

He walked outside. Gazed at the wharves, the farm buildings, the main house, and the cottage, which people had begun to call Dina's Place. Heard the swarms of people on the beach, where the launching was under way. People from the estate, children, and casual passersby. Observers and helpers. Anders and the mate were giving orders. In commanding voices.

The land toward the woods and mountainsides was now green as far as the eye could see. Behind the milky, fair-weather mist lay the mountains and the blue-green heights of Våg Peak.

Was he to leave all this?

As he turned toward the main house, with its master bedroom windows set in the facade like sparkling eyes, Dina came toward him on the tree-lined path. She wore a crimson bodice, and her hair was flying in the wind.

His eyes unexpectedly brimmed with tears, and he had to turn away to hide them.

The letter he had almost lost hope of receiving felt suddenly like a sentence of doom.

"What are you moping about?" she asked when she reached him.

"I've got a parish," he replied tonelessly, trying to meet her gaze.

"Where?"

He mentioned the place and gave her the letter. She read it slowly, then folded it and looked at him.

"You don't have to accept the call," she said as she handed him the piece of paper.

She had read him. Seen all the signs he gave her. Signs he scarcely knew he possessed.

"But I certainly can't stay here."

"We need you," she said.

Their eyes met. Hers demanding. His seeking. Full of questions she did not answer.

"The children need a teacher," she continued.

"But that's not what Mother wanted. . . ."

"Your mother couldn't see the future. She didn't know who would need you. She only knew you should make something of yourself."

"Don't you think she'd be sorry?"

"No."

"But what do you think, Dina? A pastor without a parish!"

"It's fine to have a pastor here," she said with a dry laugh. "Besides, the parish they gave you is so small it's an insult."

Later that day, Dina examined the equipment lists for the Bergen voyage. She walked around the warehouses, checking what remained to be done.

Suddenly Jacob emerged from a wall, naked. His large organ protruded like a spear.

She laughed at him for offering himself. But he stood there stubbornly, tempting her.

Had she forgotten what he was like? How he could glide into her so deeply and beautifully? How he could make her bite the sheets when passion pressed out air and sounds? How he caressed her? What was a stupid, solitary Russian, who wandered here and there like a sinker without a net, compared to Jacob's erect organ? Could she tell him that? Could she prove this Russian had better equipment? Or gentler hands than Jacob?

Something exploded in her body.

"What kind of woman are you . . . waiting for some imbecile who doesn't know if he's going to Archangel or Bergen?" said Jacob disdainfully.

His organ had grown so large it reached the list of merchandise. The papers shook in her hand.

I am Dina. Johan enters the sea with me. We are drifting. But he does not know it. I am floating. Because Hjertrud is holding me. We punish Jacob that way. Punish Barabbas.

That evening, under the pretext of needing to discuss Reinsnes and Johan's future, she brought a bottle of wine from the cellar and invited Johan to her veranda in the midnight sun.

She wanted to show him the whole place, let him see how comfortably she had furnished it.

He absolutely must see the small room facing the sea, where she slept.

He followed her. At first he wondered how to put her off without hurting her feelings. It was not certain that she was thinking what he was thinking, after all. . . . Dina was so direct. She did the most improper things in broad daylight. Like showing her stepson her bedroom. Alone. Like standing so close to him that he did not know what to do. In the process, he forgot how to say the simplest words.

She captured him like a cat that gives a bird a dizzying blow in order to have a plaything. Held him in her claws a few minutes. Tossed him between the lace curtains and the bed. Then she came even closer. Finally, she attacked.

"Dina! No, Dina!" he said firmly.

She did not answer. Simply listened toward the courtyard for a moment. Then she closed his mouth greedily.

Jacob came from the wall and tried to protect his son. But it was too late.

He had inherited Jacob's tool. Although in other respects he was built smaller and thinner.

His amazingly large, strong organ rose into the air. It was well formed, with powerful blue veins. Like a net to hold everything that exploded.

She guided him.

He did not have much to give her. Other than a large organ. Even before she undressed him, there was a great void in his soul. Which he tried to hide from them both. With shyness.

But he was willing to learn. He was related not only to Jacob but to the old Adam. Once he let himself be taken.

Afterward, he lay in the shimmering light behind white, drawn curtains and gasped for breath, knowing he had betrayed his God, his calling, and his father. He felt weightless, like an eagle floating high above the sea.

At first he was overwhelmed with shame for having exposed himself so completely. Not only had he emptied himself in her and over her; he was half naked and in a sorry state. And he did not know how to catch his breath again.

He saw from her expression that he must bear this sin alone.

And at last he understood his endless longing for home all the years he was a stranger in Copenhagen and did not dare to return to Reinsnes.

She sat in her underwear with naked thighs, smoking a big cigar and looking at him with a smile. Then she calmly began to tell him about the first time she lay with Jacob.

At first Johan felt sickened. It was so unreal. The words she used. The fact that she was speaking about his father. But little by little, the story titillated him. Made him a voyeur through his father's keyhole.

"It's a waste of time for you to be a pastor," she said, leaning back on the bed.

He attacked her furiously. Pulled her hair. Tore at her underwear. Scratched her arm.

Then she drew him to her and hid his face between her breasts and rocked him back and forth. She did not say a word. He was home. Things could not get worse, after all.

The worst had been done — and could not be undone.

When finally he left, he did not leave by the back door. Despite the fact that people were awake and could see him. Dina was adamant.

"Anyone who leaves by the back door is hiding. You have nothing to hide. Remember that. You have a right to come and go as I please. We own Reinsnes and everything about it."

He was a naked castaway who was safe ashore, but at great cost.

The sun had already bathed in the sea. Now it came running across the fields.

Johan did not understand children. He had never known any.

His lack of experience was one thing. But he never saw them in time to make contact with them.

They were always in motion. Before you knew it, they had moved both their bodies and their thoughts. And were out of reach.

Johan did not think his lessons resulted in much learning.

Benjamin soon discovered ways to divert the teacher and disturb Hanna. Or make her laugh.

They sat at the table in the main parlor and gained little book knowledge, but they learned a great deal about intrigues and making secret signs.

The room became a ghetto of glances, impudence, and subversion.

They had struggled with the catechism and the commandments.

" 'Thou shalt not covet thy neighbor's wife. Thou shalt not covet thy neighbor's house, nor his lands nor his man servant nor his maid servant, nor his oxen nor his ass, nor anything that is thy neighbor's,' " Hanna chanted brightly, as her index finger glided under the row of letters.

"Why don't you have a wife or lands, Johan?" asked Benjamin when Hanna stopped for breath.

"I don't have a wife, but I do have lands," he replied.

"Where are your lands, Johan?"

"I own Reinsnes," said Johan absentmindedly, and nodded for the boy to continue the reading.

"No; Dina owns Reinsnes," Benjamin insisted.

"Yes; Dina and I own it," Johan corrected him brusquely.

"You're not married!"

"No; she was married to Jacob, who was my father and your father."

"But she's not your mother, is she?"

"No, but we own and manage Reinsnes together."

"I've never seen you manage anything at Reinsnes," said the boy laconically, shutting his catechism with a loud clap.

Before he realized what he was doing, Johan slapped the boy's face. A red stripe appeared on Benjamin's cheek. His eyes became black buttons.

"You'll pay for that!" he snarled, and rushed out the door. Hanna slid from her chair and ran after him like a shadow.

Johan stood there, his right palm still smarting from the blow.

Johan realized this could not continue. He took out the letter with the royal seal and thought sadly about his situation.

He had gotten looks and questions. People wondered why he did not have a parish yet. And how he, with his bright mind and his theological degree, passed the time at Reinsnes.

The sheriff had bluntly declared it was not good for a grown man from a respected family to settle down as a tutor for his stepmother.

And Johan had winced, without answering. The son of Ingeborg and Jacob had never learned to defend himself.

Johan wrote and accepted the parish. He was careful never to have errands in the office and never to be alone with Dina.

Dina and Johan were strangers to each other during his final days at Reinsnes. The last evening, he stood by the door and mumbled to everyone in the parlor that they would wait to say good-bye until the following morning. Anders and Mother Karen sat perplexed. Johan's decision to take the call had been made much too suddenly. The air was heavy.

Stine rose and walked over to the pale, black-clad man, took his hand in both of hers, and curtsied deeply.

Touched by the gesture, Johan turned and walked out.

Dina followed him immediately, without saying good night to anyone. She reached him halfway up the stairs. In a flash, she had grasped his coat and held him fast.

"Johan!"

"Yes."

"There's something we haven't discussed."

"That may be."

"Come! Come with me . . ."

"No," he whispered, peering to see if the walls could hear and see.

"Johan . . . ," she pleaded.

"Dina, it was such a terrible sin . . ."

He put one foot in front of the other. Up the stairs. At the top, he turned and looked at her. He was dripping with perspiration. But saved.

From then on, she was a holy whore for him. A guardian for his lust. She was to stay at Reinsnes and manage everything, while he left to serve the Lord as his mother had wished. He would take the sin with him and atone for it. But because she was so depraved, had such vulgar sensuality and no thought of acting like a mother to him, he forgave himself. The Almighty perhaps understood there were limits to what a man could resist.

They saw him off the next day. Dina went to the beach too. Which was unusual. Somehow she made it seem as if he were a departing guest.

Johan boarded the steamboat and raised his hat in farewell. Then the store manager rowed back to shore.

Benjamin had to knock when he wanted to visit Dina. Stine said so. The first evenings after his mother moved to the cottage with all her belongings, he cried and refused to go to sleep. Then he shifted to a cunning strategy. He used all his tricks and all his charm to manipulate the women in the main house, one after another. Began with Stine, who saw through him and disciplined him into obedience with calm eyes.

Then he clung to Mother Karen's thin lap. She was his grandmother. Wasn't she? She was his grandmother alone! Not Hanna's. Just his. He made Hanna cry, because Mother Karen belonged only to him. With her silver-handled cane, her bun, her lace collar, and brooches and everything. And once again Hanna understood that her status in the house depended on the others' feeling good and not paying attention to who she was and what rights she had.

Mother Karen reprimanded Benjamin, but she had to agree that she was only "sort of" Hanna's grandmother.

Then there was Oline. Factual information about family or status had no influence on her, but she could be charmed until she forgot her intentions. And that meant he could sit in the kitchen drinking honey tea even when he should have been in bed hours before. As long as he walked quietly enough on bare feet and listened outside the door to make sure Oline was alone, he could succeed anytime.

Tomas was also a possibility. But it had to be when he was tending the animals. For Tomas went so many places and was not always easy to find. He could look at Tomas with big, grave eyes and politely ask to sit on the horse while it was led into the carriage shafts or out to the field. And if that was not enough, he could slip his fingers into Tomas's large hand and just be there.

Benjamin developed the habit of climbing onto the windowsill and opening the window in the small room that faced the cottage. He sat quite still behind the crosspiece, looking down at Dina's windows.

But soon Stine came, set him on the floor, and shut the window. Without a word.

"I just want to talk to Dina," he said miserably, trying to climb up again.

"Dina doesn't talk to children so late at night," replied Stine, and marched him off to bed.

And suddenly he felt too tired to express his rage. He just sniffled a little and lay completely still until she finished the bedtime prayer and pulled the blanket over him.

Then the night was filled with light and seagulls' shrieking. And he was alone with the goblins and trolls. He had to make himself go to sleep to put an end to it.

Chapter 6

Upon my bed by night
I sought him whom my soul loves;
I sought him, but found him not;
I called him, but he gave no answer.
"I will rise now and go about the city,
in the streets and in the squares;
I will seek him whom my soul loves."
I sought him, but found him not.

— The Song of Solomon 3 : 1–2

*T*he light bothered Dina more than usual this year. They heard her pacing outside and inside. Like an animal.

It began after Leo left. Became a fixed habit after an event which made clear that Leo would not return this summer. A Russian *lodje* anchored in the sound unexpectedly. And the captain and the mate came ashore to deliver some boxes and barrels. At first everyone thought the goods were for barter or for sale. But they were gifts from an anonymous friend.

Dina had no doubt about the sender's identity and knew he sent gifts because he was not coming himself.

There was the finest rope for Anders and a solid wooden box filled with German books for Mother Karen. Oline received an elegant French lace collar. A leather roll with Dina's name on it contained music for cello and piano. Russian folk songs and Beethoven.

Dina locked herself in her room and left the Russian guests to Mother Karen and Anders.

The Russians liked Reinsnes and decided to stay a few days. The mate spoke some Norwegian and entertained everyone with stories and questions.

He knew what was happening in politics and trade in the north and east. Russia and England were at odds. Because of Turkey, wasn't it? In fact, those Turks had caused unrest for a long time. But he could not explain why.

Anders had heard that the Russian czar had been autocratic toward Turkey.

"You can't just come and do whatever you please, even if you're the czar," he said.

The second evening, Dina ate with them. She played a couple of the new pieces on the piano. The rafters reverberated with the Russians' singing. And the *punsj* sold well.

The mate had a handsome bearded face with lively eyes. He was past his youth but still a vigorous man. His unusually large ears thrust out of his magnificent hair and beard with surprising stubbornness. He handled drinking glasses and silverware as if they were doll dishes.

It became a lively party. Cigar smoke lay thick in the parlor long after Mother Karen had said good night.

Sea gulls shrieked to them through the open windows. And light rested like a feather on the rough homespun clothing. Revealed the sailors' tanned skin, played with Stine's dark eyes and golden cheeks. Leaped over Dina's hands as they moved across the keys. And caressed the gold wedding band from Jacob that she wore on her left ring finger.

Stine's eider ducks cocked their heads and listened to the voices and the clinking glasses with glistening eyes and quivering, downy breasts. It was May, and the southern sky was newborn.

Dina tried to ask the Russians where they had taken aboard the gifts from Leo. But none of them could understand her questions. She tried time after time.

Finally, the mate said the gifts were taken aboard in Hammerfest. From a *lodje* that was headed east. None of the Russians could say who had sent the gifts. But they had been given precise information about where to unload the merchandise. And were told they would receive royal hospitality!

The new store manager at Reinsnes nodded eagerly. He was a lean, thin-haired man of thirty. Slightly hunchbacked, with eyes that looked in two directions at once. He wore a monocle and a watch chain without a watch. Now, after a fine dinner and three glasses of *punsj*, he showed a side of himself they had never seen. He laughed!

And before they knew it, he began to tell a story about a merchant from Bremen who noted that many sailors on Russian *lodjes* had simple crucifixes made of rough, stained wood and pictures of Christ on chased tin gilded with brass.

The next year he filled his merchandise crates with similar crucifixes and pictures, expecting a good business. But the Russians did not want these wares. When he asked why, he learned it was because Christ's head hung to the left and he was as beardless as a child. The Russians wanted nothing to do with this blasphemous Christ! They did not think he could be much help to a Russian sailor.

However, the merchant was not without recourse. He immediately turned to the Nordlanders, who thought they got a wonderful bargain when they bought the crucifixes for half price. Good Lutherans that they were, they did not need a Christ with a beard. And soon this version was found in all the houses along the shipping lane.

Everyone laughed heartily. And Anders said he thought he had seen such crucifixes in places where he had been. So the story might well be true.

The Russian captain's experience in doing business with Nordlanders had been different. Beard or no beard.

They drank toasts to cooperative trade and hospitality. Later they drank toasts to the barley from Kola, which was of unusually high quality and ripened faster than barley from other regions.

Eventually the party moved outside to see the midnight sun. It was already clinging to the bluff where Jacob had disappeared.

Dina turned to the mate who spoke some Norwegian and tried once more to question him about Leo.

But he shook his head regretfully.

She kicked a stone in passing, smoothed her skirt with an irritated gesture, and asked him to greet Leo and say they expected him before Christmas. If he did not come, he could forget about sending gifts.

The mate stopped short and took her hand.

"Patience, Dina of Reinsnes. Patience!"

Dina said good night immediately afterward. Then she went to the stable and untied Blackie. The horse was disgruntled.

She found a piece of rope and tied up her skirt, swung onto the horse's back, and trotted into the birch grove. She gave the horse a kick with her pointed boot. Blackie stretched his neck and whinnied. Then the spring wind caught his mane. They flew.

* * *

Standing on the rocks by the boat landing, the sailors stared after the mistress of Reinsnes.

"She's more Russian than our own women," said the mate, stroking his beard.

"She's a little too masculine," the captain observed. "She smokes cigars and sits like a man!"

"But she has beautiful pink fingernails," said the second mate, with a loud belch.

Then they got into a boat and rowed toward the heavy *lodje* that floated proudly in the dead-calm sea.

Their harmonized songs filled the air and were borne far out on the water. Rhythmic, plaintive, and foreign. Almost tender. As if they were singing for a child.

That May night it was decided. She would go to Bergen with the cargo boat. The decision made the night worthy of sleep.

She turned the horse and rode home.

The marshes were about to bloom. The birches along the gully had mouse ears.

A thin column of smoke rose from the kitchen chimney at the main house. So Oline was on her feet, preparing breakfast for the workers.

Jacob came as she was pulling off her boots. Recalled their trip to Bergen. The ride they took in the guest bed at Helgeland on their way north.

But he was obviously worried about this new voyage. For there were men in Bergen. Men along the entire shipping lane. Men, and more men.

Three days before the cargo boat was due to sail for Bergen, Dina announced she was going along on the trip.

Mother Karen was dismayed at the news.

"It's irresponsible, to leave just like that, Dina dear! The new man at the store doesn't have enough experience to manage both the bookkeeping and the merchandise. And who'll oversee the haying and the barn, since Tomas is going on the Bergen trip?"

"A man who can walk across the mountain to visit his father each Saturday and return each Sunday, in all kinds of weather, is certainly able to take care of inanimate objects in shelves and cupboards. And as for Tomas . . . he's not going along."

"But, Dina, that trip is all he's talked about recently."

"It will be as I say. Since I'm going to Bergen, Tomas is needed here even more. He'll stay home!"

"But why are you in such a hurry to go to Bergen? Why didn't you say something before?"

"I'm being suffocated!" said Dina furiously, and was about to leave.

Mother Karen had called Dina into her room. The old woman sat by the window in gentle evening light. But her mood did not reflect that.

"You've had too much to do. You need some relaxation. I can understand that. . . . But a voyage to Bergen is no way to relax. You know that, Dina."

"I can't sit here rotting at Reinsnes! Year after year! I need to see something else!"

The words were small cries that came in fits and starts. As if only now, for the first time, she realized what was the trouble.

"I've seen that something was wrong. But that it's so wrong. I didn't realize."

Dina hesitated by the door. Stood as if on pins and needles.

"You traveled a lot when you were young, Mother Karen?"

"Yes."

"Is it fair for me to be stuck in one place all my life? I must do as I wish, or I'll become dangerous. Do you understand?"

"I understand that it may seem you don't get much out of life. Perhaps you should find yourself a man? Go to Strandsted more often? To the sheriff's? Visit people in Tjeldsund?"

"There's no reason to go there. Men with the right qualifications, men I could take home with me, don't grow in the birch groves of Tjeldsund or Kvæfjord!" said Dina dryly. "After all, you've been a widow ever since you came here, Mother Karen."

"Yes, but I didn't need to oversee a farm, an inn, and cargo boats. I didn't have responsibility for people and animals and business enterprises."

"I have no desire to go all over the place looking for someone to fight with me about how everything should be done. As long as we have enough workers here, I'd rather travel for pleasure. . . ."

"But why did you decide so suddenly, Dina?"

"One must do what one has to, before beginning to doubt," she said.

Then she left the room.

* * *

Tomas had packed his trunk. He had never been outside the parish. His whole body tingled with anticipation. It was like lying in a juniper grove.

He had talked about the trip to customers at the store. Had been home to Helle, where his parents gave him their blessing and his sisters gave him provisions. Oline and Stine, each in her own way, had made sure his trunk was filled with wonderful things.

He stood grooming the horses while he reviewed all the rules and procedures with the stableboy.

Then Dina entered.

After watching him for a while, she said in a friendly tone:

"When you're finished, Tomas, you can come to the veranda and have a glass of raspberry juice."

"Thank you!" said Tomas, and the grooming comb sank. The stableboy stared at him, awestruck. To think one could be invited to Dina's veranda.

Tomas thought his visit to the veranda would be an acknowledgment. An encounter. But it was merely a matter-of-fact statement that he could not go to Bergen, after all, because he was needed at home.

"But, Dina! How can you say that? I've made plans, and given tasks, and hired a new barn boy who knows both the barn and the stable. And my father is coming to help with the haying, and Karl Olsa is coming from the farm at Nesset and will bring his two sons and work much more than his cotter's quota. I don't understand!"

"There's nothing to understand," she said brusquely. "I'm going myself. Which means you can't go!"

Tomas sat near the open veranda doors with a half-empty glass of raspberry juice on the table in front of him.

The sun blazed down on his face. He felt himself beginning to perspire inside his coarse shirt.

He rose from the chair. Clutched his cap and pushed the glass to the middle of the table.

"I see! You're traveling! And so I can't? When couldn't you manage without me? Tell me that!"

"You're not indispensable," said Dina quietly. She stood up too. Half a head taller than he.

"What do you mean? Then why should I . . . ?"

"People are indispensable only when they do what they should," she said firmly.

Tomas turned away. He walked out the door. Down the veranda

steps. He clung to the white handrail with ocher palings. As if trying to squeeze an enemy to death. Then he went straight to the servants' quarters, sat down on his cot, and took stock of the situation. He considered taking his bag and trunk and all his possessions and going to Stransted to find work. But who would hire a young man who had left Reinsnes without the slightest reason?

He made a brief visit to Oline in the kitchen. She already knew. Did not ask questions. Just poured a stiff brandy into a cup of coffee for him, right in the middle of a sunny day. The man with one brown and one blue eye did not look good.

When he had sat there without a word for the time it takes to prepare a wheat dough, Oline remarked:

"I must say you're very patient and wise, for a redhead."

He looked at her. In utter need. Nonetheless, he laughed harshly. A bitter laugh that began far down between his thighs and ate itself out of his body.

"Dina suddenly decided she wants to take a trip to Bergen! So I can't go! Had you heard that?"

"Yes. I hear all sorts of things these days. . . ."

"What's going on?" he asked heavily.

"Dina has started to torment you, now that Niels is no longer here."

Tomas turned pale. The kitchen was no place to be right now. He thanked Oline and left. But he did not go to Strandsted.

Tomas was in the woods the day the cargo boat sailed south.

Chapter 7

I opened to my beloved,
but my beloved had turned and gone.
My soul failed me when he spoke.
I sought him, but found him not;
I called him, but he gave no answer.

— The Song of Solomon 5 : 6

*P*eople talked about war. It suddenly crept into the baking trough. That summer the White Sea was blockaded and Russian *lodjes* could not export flour. The situation had long been rumored to be so serious that Tromsø merchants considered sailing east for flour. Hard as they tried, people could not understand why a war in the Crimea needed to punish people in Nordland.

Meanwhile, the *Mother Karen* of Reinsnes was ready to sail south to Bergen. The vessel had cost Jacob the substantial sum of three thousand *speciedaler*. He bought it the year he saw Dina play the cello at Fagerness.

Jacob had been very satisfied with his purchase of the new Salta cargo boat. It was 48 feet long and carried 33,673 pounds of fish.

The vessel usually had a crew of ten.

Years had passed. The *Mother Karen* darkened in color, but it was well built and strong enough to bear its cargo in all kinds of weather. Broad-beamed, with lap-jointed timbers and solid iron nails. It lay loaded to capacity, awaiting the crew and the last round wooden food boxes with handled lids.

At the cross-notched sternpost was a small white cabin with round windows. Jacob had ordered a man from Rana to install the traditional style. For Jacob did not like the modern custom of having square windows. Squares did not belong on a boat, he said. It was contrary to faith in God and sea specters.

Anders had not objected. His main concerns were the spread of the canvas, the helm, and the cargo capacity. That had not changed. Inside the cuddy were two bunks and a table. Each bunk had a draw curtain and was wide enough for two persons if necessary.

This was where Dina and Anders would sleep. The mate, Anton, had to move to the crowded crew's cabin in the bow on short notice. But he accepted that cheerfully.

Above the cuddy and the crew's cabin was a small quarterdeck. The rest of the vessel was open, designed to carry cargo rather than to be comfortable.

The *Mother Karen* was well laden, by men accustomed to such work.

At the bottom of the hold were the heavy barrels of cod-liver oil and the furs. Piles of dry fish rose higher than the rail. They had to be covered to protect them against sea spray and dampness.

A length of strong planking along the side from bow to stern, between the cuddy and the crew's cabin, shielded the cargo from sea and weather.

The mast had been Jacob's pride. A single tree trunk towered above the deck. He had gone to Namsos to choose it himself. Six shrouds buttressed it, as well as backstays and stays. The mast reached down to the keelson, where it was held securely in a huge block of wood.

The square sail was twelve meters wide and sixteen meters high. When less sail was needed, the bonnets were unlaced. In heavy weather one often had to lower the sails completely.

But a topsail could be raised too, if necessary. Then the whole crew had to pull the block and tackle.

The flagpole on the stern still flew the old Danish flag with the Norwegian lion, used before Denmark ceded Norway to Sweden in 1814. The flag was in honor of Mother Karen. She could never resign herself to the new Swedish king, Oscar. He was too light, she said without further details. She and Anders had several discussions about the matter. But the Danish flag kept flying on the *Mother Karen*, even though it caused many smiles along the shipping channel. Her wishes regarding the flag were respected, for it could cause bad luck to anger the woman for whom the vessel was named.

The mate, Anton Dons, was a short, thickset man with much good sense and even more good humor. Still, nobody meddled with him. For his disposition had another side. And an annual outbreak of wrath usually struck during the voyage to Bergen. Especially if one of the crew members tricked or cheated him.

Drinking liquor at sea was a mortal sin. The mate thrashed the miscreant himself if necessary. Never waited until the poor man was sober enough to defend himself. A blue Monday aboard the *Mother Karen* under Anton Dons's command was as bad as blue Mondays ashore with horses and wives.

Capable mates did not grow on trees, so it paid to take good care of Anton Dons. People said he knew the shipping channel as well as the pastor knew the Bible.

He was silent and steady enough in a light breeze, but in storms he was in league with both good and evil forces.

Once, as a youth, he had sailed onto a reef with such force that he sat there for three days before anyone found him. That was enough for the rest of his life.

It required great skill to maneuver the large cargo boat with its bulky form and rigging. Especially when a strong wind filled the sails. Then it took more than the name of Jesus to veer the vessel. You needed an experienced mate. One who knew the reefs and skerries and could wisely interpret the wind's direction.

People said that Anton once brought a cargo boat from Bergen to Tromsø in six days. That took more than fair winds, said Anders, chuckling.

Benjamin stood at the cottage window, watching the commotion around the *Mother Karen*. He was furious and inconsolable.

Dina's trunk had already been rowed out to the ship and placed in the cuddy. She was going far away on the ocean, to Bergen! It was unbearable.

Dina should be at Reinsnes. Otherwise everything would go wrong.

He had subjected her to every kind of attack. Crying and curses. His small body churned in confusion from the moment he heard she was leaving.

She did not laugh at his rage. Just gripped his neck firmly with her right hand and squeezed, without a word.

He did not know what that meant at first. But then he realized it was intended to comfort him.

She did not say she would buy him presents, did not say she would be back soon. Did not say she needed to leave.

And when he declared that no women went to Bergen, she simply said:

"That's right, Benjamin. Women don't go to Bergen."

320

"Then why do you have to go?"

"Because that's what I decided. You can stay in the cottage and take care of the cellos and everything while I'm gone."

"No. There are ghosts in the cottage!"

"Who said that?"

"Oline."

"You can just tell Oline that there are no more ghosts than would fit in her thimble."

"Niels hanged himself from the ceiling!"

"That's true."

"So there must be ghosts."

"No. They cut him down and lay him in a coffin and brought him to the churchyard."

"Is that true?"

"Of course. You remember that."

"How do you know the ghost won't come?"

"I live in there day and night."

"But you say Jacob is here, always, even though he's dead. . . ."

"That's different."

"How?"

"Jacob is your father, my boy. He's not sure the angels can take care of you alone, since you're so rambunctious."

"I don't want Jacob here! He's a ghost too! Tell him he has to go to Bergen with you!"

"He might be a bother. But I'll do it, for your sake. I'll take him along!"

The boy dried his tears and runny nose on his clean shirtsleeve, forgetting that it did not annoy Dina. It was Stine who got angry about such things.

"You can change your mind and stay home!" he bellowed, when he discovered the conversation had taken an unexpected turn.

"No."

"Then I'll go and tell the sheriff that you left."

"The sheriff doesn't care about such things. Roll up your sleeves and help me carry this hatbox, Benjamin."

"I'll throw it in the ocean!"

"There's no point in that."

"I'm going to do it!"

"I heard you."

He picked up the hatbox with both hands and carried it across the room and out the door with stifled rage.

"Maybe I won't be here when you come home," he said triumphantly.

"Where would you be?"

"I won't tell you!"

"Then it will be hard for me to find you."

"Maybe I'll be dead!"

"That would be a short life."

"I don't care."

"Everybody cares about their life."

"Well, I don't! I'm going to haunt you. Just so you know."

"I surely hope so. I don't want you to disappear."

He sniffled the rest of his tears as they walked toward the pier.

Just before they reached the cluster of people who stood waiting to wave good-bye, he said miserably:

"When are you coming back home?"

She leaned over, gripped his neck firmly again, and rumpled his hair with her other hand.

"Before the end of August, if you pray for good winds," she said cheerfully.

"I'm not going to wave good-bye to you!"

"No, that's asking too much," said Dina gravely, and turned his face to her. "You can go and skip stones. That helps."

They parted that way. He did not hug her. Just ran up the hill. His shirttails were wings behind him.

He refused to see Hanna all day.

That evening he was impossible. He hid from everyone, so they had to hunt for him. He received many scoldings and much attention. Finally, he let himself be comforted in Stine's lap.

"Damn! Damn Dina! I don't care about her at all!" he shouted until he fell asleep.

The *Mother Karen* of Reinsnes had been at sea early that year. Anders had sailed to the Lofoten Islands, where he had provisioned fishermen from Helgeland and Salta.

He had delivered merchandise to twenty fishing crews and carried home a huge cargo of fish, roe, and livers. He had also rented gear to a few crews in exchange for a share of the catch.

Dina had thumped his ribs contentedly when he arrived home. They understood each other's gestures.

*　　*　　*

Anders made sure his customers got a proper contract for the goods they sent with his cargo boats. And if he did not have sufficient space to guarantee safe shipment, he would arrange for another skipper to carry the goods.

With Dina's help, the customers were held to their side of the bargain and did not go elsewhere for their shipping needs.

Once, Anders had been fooled about some promised cargo. A customer from Strandsted took his dried fish to a skipper from Kvæfjord instead. But Dina charged him a penalty for misleading them.

Her action caused some ill-natured remarks. People said it was easier for the sheriff's daughter to collect such a fine than it would be for others.

They joined a convoy of four cargo boats heading south to Bergen. Then two swifter-sailing vessels caught up with them from farther north. Three more joined the flock in Vest Fjord. The weather was calm, with a northeast wind.

The mood was excellent. Each man had his tasks, and each had his section of the cargo to protect. With midnight sun, they did not need to sail only during the day. The crew worked shifts around the clock.

The merchandise from Reinsnes lay heavily between the ribs of the ship. Forty bushels of feathers and down. Cleaned, packed, and prepared by Stine. Five kegs of cloudberry preserves, gathered by the farmworkers, cooked and sweetened by Oline. Carefully watched in the cellar all winter. To make sure that mold or vermin did not depreciate it. Fifty reindeer pelts and two barrels of reindeer meat, which had been bartered or bought from Lapps who came to Reinsnes looking for food. Tomas sent ptarmigan and fox pelts. And there were seventy-five barrels of cod-liver oil and 16,836 pounds of dried fish.

Dina often stood on deck, watching the mountains and the small islands glide past. She had sloughed off an outer skin. The wind laughed to her, and all the things that had irritated or infuriated her at Reinsnes were drowned cats in the vessel's wake.

"People should live like you, Anders! It puts one in a good humor!" she shouted from the cabin doorway, as Vest Fjord widened and suddenly became a sea.

Anders turned and squinted toward her in the bright sunlight. His large, stubborn chin protruded more than usual. Then he continued what he was doing.

He and Dina shared the cabin and the table, and they downed a few mugs together. There was a responsible easiness between them. He was remarkably unembarrassed about having a woman in the cuddy. Made no fuss about it. But was sensitive to a woman's ways. He always knocked on the door and waited until he received an answer. And he was careful to hang his working clothes outside, under the cabin's eave.

The first time Dina had sailed with Anders, he was relegated to the crew's quarters. She and Jacob had rolled across stretches of open sea. And did not even notice that the winds were more than brisk on Vest Fjord. This time, Jacob had to remain on deck. While Dina observed Anders's stubborn jaw and gentle mouth. With the keen senses of a wolf bitch.

Chapter 8

He delivers the afflicted by their affliction,
and opens their ear by adversity.

— Job 36 : 15

*T*he fog lay like a sheepskin cap over the seven mountaintops. Anton knew which warehouse was their destination. Smells and sights assaulted them, familiar and enticing. During the past months the crew had pushed all that away for a while. Now it pressed in on them. A spring tide of old excitement — and pleasant memories.

The men did their work while enjoying the sight of the Promised Land. The wharves! The city! The ships and cargo boats lay close together. Lively shouted commands carried across the Bergen harbor and could be heard above the rumble of wagon wheels on the cobblestones.

Now and then the block and tackle whined solemnly above the open unloading doors at the warehouses. The old buildings stood side by side. Majestic and natural, like an ancient landscape, they leaned toward one another all along the harbor. The gray Bergen fortress was a giant that had lain down for the rest of its life. In full view of high and low. Immovable. Kin to the mountain itself.

Even before the *Mother Karen* found a mooring, small boats glided alongside it.

Bold, cheerful Bergen women came to sell their pastries and pretzels. Amid laughter and shouts, they were helped onto the deck.

They clutched their baskets in both hands. And it looked almost as if they would rather throw themselves in the sea than let go of a single pretzel without payment. But once the purchases were made, broad smiles emerged beneath the kerchiefs and bonnets. And plenty of post-trading pastries and respectable flirting followed.

One woman who stepped over the railing was quite young. In her pale-green cotton dress and gaudy blue silk bonnet adorned with purple rooster feathers, she overshadowed all the elegant Bergen ladies.

Dina shuddered at the sight. And she and Anders exchanged a laughing glance when Anton went out of his way to please the young pastry vendor.

The sunshine was a newly minted coin in a glittering pouch. The men had changed into white shirts. Their hair was slicked down with water, and they wore no caps.

Arriving in Bergen made it a holiday.

Dina wore a wide-brimmed hat and a green traveling outfit. For once, she had pinned up her hair. But some of it fell heavily, and a bit haphazardly, from beneath her hat.

Anders teased her about her fine clothes and hairdo.

"Now you look like a proper shipowner's widow!" he said approvingly when she came out on deck.

"You're going to make the prices for our fish go extremely high," he added.

She gave him a bright look and hurried across a plank to the neighboring cargo boat and then ashore. But when they strolled along the wharves, she tucked her hand firmly under his arm.

Unfamiliar smells swept past her nose. Even the sea smell was different here. Mixed with the odors of decay and stinking gutters, fish and tar-sated ships. The small shops along the harbor bulged with assorted wares. And everything secreted this wild, mingled odor of the city.

Outside a wagonmaker's workshop, an immaculately dressed man leaned on an umbrella in the hot sun and vented his anger at the proprietor. He pointed furiously at his horse, which stood by an unhitched wagon, munching hay from a feed bag, and berated the wagonmaker for giving him defective harness pins.

Dina tugged Anders's arm and stopped, listening to the accusations. The wagonmaker began to defend himself. But he was less practiced than the other man.

Suddenly Dina walked over to them.

"You should use goat-willow harness pins," she interjected.

The two men raised their heads, as if on command, and stared at her. Dina's interruption so confused the gentleman that he lost his train of thought.

The wagonmaker, on the other hand, cleared his throat, made a slight bow, and politely said that she was undoubtedly correct. . . .

"It's resilient. Goat willow, that is," Dina commented, and walked over to examine the harness pin in the carriage fastenings.

The men stared. But found nothing to say. Their ability to speak had vanished into the bright air.

"The pin broke on a branch," she said. She pulled out the splintered pieces and gave them to the wagonmaker.

He took them in his tar-stained hands. Dina nodded and walked back to Anders without turning around.

The silence continued after she left.

There were taverns nearby. And hotels and rooming houses.

A watchman roamed the street, shouting that he knew the best lodgings. He pronounced a few names with grand gestures and a deep, inviting voice. Clearly, he received some skillings for this work.

The fish market was a beehive of activity. The smells here were stronger than outside the manure cellar when the doors were opened to the spring sunshine. Fishwives shouted their prices. Shrill voices from ruddy faces. Ample bosoms with wool shawls crossed over them, despite the heat.

Class distinctions were more evident here than in church at home. The market women and unmarried girls in their colorful costumes outshone everyone else. Here and there, a white lace dress swayed under a wide-brimmed straw hat. Adorned with ribbons, rosettes, and baubles. Small, neat silk or leather shoes mingled with the clatter of wooden clogs and the shuffling of leather toe slippers on the cobblestones.

A loud voice repeatedly recommended smoked salmon and tongue for supper.

Farther on, they came to boulevards and large, luxurious homes. Wide driveways and well-clipped hedges.

Dina exuded a certain disdain as they walked. Anders could not really understand what caused it. But he was embarrassed whenever they met anyone.

All of a sudden, she laughingly began to tell him about the time she and Jacob stayed at a hotel that was reputed to be excellent.

There, they had amused themselves by making disparaging remarks about the porcelain washbowl, which was no larger than a potato basin. And about cream being spooned into their coffee rather than poured from a pitcher.

The owner had never even heard of egg cups.

Their polite but haughty complaints led to the rumor in the kitchen that they were British.

But Jacob absolutely refused to let anyone think such a thing. So he marched over to the barmaid and explained who they were.

The hotel staff immediately became more sociable. And on the last morning, the coffee was served with a pitcher of milk.

In the midst of this story, a coachman stopped his carriage and offered them a ride, for a price. She shook her head, and Anders said no, thank you.

They wandered up the steep streets, which gradually grew narrower. Dina's shoes were stiff and warm, so when they found a bench under a tree they sat down. They had a view over the whole town. Anders explained and pointed. The Bergenhus fortress, with its tower and royal palace. Vågen harbor, with all the cargo boats and swaying booms. Innumerable ships lay at anchor outside the harbor. Two steamboats plodded toward the bright sky with churning paddle wheels and black smoke. A cargo boat glided into the harbor, dropped its sail, and silently slid into place in a row of other vessels.

Slowly they made their way down the hill, found a carriage, and hired a ride to the wharf. They had to watch the time. For they were going to meet Anton and have refreshments at Klevstuen, a favorite meeting place for merchants. It was a gesture they could not neglect.

"It's important to follow the custom," Anders said.

When they arrived at the harbor, Anders pointed out cargo boats from Kjerringøy, Husby, and Grottøy.

Directly behind the wharves stood a church with two towers, its jagged profile outlined against the sky.

"That's Maria Church," he said.

Their glances met. As if this were the first time they had seen each other.

"I've never traveled with anyone before!" he said in confusion.

"You mean, you've never traveled with a woman?"

"Yes. It's different."

"How so?"

"You see things I didn't realize had meaning. You ask questions I didn't know I could answer."

"You're a strange man!" she said firmly. "Niels was lucky to have you for a brother."

*　　*　　*

The businessmen and innkeepers became middlemen between the Bergen merchants and those who shipped goods there.

Although Bergen prices rarely rose or fell dramatically, there was always some suspense about what news the ship charterers would bring home. They preferred to avoid having to haggle over prices, however.

It certainly happened more than once that fishermen were thoroughly deceived about measures and prices.

Merchants and cargo boat owners, on the other hand, learned the tricks of the trade. They had enough time and experience to wait for the best bid. And they knew which Bergen inhabitants it paid to do business with in the long run.

Cargo transporters were entertained at Klevstuen tavern. Porridge with syrup. Clay pipes and lively talk.

The merchant had a potbelly and an extra chin besides the one provided by the Lord. It tumbled over his frilled shirtfront when he gestured or laughed.

Dina recognized him from her trip with Jacob. They often mentioned his name at Reinsnes. Mr. Rasch. She had entered his name in the ledgers for years.

The last time Dina had seen him, he was with a buxom, domineering woman.

She had died from a mysterious illness that nobody understood, he told them. She just shriveled up like a forgotten summer apple. Some said it was due to nervousness and mental illness in the family. But the merchant knew of no such history and willingly expressed his opinion that slander and gossip caused people to reach such conclusions. . . . He himself thought it had something to do with her bile. At any rate, he had been a widower now for four years. His wife had come from a wealthy family in Hardanger and had a sizeable inheritance. But people exaggerated the amount, the merchant said.

Dina, Anton, and Anders had not heard about the inheritance, but they listened eagerly to all the gossip about what could befall a poor Bergen dweller these days.

There seemed to be no respect for anything in this world. People talked about sorrow and misery as if it were dirt! That was not right!

The merchant's face grew flushed during this long monologue. His extra chin spread sorrowfully around his frilled collar. First to one side. Then to the other.

Dina stared unabashedly. But it appeared she had decided to like him.

He, for his part, remembered the young wife Dina Grønelv.

"That's nothing to talk about," he said quickly, giving her a flirtatious look.

Eventually Anders, Anton, and Dina were singled out from the rest of the guests and invited home with Mr. Rasch.

Just as Anders had predicted, *punsj* was served immediately. The merchant ordered Madeira for the lady, but Dina declined the offer. She would like a small glass of *punsj* and a pipe.

The merchant was astonished but quickly recovered. He filled the pipe for her himself, while telling about a Danish noblewoman he knew in his youth. She had smoked a pipe and worn men's hats.

"No comparison," he added good-naturedly, nodding at Dina's hat. "You didn't buy it there in the far north?" he asked.

"No, it was bought on the basis of detailed drawings and sent by messenger from Bremen. We buy hats and stoves from Bremen, and books and sheet music from Hamburg. And paintings from Paris. To meet Mother Karen's tastes!" she said with a smile.

Anders sent her an uneasy look. But she walked over to the merchant and tucked her arm companionably under his.

After a moment he smiled uncertainly and lit her pipe for her. Then he invited them to be seated in the parlor, so they could discuss "timely matters," as he put it.

Dina paid careful attention when Anders negotiated quantities and prices. He described the quality and amounts of fish and roe, furs and eiderdown, he had for sale.

But she did not participate in the conversation.

The expression in Anders's eyes was so honest it would make any merchant suspicious. But these two men had done business together before.

Anders's face was smooth as moonlight when he suggested a price. He was just as regretfully honest when he shook his head because the merchant's offer was too low. Respectful, as though speaking to the pastor. Firm, as though giving vital orders to his crew.

The merchant sighed eloquently, and said they would see . . . until they agreed on the prices. It was the same ritual. Year after year. Without exception. The merchant clapped Anders on the shoulder, bowed to Dina, and said good-naturedly:

"Perhaps, when you calculate everything, Dina Grønelv of Reinsnes is the wealthier of the two of us."

"We're not talking about wealth but about business," Dina reminded him.

Once again Anders shifted uncomfortably.

"Wealth is a complex matter. Some people even receive love as a free gift," she said, looking deeply into the merchant's eyes.

His glance wavered. He did not know how to handle the situation. He was not used to doing business with young women. But he could not help liking some aspects of it. He did not understand this innkeeper's widow from Nordland. And had an uncomfortable, sweaty feeling that she was making a fool of him. Though he could in no way prove it. Still, they got a good price. Especially for the dry fish. Just as Anders had predicted.

They ordered a sewing machine for Stine from one of the merchant's acquaintances, at a considerable discount.

In return, a whole barrel of cloudberry preserves was rolled ashore for the merchant's private consumption. "Free and clear," as Anders put it.

While the cargo boat was being unloaded and then loaded again, Dina wandered around the city on her own.

She wanted to see the leper hospital, which Mother Karen had mentioned several times.

She walked back and forth in front of the entrance. Three times. As a victory over herself. In order to tell Mother Karen she had kept her promise, to pray for the sick to God the Father!

Her prayers had not been very satisfactory.

I am Dina. Hjertrud's book says Job is surprised that God can be so harsh toward human beings, who have such short, restless lives. Job suffers a great deal. He cannot understand that God punishes the righteous and does not punish the ungodly. Job consumes much time and energy wondering about his fate. Here, they pace from wall to wall with their sores. All people do not draw as much attention to themselves as Job.

In front of every house in Bergen stood a bucket of water. Dina finally asked a shopgirl about this custom.

"It's because of the fire this spring," she replied. "Everyone's afraid of fire."

"You're not from Bergen?" the girl added.

Dina smiled. No, she was obviously not from Bergen.

"Good Lord, how naive to think a few drops of water in a bucket can protect you if fire breaks out!"

The shopgirl pursed her lips but said nothing.

Dina bought twill tape, lace, buttons, and the other things on the list Stine had sent with her.

Then she hired a carriage to take her to the area where, on the thirtieth of May, one hundred twenty houses had gone up in flames. A devastated but exciting place.

It lay like a leprous sore, with the healthy city pulsing at its edges. Ragged beggars wandered about, searching for treasure. They bent over and dug with pieces of wood. Now and then they straightened their backs and put something in their bundles.

"There are so many poor, wretched people here! Besides the lepers!" Dina said to Anders in the cuddy that evening.

"And whores!" she added. "They loiter where the men go ashore, or they come aboard."

"That must be a hard occupation. Not much profit in it, apparently," said Anders.

"At least Job didn't have to be a whore!" said Dina.

Anders gave her a strange look.

"Where have you been today?" he asked.

She told him about her prayers at the leper hospital and about visiting the site of the fire.

"You shouldn't go to that area. It could be dangerous," he said.

"Dangerous for whom?"

"For young women wandering around alone," he replied.

"Not for men?"

"For men too," he said pleasantly.

"Who does it?" she began.

"Does what?"

"Visits whores."

Anders stretched his neck bashfully.

"Fellows who don't have what they need," he replied slowly. As if he had not thought about this until now.

"You mean, someone who doesn't have anybody finds it easier to have many women?"

"Yes," he said, feeling embarrassed.

332

"And what else are men looking for?"

He rubbed his neck and ran his hand through his hair.

"It differs, I guess," he said finally.

"What are you looking for?"

He gave her the same straightforward gaze he had given the Bergen merchant.

"I'm not looking for anything!" he said calmly.

"Never?"

His face flushed slowly beneath her scrutiny.

"Why do you ask these questions?"

"I'm not sure, Anders. I guess I want to know what's inside men. What they think . . ."

He did not answer. Just looked at her.

"Do you visit whores?" she asked.

The question hit him in the face. But he recovered.

"It's happened . . . ," he said at last.

"What was it like?"

"Nothing to write home about," he said in a low voice. "I guess I'm not like that," he continued, even more quietly.

Anton knocked at the door, wanting a word with Anders. A light rain fell softly on the roof. Dina sat with one more question in her lap.

The loading had gone well, and the prices they got for dried fish were the best in several years. Most of it sold as the finest quality, a premium product.

The men were content, and conversation was lively when they came aboard.

Dina, Anders, and Anton also slept on board that last night. The rest of the time they had rented rooms ashore. Treated themselves to living in a city, as Anders put it.

The city sounds were different in the cargo boat. Accompanied by the smack of small waves and the creak of sleeping boats. It entered your blood. And remained there, like a throbbing fever, until the next time you sailed into Bergen harbor.

Chapter 9

I lift up my eyes to the hills.
From whence does my help come?

— Psalms 121 : 1

*T*hey had a fair wind sailing north. The mood was peaceful and tolerant.

At the tiller, the vessel's pride, an ornamental figure in plumed helmet and full uniform, "The Helmsman," stared straight ahead. And on the flagpole, the old Danish flag, smooth as an ironed tablecloth, pointed northwest.

Shortly after they rounded Stadtland, Dina exploded her bombshell. She wanted to stop in Trondheim. Anton and Anders were standing outside the cuddy when she announced her intention.

"Trondheim!" shouted Anton, staring at her incredulously. "What do we need to do in Trondheim?"

She had an errand there, Dina said. Besides, she wanted to see the cathedral. So they would make a brief visit.

Anton and Anders talked simultaneously. Anton's voice grew louder and louder. Anders's was deep and penetrating. Did she realize the trouble this would cause? Entering that infernally long Trondheim Fjord, while all the other cargo boats sailed home with good winds? Struggling to maneuver in the fjord's backwaters, with absolutely nothing, neither wind nor sails, to help them navigate! Did she realize it could take ten days extra, at least?

"And it's already the end of August!" said Anders.

"No, I haven't figured the number of days. But there's no special reason to go home. We'll get to Reinsnes eventually!"

Anton forgot he was a congenial fellow. He sputtered furiously. The wind caught his stiffly waxed mustache and threatened to tear away his skin.

Anders took everything more calmly. He had seen Dina break tougher branches than Anton.

"We sail to Trondheim!" Dina said curtly. Then she gathered her skirts and returned to the cabin.

All night long, Anton stood at the helm in a blind rage. He was so furious that he almost refused to go to bed when Anders came to relieve him at the dogwatch.

"There's no need for all of us to lose our wits!" Anders commented dryly.

"Damn it, you were the one who wanted to take along a woman!" Anton bellowed into the air.

He stood bareheaded, wearing a dark-blue pea coat he had bought in Bergen. The collar was turned up, and the padded shoulders were as wide as a barn door. The brass buttons smelted before their eyes as the morning sun rose.

"Dina owns both the vessel and us," Anders said brusquely, as he took the helm.

Anton sputtered oaths like water on a hot anvil. But he went to his bunk and snored so loudly all morning that the crew's cabin creaked and writhed in pain.

Upon their arrival in Trondheim, they were greeted with the news that Bomarsund, the Russian naval base on Åland, had been attacked by French and British naval vessels. Shipyards and stores of seasoned timber on the Finnish coast had been burned as well.

The Finns were said to be loyal to Russia. They defended both their own and Russian interests like raging beasts. Now, according to those who understood the matter, the king of Sweden-Norway wanted to bring his country into the conflict.

Anders was concerned about the Finns. Because his family included people of Finnish stock. He thought it was not so much a matter of the Finns sympathizing with the Russians. Rather, they were angry because Western naval powers had scorched Finnish crops and confiscated Finnish ships.

"Who wouldn't defend himself if a madman set fire to the entrance of his home?" he said angrily.

Dina could not imagine why the British and French were using their gunpowder in the Baltic Sea.

Anton had calmed down and was on speaking terms again. But

he did not have much interest in the matter. He talked only about things he could understand, he said. Ladies and sailors should not discuss world politics. They should just finish their tasks and get home again.

"Leo once said . . . ," Dina recalled, ignoring Anton. "He said the French and the British sided with the Turks in the endless Turko-Russian war. And that was dangerous for the whole world. . . . He said the Finns would never ally with Sweden, no matter what. And the king was stupid not to understand this. He said Czar Nicholas hadn't invented gunpowder. And that the war began with a ridiculous quarrel between two monks. A Greek Orthodox and a Catholic."

"What did they quarrel about?" asked Anders.

"About who owned the holy places in Palestine." Dina laughed.

"But what does that have to do with the war?" Anton sounded impatient.

"Holiness always has something to do with some war," said Dina calmly. "The Bible, Christ, the Virgin Mary, the temple in Palestine . . ."

Suddenly she doubled over, as if someone had hit her in the stomach.

"Are you ill?" asked Anders.

"No!" she said curtly. "But how did they get the king and the czar involved in all that?" she continued, straightening her back.

"When there's a war, someone always sits on the fence and collects rich gifts, or gets rid of trash," said Anton.

"How do you suppose Leo learned who started the war?" Dina asked Anders.

"He travels so much, you know. He must hear many things."

Dina floated away from them. The war had come nearer than anyone liked.

Hundreds of years ago, a king had given the town the area between Kongens Street and Erling Skakkes Street. In order to gather in one place all those who otherwise would slouch in alleys and back rooms. The lepers, the poor, the demented, the old, the orphans.

Good citizens of Trondheim had willed their gifts and made sure that order was brought into all this misery.

A comforting complex of walls and wood. Buildings filled with human refuse and wretchedness. It looked very respectable. From the outside. But the fence was high and the entrance guarded.

Dina was allowed to enter when she stated her errand. This was a world unto itself. Hidden from ordinary people. Hidden from those who had to go there for whatever reason.

Two-story wooden buildings. With an occasional brick building among them. The red tile roofs bound the buildings together in an outward common fate.

The "criminal asylum" or "penitentiary" was a large two-story building with French Empire windows and doors.

Dina was admitted to an oval room on the ground floor. A cacophony of sounds came from the adjoining rooms. She breathed quickly, as if the air held anticipation, or catastrophe.

The first person she saw, besides the guard, was a huge male-like figure puttering with some rags in a box. He kept pointing at something inside the wall and discussed with himself whether or not he needed to go to town. He asked and replied in separate voices, seeming totally immersed in two different roles. One was coarse and trembling with indignation, the other gentle and refined. Now and then he punched the air powerfully and said: "Tjo! Tjo!" as if showing he had hit something with his clenched fist.

His head was smooth-shaven, giving the appearance of just having undergone a brutal delousing. But the gray, sunken cheeks had a two- or three-day beard.

Dina stood there. An atmosphere of sinister cheerfulness surrounded her. She tensed her body, in preparation for what would occur when the man saw her. But nothing happened.

The guard returned and said the director was about to leave the building, but he would talk with her here. He would arrive in a few minutes. It was a clear rebuff. He did not know Dina Grønelv. And he probably had no understanding of the fact that she had said she wanted to know when they expected Leo Zjukovski.

While waiting for the director, she asked questions about the asylum. The guard talked willingly. Occupants of the ground floor had working rooms, dining rooms, and a prayer room. On the second floor, the "inmates" or "those people" were kept in prison cells.

"Some cells are black as a grave," said the guard. His smile revealed a sparse set of teeth but was otherwise open and friendly.

"There's not much you can do about those on the second floor," he continued. "But each one has his own iron stove. We make sure of that!"

Sounds from upstairs tumbled onto their heads. Scraping, thumping, and a loud, furious voice.

"Things aren't always good up there," the guard said with a derisive grin.

The poor wretch by the wall was still puttering with his rags, utterly oblivious of them. The guard followed Dina's eyes and said:

"Bendik is out of it today. But he's not dangerous, whether he's out of it or not."

"Why is he here?" she asked.

"He's crazy! But he's not dangerous. They say he had a sad history in Nordland. Something about a woman who burned to death. That's when it started. But he hasn't so much as tormented a wild cat here. He just keeps to himself. The ones in the black cells upstairs are another matter. I wouldn't want to look them in the eye without some barrier between us!"

Dina began searching for something in her bag. It was like a marsh. Dark and deep and bottomless.

"You must have an important errand, to come to such a place. And all the way from Nordland!"

Dina raised her head. And explained she was on a voyage to Bergen with her cargo boat. So it was no problem to sail to Trondheim to take care of some business.

"You own a cargo boat?" he exclaimed enthusiastically, looking at her with respect. As a matter of fact, he knew a woman who owned a paddle steamer. He sent Dina an oblique, questioning glance.

When she made no comment, he added:

"She's the richest widow in the city!"

Dina scanned the walls and clearly indicated she had no intention of discussing rich widows and their paddle steamers. Instead she asked dryly:

"What's your job here?"

"I make sure the rabble doesn't escape!" he replied briskly.

"And what have they done? Those who are kept here . . ."

"Murder and arson, madness and theft," he said, as if reciting a hymn by heart.

"Where do they come from?"

"Mostly from the inlets around the city. But otherwise from everywhere!"

Just then the poor wretch rushed toward them, dragging his rags.

It happened so fast. Before the guard could prevent it, the huge fellow grasped Dina's arm and stared at her. Then the guard pulled him away.

The man stood with outstretched hands. Gray cloud banks drifted past in his eyes. And mirrored deep in them, Dina saw herself.

On sudden impulse, she raised her gloved hand and laid it on the man's shoulder.

There was a glimmer in his eyes, as if he remembered something important. His face lit up, and he gave her a toothless smile. His huge back was bowed by an invisible burden, which he had probably borne for many years.

"You . . . you finally came . . . ," he mumbled, and reached for her again. Like lightning.

The guard tugged at the man, and said a few harsh words.

Dina stood there. Her jaw twitched, and her face slowly turned white. She pulled from the man's grasp but could not free herself from his gaze.

The guard took the madman to the courtyard.

I am Dina. There is a washhouse stove with a kettle of boiling water on it! I am in the steam. That is why I am perspiring. My skin is scraped away continually. I am washed into nothing. And Hjertrud's screams never stop.

The director appeared out of nowhere. As if he simply arose then and there. He strode across the room with dignity and extended his hand.

A tall, thin man with a severe, well-clipped mustache. It seemed glued to his face.

No suggestion of friendliness or a smile. His handshake was as dry and proper as the rest of him.

His thick, dark hair was slicked down on his round head. This was a man who lived for his hair.

He nodded courteously and shifted his walking stick back to his right hand. How could he be of assistance? He looked at her, and all vestiges of the steam disappeared. His voice was calm and dark. Like wood chips in a stove before the fire is lit.

A glint of antipathy flashed from Dina's gray eyes. He had not done anything to her. Other than save her from the steam.

She told him her reason for coming. Had a package containing Pushkin's book and a sealed letter to Leo. But hesitated slightly before taking them from her bag.

The director expressed his surprise a little too quickly. As far as he knew, they had not hired someone named Leo Zjukovski to transport prisoners. Definitely not. They had made such transfers only a few times while he was there. And a Russian? No!

Dina listened to his reply and asked how long he had been the director of "this place."

"Three months," he replied indifferently.

"That's not exactly a long time. . . ."

The man cleared his throat, as if he had been caught cheating.

"You can't tell that Leo Zjukovski is a Russian," she said. "He speaks Norwegian!"

Her voice lay like frost in the room.

I am Dina. The large birch trees outside are rustling too much. They clamp their branches around my head so I cannot think. The church bells thunder. Nearby. I count the doors that exit from this room. But the number disappears in all the sounds and voices from the cells upstairs. Is a madhouse director a human being? Why does he refuse to know about Leo?

The director said she should inquire in the prison, or with the prison director. He could take her there himself, if she wished. The building was nearby. But it was best that he accompany her across the courtyard and through the entrance.

Dina went with the man. They wandered futilely through the heavy arches and huge doors. Past the guards with empty gazes. It did not bring her closer to Leo. Nobody knew a Russian named Leo Zjukovski who spoke Norwegian and accompanied prisoners to or from Vardø Fortress.

When they stood once again in the oval room, she took out the package. Pressed it into the director's limp hand, until he was forced to take it.

She looked at him as if he were one of the farmhands at Reinsnes. Gave him a firm order. Which he could not refuse without being extremely impolite toward a woman.

"When Mr. Leo Zjukovski arrives, give him this package. It's sealed, as you see. . . ."

The director shook his head but closed his fingers around the package so it would not fall to the floor.

She straightened her hat, adjusted her bag on her arm. Pulled on her right glove and thanked him. Then she said good-bye and walked briskly toward the door.

*　　*　　*

Farther along the street, the carriage passed a building constructed in the form of a cross. It had large windows, a heavy tiled roof, and an elegant arch above the entrance. High on the three-story main wing was a large window shaped like a half-moon.

Dina leaned forward and asked the coachman:

"What's that building?

"The Tronka. A hospital for the insane," he replied listlessly.

"Why is it called the Tronka?"

"They say it's because there once was an alms box at the entrance. *Tronc* is the French word for alms box."

The coachman became more lively as he spoke.

"Why did the hospital have a French alms box?"

"People just like to use fancy words. I'm sure the box came from around Trondheim. And now there's riffraff and crazy people inside, even if it's got a fine French name!"

He cracked his whip over the horses, who had slowed their pace. From somewhere came a heavy sighing like the sound of wind. The driver turned around a few times. Because the woman did not speak again. She sat doubled over, rocking back and forth.

Soon afterward, he stopped the carriage and asked if she was ill.

Two blank, glassy eyes were her only response. But she paid well when she got out.

Am I Dina? A true dreamer of nightmares? Forged by Bendik? Why do I find everything imaginable, but not Leo? Am I Dina? Who cuts out a piece of her heart and places it in a madhouse director's hands. Why am I here, when I have a wound that will not bleed? Where is Hjertrud now?

Dina stayed in the cuddy the rest of the day.

That night Anders was awakened several times by groans that came from behind Dina's curtain. He spoke to her.

But she did not answer.

The next morning, she was gray and withdrawn.

But they hired a carriage and drove to a factory by the Nid River to buy a new bell for the *stabbur*.

The old one had been cracked for a long time. But during the past spring, half of it had fallen, causing major damage to the roof.

They found a bell that was the right size and had the year inscribed on it and a good clang.

The owner of the factory had been a friend of Jacob's.

Dina had let him know in advance that they were coming. So he received them with all due propriety, offered refreshments, and gave them a tour of the factory. Mr. Huitfeldt regretted that his partner, an engineer, was on a brief trip to England and, therefore, could not entertain her.

The man ignored Anders. It was clear that Trondheim citizens did not follow the same rules for tact as Bergen merchants.

Anders took it calmly. He had met such people before. Who did not understand that one could not take ships ashore to demonstrate one's worth.

The factory owner told at great length about his company's fantastic success with stoves, farm bells, and machine parts.

He enjoyed the new times, he said, laughing. And furthermore, he had the demanding task of casting machine parts for the *Nidelven* steamboat.

Anders and Dina exchanged a look as they seated themselves in the carriage again.

"I'm not sure it's worth mentioning. But people of Trondheim seem odd in many ways," Anders remarked.

"Although not everyone in Trondheim is from Trondheim," said Dina.

They laughed.

Dina suddenly kicked his leg with the pointed tip of her shoe.

"Why do you let yourself get run over by such megalomania?"

"Oh, I don't know. . . . It may pay off. In the long run."

"You're really a merchant at heart, aren't you, Anders?"

"Perhaps. But if so, one without capital."

"Do you wish you had capital?"

"No. You see what they become. People with capital."

"Am I like that too?" she asked abruptly.

"No. But you have your difficult sides," he replied truthfully. "Since you ask."

"What do you mean? I'm stingy?"

"No. But closefisted. And stubborn. Take this Trondheim detour, for example."

She did not reply.

The wheels rumbled on the cobblestones. The city clamored around them.

"You went off on your own yesterday. . . . May I ask where?"

"I made a quick visit to the asylum."

Anders turned toward her, not just his face but his whole body.

"You're joking! Why would you go there?"

"I delivered a package for Leo. A book he forgot . . . He has a habit of forgetting books."

"Was he there?"

"No, but he'll go there, I'm sure."

"How do you know that?"

"Because they said he wasn't coming . . . ," she replied thoughtfully.

"They said he wasn't coming . . . and that's why you're sure he's going there? What do you mean, Dina?"

"Something's not right. The director didn't like that I came. That I knew Leo was coming."

"You've become a bit strange on this trip."

"Do you remember that Leo said he was going to take a prisoner to Vardø Fortress?"

"Yes. . . . Now that you ask. But that was just something he said."

"In any case, he comes to the asylum here in Trondheim."

"How do you know?"

"I know!" she said firmly.

They sat without saying anything, while the coachman fell into line with a whole procession of carriages that would not move out of the way.

Anders looked intently at everything happening around them for a while. Then he said:

"Have you decided on the Russian?"

"You don't put any wrappings around your question, my dear Anders."

"No. What's your answer?"

"That I don't display my decisions in public."

"But you want him. I've seen that."

"What you've seen, you don't have to ask about," she retorted.

He crossed his arms on his chest and kept silent.

"We were talking about capital . . . ," she continued after a few minutes.

"Yes," said Anders readily.

"Do you know what your brother did?"

"Niels? Do you mean how he . . . passed away?"

He looked at her in surprise.

"You and I both know how he died," she replied firmly. "I'm talking about something else."

"What do you mean?"

"He embezzled money for years, your brother did!"

She looked straight ahead.

"What . . . what are you saying?" He stared at her, wide-eyed.

She did not reply.

After a moment, he grasped her hands. The veins pulsed in his neck, but his face was pale.

"Why do you say something like that, Dina?"

"Because it's true," she said brusquely, and told Anders about the space under the floorboards.

Anders's hands gripped hers and squeezed hard.

"How much was it?" he asked hoarsely.

"Enough for a trip to America."

"And where is it now? The money?"

"In the bank."

"Why on earth did he . . . ?"

"He wanted capital."

Anders stared.

"It's unbelievable!"

"In a way, he was right," she continued. The words tumbled out.

"Right?!"

"His reputation was ruined. Because of that business with Stine."

"But good Lord!"

"He had to go away. Far away. Couldn't travel like a tramp. Leo did say he was going to America. Stine found a map. . . . So he must have been planning to leave. He couldn't go to prison. Hjertrud would never have allowed . . ."

"Hjertrud? Dina dear . . . But then, why didn't he leave? Why . . . ?"

"He hung himself because he knew that I knew."

"That you knew?"

"I gave him a chance to return the money."

"Do you mean he took his life because . . . ?"

"Because of the shame."

"Did he think you'd report him?"

"He had no reason to think otherwise."

"Dina! Did you drive him to it?!"

He could go no further. His hands clenched tighter and tighter. His nails cut into her skin.

She leaned back against the seat. As if giving up.

"I don't know," she said angrily, and shut her eyes tight.

Anders put his arms around her and held her close.

"Forgive me!" he begged. "Of course it's not your fault! People who do shameful things must bear the responsibility themselves. But to think that Niels . . . that he could do such a thing! Without a word to me."

He sighed. But did not let her go.

Two children sharing an old misfortune.

"The streets in Trondheim are wider than in Bergen," Dina observed.

"But unloading is more difficult, and it's hellish going in and out of the fjord!"

Anders was grateful to change the subject.

"The harbor is too shallow!" he added emphatically.

They both stared at the greasy column of smoke that rose from the steamboat as it puffed toward the harbor.

They drove down a narrow side street, past small, miserable houses. A sailor staggered across the lane in front of the carriage, and a hysterical woman shouted at a stout man in a tight jacket, telling him to hurry because the steamboat was already under way. He heaved like a bellows and lost a hatbox. They sprang in front of the horses as if asking to be run over.

The carriage stopped, and Anders paid the coachman. They walked the final distance to the harbor.

The bickering couple reappeared at the wharf, where the woman intimidated a ferryman into taking them to the steamboat. They stumbled over the thwarts. For a moment, it seemed they would overturn the flimsy ferryboat. And all the while, they argued and shouted at each other.

People swarmed along the sixty-foot unloading pier and the small shipping office. Gradually, others besides the first couple begged a ferryman to row them out to the steamboat before it departed. The large vessel was not allowed at the pier because of the risk of fire.

Anders was glad to have something on which to vent his despair.

"This is just a tea saucer of a harbor!" he grumbled, without anyone asking his opinion.

Dina gave him a sidelong glance and said nothing.

A man with a raised butcher knife ran barefoot along the pier after a boy clutching a bottle of rum. The police arrived and seized them both, with much shouting and commotion. People withdrew to the sidelines to avoid getting involved. Some were almost pushed off the pier.

Anders was filled with sorrow. Dina's wounds would not bleed. There were deep rifts in the sky, but no sun. Thoughts fell like rain.

They sailed the next morning.

The winds were favorable. But even so, Anton was not at his best.

"There's a storm coming. I feel it in my hip," he complained. He was a badly butchered cow standing at the helm.

They left him to his surly mood but were careful not to cause him trouble.

Anders and Dina had other problems. A tension between them that was both good and bad. New and untried. The conversation in the carriage was not finished. It was the prelude to something that was hard to approach when they had to be in the same cabin.

Anders's eyes were a Bible verse under a magnifying glass. It said: We are brother and sister! Something disturbed our roles. We ought to know where we each stand.

He admitted things to himself. That for years he had longed for Dina to confide in him. Ask him for advice.

Now she had confided that Niels was a scoundrel. Anders felt bewildered, and ashamed, for he was more happy about Dina's confidences than concerned about Niels's last days.

Dina was an eagle that sat in its tree and disliked the daylight.

Chapter 10

Then the Lord answered Job out of the whirlwind:
"Who is this that darkens counsel by words without knowledge? . . .
Where were you when I laid the foundation of the earth?
Tell me, if you have understanding.
Who determined its measurements — surely you know!
Or who stretched the line upon it?
On what were its bases sunk,
or who laid its cornerstone,
when the morning stars sang together,
and all the sons of God shouted for joy?
Or who shut in the sea with doors,
when it burst forth from the womb;
when I made clouds its garment,
and thick darkness its swaddling band,
and prescribed bounds for it,
and set bars and doors,
and said, 'Thus far shall you come, and no farther,
and here shall your proud waves be stayed'?
Have you commanded the morning since your days began,
and caused the dawn to know its place . . . ?"

— Job 38 : 1–2 , 4–12

*T*hey rounded the Trondheim Fjord and set the bow northward. Anders saw a storm gathering ahead. It was almost a relief.

By the time they could see neither flat Ørland to starboard nor Agdenes to port and were alone with the elements, they had light fog and a stiff wind.

The weather would not relent. Came like a dull gray ghost, bringing a northwester and rain.

The broad-beamed vessel was tossed into the troughs of the waves as if it were a drifting coffee cup without a handle. The sea rinsed the starboard bow.

Precious cargo was lashed more securely and covered as well as possible.

One boy from a cotter's farm at Reinsnes already lay in his bunk. The poor fellow had vomited in the bedclothes. Causing a great commotion from the man lying next to him. But no one took sides. They all had enough to keep them busy.

Deep in the sturdy vessel there was creaking and crashing. The sails and crossbeams moaned and wept.

Hours passed, under water more than above it. Still, Anton would not seek harbor. He steered into the Fold Sea, as if it were a personal test of strength.

Then everything broke loose.

Dina sat alone in the cuddy, clinging to the table.

The walls constantly shifted direction.

She pressed a pillowcase between her thighs when she saw blood dripping on the floor. Then she toppled onto the table for a moment.

A frightened pool of blood kept changing its course on the restless floorboards. Ran toward east and west, north and south, according to how the vessel heeled. A viscous, brownish river gradually formed between the cracks in the planks.

Am I Dina? Who was a pipe organ last night. With many chorales coming from my body! Because that is what I wanted! Today the knives cut slash after slash. I am a river that does not know where it is going. There are not even any screams. I drift so terribly quietly. Where is Hjertrud now?

Mother Karen's carved likeness, a stately, high-bosomed woman with thick hair gathered into a loose knot, disappeared into raging billows.

But she rose proudly again. Shook off the foaming, long-crested waves. Time after time. The eyes, chiseled by a local artist in Vefsn, stared alternately into the ocean depths and at the sky.

This was the Fold Sea showing its true, malicious nature. At least two months earlier than usual.

Anton ordered the crew to remove the bonnets and four yards. Anders watched the gusts of wind, like a hawk, through the heavy spray.

The weather was merciless. To head toward shore would be folly. There were reefs and skerries everywhere.

Anton prepared to sail the high sea. He had no other choice.

348

The wind was uneven and capricious but would have to surrender, because after years of experience, Anton and Anders knew its behavior.

Each time they eased the vessel and had it under control, Anders felt as if someone bit the back of his neck. Dina!

Time after time, the battle with the storm filled him with desire. For hours, he felt it. As they mastered the waves, mastered the wind. The boat and the sail.

Never before had he experienced such close-hauled sailing. His lower jaw thrust forward. His brows grew bushy with salt spray. Outwardly, he was a sea weakling tied to a line in the storm's wake. Within himself, he was an iron stake. Even if everything went wrong. He knew how to sail!

Dina lay behind her curtain and saw nothing through the streaming windows.

Every loose object danced its own dance. She had put an oilskin under her on the bunk and held fast with both hands during the birth pangs.

Alexander Pushkin entered through the window and talked to her about death. When it struck a poor little one in the womb! He brought his book of poetry. As a gift from Leo. His laughter thundered in the hull. Then he thumped his book hard on her stomach. Went in and out the cuddy's round window and always brought a new book. They became heavier and heavier, and had sharper and sharper corners.

In the end, her lap was a bloody mass that hung from the edge of the bed in thin shreds of flesh.

She tried to hold them together, but that did not help. He was so quick, this dark man with the sharp books.

He shouted his great hatred of women in a ringing, desperate voice or called her the "Bronze Rider's whore" and "my dear Natasha" through clenched teeth.

He had Leo's voice and came out of the gusty wind. Loudly. As if he were using a megaphone. Shattered her head into thousands of tiny pieces.

He was a sea specter! Who had the smith's hands, and Leo's scar across his cheek. Finally, he drew Tomas's rifle from his cape and aimed at her. Bang!

But it was Hjertrud he hit! Hjertrud stood in the corner, her face a large, gaping hole! How could that happen?

*   *   *

Warm liquid ran between Dina's thighs. And gradually turned into icy scourges.

The wind had dropped a little.

Dina raised herself enough to gather the sheet together and hold it between her legs. Then she tottered to the door and shouted for Anders. Her lungs burst in her throat. The cries were witches on the way to their age-old meetings on Brocken Mountain. They cut through the wind and the whirling sea.

There could be no doubt. Something was wrong.

Anders was cold, tired, and bleary-eyed. But he found someone to relieve him. And struggled to the cuddy, where Dina roared his name furiously.

Once inside the door, he stood gasping for breath. Water dripped rhythmically from his oilskins.

The southwester had swept across the sea in violent squalls several hours before. Rivers ran down his face and neck from his blond, salt-caked hair. It was plastered to his skull and made him look like an angry seal. His chin thrust forward more than usual.

He stared at the woman on the bed. At first did not believe what he saw.

Daylight entered defiantly through the salt spray on the windows. It revealed Dina's naked thighs. The white sheet soaked with blood. Her groans were a loose boom in rough weather. She stretched her arms toward him. Her eyes pleaded.

"Good Lord!" He fell to his knees beside her.

"Help me, Anders!"

She did not try to cover herself. He reached for her in a daze, murmuring desperate sounds.

"I'm ripped to pieces. Ripped to pieces, here inside me . . . ," she whispered. Then her eyes drifted away.

Anders got to his feet and was about to rush to the deck for help. Because this was more than he could manage alone.

But she opened her eyes, looked at him sharply, and hissed through her teeth:

"Shh! Quiet! Not a word! Help me!"

He turned and stared at her, confused. Then he understood the order. He recalled various stories. About women's ways. Women's troubles. Women's fates. Women's shame.

For a long moment, he stood dumbfounded. Then he nodded

palely. Opened the cabin door, cleared his throat of six hours of storm on the Fold Sea, and shouted an order to Anton.

"Dina's sick. Tollef will relieve me! Tell the boy to heat some water!"

Out in the gale, Anton was angry. Damn women at sea! They got sick and vomited, and made detours to Trondheim! Storms and deviltry! Misery and punishment!

The seasick cotter's son came with a wooden bucket of hot water, but he had lost half of it on the way. Anders met him at the door. Both were pale and trembling. For different reasons.

Anders had drawn the curtain around Dina's bunk. He had taken off his oilskins and stood bare-chested as he took the bucket. He did not allow the boy to enter. Just brusquely ordered more water.

The boy was tired. Weak from vomiting, frightened, and sad. His face was a bare hand working with iron in black frost.

"Hurry up, fellow!" Anders shouted. He sounded so unlike himself that the boy rushed away immediately.

She was lying utterly still now. Allowed him to roll her over so he could remove the soiled sheets. Everything was soaked with blood.

Its sweet, cloying odor pervaded the cabin. For a moment, he felt nauseated. But swallowed the feeling.

"Who the devil planted this in Dina?" he asked himself. "Who did it? The Russian?"

Thoughts whirled in Anders's head as he washed and tended her. He had never been so close to a woman. Not this way . . . Was clumsy, shy, and furious.

He placed an old fur coat under the one clean sheet he found in Dina's trunk and lifted her onto it. She had gradually become listless and impassive. Did not open her eyes, just breathed heavily and clutched his wrists. He had to pull himself free to help her.

The blood no longer spurted from her. But it flowed evenly. He shoved the soiled bedclothes into a corner with his boot.

Suddenly, amid all the red, he saw something bluish, membrane-like. He shuddered. Who the hell was responsible for this? He clenched his teeth to keep from shouting the question aloud.

She was already unconscious. Must have been bleeding for a long time. Just so she did not . . . He did not complete the thought. Just thrust his chin forward and wadded a coarse workman's blouse between her legs. The wool drew to itself both the similar and the dissimilar textures. He pressed it against her body. With every prayer he knew.

Now and then she regained consciousness and gave him a glassy stare. Horror and desolateness crept across the floor and into the bed.

Then he said the prayers aloud.

The wind abated, and the *Mother Karen* rode the heavy seas.

Anders noticed that they managed the sails without him. Which lessened the pressure only a little. For she was still bleeding.

One after another, the crew members came to the cuddy. But he met them at the door. Just ordered hot soup and warm water.

Finally, Anton shouted that Anders had better get the mistress of Reinsnes on deck, so she could spit in the sea like other folks.

Anders yanked open the door and swung his fist past Anton's jaw. Then he slammed the door so fast that, for a moment, the mate's large nose was dangerously close to being caught in it.

Outside, things grew quiet. The ship plowed the waves. Soup was brought to the cuddy. Water as well. The men managed the braces. Eventually everyone realized that the problem was more serious than seasickness. They fell into their routine again.

Hours became a day. The sun appeared in the sky, and the wind rushed southward.

Inside the cuddy, Dina dozed constantly. The bleeding finally stopped.

Anders had given up trying to keep her clean, but now at last he could move her aside and spread fresh sheets on the old fur coat. She put her arms around his neck as he lifted her. He kept watching to see if she started to bleed again.

She did not try to hide her nakedness. That was not necessary, after several hours in the same pool of blood.

Dina's dignity did not depend on such things, apparently. She left everything in the man's hands. At times she fainted. And then regained consciousness and called him softly. Once, she murmured something he could not hear. It sounded as if she was calling the thief from the Bible. Barabbas!

He got her to eat some soup. She drank water in large, greedy gulps. It dribbled down the corners of her mouth and made wet spots on the linen. Her hair was disheveled and soaked with perspiration. But since he did not know how to comb it, he let it be.

Now and then he shook her gently, to make sure there was still life in her. And when he saw that the light bothered her, he drew the window curtains. Even in the semidarkness he could see she had a yellowish pallor. The dark shadows on her eyelids reached far down her cheeks. Her nose protruded. Stubborn and white at the nostrils.

Anders could not conjure health for someone. He was not particularly good at praying either. But this Sunday morning he sat in a vapor of old blood and prayed for Dina's life.

Meanwhile, the crew resecured the cargo, and the *Mother Karen* sailed past Vega on her way home.

Whether because of the prayers, or something else, her breathing became even. Her long white fingers lay on the blanket. He could see the veins branching to her pink fingernails.

He touched her eyebrow gently, to see if her eyelid would move. She opened her eyes and looked at him. Close, close to his face. As if she had appeared out of the mist.

He thought she would begin to cry. But she just inhaled with a deep sigh and closed her eyes.

He wondered if she ever cried, since she did not do so now.

This initiation into women's life made him somewhat uncomfortable. In a way, he was grateful she did not cry.

"What's the damn disease in the cuddy?" Anton asked. He had calmed down, along with the wind. Now he wanted to know what was happening.

Anders closed the door and stood on deck with him.

"She's sick. Very sick. Vomiting and terrible bleeding. It's her stomach. She's got something awful in . . . in her stomach. She's completely exhausted. Poor thing . . ."

Anton cleared his throat and apologized because he had not realized it was so serious. But as he had always said: Women aboard ship . . .

"She could have died!" said Anders, and kicked a wooden cask that was rolling around the deck.

"Tell the boy to lash things down, so they don't go flying out to sea. And keep your damn opinions to yourself. This has nothing to do with you!"

"I didn't know that it . . . that it was so . . ."

"Well, now you know!"

Anders returned to the cuddy. As if he was no longer expected to work on deck.

The most soiled sheets were surreptitiously thrown overboard. Anders waited until the weather improved sufficiently so everyone was not needed on deck. Saw his chance when nobody was around.

Lacework, embroidery. He dumped it all. The bluish clump disappeared for all time.

They had not mentioned the clump to each other. Not a word. But they had both seen it.

She focused two water-colored eyes on him. He sat down on her bunk. Its high edge made sitting there uncomfortable. Above them, the rigging clanked noisily.

He had opened one of the round windows to get some fresh sea air.

Sweat trickled from her dark hairline and down her neck. There were shadows around her eyes, and her pupils flickered.

High on each of her yellow cheeks flamed an angry red spot. They did not look good.

Anders had seen many things. Scurvy, smallpox, leprosy. He knew that cheeks like Dina's were a sign of fever. But he did not mention it. Just wiped her face and neck with a damp cloth.

For a moment, an expression that could have been gratitude flickered in her eyes. But he was not certain. With Dina, one could never be certain. Still, he ventured to take her hand.

"You haven't asked about anything," she whispered.

"No. It's not exactly the time for anything like that," he said, and looked away.

"But you're not so stupid that you don't understand?"

"No, I'm not so stupid. . . ."

"What are you going to do when we get home?"

"Bring you ashore and then tend to the ship and the cargo."

He made his voice reassuring.

"And then?"

"What do you mean?"

"When they ask what's wrong with me?"

"Then I'll say your stomach played tricks on you and you spit up a lot of blood. That blood came out both ways. But it's over now, and I'm sure it's not infectious."

He cleared his throat after such a long speech and took her other hand as well.

A long, warm shudder went through the bunk. And spread to him. She appeared to be crying. With her body more than her eyes. Like an animal. Silently.

Anders felt as if he had been at church and taken Communion. As if someone had given him a gift.

For years, he had lived in a house with a person who never showed anything but stubbornness or anger. Never showed warm feelings. They had gotten so used to this that they did not even think it strange they knew her so little.

He put his arms around her and recognized himself. It made him strong.

He could sail any sea, in any weather the good Lord chose to send. For he had seen something that was worth understanding.

He wanted to weep for his dead parents. For Niels. For his own stubbornness. Which had made him skipper of the Reinsnes cargo boat. Despite his hatred of the cursed sea. Which had swallowed his parents and given him lifelong nightmares about huge waves devouring them all in the end. He wanted to weep about God! Who sat on the bottom of every capsized boat and saved only Himself.

He held her until the trembling stopped. Sounds from the deck reached them as a distant, meaningless echo. The sea gull was submissive as the large, low August sun finally blazed on the cuddy roof.

"You'll spare me the humiliating ordeal in church and explaining my fornication," she said bitterly.

"Oh, you've probably punished yourself enough."

"Stine barely escaped bread and water. Because it was the second time."

"Who counts the times? Tell me, who in God's name is pure enough to count the times?" said Anders.

"Niels denied his guilt. So they had nothing on him."

"Niels is dead, Dina."

"Stine's living in shame!"

"Nobody remembers that now. Don't think about it. Everything's over."

"Some people are put in prison too," she continued.

"Not these days."

"Oh, yes. Kirsten Nilsdatter Gram was in prison for three years in Trondheim because she sheared nineteen sheep belonging to her neighbor and helped herself to flour and salted meat in their *stab-*

bur. . . . Niels had a fortune hidden away . . . and let Stine bear the shame."

Anders realized she was not fully rational.

"Niels was all I had . . . ," he murmured, mostly to himself.

Suddenly she was completely lucid.

"You have me," she said, gripping his hand with surprising force. "You mustn't feel sorry . . . about anything, Anders!"

They exchanged a look. Sealed a pact.

When they reached Tjeldsund, no one had yet dared to disturb them. He had made everyone understand that Death had made a brief visit. But had turned in the doorway.

And the cook, who was the only one allowed to come with the soup kettle and water, readily confirmed that Dina was too sick and weak to talk to people.

The men walked quietly when they were near the cuddy. Their coarse talk and the joy of seeing their home channel were noticeably dampened. They planned how to get the mistress ashore.

Anders had helped her sit up in bed so she could glimpse the world outside.

The landscape teemed with late-summer fertility. Dina bore no fruit.

They passed a warehouse balancing on posts in the sea.

"That's Christensen's wharf and store. He sent some winter barley all the way to the international exhibit in Paris! He's quite a fellow! 'Winter barley from 68.5 degrees north,' he wrote on a small identification tag," Anders told her.

Dina smiled weakly.

When they neared Sandtorg, Anders wanted to go ashore and get the doctor. But Dina snarled.

"He has a habit of spreading news about what's wrong with his patients," she said.

"But if you die, Dina? If you start bleeding again?"

"That will settle everything," she said.

"What blasphemy, Dina! Surely a doctor doesn't have the right to say anything to others?"

"People talk about many things, whether they have the right or not."

"You're harsh, Dina! Aren't you worried about your health? Aren't you afraid of death?"

"That's a foolish question right now, Anders. . . ."

He stood in the middle of the cabin and looked at her for a moment. In case she changed her mind. But she did not even open her eyes. Finally, he went outside and closed the door behind him.

She began to improve as they sailed through Våg Fjord. Wanted to continue sitting up in bed. But the fever spots did not disappear. And her eyes were unpolished glass.

The birch-covered ridges were fenced in by white, sun-baked beaches. Carefree islands and mountain peaks swam past. Small waves slapped the sides of the vessel.

She dozed occasionally. But when she awoke, Hjertrud's head with its immense dark scream stood over her. And thick, nauseating steam enveloped the bunk. So she tried to stay awake.

I am Dina, who sees the nerves in a newborn birch leaf. But it is autumn. Oline makes a sweet drink from my blood, and pours it into bottles. She seals them well and says they must be carried to the cellar for the winter. The green bottles are full and heavy. The maids cannot carry more than one bottle at a time.

The men were in fine spirits. Each lost in his own thoughts. It was good homecoming weather. The sea rippled, and the sky was spattered with thick cream. The rich white cream floated around the mountains, without blocking a single ray of sunshine. Forests rose along the headlands and coves. Glistening green after the rain. In Strandsted near Larsnett, life moved slowly, and the church was a safe white giant amid all the green and blue.

The flag waved with dignity when they rounded the headland and caught sight of Reinsnes. Someone had been watching and had seen them enter the sound.

Anders tried to help Dina comb her hair. But had to give up. They tucked it under her hat.

The men wanted to put her on a fish pallet and carry her ashore. But she refused.

When she tottered from the cabin with her arm heavily around Anders's neck, they knew it had been serious. For no one had ever seen Dina like this.

She looked like a seabird that had pulled itself loose after being trapped in a net — for a long time. Her hat was askew. And it was far too large and elegant to tolerate the humiliation of having its owner practically carried into the longboat and set ashore like an inanimate object.

Dina tried to mitigate the impression with all the dignity she could muster. But the only result was that she fainted. The men turned away to make it easier for her.

Anders helped her over the slippery, seaweed-covered stones. She stopped for a moment among the silent, staring people. Stubborn as a goat that had seen three blades of green grass farther up the scree. Then she continued walking.

Mother Karen waved from a bench in the garden. Stine stood with her face toward the sun. Benjamin's suntanned hands found the folds of Dina's skirt. Anders walked beside her.

But Tomas stayed in the stable.

Welcoming shouts flew over the ship's railing. The crew came ashore. But their arrival was more subdued than usual. Everyone's eyes were on Dina.

What was wrong?

Anders made explanations. Confidently. As if he had been practicing across every meter of Våg Fjord. His arm muscles trembled around Dina.

Then they stretched out their arms and embraced her. Stine. The maids. It seemed to make her weaker. Her legs would not support her. Small sighs drifted among the seaweed-covered stones as she fell.

She was home.

Dina was put to bed under Stine's supervision. At last the men could escape.

Anders felt the burden lift from his shoulders. It had been heavy. He had survived storms and saved people from drowning and other deaths. But he had never experienced anything like this voyage.

Anders never talked about his own achievements, so it was not hard for him to say nothing about this one. Instead he busied himself being a merchant and skipper for Dina. She lay in the cottage unable to do anything, after all.

He had the expensive gifts brought from the ship. They had been well protected during the storm. Gifts from Bergen and Trondheim. Packages and trunks.

Stine's sewing machine was admired. Ornate cast iron marked Willcox & Gibbs, mounted on the finest walnut. Such as she had seen advertised in the newspaper for fourteen *speciedaler*.

Stine was beside herself. Walked from room to room, clasping her hands. Her face was flushed, and she went to Dina's cottage four times to thank her and insist it was far too much.

The parlors at Reinsnes hummed a happy welcome. Glasses gleamed and clinked. Tissue paper crackled, locks clicked, and dress material rustled.

Coffee and brown sugar were properly sampled. Kerchiefs and shawls with long fringes and red roses were modeled, admired, and caressed. Rings and brooches were pinned on, taken off, and pinned elsewhere.

The cotter's boy, who had now taken his first voyage, was thoroughly scrutinized because his chin had sprouted a beard while he was in Bergen. He blushed and tried to escape, but the girls held him fast and rummaged in his pockets for a Bergen pretzel.

Hanna clutched a doll with a sad white face. It had a red velvet dress, cape, and bonnet. Its wooden head and limbs could move. They clacked cheerfully under the doll clothes whenever Hanna wandered.

Benjamin's present was a steam engine fastened to a board. With Anders's expert help, it spewed steam and smoke into the room. But Benjamin had no interest in an engine that Dina did not stoke.

The tin of Bergen pretzels was passed around until it was empty. Out in the courtyard, men removed the new dinner bell from its wood-chip packing and hung it on the grindstone axle to test the sound.

Benjamin rang it. Time after time. People stood around him, smiling. Mother Karen was a piece of lacework in the parlor window. She fluttered with all the activity.

"It has a sharp tone," said Oline, who was skeptical about the bell.

Anders thought the bell would sound different once it was in place under the *stabbur* roof. It had a better clang when it hung on a wooden beam, he said.

Glancing sidelong at Dina's room just then, he noticed the window was open and pulling gently on a white lace curtain. The delicate material had caught on the building's rough wooden exterior and was struggling to get free.

A strange thought struck him: It would be sad for the curtain if the wind tore it to shreds. . . .

Tomas was invisible today. He had prepared himself for weeks. No longer felt the pain. Actually, it had always been that way when the cargo boat returned from a long voyage.

A large estate needed to have men at home in the fields when the cargo crew went to sea. To Bergen and Trondheim. And when the crew returned, there were many men around!

Tomas found important tasks in the stable and barn. He said nothing about how things were on the estate until he was asked. And that did not happen for a while.

He had seen her as she entered the cottage. Such a total stranger. With no face or expression. A bent, small bundle of a person. Iron claws and sharp fishhooks twisted in him.

All during the welcoming celebration, Tomas busied himself wherever Stine happened to be. To ask about Dina. What was wrong? Was it true she had been violently seasick and cut her stomach to shreds in a storm on the Fold Sea?

Stine nodded. Apparently that was true. But the worst was over. She would give Dina a brew made from roots she had just dug. Her body would certainly heal . . . eventually.

Her dark, moist eyes stared straight through him without seeing him. Hid all her thoughts behind seven sails and many seas.

Chapter 11

If the righteous is requited on earth,
how much more the wicked and the sinner!
— Proverbs 11 : 31

*T*he days were busy. They brought the cargo ashore and distributed it to the proper recipients, stored it, or set it aside.

Anton stayed a few days to assist them. He would also help to pull the vessel ashore. The cargo boat would not be used again until the Lofoten fishing trip. They might as well get it to dry land while there were enough men for the task. To leave it at sea was not a good practice. Maggots quickly infested waterlogged cargo boats. Besides, the weather was unmerciful to vessels that lay untended, objects of public ridicule.

It took two days to pull the cargo boat ashore this fall. With the good aid of men and brandy. That the skipper should have more brandy than the others during such important work had been decreed by the honorable District Governor Knagenhielms as early as 1778. But Anders shared all gifts like a brother.

There was no spring tide to help them, but they managed anyway. With coaxing, curses, and blessings. As well as practical equipment like block and tackle, ropes and capstan. Little by little, grasp by grasp. Hand over hand.

Oline took care of the men. Did not let them languish on sea biscuits or the Bergen pretzels, which were quite dry by now. She cooked pots of salted meat and stoked the washhouse stove to bake bread and provide warm water for bathing.

Salted meat made the men thirsty, she knew. But that did not concern her. She was generous with fruits drinks and coffee.

They came riding, walking, and rowing. Everyone who had sent goods to Bergen or who knew it could be useful to do a day's work at Reinsnes.

361

You might profit well from coming. And you would be penalized sooner or later if you stayed away without a good reason. That was the way things were. Ancient, simple rules.

But it was not all work. It was a celebration too. There was dancing at Andreas Wharf when the task was finished.

And then there were the generous meals! The laughter. The fun.

Servant girls at Reinsnes were something special. They were watched more carefully than other maids. But were soft and cheerful as butter in the sunshine. So people said.

Anders went back and forth, taking charge of everything. Dina lay in the new widow's bed.

A strange mood fell on the estate when people realized she would not be present. Would not play the piano, or give orders for pulling the block and tackle, or furrow her brow like an old shoemaker when something broke.

Usually this was something unique to tell people from other districts. That the tall woman stood with her hands on her hips and participated in the work. Such things did not happen at other estates.

Dina's illness was hard for Mother Karen. She walked stiffly across the courtyard and spent a few hours with her each day, talking and reading aloud.

Dina accepted it with a twinkle in her eyes. She complained to Mother Karen and Stine about being unable to drink wine. It made her ill.

The fact that she even thought about it was a sign she was getting better, Stine thought. But Mother Karen said it was blasphemous to complain about such a thing after she had been so sick.

Oline fed her liver, cream, and fresh blueberries. To prevent the fever from recurring and put more blood in her veins.

Mother Karen wanted to send for the doctor, but Dina just laughed. She was over the worst now. All she needed was some time to heal.

Stine helped her brush her hair twice a day, just as she did for Mother Karen. She understood more about Dina's illness than she said. As if they would be punished for allowing the words inside the walls. The room, and every object, had ears.

Stine knew to whom she owed her position at Reinsnes. From beneath thick black eyelashes, she sent Dina quick glances. Golden as amber. Soft. Like ripe cloudberries on the mountain bogs in September.

When Dina asked her to bring the pieces of soap she had saved from Jacob's trips to the city, Stine got the cardboard container and removed the cover. Fragrance burst into the room like flowering fields and filled the air.

Stine smoothed the pillows. Brought blueberry juice in the old crystal pitcher.

She had Oline decorate the tray with glazed raspberries. And she told Hanna how to find wild strawberries in the pasture. Which they threaded on a straw and served to Dina on a plate with gilded edges, along with a white linen napkin and a glass of Madeira.

Dina once had found a girl at the marketplace and brought her back to Reinsnes because of her wonderful singing voice. She had stayed to help Dina in the cottage.

Now she was placed under Oline's supervision. For Stine intuitively understood that to have a healthy, well-built woman moving about the cottage would be too much for Dina. The girl's strong femininity, her aromas and activity, made the room hold its breath. This was precisely what Dina did not need in her condition. Stine aired out the smell of the girl entirely.

So only Jacob's soaps and Stine's comforting fragrance filled the bedroom. Stine smelled of heather and air-dried sheets, green soap, and various dried herbs. Smells such as one notices only when they disappear.

A few days later, Dina sent for Anders. He entered her bedroom in his stocking feet and seemed like a complete stranger. As though he had never seen her in any situation other than lying in the large bed with its German lace curtain and matching coverlet. As though he had never removed a single clump of blood from her or tried to clean her after the deluge on the voyage across the Fold Sea.

He stood bareheaded, his hands behind his back, and was somewhat ill at ease.

"You're starting to feel better?" he asked.

"It's going fine," she said, and motioned him to the bed. "Sit down, Anders. I have some business to discuss."

His shoulders sank with relief. He reached eagerly for a chair and sat down, at a proper distance from the bed. Then he sighed and gave her a broad smile.

"I haven't been able to check the figures at the store since before the Bergen trip," she said.

He nodded understandingly.

"Can you help me go through them? I can't do much yet, you realize."

He nodded again. Resembled the poor fellow in Mother Karen's weather house who leaped out and bowed from the waist in bad weather.

"I'll soon be back on my feet and able to do it myself. But we need to place orders for the winter and send notices to those who must pay their bill before getting more provisions. There aren't many such cases. But you know . . ."

She leaned back on the pillow and gave him a direct, searching look.

"The cotters don't need to pay, or they can pay by doing day labor during the Christmas rush. . . ."

Her mouth trembled, and her eyes wavered for a moment. She stretched out her hand.

He did not move, as if uncertain about the situation. Then he pulled the chair closer to the bed and took her hand.

"Anders?" she whispered suddenly.

"Yes," he whispered in return.

"I need you, Anders!"

He swallowed and looked away. Became a little boy with a stubborn chin, a protruding jaw, and serious blue eyes. Who, for the first time, was allowed to go to the altar and watch all the large candles being lit.

"I'm here," he said, squeezing her hand between his.

"You must send for the sheriff. I want to write my will."

"Dina, what are you thinking? You're not thinking you'll . . . You're going to get well."

"Death never harvests according to a person's age or value around here," she said.

"What a terrible way to talk!"

"Don't worry. I just want to write down my wishes regarding the things I own."

"Yes, yes . . ."

"I want you to have the *Mother Karen*, Anders. The cargo boat is yours! She'll outlive both you and me."

He took several deep breaths.

"Do you mean it?" he finally managed to say.

"Obviously I do, since I said it."

The light struck the porcelain washbasin and created a haze over the roses painted around the edge. It climbed into Anders's wiry blond hair. Revealing white hairs at the temples.

He was no longer the little man in Mother Karen's weather house. He was the cherub with a lighted torch on her bookmark.

"Have you heard anything?" Dina asked, after a long pause.

"Heard? Heard what?"

"Does anybody wonder?" she said in a hard voice. "Wonder what's wrong with me?"

His lower lip curled.

"No. Nobody! I explained what happened. How it started. And how long it lasted."

"And if, in spite of that, there's a hearing . . . ," she whispered, forcing him to look at her.

"Then I'll swear to it under oath," he said firmly.

She sat up with sudden energy. Leaned forward and grasped his head with both hands. She pulled it down to her, hard, as if in a vise. And stared him straight in the eye.

For a wild moment, something trembled between them. And for the second time, they sealed a pact. Understood one another's ways.

Then it was over.

He pulled on his boots in the entry and went out into the dusk.

His lower lip was soft today. He had shaved his beard, as he always did when he returned from a long trip. And the less tanned part of his face was slightly flushed.

As he walked across the courtyard, his shoulders were unusually erect.

Chapter 12

The hand of the diligent will rule,
while the slothful will be put to forced labor.

— Proverbs 12 : 24

By the end of October not even a tiny birch leaf remained on the trees. The snow blew across the sea before blanketing the ground, and frost settled in the large water barrel in front of the washhouse. Stoves were kept burning from early morning until people went to bed. The hunting season was spoiled, and the lingonberries froze.

But Dina finally got back on her feet.

Mother Karen received a letter from Johan. A pitiful letter. He was unhappy in Helgeland. The parsonage was in poor condition. The roof leaked, and he lacked the bare necessities of life. It was impossible to get servant girls, even if you paid in gold. And the congregation provided little help, financially or otherwise. If Mother Karen could spare some amount, large or small, to supplement the annual allowance he received from his inheritance, he could buy a new chasuble and some bed linens.

Mother Karen went to Dina and read the letter aloud, with a mournful expression on her face. She wrung her hands and sat close to the white stove, wrapped in her shawl.

"Your bun is slipping, Mother Karen," Dina said calmly, and sat down too.

Somewhat bewildered, Mother Karen tried to fix her bun.

The flames leaped inside the open doors of the tile stove. Eternally searching for something to consume.

"He's been unfortunate with this parish," Mother Karen said sadly, and sent Dina a pleading look.

"There's no question about that," Dina agreed. "And now he wants a little of Mother Karen's annuity?" she added, with a sidelong glance at the old woman.

"I don't have much left to give," she said with disappointment. "He got most of it when he was studying. It was so expensive in Copenhagen. So extremely expensive . . ."

She rocked back and forth and sighed.

"Knowledge is easy to bear, but it's a dearly bought friend," she added.

"Perhaps Johan wants some more of his inheritance," said Dina good-naturedly.

"Yes, that would probably be best," said Mother Karen, relieved that Dina addressed the matter so quickly and did not make her beg for Johan.

"I'll talk with the sheriff and ask him to calculate the figures and find reliable witnesses."

"Do we need to be so precise?"

"Yes. When it concerns inheritances, nothing is precise enough, Mother Karen. There are several heirs to Reinsnes."

Mother Karen glanced at her and said uncertainly:

"I thought it would be possible to give a small gift . . . without deducting it from his inheritance."

Dina gave her a penetrating look. Forced the old woman into a corner.

"Do you want Benjamin to give part of his inheritance to his grown half-brother, an ordained pastor?" she said quietly but very distinctly.

Mother Karen bowed her head. The white bun meekly pointed straight up in the air. Silver curls quivered at her ears.

She fingered the cross she always wore around her neck.

"No, no. I didn't mean it that way," she said with a sigh.

"I know. We just misunderstood each other," Dina said lightly. "I'll have the sheriff arrange for the witnesses and signatures. So Johan can get an advance on his inheritance, in addition to what he's already received."

"It will be hard for him to divide his land and inheritance that way," said the old woman sadly.

"It's never been easy to live beyond one's means. At least not afterward," said Dina brusquely.

"But, Dina dear, Johan has surely never . . ."

"Oh, yes, he has!" Dina interrupted. "He had a regular allowance while he was studying. Plus, you gave him your entire annuity!"

There was a silence. The old woman sat as if someone had struck her. She lifted her palms toward Dina. Wanting to protect herself.

Then her hands fell into her lap again. They trembled as she folded them tightly.

"Dear, dear Dina," she said hoarsely.

"Dear, dear Mother Karen!" replied Dina. "Johan needs to do a little work before he dies. I mean that sincerely. Although I like him very much."

"But he's serving a parish. . . ."

"And I had all the responsibility at Reinsnes while he was here satisfying his spiritual life and his hunger pangs! Without lifting a finger!"

"You've become very hard, Dina. I hardly recognize you."

"Compared to when?"

"When you were newly married and wanted to sleep all morning without doing a bit of work."

"That's several lives ago!"

All of a sudden, Mother Karen rose from the high-backed armchair and took a few uncertain steps to Dina's chair. Leaned over and stroked the tall woman's hair.

"You've got too much to think about, Dina. Too many responsibilities. I know that's true. And I understand better than anyone else. Because I knew you then . . . You should get married again. It's not good to be alone, the way you are. You're still young. . . ."

Dina laughed harshly but did not pull away.

"Maybe you know a suitable man?" she said, looking away.

"The Russian traveler would have been suitable."

Dina blushed intensely.

"Why do you say that?"

"Because I've noticed that you run to the flag knoll and look out to sea, as if you're waiting for someone. And because the Russian made your eyes shine as bright as the lighted tree last Christmas. And because you became bad-tempered, if I may say so, the moment the Russian left last spring."

Dina began to tremble.

"Yes, yes . . . Yes, yes," murmured Mother Karen, continuing to stroke her hair. "Love is crazy. That's always been true. It doesn't stop. It doesn't even stop when it's tested in storms and everyday life. It's painful. Sometimes . . ."

It was as if she were talking to herself or to the stove. Her eyes roamed fitfully around the room as she shifted her weight from one foot to the other.

Finally, she sank onto the armrest.

Dina suddenly threw her arms around Mother Karen, drew the frail body into her lap, and began rocking back and forth.

The old woman sat like a little girl in the ample lap.

They rocked one another. As their shadows danced across the wall and the flames slowly subsided.

Mother Karen felt as if she were a young woman again, sitting in a rowboat that was taking her to a sailing vessel for her first trip to Germany with her beloved husband. She smelled again the sea and mist as she sailed out of the Trondheim Fjord in her bonnet and traveling outfit.

"He had such a sensitive mouth, my husband did," she said dreamily, letting Dina rock her.

Her eyes were closed and her legs dangled slightly.

"He had such blond curls," she added, smiling toward the veins inside her eyelids. They gave a reddish pulse to the dreams.

"The first time I sailed to Hamburg with him, I was two months pregnant. But I didn't say a word to anyone, for fear of not being able to go along. People assumed my symptoms were seasickness," she said, bubbling with memories and laughter.

Dina leaned against Mother Karen's neck. Pulled her more comfortably into her lap and rocked her rhythmically in strong arms.

"Tell me about it, Mother Karen! Tell me!" she said.

Strong gusts of wind buffeted the cottage. Winter had arrived. The shadows of the two figures in the armchair slowly merged into one. Jacob sat there patiently, causing no trouble.

Meanwhile, love searched endlessly along the Russian roads, in the Russian forests and great cities.

"But I can't propose to him, Mother Karen!" she said desperately. Right in the midst of the old woman's story about how they arrived in Hamburg and when Jacob's father learned she was pregnant he threw her into the air like a feed sack and caught her as if she were a piece of delicate glass.

Mother Karen was lost in her own thoughts and blinked several times.

"Propose?"

"Yes, if Leo comes back."

"Of course Jacob's widow can propose to the person she wants to share her life. No question about it. Of course she can propose!"

The old woman's outburst made Jacob uneasy, and he disappeared into the wall.

"But if what if he says no?"

"He won't say no!"

"But if he does?"

"Then the man has good reasons that I don't know about," she said. Dina bent her head toward the other woman.

"You think I'll get him?"

"Yes. You can't let love disappear from your life without lifting a finger."

"But I've looked for him."

"Where? I thought you were waiting for some sign of him. And that was why you were acting like a caged animal."

"I looked for him, in both Bergen and Trondheim . . . ," Dina said humbly.

"It would have been quite a stroke of luck if you'd seen him."

"Yes . . ."

"Do you know where he might be?"

"Maybe at Vardø Fortress, or farther east . . ."

"What's he doing there?"

"I don't know."

There was silence for a moment. Then Mother Karen said in a firm voice:

"I'm sure the Russian will come back! With his powerful singing and disfigured face. I wonder how he got that scar."

Johan received a large sum. As an advance against his inheritance. It was meticulously recorded in the presence of witnesses.

Mother Karen wrote letters. In utter secrecy. To try to locate Leo Zjukovski. But found no trace of him anywhere.

This detective work on behalf of Dina and Reinsnes made her feel healthy and useful. She also undertook to tutor Benjamin and Hanna in reading and writing and got Dina to teach them arithmetic.

And so the winter continued, with snowdrifts and lighted candles, with preparations for Christmas and for voyages to the Lofoten Islands.

One day Dina went to the stable to find Tomas.

"You can go on the Lofoten trip with Anders this year," she announced unexpectedly.

Rime covered the windows. The inside of the stable door was laced with frost. Howling winds whipped around the corners of the building.

370

Tomas did not want to go anywhere. He stared straight through Dina with one blue and one brown eye and continued feeding the horses.

"Tomas!" she said gently, as if she were Mother Karen. "You can't just throw yourself away here at Reinsnes!"

"Do you think I'm throwing myself away?"

"You aren't anywhere. Don't see anything. . . ."

"I was supposed to go to Bergen last summer. That didn't happen."

"And so now you're not going to Lofoten?"

"I'm no Lofoten fisherman."

"Who says so?"

"I do!"

"How long are you going to be angry that you didn't get to Bergen?"

"I'm not angry. I just don't want to be sent away when you think it's too hard to have me here!" he said, almost inaudibly.

She left the stable with a wrinkled forehead.

Dina grew restless when Anders left for Lofoten that year. She paced around the cottage nervously and had no one with whom to share a carafe of wine and a cigar.

She began rising at the crack of dawn to start working. Or she sat under the lamp with Hjertrud's book. She read it fitfully. The way one drives sheep down the mountain in autumn or climbs steep slopes, just to be done with it.

Hjertrud rarely came. And when she did, it was with the terrible scream. It tore through the bedroom like a blast of wind. The curtains stood straight out, and the glasses shuddered. Then Dina would get dressed and go down to Andreas Wharf, to comfort and to be comforted.

She brought the small, gleaming mother-of-pearl shell. Let it glide slowly between her fingers, while the lantern drew Hjertrud from the eastern corner. Where the herring nets hung, side by side, from the ceiling. As immobile as sad thoughts. The waves washed beneath the floorboards in powerful, rhythmic surges.

Now and then she sat on the enclosed veranda and drank wine. Until the moon was full and she toppled over.

* * *

When the light returned, Johan returned too. He would rather be at Reinsnes teaching the children than freezing to death among strangers who had no education or faith in God, he said. But his mouth trembled as he glanced at Dina.

Mother Karen was dismayed that he had left the Lord's calling so abruptly.

Johan said he had a legitimate reason for leaving. He was ill. Had been coughing for several months and could not live in the drafty parsonage. Only one stove worked, and that was in the kitchen. Was he supposed to sit in the kitchen with the maid when he planned his sermons and did his official correspondence as a servant of the state church?

Mother Karen understood. She wrote a letter to the bishop about the matter, and Johan signed it.

Benjamin distanced himself from the grown-ups. Developed a forbidding look. And a sullen, know-it-all attitude that annoyed Johan intensely. But the boy was intelligent and an apt pupil when he wanted to be. He was happy with only three people: Stine, Oline, and Hanna. Three generations, which he utilized for different, but complementary, purposes.

One day Stine discovered him avidly exploring Hanna's lower body as she lay quietly with her eyes closed on the bed that the two children shared.

Stine immediately decided that Benjamin would sleep in a room by himself. He wept bitterly, over the separation more than over the shame that people foisted on him.

No explanations were offered. But Stine was adamant. Benjamin was to sleep by himself.

Dina, who did not hear the commotion, let Stine's word be law.

That evening as Dina came from the office, she saw the boy in the moonlight. He was standing naked at a window on the second floor.

The window was open, and the curtains wrapped around him like banners. She went upstairs, stood behind him, and said his name. He would not go to bed. Would not be comforted. Would not let anyone talk to him. And he did not howl in rage, as he usually did.

He had ripped the soles off his best shoes and cut apart the rose leaves and stars in the crocheted bedspread.

"Why are you so angry, Benjamin?"

"I want to sleep with Hanna. Like I always did."

"But you carry on with Hanna."

"Carry on how?"

"You take off her clothes."

"I have to take off her clothes when she's going to bed. I always do that. She's so little!"

"But she's too big for that now."

"No!"

"Benjamin, you're too big to sleep with Hanna. Men don't sleep with women."

"Johan sleeps with you!"

Dina took a step backward.

"What did you say?" she asked hoarsely.

"He sleeps in your bed. He doesn't like to be alone either."

"That's nonsense!" she said sternly. And held the most sensitive hairs on his neck until he climbed down from the windowsill.

"No! I saw it myself!"

"Hush! And go to bed now, before I give you a shaking!"

Terrified at the sound of her voice, he stood staring at her. And like a flash, lifted both hands over his head as if expecting a blow.

She let go of his hair and walked briskly out of the room.

All evening he stood by the window. Motionless. Staring at the cottage.

Finally, she went back to him. Dragged his trembling body from the windowsill and put him to bed. Then she gathered her skirts around her and calmly lay down beside him.

The bed was wide enough for two. It must seem terribly large to someone who was used to sleeping with Hanna's warm body.

It was the first time in years that Dina had seen Benjamin asleep. She stroked his moist forehead and stole downstairs, across the courtyard, and back to her own room.

Hjertrud needed her that night, so she paced the floor restlessly until morning was a gray sail at the window.

Chapter 13

Be broken, you peoples, and be dismayed;
give ear, all you far countries;
gird yourselves and be dismayed.

— Isaiah 8 : 9

*T*he Crimean War created excellent economic conditions for shipping, trade, and fishing. But it led to a break in the usual trade with Russia. The White Sea had been blockaded the previous summer. And it appeared the same would be true this year. Russian cutters could not leave.

The past autumn, Tromsø cutters needed to go all the way to Archangel to get grain.

Anders had planned to sail with an eastbound ship after he and Dina returned from Bergen. But instead he took charge of equipping the Lofoten fishermen and otherwise did what he was "suited for," as he put it.

Dina watched the newspapers all spring to see if, once again, the war would require sending cutters to Russia. She tried to contact skippers in Tromsø who were willing to procure supplies. But it was like skinning live eels.

"I should be there myself to negotiate an agreement," she said one day, when she and Tomas were discussing the matter with Mother Karen.

Although several places in the parish had harvested a bumper grain crop, with twenty- to twenty-five-fold yields, it did not help much.

They did not cultivate grain at Reinsnes. Had just one small field, because Mother Karen insisted on it. Tomas found the enterprise more trouble than it was worth. Every year, alone in his room, he lambasted Mother Karen's grain field.

But the good harvest encouraged Mother Karen to try to convince the others that they should increase the size of their grain field. Especially in view of the dangerous blockade.

Today she triumphantly read aloud to Dina and Tomas an article in the newspaper. Chief Magistrate Motzfeldt wrote that the war had made people aware of their gifts, and he emphasized the uncertainty of harvesting only ocean fields. He challenged them to the heroic achievement of surviving without Russian grain sacks. Our people must be frugal about bread, the chief magistrate wrote. They must harvest grain from their own earth and eat it in the sweat of their brow.

"That's what I've always said. We should have a bigger grain field," Mother Karen remarked.

"Reinsnes isn't suited to growing grain," said Tomas meekly.

"But people should be self-sufficient, as far as possible. That's what the chief magistrate says."

Oline had come to the door. She peered toward the newspaper and noted dryly:

"That Motzfeldt doesn't sweat as much for his food as we do at Reinsnes, I'm sure!"

"None of us knows much about growing grain," said Dina. "But if Mother Karen feels we absolutely should have a bigger field, I'm sure we can get good advice from the Agriculture Association. And we'll do what we wish with it. But growing more grain means the tenant farmers must put in more work for the estate. Do you think that's fair, Mother Karen?"

"Surely we can hire people?" replied Mother Karen, who had not thought much about the practical aspects.

"We must consider what's profitable. We can't grow hay for just as many animals and cultivate grain at the same time. We know that here in the north not every year has a good grain harvest. But we certainly could have a somewhat larger field. We could plow more ground in the south field, even if it's open to the sea winds."

"It will take a lot of work to make that ground near the birch grove yield a profit," said Tomas.

"Reinsnes is a trade center. That's what is profitable, as all the figures show," said Dina. "I know Mother Karen means well, but she's no grain farmer, even though she's met the chief magistrate and likes him very much."

"He doesn't realize that we can't depend on the first frost coming late!" said Oline.

Mother Karen found nothing to say but was not angry.

When Anders returned from Lofoten with the crew and the catch in the longboat and cargo boat, Dina had decided to go to Tromsø on business.

It appeared this war would continue, so she had to arrange to purchase flour in Archangel, she declared.

It was not going to be like the previous year, when they had to pay exorbitant prices for Russian flour, which the Tromsø merchants had procured. This year she would hunt the bear, lure it out of hibernation, and try to get her share of the pelt.

She did not want yet another winter in which they had to pay four to six *speciedaler* for rye and three to six *speciedaler* for barley. Anders agreed with her.

So they went through the Bergen transactions and calculated their Lofoten fishing profits. Then they made a rough estimate of how much Archangel flour to purchase. They had plenty of storage space.

Dina planned to buy more flour than they needed for provisioning ships and selling in the store. She wanted to make sure they had a reserve for the spring. Flour might be in scant supply, both in Strandsted and along the sound.

Anders said that if she offered cash to Tromsø merchants when they needed it for supplies, it would be easier to negotiate a price for flour.

Several merchants brought grain from Archangel and did it well. The best would be to start with old business contacts. It was simply a matter of talking with them.

He was sure Dina would manage better than he. She just had to watch her sharp tongue. Tromsø merchants understood her speech more easily than people in Bergen. She must remember that.

The task was as if made to order. She did not mention that she planned to go north to Vardø Fortress. Only Mother Karen knew that. She had no idea how she would get from Hammerfest to Vardø Fortress. But there was always a ship sailing east in the shipping channel.

*   *   *

The fact that Dina gave Anders a percentage of the Bergen cargo profits, and also let him carry on his own business by floating lumber from Namsos, caused much speculation and a great deal of envy.

Could there be something between them that nobody knew about? And that could not stand the light of day?

The rumors grew stronger. Especially after Anders was deceived by a timber merchant in Namsos and Dina settled the bill. He had paid for lumber he floated home with him the previous spring, without knowing the timber merchant was bankrupt and selling lumber he did not own. The new owner demanded payment as well. Since Anders had no witnesses to the original settlement of the account, there was nothing to do but pay once more.

The story was like a warm cowpie in the spring, flies buzzing around it. People let their imaginations run wild.

There must be something special between the two, since Dina Grønelv, who was so tightfisted in business dealings, shared her skipper's financial loss. And as if that were not enough, she drew up a will in which she gave him her finest cargo boat.

Coarse rumors reached Mother Karen's ears. The old woman sent for Dina, wrung her hands, and asked if the rumors were true.

"And if they were? Would that matter? Who's powerful enough to do anything about it?"

But Mother Karen was not satisfied.

"Are you thinking of marrying Anders?"

Dina bridled visibly.

"Do you want me to marry two men? After all, haven't you given me your blessing to go and find Leo?"

"You must understand, the gossip is not good. That's why I ask."

"People have a right to talk when there's nothing else they should be doing."

But the thought was put into words. The thought of Anders as the master of Reinsnes.

Dina paced under the beam where Niels had dangled and made him appear.

He was meek and full of explanations. But she did not accept them. Just hung him back on the rope and nudged him so he swung like a pendulum without a clock.

She reminded him that he was not safe, even if he was no longer a boarder at Reinsnes. Because she held his reputation in the hollow of her hand. Before she went to bed, she made it clear that if he did not stop all the rumors she would take him at his word. Marry Anders. Publicly and with great festivity.

And Niels grew limp and distant and disappeared.

Whether or not Anders had heard the rumors, he did his work and seemed calm and untroubled.

He suggested whom to approach about buying flour and gave Dina the names of people with whom she should not do business under any conditions. Bent over lists of merchandise and numbers with her. Brushed her hand, without noticing it.

They discussed how much they could pay for Russian flour without having to charge exorbitant prices at their store to make a profit. And how large a stock they should keep on hand until spring shortages occurred.

He ran his hand through his thick blond hair and nodded energetically now and then to emphasize his words. His eyes were clear and open. He looked as if he had just been to Communion and received forgiveness for all his sins.

When they had finished, she brought a small glass of rum for each and asked bluntly if he had heard the rumors that were circulating.

He smiled broadly.

"I've heard that people in Strandsted and on the cotters' farms are trying to marry off the bachelor at Reinsnes. But that's nothing new."

"And what do you say to that?"

"I make sure I don't have to say anything."

"You'll let it hang to dry for a while?" she wondered.

He looked at her in surprise. Then shut the ledger without a word.

"Do you find such rumors amusing?" she asked a little later.

"No," he said at last. "But they're not exactly sad either."

He gave her a teasing look. Then she gave up. They laughed. Clinked their rum glasses and laughed. But it was hard to erase the conversation.

" 'Prince Gustav' looks like a woman," Benjamin declared savagely, and hooked his fingers around his suspenders, as he had seen Anders do.

"That's just a figurehead, not the real Prince Gustav," explained

378

Hanna, stretching her neck, curious as an ermine, to see everything that was happening.

She tried to hold on to Benjamin, but he pulled himself free and ran to Dina, who stood on the pier, dressed for traveling.

" 'Prince Gustav' is a woman! Are you traveling with a woman?" he shouted at her furiously, and kicked a stone so it flew close to Stine's head.

Dina was silent.

He did not give up, despite the fact that many people had come to say good-bye to her.

"Are you going to come home like a crow this time too?" he hurled at her fiercely.

"Hush now," she said quietly, dangerously friendly.

"The last time, you stayed in bed for weeks after you came home."

He was crying openly now.

"That won't happen this time."

"How do you know?"

"Because!"

He threw himself against her and wept loudly.

"You're making a lot of noise!" she said firmly, and grasped the back of his neck.

"Why are you going there?" he raged. "Mother Karen says it's winter all year long. And nothing but seagull poop and uproar," he added triumphantly.

"Because I must go. And want to go."

"I don't want you to!"

"I hear that."

He pulled and tugged at her, cried and struggled, until she got into the rowboat and Tomas put the oars in the oarlocks and pushed away from shore.

"That little fellow isn't afraid to show his feelings," she said to Tomas.

"He wants his mother at home," said Tomas, and looked away.

"I guess that's true."

Dina held her hat as he rowed against the wind and neared the steamboat with long, powerful strokes.

"You'll take care of everything?" she asked in a friendly tone. As if he were a distant acquaintance of whom she was forced to ask a favor.

"I expect we'll manage. But it's hard when Anders is on a trip to

Bergen and you're away too. There are many people to oversee in the haying season and . . ."

"You've managed before," she said firmly.

"Yes."

"I'm depending on you. Take good care of the horse," she added suddenly. "Ride him a little now and then."

"He won't let anyone except you ride him."

She did not reply.

"Isn't that Mother Karen sitting in the window?" she asked, and waved toward the main house.

The spacious, smoke-spitting vessel had been named *Prince Gustav* after Crown Prince Oscar's youngest son. Which was why the round-cheeked figurehead adorned the bow. Not very pretentious, but clearly visible. The prince's name was painted on the paddle wheel. In neat letters, with a crown over them.

The paddle wheel began churning. On the shore, caps and hand-kerchiefs were tossed into the air as if at a signal. Voices hummed on every side. Dina raised a white-gloved hand.

Although there was scarcely a breath of wind, the big chokecherry in the garden swung back and forth.

Benjamin sat there, howling. Howling and shaking the tree. He attacked and abused it. Tore off branches and trampled boughs. So she would see what he had done and feel sad about it.

Dina smiled. A light breeze caressed the rippling sea. The steamboat was on its way north. Mother Karen had given her blessing. Would it help?

She greeted the captain just before they came to Havnviken. Expected to meet the man with the enormous, grizzled sideburns whom people called Captain Lous.

Instead she met a tall man who reminded her of a workhorse in his movements and appearance. His nose loomed bravely in a large, long face. His lips were a muzzle. Generous and constantly in motion, with a dark cleft between them like an old woman's breasts. Two kindly round eyes were hidden behind bushy brows.

He expressed his regrets in a refined manner when she asked to speak to the old captain. Clicked his heels and offered her a slender, well-formed hand, which bore no resemblance to the rest of the man.

"My name is David Christian Lysholm," he said, as his blue glance swept over her from head to foot.

He showed her around the ship as if he owned it. And praised Nordland as though it were her private property, where he was a guest.

Times had not changed here in the north. The gentry could still travel in a manner befitting their status. That was certainly not possible on the miserable roads farther south, he said.

He stroked the highly polished brass railings and nodded at his own statements. Then asked if he would be permitted to smoke a pipe in madam's presence.

Of course he would, Dina said. She enjoyed smoking a pipe herself. He smiled like a new moon and seemed lost for words. Dina did not go to get her pipe from the cabin. There was no need to make a spectacle of herself.

They were still standing inside the brass railing that separated first class from the "other travelers."

People are given space according to their status, not according to their pocketbooks, the captain said. And took her arm as though it were the most natural thing in the world.

In Havnviken they were met by several small boats filled with young people.

The captain stood at attention to welcome the only new passenger. The bailiff. He came aboard with his pigskin portfolio and an air of great authority.

They greeted each other as old acquaintances, and the captain introduced Dina.

Meanwhile, the postmaster stood by the ladder, talking with a local tradesman about two letters that did not bear the proper stamps. He insisted on four skillings postage.

Then the ship's bell rang for the third time, and the paddle wheel began churning. They glided through salt water. People ashore were like ants. Mountains drifted past.

The travelers stared at one another surreptitiously. Some with a self-contained expression, others curious or seeking. All had some reason for being on the move.

"What brings the bailiff north?" the captain wanted to know.

Evidently the Russians had pushed across the border between Norway and Russian Lapland in two or three places. Settlers there in the north complained that the foreigners had usurped Norwegian territory. And had even insisted the land belonged to Russia! Now the invaders had come as far as Tana. And local efforts to make them leave were unsuccessful. So the bailiff was on his way north.

"Are the Russians violent or peaceful?" Dina asked.

"They're as pesky as horseflies — that's what they are!" said the bailiff.

The postmaster chewed thoughtfully on his mustache and pushed his cap farther back on his forehead. He had heard that the Russians acted as if the northern region of Finnmark belonged to the czar and that many Finnmarkers wished it were true. For the government in Christiania did not look good in the matter. The shrewd Russian diplomats arranged everything. And the government officials never bothered to lift a finger. They did not know anything either. Had never been to Finnmark to see conditions there.

The postmaster bowed three times to the bailiff as he spoke. As if he realized that he did not know for certain where the bailiff's sympathies lay, with the government or with the Finnmarkers. It was just as well to act courteous, even if you said what you believed.

The captain was embarrassed. But the bailiff was not. He looked at the postmaster good-naturedly and said:

"This is a long country. It's hard to keep a close eye on everything. People in the north, especially Finnmark, are dependent on a good relationship with Russia. It's their source of important products, such as grain and rope. But of course, there's a limit to everything. We can't allow our country to be invaded."

The bailiff turned to Dina and asked how things were in her district. And about the health of her father, the sheriff.

Dina replied briefly.

"The sheriff has never been sick a day in his life, except that sometimes his heart gets out of rhythm. This spring was a nightmare of snow and food shortages. But it's over now."

The bailiff seemed to be enjoying himself. His brow wrinkled attractively, and he asked her to give his greetings to the sheriff if she saw him before he did.

"What happened to the pirates who plundered Raft Sound a while ago?" asked Dina.

"The case is going to court in the fall. But they're already sitting in chains in Trondheim."

"Is it true that two women were involved?" she wanted to know.

"Yes, there were two women in the band. Gypsies, I'm sure."

"How do you transfer such dangerous prisoners to Trondheim?"

"It takes husky fellows. And we keep the prisoners in irons," he said, seeming surprised at her question.

Dina said no more, and the men began their usual talk about the weather.

Aside from the serving girls and two young sisters traveling in third class, Dina was the only woman aboard.

She withdrew to the women's cabin in first class, which she had to herself for now. Opened her travel bag and carefully chose a dress and jewelry. She even pinned up her hair and wore a corset. But she did not wear a hat. She twirled around and nodded with satisfaction.

It should be possible to get eastbound transportation with the bailiff! She regarded the evening ahead as a chess game.

There were two coastal pilots on board. But only one was sober. That was enough, the captain said good-naturedly. The other lay snoring in a bunk. With one pilot on the bridge and another belowdecks, the trip would go safely.

A bewildering array of languages was spoken. German, English, and Danish, in addition to Norwegian.

The third-class passengers had gathered around the black smokestack. They sat on boxes and chests. Some dozed in the fine weather. Others had taken out their picnic boxes and were calmly eating food they had brought with them.

Soot from the smokestack slowly settled on them, but they paid no attention. One of the girls sat demurely knitting with brown yarn. A tangle of red hair escaped from her kerchief onto her forehead.

Her sister guarded a box of potted plants, which had been taken aboard with much shrieking and commotion. Carnations and geraniums. The flowers protruding over the edge of the box looked amazingly sturdy. Virulent green, with red clusters of flowers. They transformed third class into a hidden windowsill.

Dina stood on the bridge, watching for a while. Then she went to the dining room, where a table was set. Fish was served for the evening meal. Platters of salmon and herring. Ham, cheese, bread and butter. Coffee, tea, and beer.

A large bottle of brandy stood in the middle of the table. They did not drink such things at Reinsnes. Dina had been served brandy in Bergen. It was too sweet for her taste.

Three servants slipped back and forth, filling platters and exchanging full bottles for empty ones.

Dina hesitated in the doorway, exactly long enough. The captain rose and invited her to the table.

She allowed him to escort her. Half a head taller than most of the men. They stood rigidly at attention and remained standing until she was seated.

She took her time. Jacob was there, whispering in her ear how to behave. She offered them her hand, one after another, and looked each man in the eye.

A Dane, with far too much flesh on his face, introduced himself with a count's title and did not want to release her hand. It was clear that he had already helped himself from the bottles on the table.

His fur coat lay on the chair beside him, and he had servants with him.

Dina observed that such bulky clothing must be warm at this time of year.

But the Dane said that voyages so far north could run into all sorts of weather. In an impressively short time, he managed to inform her that he was a doctor of philosophy and a member of the Copenhagen Literary Society. He thought the people in Nordland were friendly and not as commonplace as he had feared. But there were few with whom one could speak English.

He gestured eagerly, so they could see all his rings.

Dina furrowed her brow like a newly plowed potato field, but this had no effect on the man holding her hand so tightly.

She finally escaped. Because an older man offered his hand and bowed. His face was the color of a young boy's who had played outside in the cold all day.

He was short and stocky and spoke German. Nodding toward a sketch pad on the chair beside him, he introduced himself as a chamberlain and painter. For the rest of the evening he kept an eye in Dina's direction, no matter to whom he was speaking. It turned him into a cross-eyed merchant from Hamburg. But he proved to be quite talented in various ways.

Another guest at the table was a British salmon fisherman. Who was actually a real estate agent. He claimed he traveled extensively.

Dina said she understood that the British traveled a great deal. One often encountered them along the shipping channels.

The captain acted as interpreter. The real estate agent chuckled

and nodded. He had sat with a crooked smile while the other men
flirted with Dina according to all the rules of the art.

Now the meal could begin.

*I am Dina. I feel the folds of my clothing. All the seams. All the hollow
spaces in my body. Feel the strength of my bones and the suppleness of my
skin. I feel the length of each hair on my head. It is such a long time since I
could float away from Reinsnes! I draw the sea close to me. I carry Hjertrud
through wind and burning coals.*

During the meal, the men addressed most of their comments to Dina.
The conversation was a complicated mixture of languages. But they
all did their best to follow it.

The Danish count soon dropped out of the conversation. Simply
because he fell asleep. The bailiff asked Dina if he should have the
gentleman removed from the dinner table.

"A sleeping man rarely gets into mischief," she replied.

The men were clearly relieved that the lady was so tolerant about
such matters. And the conversation continued to flow easily.

The captain began talking about Tromsø. It was a lively city and
offered something for everyone's taste. The best place along the
shipping lane, in his opinion.

"You really should visit Mr. Holst, the British vice consul," he
recommended. "The man is not without resources. He owns the
valley across the sound. . . ."

Everyone listened attentively to hear whom it might be worthwhile to visit in Tromsø.

"Some of the merchants subscribe to British newspapers," the
captain continued, turning to the real estate agent from England.

"And Ludwigsen's hotel is not uncomfortable. Not at all. It has
a billiard room!" he added, with a nod toward the others, who could
not expect to visit the British vice consul's home.

"Ludwigsen is a captain too, and speaks English," he said, again
directing his comment to the Englishman.

The others listened politely at first but then began to talk among
themselves in low voices.

They gently nudged the Dane's arm to awaken him. He looked
around, embarrassed, and excused himself, saying he had been on
deck very early that morning. Because the midnight sun had awakened him.

Dina suggested that perhaps it was the early-morning sun. But the Dane gravely insisted it had been the most beautiful midnight sun. At four in the morning, and the world had been incredible, with a calm shining sea and islands reflected in the water. *Skål!*

They all raised their glasses and nodded.

I am Dina. Tonight I have them in my bed. All at the same time. Leo is closest. But Tomas steals under my arm and pushes the others away. I lie with my thighs spread and my arms straight out from my body. I do not touch them. They are made of spindles and ashes.

Jacob is so moist that I start to shiver. Anders lies in a tuft of wool, warming himself in my hair. He does not move. Still, I feel his firm hips pressing against my ear.

Johan has turned his back to me but keeps edging closer. In the end, we have skin and arms in common. He hides his head against Leo and refuses to look at me.

While the others lie with me, Anders is a bird nesting in my hair. His breath is a soft whisper.

Leo is so restless. He probably wants to escape again. I reach for him. Grasp the hairs on his chest firmly.

Then he thrusts the others aside and places himself over me like a lid. The rhythm of his body surges through my veins. Through the bed. So powerfully that Anders falls out of my hair and the others wither like rose petals in a bowl. They drop silently to the deck.

Music streams from Leo, as if from an organ. Rises and falls. His voice settles in my skin like a gentle breeze. Glides through my pores and into my bones. I do not have the strength to defend myself.

The pastor stands before the altar, and all the wooden figures and paintings enclose me — with Leo. In the organ. The cast-iron bells peal like thunder.

Then the sun rises from the sea. Frosty mist drifts past. And we are seaweed wrack on the beaches. That climbs the mountains and the church walls. Pours through the tall windows and through all the crevices.

We are still swaying and alive. In the end we are just a color. Red brown. Iron and earth.

Then we are in Hjertrud's embrace.

Chapter 14

Many waters cannot quench love,
neither can floods drown it.
If a man offered for love
all the wealth of his house,
it would be utterly scorned.

— The Song of Solomon 8 : 7

*D*ina fastened her hat firmly with two hatpins, for a brisk wind was blowing across Tromsø Sound. She had drawn her corset no tighter than would allow her to breathe easily but had pushed up her breasts so they could divert difficult discussions if necessary.

She stood for a moment before the small mirror in the cabin.

Then she went to the deck and said good-bye to her traveling companions and the ship's officers.

A sailor carried her large travel bags ashore. She turned a few times, as if wanting to help the thin fellow with his burden.

Numbers, manipulation, and tact were what mattered now. A head for figures on a woman's body should be checkmate for someone who had not mastered this game.

The days in Bergen and Trondheim had not been wasted. The tricks came to mind like lively musical notes. It was merely a question of sorting them and fitting them into the present context.

"In business, you say no more than is absolutely necessary. If you have nothing to say, just let the other person talk. Sooner or later, he'll make a slip of the tongue."

Those had been Anders's last words to Dina.

Tromsø proved to be several conveniently located clusters of white buildings. Innumerable gurgling brooks flowed down green slopes and formed natural borders between them. Higher up was a birch forest. Lush and green as if it had come from Paradise.

But here, too, Paradise had not lasted once human beings inhabited it.

Dina hired a carriage to drive her around in the sunshine so she could orient herself. South of the city limits, near the beach, were two or three rows of small cottages.

In answer to her question, the young coachman, with a red knitted cap pulled over his ears, explained about the city.

The main road went along the sea, across Prost Point, around the parsonage, and on to Sjø Street. Strand Street was the longest in the city. Grønne Street ran parallel to it. But at the market square the road ended by the courthouse, which lay between the pharmacy and Holstgården.

A stream flowed through the area south of the marketplace, from Vannsletta, past L. J. Pettersen's estate, and then into the ocean. It bore the pretentious name Pettersen's River.

Beyond the pharmacy was a terrible mud hole. The coachman said that when the Pettersens held balls, the men had to wear high boots and carry the women across the muck. Nevertheless, or perhaps precisely therefore, it was fun to be invited to a ball at Pettersens'.

Warm weather and wind had dried the mud hole this summer, so people could walk across it.

Dina took lodgings at Ludwigsen's Hotel du Nord, or Hotel de Bellevue. It clearly catered to the gentry.

J. H. Ludwigsen wore a top hat and used a long-handled umbrella as a walking stick. He was always at her service, he said with a bow. He had thick sideburns and a broad face that inspired confidence. His hair was properly brushed into high waves that fell from an irreproachable left part.

He mentioned several times that if there was anything Madam Dina Grønelv desired, she should just let him know.

Dina sent a messenger with greetings and a request for a meeting to two merchants. This was how Anders had recommended she proceed.

The next morning, she received a message on a visiting card saying she was expected at Pettersen's office. And a short letter informed her that she was awaited at Mr. Müller's.

Mr. Pettersen received her. He was in excellent humor. He had just been named vice consul in Mecklenburg and would leave soon to attend to his official duties. His wife would accompany him, but he also planned to do some private business. He owned a ship with his brothers.

Dina offered profuse congratulations and asked him about his new appointment.

Behind his jovial tone, the man was obviously a shrewd businessman.

Finally, she stated her reason for coming. Asked questions about capital and provisions. Crew. Shares. Percentages for the shipowners. What price would he charge for the flour? How much merchandise could he carry, safe and dry, belowdecks?

Mr. Pettersen sent for some Madeira. Dina said nothing but refused with a gesture when the maid wanted to pour her a glass. She did not want to drink wine so early in the day.

Pettersen took a glass himself and ordered tea for Dina.

He was clearly interested. But too quick with his words. As if he were trying to reassure her before she had indicated any need for that. Furthermore, he could not guarantee a definite flour price.

She looked straight at him and said it was strange he, the vice consul, did not know more about prices.

He ignored her tone and asked how long she would be in the city. Because he could certainly give her a better answer in a few days. They expected Russian *lodjes* any day now.

She balanced his hospitality on a sharp knife when he invited her to stay with his family. Said she already had a roof over her head, which she could not reject. Thank you! He would hear from her if she could accept his offer to buy and ship flour from Archangel without a set price.

Hans Peter Müller was the second name on her list.

Dina went to the stately house in Skipper Street the following day. It was replete with wealth and luxury. Mahogany furniture and porcelain.

A frail young wife, who spoke with a Trond district accent, entered the office to greet her. Her eyes were as sad as those of the child ghost at Helgeland. She glided through the rooms. As if she were mounted on a rolling pedestal and pulled by invisible strings.

The cargo boat *Haabet*, which lay on the Müller beach, would sail to Murmansk with products from their own cod-liver-oil distillery. Müller gave Dina a guaranteed maximum price. But admitted that he could get better prices for himself.

Dina gave him a firm handshake. That he even talked about his calculations indicated she was dealing with someone who accepted her as a partner. She did not have to play games by pushing up her breasts for the occasion. One could talk business with a man who already had an angel in the house. Dina took a drink to seal the bargain.

The air in the house was good to breathe. She accepted their hospitable invitation to stay in one of their guest rooms for a few days.

It turned out that Müller also owned a black horse. A creature as gleaming as the mahogany furniture in the parlors. The horse received Dina's hips and thighs as if they had been carved from the same piece of wood.

Dina got along well with the young wife, Julie, from Stjørdal. She did not chatter constantly and looked straight at people. But she did not mention why she had such sad eyes.

Dina stayed longer than she had planned.

The bailiff had already continued his travels, so she had to look for another means of transport. Müller thought he could get passage for her on an eastbound vessel the following week.

The first day Dina was at the Müller home, she and her host sat in the sitting room smoking, while Madam Julie rested.

He talked about the difficult winter. About how ice had formed in Gi Sound and prevented the *Prince Gustav* from entering. On May 10 they had sawed an open channel of 120 feet so the steamboat could get through. But fortunately, the ice had not had affected sailing-vessel trade.

Two of Müller's vessels had just returned safely from the Arctic Ocean. He had a ship on southern waters too, he said in passing. As if he had almost forgotten.

The problem the previous year had been to find reliable maps for the voyage to Archangel. And men who knew the area sufficiently did not grow on trees. . . .

Dina acknowledged her good fortune in having Anders and Anton on her cargo boats. But of course, the problems they encountered sailing to Bergen were not worth mentioning. Compared with a voyage to Archangel.

Her host grew talkative. Told how the steamboat had arrived from the south on May 17 with all its paddles nearly ruined. It had to be repaired at the shipyard. That had provided work for several men, which was a blessing.

He himself had lost his ketch *Tordenskjold* with twelve men and a full catch east of Moffen. Still, over the past few years he had made a gross profit on his Arctic Ocean fishing of 14,500 *speciedaler!*

Dina nodded thoughtfully and blew an expert smoke ring, which settled around her head.

Later he talked about how everything had improved after Czar Nicolas drew his last breath. Trade had increased, more than one could have dreamed.

Dina said it had more to do with the war than with the czar.

Müller pleasantly insisted that the two things were related.

Dina maintained that the unusual aspects of the situation, the war and the blockade, were precisely what created profitable times for business.

The man nodded thoughtfully and in no way disagreed. But he did not change his opinion with regard to the czar.

Meanwhile, the host's best cigars went up in smoke.

Dina settled into the rhythm of the house, like a cat that had suddenly found a sun-warmed stone. Strangely enough, Madam Julie showed no sign of jealousy toward this woman who invaded the house and captured her husband's interest. Quite the contrary, she said there was no need for Dina to travel east so soon. Since she only wanted to look around in Vardø Fortress.

Dina kept informed about ships that arrived from the south and the east.

Mr. Müller asked if she had decided yet whether she was actually going to Vardø Fortress, since she inquired about vessels traveling both north and south.

But Madam Julie knew the answer.

"Dina is waiting for someone," she said.

Dina stared at her. Their eyes met in understanding.

I am Dina. Julie is safe. Death lives in her eyes. She constantly begins to ask a question she never completes. Then she looks at me, wanting me to answer. She wants me to show Hjertrud to her. But it is not time for that. Yet.

*　　*　　*

Dina rode out of the city on the black horse. Wearing Mr. Müller's leather trousers.

At first Julie had offered her an elegant riding outfit with a black cashmere skirt, white blouse, and white pantaloons with a strap under the foot. But that was not acceptable.

Dina agreed to wear a skirt over men's leather trousers. It was very full, and open front and back. Just to cover oneself, as her hostess said.

When Dina returned, Julie was waiting with a glass of good Madeira before they dressed for dinner. She herself drank tea.

In her subtle way, Julie told about life in Tromsø. She saw it clearly and objectively, because she was an outsider.

Dina did not need to fear she would offend her hostess if she wondered about something or laughed at the people and their customs.

She asked about Ludwigsen.

"He owns a fortune and looks like he was clipped from a magazine," said Julie, with some interest and warmth.

They giggled together, like little girls. Among many beautiful, lifeless things in a much too solemn parlor.

During the 1840s, when drinking morals in Tromsø were at their worst, the municipal council restricted the number of places that could serve alcohol. So now there was only one chandler and one liquor merchant in the city. They did a thriving business.

"Respectable people go to Ludwigsen's. Quite frankly, they go there to be seen," Julie told Dina.

She looked like an angel, which she was. Always dressed in either cotton or silk sateen. But the angelic curls at her ears contrasted with the ironic corners of her mouth and her serious eyes.

Usually she told about balls and dinners at the homes of government officials and leading citizens. About interesting episodes when people of different backgrounds dined together. She had many such experiences to choose from, for the Müller family was highly regarded by everyone.

Dina breathed in all the new things as if they were strange spices from distant latitudes.

"Don't get acquainted with people too quickly," Julie advised. "Or they'll be after you like dogs. It does no good to withdraw or to think you can undo the acquaintance once you've made it. You'll never get rid of these people, who have nothing in common other than that they enjoy good food and drink."

The second day of Dina's visit, the new doctor came to call. He was in charge of the hospital, which had a temporary asylum. The "crazy cage," or the Tronka, people called it.

Dina showed interest in both the work and the building. Which livened the doctor's enthusiasm. He talked about the "caretakers," as he called them. About constant improvements for the poor inmates, who were completely out of their minds.

He told about a religious fanatic they had in custody. He had lost his mind when Hætta and Somby were executed in '52. The reverberations caused by the execution, by the law and the church, and by Læstadian religious fanatics were still felt. People withdrew in horror and dismay. Their society was too small for two death sentences.

"Some people even withdrew from the state church," said Julie.

"But now we've gotten a new bishop to clean up the apostasy. His wife is also pious and good," said the doctor.

The hollows at the corners of Julie's mouth were deep and pointed upward. She and the doctor had obviously discussed the matter before. They complemented one another.

Müller did not say anything.

"Is he dangerous?" Dina asked suddenly.

"Who?"

The doctor was confused.

"The religious madman."

"Oh, he . . . He's dangerous to himself. He pounds his head against the wall until he's unconscious. I don't know what drives him. I'd say he's violent. He calls on God and the devil without much distinction between them."

"Why is he locked up?"

"His behavior threatens his family and . . ."

"May I see your asylum?" she asked.

Surprised by the request, the doctor agreed. They made an appointment.

Four cells on each side of a corridor. The same sounds as in Trondheim, but not as deafening.

Both insane and regular prisoners were incarcerated here. Women should not talk to such people, the doctor said. Someone called to him urgently. He asked Dina to excuse him. Then jangled his keys, unlocked the door, and disappeared.

The caretaker called to a person named Jentoft through a small opening in a door.

A smooth-shaven head and the filthy arm of a burlap kirtle appeared in the opening. The fellow squinted toward the light. His eyes were more alive than one would expect of a caged human being.

He grasped for the air around Dina, because he could not get his hand through the grate.

When the caretaker said that Dina Grønelv wanted to talk with him, even though he was crazy, he blessed her and made the sign of the cross.

"God is good!" he shouted.

The caretaker told him to lower his voice.

"Do you know God?" Dina asked quickly, with a glance at the caretaker, who was utilizing the time to tidy the shelves along the corridor.

"Yes! And all the saints!"

"Do you know Hjertrud?" Dina asked earnestly.

"Know Hjertrud! God is good! Does she look like you? Is she coming here?"

"She lives everywhere. Sometimes she looks like me. Sometimes we're completely different. The way people are . . ."

"To God, everyone's the same!"

"Do you believe that?"

"The Bible! That's what it says in the Bible!" the man said loudly.

"Yes. That's Hjertrud's book."

"It's everyone's book. Hallelujah! We'll lead them to the pearly gates, one and all. We'll force them from this sin and sorrow! All who resist! All who are not converted will fall before the sword!"

The caretaker looked at Dina and suggested it was time to end the visit.

"This lady has come to talk with you, Jentoft," he said, as he walked over to them.

"The cherubs will rush forth and cleave them in two. From head to foot! One and all! The axe now lies at the root of the tree. . . . God is good!" the man intoned.

The caretaker looked at Dina apologetically. As if the prisoner were his personal property that had gotten in her way.

"Calm down, Jentoft!" he said firmly, and closed the small opening, right in the agitated man's face.

"A prisoner needn't always be imprisoned completely alone," said Dina gravely.

The caretaker gave her a blank look.

"Aren't you going to wait for the doctor?" he asked.

"No. Say thank you and good-bye to him!"

The Müllers held a dinner party for Dina.

She was introduced to a bookseller named Urdal. It would be wrong to say he was a social lion. But he had been a hired hand for the great Norwegian poet Henrik Wergeland and ran a bookstore in Lillehammer. So he was, by all means, a member of good society.

He published old, sad folk songs. Took fishermen into his back room and taught them the melodies. And so Urdal's songs became widely known. Dina knew them too.

While they were waiting for dinner, Dina played the piano and the bookseller sang.

The bishop and his wife were also invited.

When people looked into the wife's large gray eyes, something seemed to fall into place. Madam Henriette had a large, strong nose with an unusually broad base. The cleft between her nose and mouth brimmed with sadness. Under a white kerchief, her dark hair had an impeccable center part. A lace collar was the only ornamentation she wore, except for her wedding ring.

She was a refuge for all women, regardless of their family or social class, Julie said.

Madam Henriette's eyes rested briefly on one person after another. Like a cool hand on a fevered brow. She was not the least pretentious about her position as the bishop's wife. Nonetheless, her presence at the table was extremely dignified.

"You've been a widow for many years, even though you're so young?" the bishop's wife asked gently. She poured coffee into Dina's cup herself, as if she were the servant of all.

"Yes."

"And you manage an inn and a cargo boat enterprise and oversee many people?"

"Yes," whispered Dina. That voice! Those eyes!

"It must be difficult."

"Yes . . ."

"Do you have anyone to help you?"

"Oh, yes, I do."

"A brother? A father?"

"No. The workers at Reinsnes."

"But nobody close to you?"

"No. I mean . . . Mother Karen . . ."

"Is she your mother?"

"No, my mother-in-law."

"That's not the same, is it?"

"No."

"But you have God. I can see that clearly!"

Madam Julie began speaking to the bishop's wife about a woman in the community who wanted to visit the parsonage but did not dare to come on her own initiative.

The older woman turned slowly toward Julie and, seemingly by chance, laid her hand on Dina's. Light, cool fingers.

The day was a gift.

When the bishop looked at his wife, his broad face grew gentle and his eyes almost overflowed. Slender threads connected those two and pleasantly affected the rest of the party as well.

Dina skipped the cigar after dinner and did not provoke anyone.

There was no defiance in her the following day either. But she could have left for Vardø Fortress! Instead she rode Müller's horse to exhaustion. On the island. Around a lake. Thundered through woodlands and thickets. The smell of summer was so strong that all her senses burned.

Chapter 15

The watchmen found me,
as they went about in the city.
"Have you seen him whom my soul loves?"
Scarcely had I passed them,
when I found him whom my soul loves.
I held him and would not let him go
until I had brought him into my mother's house,
and into the chamber of her that conceived me.
— The Song of Solomon 3 : 3–4

*T*he day Müller had arranged that Dina would sail to Vardø Fortress, a terrible southwest gale beset them. The bay seethed.

Vessels that had not planned to stop in Tromsø sought safe harbor there. One after another. There were so many masts in the harbor that one could hop far across the water dry-shod. Had it not been for the rain!

Aboard a Russian *lodje* headed south to Trondheim was a person who would have been glad not to go ashore in Tromsø. He had business elsewhere.

He took a room at Ludwigsen's hotel to get away from the sailors' crowded quarters. He wore a broad-brimmed felt hat and leather trousers. After settling into his room and informing the hotel that he did not want to share the room with anyone, he went to the pharmacy. To buy something for a finger that had become infected and swollen on the voyage from Vardø.

He was standing at the counter, waiting to be served, when the door chime announced another customer. Without turning around, he realized it was someone wearing a skirt.

The rain had stopped, but the wind came through the open door and blew his hat off his head.

It was July 13, 1855, three days after Dina had sat at the Müllers' table and witnessed love.

Perhaps it took three days for the blessing of the bishop's wife to be fulfilled? In any case, Dina picked up Leo's hat and weighed it in her hand, as she looked at it with repressed interest.

The pharmacist hurried over and slammed the door behind her. The door chime was furious. Its uneven peals reverberated from the walls.

Leo's eyes zigzagged up Dina's cape and body. As if he did not dare to see her face immediately.

They caught their breaths simultaneously and stared at one another for a moment. Then they just stood there, two steps from each other.

She holding his hat like a warning. He looking as if he had just seen a horse flying through the air. Only when the pharmacist said, "May I help you?" did a sound come from Dina. Laughter. Rippling and free.

"Here's your hat!"

The scar was a pale new moon in a brown sky. He stretched out his hand. Suddenly the rest of the world did not exist. His fingers were cold. She stroked his wrist with her index finger.

They went out into the wind without buying drops for Mother Karen or bandages and iodine for Leo's finger. The friendly pharmacist stood behind the counter, staring openmouthed, and heard the door chime as they left.

They wandered along a narrow, muddy street. Men were laying sidewalks at the lower end of it.

They did not say a word at first. He took her arm and tucked it securely under his. Then, finally, he began to talk. In that deep, remarkable voice that carried so well. That used such clear words. But always held back something.

At one point, she slipped in the mud. His strong arm kept her from falling. Pulled her close. Her skirt dragged in the dirt, because she was holding her hat instead.

He did not notice. Just observed absentmindedly that mud clung to the hem of her dress, more and more greedily with each step.

They walked up the hills. Until the city and the mud were left behind and meadows and birch forests took over. They walked holding on to their hats. Until Dina let hers fly with the wind. He ran after it. But had to give up. They watched as it flew north, its ribbons fluttering. A lovely sight.

He planted his large black hat on her head and pulled it over her ears.

The city lay below, but she did not see it. For Leo's mouth was red. With a sore, brown stripe around it from overexposure to the sun.

She stopped and put her hand on his mouth. Slowly brushed her fingers over the sore skin.

He closed his eyes, while still holding the hat on her head with both hands.

"Thank you for the gifts the Russian *lodje* brought last spring!" she said.

"The music pieces? Did you like them?" he asked, his eyes still closed.

"Yes. Thank you so much! But you didn't write anything."

He opened his eyes at that.

"No, it was difficult. . . ."

"Where did you send them from?"

"Tromsø."

"You were in Tromsø, and you didn't come to Reinsnes?"

"It was impossible. I went inland. To Finland."

"Why did you go there?"

"For adventure."

"You don't find adventure at Reinsnes anymore?"

He laughed quietly but did not answer. His arms were still around her shoulders. In order to hold the black hat, apparently.

Little by little, he leaned toward her.

"Were you planning to come to Reinsnes for a while?" she asked.

"Yes."

"Are you still planning to come?"

He gave her a long look. Then he tightened his arm around both her and the hat.

"Will I still be welcome?"

"I guess so."

"You're not sure?"

"Yes!"

"Why are you so hard, Dina?" he whispered, and leaned closer. As if afraid the wind would fly away with the answer.

"I'm no harder than necessary. You're the one who's hard! You make promises and lie. Don't come when you say you will. Let people wait in suspense."

"I sent you presents."

"Oh, yes. Without even a scrap of paper to indicate who sent them!"

"That was impossible right then."

"I see. But it was cruel."

"I'm sorry!"

He put his hand with the swollen finger under her chin. Was embarrassed that the hand was so coarse and let it fall again.

"I went to the prison in Trondheim to ask about you. And I left a letter."

"When were you there?" he said into the wind.

"A year ago. I was in Bergen too. . . . You weren't there?"

"No. I was stuck on the Finnish coast and saw the British playing with dynamite."

"You had a job to do?"

"Yes," he replied candidly.

"Did you sometimes think?"

"I never do otherwise."

"What did you think about?"

"About Dina, for example."

"But you didn't come?"

"No."

"Something was more important than Dina?"

"Yes."

She pinched his cheek angrily and kicked a stone so it struck his calf. He remained impassive. Merely moved his foot a little. And put the hat back on his own head.

"I think you're doing dark deeds!"

She snarled like a judge who encounters a stubborn defendant. He gave her a long, searching look. But with a broad smile.

"And what will you do about that?"

"Find out what's going on!" she exclaimed.

Without further ado, he began to recite a poem he had translated for her the last night he was at Reinsnes:

When she sees the bait, she'll howl and rage
like wild beasts in an iron cage.
Though restrained by rocks, silent and grim.

On wings of hope she hurls toward the rim
and hungrily licks each hill.
Her voracious longing is never still.

Dina glared at him.

"That's a description of a river, remember?" he said. "Pushkin accompanied a Russian division on a military campaign against Turkey. Do you remember I told you that?"

She nodded.

"You're like a wild river, Dina!"

"You're making fun of me," she said crossly.

"No . . . I'm trying to make contact."

I am Dina. Pushkin's poem is soap bubbles that come out of Leo's mouth. His voice keeps them floating in the air. For a long time. I slowly count to twenty-one. Then they burst and fall to the ground. Meanwhile, I must rethink every thought.

Not until they were returning to the city did she ask where he was going now.

"South to Trondheim," he replied.

"Without stopping on the way?"

"Without stopping on the way."

"Then you can get your underlined book at the asylum there," she said triumphantly. "Because it's connected with those dark deeds that you can't talk about. That keep you from including a name or a greeting when you send gifts. That result in nobody knowing who you are when I ask."

"Who have you asked — or talked to — about me?"

"Russian sailors. Bergen merchants. The people in charge of the asylum and prison in Trondheim."

He stared at her.

"Why did you do that?" he whispered.

"Because I had a book I wanted to return to you."

"And that's why you went to all that effort from Bergen to Trondheim?"

"Yes. So now you can get the book yourself!"

"I certainly can," he said, calm and trembling. "To whom did you deliver it?"

"The director."

He knit his brows for a moment.

"Why?"

"Because I don't want it any longer."

"But why did you give it to the director?"

"Who else would I give it to? But the package is sealed," she said with a mocking smile.

"I said you could keep it, you know."

"I didn't want it. Besides, you were so worried about that book. . . ."

"What makes you think that?"

"Because you pretended to be so indifferent."

There was a pause.

He stopped and stared at her for a moment.

"You shouldn't have done that," he said gravely.

"Why not?"

"I can't explain, Dina."

"The director isn't your friend?"

"I have no confidence that he's the right person for Pushkin. . . ."

"Do you know him?"

"No. Now will you please stop asking questions, Dina?"

She turned like a flash, walked over to him, and gave his cheek a resounding slap.

He stood there. Riveted to the gravel road.

"You shouldn't hit people, Dina. People, and animals, shouldn't fight."

He began to walk slowly down the hill. His right hand holding his hat. His left hand dangling like a dead pendulum.

She did not move. He heard the silence. Turned and said her name.

"Why do you have to be so secretive about everything?" she screamed down the hill at him.

Her throat was extended, like that of a goose that does not want to be slaughtered. Her large nose protruded into the air like a beak. The sun had slashed the clouds. The wind was increasing.

"You wander here and there, letting people get attached to you. And then you disappear without a trace! What sort of person are you anyway? Eh? What sort of game are you playing? I want to know!"

"Come here, Dina. Don't stand there shouting."

"I'll do what I wish. You come here!"

And he came. As if humoring a child whose tears he had caused.

They walked down the hill. Close to each other.

"You don't often cry, do you, Dina?"

"Not because of you!"

"When did you last cry?"

"In a storm on the Fold Sea last summer," she snarled.

He smiled a little.

"Shouldn't we stop the war now?"

"Not until I've found out who you are and where you're going."

"Don't you see me here, Dina?"

"That's not enough!"

He held her tightly in his arms and said simply, as though commenting on the weather:

"I love you, Dina Grønelv."

Several decades before someone had placed a large curbstone exactly where they stood. Otherwise she would have sat down in the mud.

Dina sank onto the stone. Pulled and tugged at her fingers, as if she did not want them.

"What does that mean? What does that mean? What does that mean?" she shouted.

He accepted her hysteria. With apparent calmness.

"Isn't that enough either, Dina?"

"Why do you say words like that? Why don't you come to Reinsnes more often instead?"

"It's a long way," was all he said. He stood in front of her, perplexed.

"Tell me!"

"Sometimes a man has reasons to keep silent."

"More than a woman?"

"I don't know about that. But I don't beg you to tell me things."

Something was stretched too far between them.

"Do you think you can come and go at Reinsnes as if nothing . . ."

"I come and go as I wish. You absolutely must stop asking about me on your trips. I'm *nobody*. Remember that!"

He was angry.

She got up from the stone and took his arm, and they continued along the road. There were still only fields and forest around them. No houses. No people.

"What do you actually do?" she asked, leaning close to him in a confidential way.

He saw through the technique immediately. Nevertheless, after a while he replied, with a sigh of resignation:

"Politics."

She picked his face into small pieces with her look. Bit by bit. Clung to his eyes at the end.

"Some people are after you. And others are trying to protect you."

"You're after me." He grinned.

"What terrible things have you done?"

"None," he answered. Looking serious now.

"Not in your own eyes, but . . ."

"Not in yours either."

"Let me decide that for myself. Tell me about them."

He threw out his hands helplessly and, finally, took off his hat and put it under his arm. The wind besieged him.

Then he said harshly:

"The world is worse than you can imagine. Blood. Gallows. Treason, poverty, and degradation."

"Is it dangerous?" she asked.

"No more dangerous than you'd expect. But more horrible than you'd believe. And that makes me a person who doesn't exist!"

"Doesn't exist?"

"Yes. Someday things will be better."

"When will that be?"

"I don't know."

"Will you come to Reinsnes then?"

"Yes!" he said firmly. "Will you have me, even if I go by without stopping and am a person who doesn't exist?"

"I can't marry a person who doesn't exist."

"Do you want to marry me?"

"Yes."

"Have you asked me?"

"We've received a blessing. That's enough."

"What would I do at Reinsnes?"

"You'd live there with me and lend a hand as needed."

"Do you think that's enough for a man?"

"It was enough for Jacob. It's enough for me!"

"But I'm not you or Jacob."

They stared at each other like two male animals staking their territory. There was no trace of courtship in their eyes.

Finally, she gave in. Looked down and said meekly:

"You could be the skipper on one of the cargo boats and travel all over, if you wanted."

"I wouldn't make a good skipper," he said politely. He still held his hat crushed under his arm.

"I can't be married to a man who's wandering around Russia and everywhere!" she shouted.

"You shouldn't be married, Dina. I don't think you're suited to being married."

"But who will I have?"

"You'll have me."

"But you're not there!"

"I'm always there. Don't you understand? I'm with you. But I can't be fenced in. You can't be the fence. That only leads to hate."

"Hate?"

"Yes! You can't confine people. Then they become dangerous. They've done that to the Russian people. And everything's going to explode soon!"

Millions of meadow grasses were flattened by the wind. Some terrified bluebells dangled back and forth.

"You can't confine people. Then they become dangerous . . . ," she whispered. "Then they become dangerous!"

She said it into the air as if it was a truth she had not realized until just this moment.

They did not need to touch one another. A bond as strong as mooring lines stretched between them.

The next day, a messenger arrived at the Müller estate with a package. For Dina.

It was her hat. It looked as though it had been lying outside all winter. But inside the crown lay a card in a sealed envelope.

"No matter how bad things appear, I'll always return."

That was all.

She took the first steamboat south. He was two days ahead of her. There was no joy in the vessel's wake. But the tranquillity was a companion of sorts.

The bishop's wife knew that love existed. And Dina had saved herself a trip to Vardø Fortress. She had heard it was a windswept, godforsaken place with a dungeon and a fort inside a star-shaped wall.

"You can't confine people. Then they become dangerous!" Dina murmured to herself. She did not have much to do besides count mountaintops and fjord entrances.

The people on board were insignificant.

Chapter 16

For my life is spent with sorrow,
and my years with sighing;
my strength fails because of my misery,
and my bones waste away.

— Psalms 31 : 10

*W*hile Dina was on her way home, Mother Karen collapsed in her wing chair and could no longer speak.

Tomas was sent across the mountain on horseback to get the doctor. And Anders rushed a message by sea to Johan, who was visiting the pastor in Vågan.

The doctor was not home. But even if he had come, he probably could not have done much.

Johan packed his travel bag and set out for his grandmother's deathbed. To him, as to everyone else, it had seemed natural that Mother Karen would never die.

Oline was beside herself. Her distress affected the food. Everything she touched was tasteless and unfit to eat. Her face was as pink and naked as a baboon's rear.

Stine sat with the old woman. Boiled herbs and fed her with a spoon. She wiped away the secretions from the old woman's pores and openings. Washed her and strewed potato starch. She filled leather pouches with dried herbs and rose petals to sweeten the air in the sickroom.

Now and then Mother Karen thought she had come to the Garden of Eden and could forget the long road she must travel to reach it.

Stine warmed wool cloths and placed them on the limp limbs, plumped the pillows and quilts, and opened the window a crack. So there would always be some fresh air.

Meanwhile, the August sun blazed, the blueberries ripened, and the final loads of hay were brought into the barns.

*　　*　　*

Benjamin and Hanna were invisible and silent, on Oline's orders. They mostly wandered along the beach, watching all the ships that might bring Dina and the presents she would have for them.

Benjamin understood that his grandmother was ill. But he regarded it as one of Oline's many exaggerations to say that Mother Karen was going to die. Hanna, on the other hand, had inherited Stine's sense of the inevitable. So one day she stood barefoot at the high-water mark, speared an overturned crab with a stick, and said:

"Mother Karen will probably die before Sunday!"

"Huh? Why do you say that?"

"Because Mama looks that way. In fact, Mother Karen looks that way too! Old people have to die."

Benjamin was furious.

"Mother Karen's not old!" he declared. Then added gently, "People just think she is. . . ."

"She's ancient!"

"No! You're crazy!"

"Why do you deny it? She should be allowed to die now, without you getting angry!"

"Yes, but she's not going to die! Do you hear?"

He grabbed her braids and twisted them right to her scalp. Beside herself with rage and pain, she plopped down on the high-tide beach and howled. Her dress and pantalets got soaked far up her back. She sat there with her legs outstretched and her bottom underwater. The cries came fitfully from her gaping mouth.

Benjamin forgot he was angry at her. Besides, he realized he had to do something if he did not want Stine to come running to see what was the matter. He stared at the girl a few moments. With a resigned expression. Then he reached out both hands, helped her to her feet, and calmed her down.

They took off her wet clothes. Wrung them out and laid them on the warm rocks to dry. And since they were sitting there like that, not really knowing whether they were friends or enemies, he began to examine her, as he sometimes did when nobody could see them. Still feeling offended, she stretched out on the rock, flicked an erring ant from her thigh, and graciously let Benjamin continue. While she sniffed phlegm and tears and let herself be somewhat comforted.

Both of them had forgotten that Mother Karen was going to die before Sunday.

*　　*　　*

Dina arrived on the steamboat the next day. She took the children into Mother Karen's room. They stood by the bed with stiff arms and downcast eyes.

Benjamin shivered in the warm room. He shook his head when Stine told him to take his grandmother's hand.

Dina leaned over Mother Karen and held the old woman's hands, one after the other, in both of hers. Then she nodded to Benjamin.

The boy put his hand in Dina's, who guided it to the old woman. Then she held both their hands in hers.

A sudden light flickered in Mother Karen's eyes. Her face was partly paralyzed. But she drew the left side of her mouth into a helpless smile. And her eyes slowly brimmed with tears.

Stine's herb pouches swung gently above the bed. The white curtain brushed against the windowsill.

Benjamin threw his arms around Mother Karen's neck and gave her a big hug. Without anyone's telling him to do so.

Anders, Oline, and the other Reinsnes workers stood inside the door. They had been to the bedside one by one.

Mother Karen never spoke again. But she let them stroke her thin hands. Large blue veins twisted across the back of each hand like bare autumn branches. When her eyes were open, they followed the people in the room. And it was clear that she heard and understood everything.

A deep peace settled on the room. People merged with one another. Mute. Like clumps of heather after the snow has disappeared, they drew themselves erect and blended together.

Johan did not reach Mother Karen before she died.

The funeral boat was decorated with leaves and adder's-tongue ferns. As well as bouquets and wreaths of flowers. They covered the coffin completely.

Oline was responsible for seeing that the funeral guests were well fed and did not go home and talk about the poor kitchen at Reinsnes. She would make sure Mother Karen did not get that posthumous reputation!

Night and day, she worked her magic with food and drink for the funeral. Nothing would be lacking. And she sighed and wept the whole time.

Benjamin thought it would never end. He had to help by wiping her eyes, so her tears would not fall into the *lefse*, the liver pâté, or the sandwiches.

Johan was imprisoned in grief. What had happened between him and Dina remained on his conscience like spots of decay. And he had never received forgiveness for it. Mother Karen's death was a dreadful warning. But Dina still existed! She could insult and subdue him merely by walking through the room. He had been unable to talk with Mother Karen about his terrible sin, and now she was dead! And he could never think about his father without great anxiety.

For a long time now, he had felt distant from God. He had tried to do penance among his parishioners on the windswept skerries. Refused a salary and gave all his earnings to the poor. But it made no difference.

His self-hatred was so intense that he could not stand to see his own nakedness. He could not even empty himself in his sleep without feeling that he was drowning in Dina's hair. Her white thighs were the entrance to hell. He saw tongues of fire licking him when he awoke, and he forced himself to remember all the prayers he had learned.

But clearly, this was not enough for Our Lord. Johan needed to confess his sin to the bishop in Nidaros or Tromsø.

After the funeral, Johan returned to Helgeland. He had avoided Dina the way one avoids ice in an open channel.

Dina ordered the barn to be cleaned. And the floors in the store and the boathouses were to be scoured.

Nobody knew the reason for this cleaning. But they understood it was an order. She sat in the office through the long fall evenings, burning expensive oil while she minutely examined expensive numbers.

She did not move into the main house, and she did not play the cello. The latter made everyone uneasy.

Benjamin knew better than anyone that this was a dangerous Dina. He tried to reach her with the same tricks she used when she wanted something.

But Dina responded by hiring a tutor. With wisdom and discipline, he forced the children to make progress. As if they were two threshing machines that should be driven to their limits.

Anders traveled here and there. He seemed invisible even when at Reinsnes, because they knew he would be leaving soon.

Mother Karen lay in her grave, with no responsibility for anything. She was more sacrosanct than ever.

Her reputation flourished, pure and white as the frost patterns on Dina's window. Mother Karen kept her distance. She did not come to Dina from the corners or from the heavy cloudbanks above the sound. She did not interfere with what Dina did or did not do. Made no demands.

It appeared she was perfectly content to be dead and had no need for any contact.

When it was rumored that bears had been seen on Eid Mountain again, Dina asked Tomas to go hunting with her. But he refused. Always had something that needed to be done.

Autumn passed.

In October winter arrived suddenly, with cold weather and heavy snowfalls.

Dina began to play the cello again. She divided her time between the ledgers and the cello.

The tones. Black signs on stern lines. Silent, until she gave them sound. Sometimes the tones came from the printed music, or from Lorch's cello, without her playing. Her hands could rest idly on the instrument, and still the melody would emerge.

The numbers. In neat, dark-blue columns. Silent, but clear enough. For initiates. They always meant the same. Had their yearly rhythm and their hidden treasures. Or their obvious losses.

Chapter 17

Then Amnon said to Tamar, "Bring the food into the chamber, that I may
eat from your hand." And Tamar took the cakes she had made, and
brought them into the chamber to Amnon her brother. But when she
brought them near him to eat, he took hold of her, and said to her,
"Come, lie with me, my sister." She answered him, "No, my brother, do
not force me; for such a thing is not done in Israel; do not do this wanton
folly. . . ." But he would not listen to her; and being stronger than she,
he forced her, and lay with her.

Then Amnon hated her with very great hatred; so that the hatred
with which he hated her was greater than the love with which he had
loved her. And Amnon said to her, "Arise, be gone."

— 2 Samuel 13 : 10–12, 14–15

*T*omas had begun to be on the lookout for Dina whenever she was
in the stable or barns.

She moved uneasily when he was nearby. As if she were avoiding
an insect. Sometimes she gave him a searching look. Generally when
he was at a safe distance.

One afternoon he approached her as she entered the cottage.

"Why are you always in my way, Tomas?" she said angrily.

The brown and the blue eye blinked several times. Then they
narrowed.

"If I'm to do my work, I need to move around."

"And what work do you have here, on my steps?"

"I'm clearing away the snow. If you don't mind?"

"Then maybe you could use a shovel?"

He turned and went to the toolshed. For hours, his spade shrieked
near the cottage.

The next day, Dina called Stine to her room.

"What about you and Tomas getting married?" she asked without
preliminaries.

Stine sank onto the nearest chair but immediately stood up again.

412

"How can you say such a thing?" she exclaimed.

"It's a good solution."

"To what?"

"To everything."

"You can't mean that," Stine said shyly, with a desperate look at Dina.

"You can live here in the cottage, like fine folk. I'll move into the main house," said Dina gently.

Stine put her hands under her apron and lowered her eyes. She made no reply.

"What do you say to the idea?" asked Dina.

"He doesn't want to," Stine said calmly.

"Why wouldn't he want to?"

"You know why."

"And what's the reason?"

"He wants someone else."

"And who might that be?"

Stine squirmed. Her head drooped farther toward her chest.

"You must be the only one who doesn't know. It's hard to make people change their hearts. And rarely leads to any good. . . ."

"You'd be a blessing to anyone, Stine!" Dina interrupted.

Stine walked slowly when she left the cottage. Her eyes were almost black and looked resolutely straight ahead. She had forgotten her shawl on the chair. But did not go back for it, even though she was shivering.

For a long while, she stood on the kitchen steps, looking at the icicles that hung from the eaves. Oline was working inside, with her back to the window.

Dina sent for Tomas and told him about his future.

He stiffened, as if someone had nailed him to the floor. His face was utterly naked.

"You can't mean that!" he whispered.

"Why not? It's a good solution. You two can live here in the cottage, like princes!"

"Dina!" he said. His eyes fumbled for her. Blindly.

"Everything Stine puts her hand to turns out well," said Dina.

"No!"

"Why not?"

"You know why. I can't get married!"

"Are you going to go around acting like a fool all your life?"

He recoiled as if she had struck him. But said nothing.

"You dream too much, Tomas! I'm offering you a solution. It will be best for everyone."

"You don't like that I look in your direction," he said harshly.

"There's no future in looking in my direction."

"But I was good enough . . . before!"

"Don't talk about *before!*" she said sharply.

"You're cruel!"

"Do you call an offer like this cruel?"

"Yes," he said hoarsely. He put on his hat and wanted to leave.

"It's hard for you to be at Reinsnes without being married, don't you see?"

"When did that start to be true?"

"When I realized you're sneaking after me everywhere," she hissed softly.

He left, without her permission to do so.

Dina paced back and forth all afternoon, despite the fact that she had work to do.

The maid came to light the fire in the bedroom. But Dina screamed at her to get out of the house.

The cottage grew dark and quiet.

Tomas was sitting in the kitchen with Oline, eating his evening porridge, when Stine came to get something.

She glanced at him and blushed. Then left quickly.

The floor burned beneath Tomas. He stared as if he had never seen a door close behind anyone before.

Tomas slumped his shoulders and chewed his porridge thoroughly.

"Well?" said Oline. "Is the porridge cold?"

"No, not at all. Thanks very much," said Tomas, embarrassed.

"You don't look very happy."

"I don't?"

"And Stine looks the same way. What's going on?"

"Dina wants to marry us off!" he burst out, before he could collect his thoughts.

Oline shut her mouth tightly. The way she closed the oven drafts every night.

"To each other, or to someone else?" she asked, clearing her throat. As if the whole idea were new to her.

"To each other."

"Have you been . . . ?"

"No!" he said furiously.

"I see. . . ."

"You can't just marry off people," he whispered.

Oline made no comment and began rattling dishes on the table. Then she observed:

"She's getting more and more like the sheriff."

"Yes!" Tomas agreed. Then he became lost in thought again.

"Doesn't she want you? Stine, that is?"

"I can't imagine she would," he said, bewildered.

"Would it really be so bad?"

"So bad?"

"It might be a good solution, you know."

He pushed his coffee cup away, grabbed his cap, and rushed out the door.

"The hell with the good solutions here at Reinsnes," he growled from the entryway.

The next morning, Tomas was nowhere to be found. Nobody knew where he had gone.

Three days later, he came down the mountain, his clothes tattered and his breath reeking of alcohol.

He helped himself to food and drink in the kitchen, then went to bed and slept for twenty-four hours.

He was awakened by Dina, shaking him. At first he thought he was dreaming. Then he stared in amazement and heaved himself into a sitting position.

Pay attention to Dina Grønelv, he thought bitterly, when he realized who was there. For years, he had meekly gathered just a look, a gesture, a word from that direction.

"Well, Tomas, you've certainly indulged yourself. Drinking and carousing! And right before Christmas, when everything needs to be done," she said calmly.

Her words thundered straight into his dulled brain.

"Aren't you afraid you'll be asked to leave?"

"No," he said firmly.

The forthright answer took her aback slightly, but she quickly recovered.

"Get to work now!"

"What does the mistress of Reinsnes recommend? Should I take her from the front or the back?"

Outside, the wind played havoc with a tin pail.

She struck him. Hard. It took several seconds before his nose began to bleed. He sat in bed, looking at her. The stream of blood increased. A red, warm river flowed down his lip and chin. Dripped onto his open shirt, after coloring the golden hairs on his chest red.

He did not wipe away the blood. Just sat there with an ugly grimace and let it flow.

She cleared her throat. Even so, her words came out like an avalanche of stones.

"Wipe your nose, and get to work!"

"You wipe it!" he said hoarsely, and stood up.

There was something threatening about him. Something completely unfamiliar. She no longer owned his thoughts.

"Why should I wipe your nose?"

"Because you made it bleed!"

"That's true," she said, unexpectedly gently, and looked around the room. She spied a towel, fetched it, and held it out to him with a sneer.

He did not take it. So she went over to him and carefully wiped his nose. To slight avail. The blood kept flowing.

Suddenly something flashed between them! Shone like flames in the dim, spartan room. A raw, keen desire! Sister to hate and revenge.

He smelled of drunkenness and the stable. She smelled of ink, rose water, and fresh sweat.

Dina pulled back her hand as if she had burned herself. Then she retreated out the door, with nostrils flaring.

"You made it bleed!" he shouted after her furiously.

The first Sunday after New Year, the banns were read for Stine and Tomas.

"Why would anyone want to have dreams?" asked Oline more than once. "Either they last only a short time and end unhappily, or you drag them with you all your life."

Dina carried the cello to the master bedroom again. The intermezzo in the cottage was over.

I am Dina. People exist. I meet them. Sooner or later, our ways part. That is what I know.

Once, I saw something I had never seen before. Between two middle-aged people, a bishop and his wife. Love is a wave that exists only for the beach it encounters. I am no beach. I am Dina. I observe such waves. I cannot let myself overflow.

Benjamin had gotten used to not living in the same house as his mother. He decided on his own to move into the cottage. Had to forestall Dina from making the same decision.

He had grown the past year. But would never be a big person. Quiet and observant, he moved about asking questions and responding like an oracle. With few, pointed words. He no longer clung to Dina. Something had changed after she went to Tromsø. Or was it after Mother Karen died?

They could not see that he specifically mourned her or missed her. But he often stole into Mother Karen's room, without Hanna.

There, everything remained as before. The bed was made. The decorative pillows were plumped and placed against the headboard. Like motionless wings of an angel that had flown away.

The bookcase still had the key in the door. Benjamin opened it and forgot everything else until someone called him.

He learned easily but avoided work whenever possible. He went to the main house now only in order to get books, or to sit cross-legged on the floor, reading by Mother Karen's bookcase. Although Johan had taken the philosophical and religious works, the novels were still there.

Benjamin read aloud for Hanna. They sat for hours by the white stove in the cottage with Mother Karen's books.

Stine did not bother them if they behaved well. Occasionally she said:

"There's not much wood left." Or: "The water bucket is empty."

Benjamin knew it was his job to be the chore boy when nobody else was around. Sometimes he was surprised when he came from the warehouses or the beach and saw the large white house. Then he quickly shifted his gaze to the dovecote in the middle of the courtyard and thought about something else.

Now and then, he knew he felt pain but he could not tell where.

Benjamin had noticed many things without really being aware of them. Such as that Tomas had always been Dina's. Just like Blackie and the cello. Until Stine and Tomas got married and moved into the cottage.

They had not spent many winter evenings sitting by the tile stove, doing their separate tasks, before Benjamin understood that Tomas no longer belonged to Dina. And did not belong to Stine either, even if he slept with her. Tomas belonged to himself.

But the idea that you should belong to yourself when you lived in the cottage was frightening to Benjamin. Dina and the cello were distant sounds in the master bedroom.

Benjamin was in the cottage to learn to belong to himself.

Chapter 18

He who finds a wife finds a good thing,
and obtains favor from the Lord.

— Proverbs 18 : 22

*A*nders went to the Lofoten Islands in January to buy fish. He had no sooner returned than he began preparing for the trip to Bergen. His life was one long sea voyage. And if he began to feel restless after a few weeks ashore, he did not trouble anyone with that.

Sometimes travelers arrived on the steamboat and needed lodging. But not as often as in the past few years.

At the Reinsnes store, however, people crossed the threshold constantly. Dina's flour imports from Archangel proved to be more than a bright idea. She earned large sums by saving flour until shortages occurred in the spring. Then the rumor spread that at Reinsnes you could get flour, fishing equipment, and various necessities in exchange for dried fish. So Anders was given firm commitments for fish shipments to Bergen.

Stine no longer ate in the main house. She prepared food for her husband and the children. But did her other tasks as always. Her smooth, continuous movements kept one from noticing that she worked from early morning until late at night.

She changed only imperceptibly, over a long time. It began the day she moved her few humble belongings to the cottage. She smiled as she carried the kettles she used for cooking salves. She crooned something in the strange language she rarely used as she transferred herbs from the cellar in the main house to the cellar in the cottage.

First she scoured and cleaned. Swept and dried. Got Hanna and Benjamin to help her cut elaborate shelf borders from colored paper. Aired the bedclothes. Placed all the household goods Dina had given her in cupboards and chests of drawers.

Stine's home was open to everyone. Whether they came out of curiosity or to seek advice about sickness and sores.

In many ways she outshone Oline. People were more likely to stop at Stine's after being at the store than to visit the blue kitchen in the main house. They came, first and foremost, for her herb drinks and salves. But also for reasons that nobody said aloud.

Stine's hands were warm and willing. Her eyes could glisten with dark joy. This spring she had more eider ducks than ever. She fed them and plucked their down. Built shelters with boards and boxes to protect them from the wind and rain while they brooded on their nests. And later she gathered the chicks in her coarse burlap apron and carried them to the seashore.

For several weeks after his marriage, Tomas was a half-stunned ox. Then he could resist no longer. His face slowly grew smooth and unwrinkled. As if Stine had washed him, morning and evening, in herb decoction and rose water. Or had used unseen powers.

When her stomach rounded visibly under her apron, Tomas began to smile. Carefully at first. But soon he glowed as brightly as the sun and his bronzed arms when he followed the plow.

Tomas initially thought it was Lapp magic. Because as the days and nights passed, it was impossible not to be affected. Warmth streamed from her.

In the beginning, she never tried to touch him. She cared for his clothes, set food before him. Was concerned that he got rest. Came to the fields with sour milk in a pail. Put it down with a gentle greeting and left again.

She had never received anything without having to pay for it. On their wedding night he took her quickly and angrily, while he thought about her having borne two illegitimate children.

Just before he emptied himself, he lay between Dina's ample thighs. Afterward, Stine covered him and wished him good night. But Tomas was not able to sleep. Lay awake looking at her face in the dim light.

The weather had been bitterly cold. Suddenly he saw that she was shivering. So he got up and put wood in the stove. To make her happy. Because he suddenly realized that she was a human being. And that she had not asked to have him in her bed.

He soon discovered that if it was a Lapp spell she had put on him, he wanted it to continue.

With shy happiness, he came to her more and more frequently. Experienced the wonder of never being rejected.

He quickly learned that the more gently he touched her, the more willing and warm she became. And even if her strange eyes lived their own life, she was with him. Day and night.

Meanwhile, the child grew within her. A legitimate child with a father both genetically and on paper. If originally she had not longed for precisely that man, she never let anyone hear that. If she knew that she had inherited him from her mistress, as she had inherited underclothing and dresses and various fragrant pieces of soap, she made him her own.

The day Stine revealed she was pregnant, Tomas leaned toward her and whispered unmanly words. Without feeling he should be ashamed. He did not know much about love. Other than that it meant waiting for Dina's word, Dina's nod, Dina's horseback rides, Dina's good humor, Dina's all-devouring desire. Such love had subdued him and made him hide all during his youth. Suddenly he was free of it.

There were days when he did not remember who owned Reinsnes. Days in the fields. In the barn. In the woods. For he was working for Stine and the child.

Chapter 19

Do not call conspiracy all that this people call conspiracy, and do not fear what they fear, nor be in dread.

— Isaiah 8 : 12

One day the sheriff's outrigger glided up to the pier unexpectedly. He was grave and gray and wanted to speak with Dina privately.

"What's happened?" she asked.

"They've arrested a Russian in Trondheim," he said.

Dina bridled.

"What sort of Russian?"

"That Leo Zjukovski, who's been a guest at Reinsnes a few times."

"Why did they arrest him?"

"Espionage! And offense to his majesty!"

"Espionage?"

"The bailiff said they've been watching him a long time. He even made it very easy for them: they arrested him near the prison. After he'd gone to the prison to get a package. Apparently the prison director knew he'd come, sooner or later. The chief magistrate thinks the previous director was a courier for subversive political activities. This Leo Zjukovski walked right into the trap. The package had been there a long time. . . . It apparently contained a coded message."

The sheriff had been speaking in a low, threatening voice. Now it became a deep growl:

"And the prison director said Dina Grønelv from Reinsnes brought the package!"

"What's this all about?"

"About the fact that my daughter can be accused of disgraceful espionage! That she was on familiar terms with a spy! And this man even ate and drank with the sheriff!"

Dina's face was cut from an old sail. Her narrowed eyes twitched nervously. Peered from the window to the sheriff and back again.

"But the book, my dear sheriff. The book I delivered was just Pushkin's poetry! Leo and I entertained ourselves by reading it together. Of course, he had to translate it, because I don't understand Russian."

"What foolishness and fabrication!"

"It's true!"

"You must say that you didn't deliver the book!"

"But I did deliver the book!"

The sheriff sighed and put his hand to his heart.

"Why do you do such ridiculous things?" he shouted.

"The underlining we did in the book isn't a secret spy code. It's just words I tried to learn."

"There was other underlining, you see. The code must have been there already."

Neither the sheriff, nor his heart, could stand to have his daughter involved in such a thing. At first he simply refused to state in his report that she had delivered the book in Trondheim. He stared at Dina from a wide crack with bushy white eyebrows above it. Icy cold. As if she had offended him personally by admitting she had left that unfortunate package at the prison. He refused to have his name implicated in any scandal!

"I must remind you that I have Jacob's name! And it's my duty not to conceal information. You surely know that, don't you?"

He suddenly collapsed, as if someone had hit him in the back of the neck with a large steak hammer. One could almost hear the thud before his head cracked against his breast. He held both corners of his mustache and pressed them together over his mouth with a humble expression.

In the end, he retreated and decided to take the whole situation as a gift. It would make him, the father and sheriff, very important in the bailiff's eyes. In fact, in the eyes of the whole Norwegian court system!

It would be a great satisfaction to shake things up and prove that this was all a ridiculous mistake. That the man was just a harmless vagabond who did not like to work. A spy? Nonsense! War and famine made people so suspicious of everything from the east. While the English and French went free, even though they actually caused all the trouble. He berated the Germans too, just for good measure. Russians, on the other hand, had never done anything wrong in the north except get drunk, sing in harmony, and ship grain!

The sheriff wrote his terse report. Dina signed her statement.

But the Crimean War continued in Dina's head. The cello music that evening showed she was trying to ride all the way to Trondheim.

The sheriff thought her testimony would help to free the fellow. No question about it. After all, he had even helped put out a terrible barn fire at Reinsnes. Thanks to his cleverness and courage.

Dina was summoned to Ibestad to testify before the chief magistrate. About Pushkin's unfortunate book of poems and all the underlining that was supposed to be a code.

The chief magistrate received Dina and the sheriff politely. A clerk and two witnesses were already in place. After the initial formalities, the magistrate read aloud from his documents.

A translation of the underlined words apparently showed that Leo Zjukovski accused Oscar I, as well as respected citizens and theater director Knut Bonde, of being in league with Napoleon III. Moreover, he tried to get unnamed persons to support a plot against the Swedish king!

Dina laughed heartily. The chief magistrate must forgive her. Her feelings about the Swedish king were supported by Mother Karen's posthumous reputation. After all, Mother Karen had sailed Reinsnes cargo boats under the Dano-Norwegian flag!

The sheriff was shamefaced. But since he was involved in the case as a father, he could not express himself. Far less, make Dina stop laughing.

"Your testimony will be written down word for word and sent to Trondheim," the magistrate warned.

"I realize that."

Calmly, he began to question her. She answered briefly and clearly. But ended almost every answer with a question.

The magistrate smoothed his mustache and drummed his fingers on the table.

"Are you saying the whole thing is merely private, entertaining insults against his majesty?"

"Absolutely!"

"But the Russian did not testify to that. He did not mention Dina Grønelv's name in connection with the code. Admitted only that she evidently delivered the book of her own free will, without his knowledge."

"I guess he wants to keep me out of it."

"Do you know this man well?"

"As well as one knows most guests who spend a night or two. Many people come ashore at Reinsnes."

"But you swear this man did the underlining in the above-mentioned book during a so-called party game?"

"Yes."

"Were there witnesses?"

"No; unfortunately not."

"Where did it occur?"

"At Reinsnes."

"But why did you bring the book to the asylum?"

"Because I was in Trondheim, traveling with my cargo boat. He had forgotten his book, and I knew he was going to Trondheim."

"How did you know that?"

"He mentioned it, I think."

"Why was he going there?"

"We didn't talk about that."

"But it's an unpleasant place for a woman to deliver a book, isn't it?"

"It's not particularly pleasant for men either!"

"Can you explain why a book would be so important to this man?"

"It's his favorite book. As Your Honor is well aware, people who like books often drag them along. Mother Karen brought two large bookcases to Reinsnes when she arrived. Leo Zjukovski knew Pushkin. He always brings his books when he travels. I'm sure he explained that himself."

The chief magistrate cleared his throat and glanced at his papers. Then he nodded.

"Who is this Pushkin?"

"He wrote the poetry, Your Honor. He wrote the book!"

"Yes, of course. Leo Zjukovski could not convincingly explain where he came from or where he was going. Do you have any idea?"

She considered the question carefully. Then shook her head.

"Was the suspect at Reinsnes just before he went to Trondheim?"

"No. The last time he was a guest at Reinsnes was the spring of 1854."

"This . . . this poetry book has been at the asylum all that time."

"Your Honor must ask the asylum director about that. But one thing is certain. Someone broke Dina Grønelv's seal on a private package."

"Hmm . . ."

"Isn't that illegal, Your Honor?"

"That depends upon . . ."

"But, Your Honor! Before they broke my wax seal, they didn't know what was in the package. So surely it was against the law to break into another person's property?"

"I can't answer that, in this case."

"And the letter? Where's the letter?"

"Letter?" asked the chief magistrate with interest.

"There was a letter in the package. To Leo Zjukovski. From me."

"I'm the one asking the questions. You are just to answer them."

"Very well, Your Honor."

"I haven't heard about any letter. I'll start a search for it. What did it say?"

"It was private."

"But this is . . . a court hearing."

"It said: 'When Mohammed won't come to the mountain, the mountain comes to Mohammed.' And: 'Barabbas must come to Reinsnes if he's going to escape the cross again.' "

"What does that mean? Is it a code?"

"If so, it has little to do with the Swedish king."

"You must remember that you're talking about the king of Norway and Sweden!"

"Of course."

"What do those words mean?"

"It's a reminder that we're still as hospitable as ever at Reinsnes."

"Was that all that was written?"

"Yes. And then my signature."

"Did you and this Leo Zjukovski have any . . . any friendship beyond normal hospitality?"

Dina looked at the magistrate.

"Will you please explain what you mean?"

"I mean, was it usual for you to exchange letters and codes?"

"No."

"I've heard that you've traveled quite a bit the past two summers. Both north and south. Have you met Leo Zjukovski on your travels?"

Dina did not answer immediately. Over in the corner, the sheriff stretched his neck. He did not feel well.

"No!" she said firmly.

"Do you believe this man is innocent of the alleged actions for which he was arrested?"

"I don't know why he was arrested."

"For having in his possession a suspicious book in Russian which experts have carefully examined and have deciphered. The codes show a hostile attitude toward the king and toward highly respected citizens and insinuate that the king and those citizens have plotted to draw the Nordic lands into the Crimean War."

"On which side?"

"That is irrelevant to this case," said the judge, somewhat disconcerted. "But Napoleon III is our ally. Please just answer, and don't ask questions."

"We've been involved in the war a long time here in the north. Your Honor can arrest me as well for the coded messages which Leo Zjukovski is accused of carrying."

"What do you mean by 'involved' in the war?"

"We've sailed to Archangel and bought grain, to keep from starving to death. As far as I know, the king hasn't bothered to ask how we're faring. And now he wants to drag us into a war that, judging from its name, they should be fighting elsewhere — not by bombarding Russians on the Finnish coast."

"Please, keep to the matter at hand!"

"Yes, Your Honor. As soon as I understand what the matter at hand is."

"Dina Grønelv, you testify that you participated in creating the codes?"

"It was an enjoyable way to learn Russian words."

"What do these . . . these codes say?"

"Your Honor read it at the beginning of this hearing, but I don't remember it word for word. We've talked about many things since then. And much water has flowed into the sea since Leo Zjukovski was at Reinsnes and taught me Russian."

"You're not very cooperative."

"I think it's crazy to arrest a man because he made fun of the Swedish king, while you don't lift a finger to reprimand those who broke Dina Grønelv's seal! And nobody will win the Crimean War! Except those who earn money from it."

Finally, the magistrate decided to end the hearing. The court proceedings were read. She accepted them. And everything was over.

"Am I charged with anything?" she asked.

"No," replied the judge. He was obviously tired.

"How will this hearing affect the charges against Leo Zjukovski?"

"It's hard to know. But your testimony weakens the code accusation, that much I can say."

"Good!"

"You sympathize with this Russian?"

"I don't like it when my guests get arrested because they try to be friendly and teach me Russian words. I won't deny that."

The chief magistrate, the sheriff, and Dina parted in a spirit of complete understanding.

The sheriff was content. He felt as if he had personally put everything in order! Persuaded first one person and then another. Come with firsthand information to both the bailiff and Dina. So the hearing could occur promptly and properly.

Today Dina was his daughter.

A rainbow curved over Reinsnes when Dina arrived from Ibestad. As the *faering* boat gradually drew nearer, one building after another slipped away and became shrouded in mist.

One end of the rainbow's arc was fastened to the cottage roof, the other was hidden in the sound.

She peered toward land. Today she was sailing alone.

Dina stood at her bedroom window, watching Stine and Tomas walk across the courtyard. Close together. It was late in April.

Nobody walked like that when people could see. Nobody!

They stopped by the dovecote. Turned their faces toward each other and smiled. Stine said something that Dina could not hear from the window. Then Tomas threw back his head and laughed.

Had anyone ever heard Tomas laugh?

He put his arm around Stine's waist. Then they strolled across the courtyard and into the cottage.

The woman behind the curtain drew a breath between her teeth. With a sharp hiss.

Then she turned away. Tramped across the room. To the stove, to the cello, back to the window.

The room grew darker and darker.

The newspapers carried articles about the Paris peace agreement. Russia licked its wounds without much honor. England licked its wounds without much triumph. And Sweden-Norway did not free the Finns. Indeed, Napoleon III was the only true victor.

One day Dina read in the newspaper that Julie Müller had died. She sent condolences to Mr. Müller. And received a long, sorrowful letter in which he said he wanted to sell everything he owned, including the horse, and emigrate to America.

Dina went to the flag knoll. Meanwhile, summer brought its blessings to Nordland.

Chapter 20

Then deep from the earth you shall speak,
from low in the dust your word shall come;
your voice shall come from the ground like the voice of a ghost,
and your speech shall whisper out of the dust.

— Isaiah 29 : 4

*B*lackie had a sore on his belly that would not heal. No one knew what caused it. The animal stood in the stable and seemed to be gnawing itself to pieces.

All Tomas's efforts to prevent the horse from tearing open the wound again with its stubborn yellow teeth did little good.

No one except Dina could get near the afflicted animal. It was obviously in pain, because the sore was infected. She put a basket over Blackie's muzzle. And each time it wanted to drink or eat, she stood there to make sure it did not tear the sore.

They heard the wild, furious whinnying night and day. And the pounding hooves in the stable made both people and animals uneasy.

Stine cooked salves to put on the sore. And Oline brought her porridge poultices.

But after a week, the horse lay down on the stable floor and refused to get up. It spit mucus over Dina when she approached, and bared its teeth to one and all.

The hoof nearest the sore lay under the animal. Its eyes were bloodshot.

Hanna and Benjamin were forbidden to go into the stable.

I am Dina. Human beings are so pitifully helpless. Nature is indifferent. Squanders all life. Never takes responsibility. Lets everything settle like slime on the surface. How can new life bear to begin in this mire? Slime begets slime endlessly, but nothing meaningful happens or is created. If only one person had raised himself from the mire and done something with his life! Just one . . .

The numbers and the notes are not subject to the mire. Are independent

430

of human knowledge. The numbers have a law, even if nobody writes it down. The notes will always be there. Whether or not we hear them.

But nature is slime. The rowan tree. The horse. Human beings. Risen from slime. To slime they shall return again. Everything has its day. Then it drowns in the mire.

I am Dina who is alone with an iron sledgehammer and a knife. And the horse. Do I know where to strike? Yes! Because I must. I am Dina who talks to Blackie. I am Dina who holds him around the neck. Who looks into his wild eyes. For a long time. I am Dina, who strikes. Deeply.

I am the woman who sits here in all this warm redness and receives the horse. Who sees its eyes slowly become glass and fog.

Tomas went to the stable to check on the horse, because everything got so quiet.

From a distance in the dim light, it appeared as if Dina had fresh, rain-wet rose petals strewn over her face and clothing. She sat on the floor holding the horse's head. Its large black body lay peacefully, the strong slim legs and hooves stretched out two by two.

The blood had gushed out in powerful spurts. Far up the wall and across the yellow hay on the floor.

"My God!" groaned Tomas. Then he took off his hat and sat with her.

She did not seem to realize he was there. Nonetheless, he stayed. Until the last trickling drops stiffened in the deep knife wound.

Then, slowly, she pulled herself free, placed the horse's head on the floor, and covered its eyes with its mane. She stood up then and brushed her hand across her forehead. Like a sleepwalker who awakens while still wandering.

Tomas got up too.

Dina gestured to him to keep his distance. Then she walked across the floor and outside, without shutting the door behind her. The sound of her iron cleats on the straw-covered floor echoed gently through the stable.

Then came the silence.

The sledgehammer and the knife were returned to their places. The stable was cleaned. The bloody working clothes were placed in the river, under a large rock. For the current carried every loose object to the sea.

*   *   *

431

Dina went to the washhouse and built a fire under the huge kettle. Sat on a stool close to the stove until the water was hot enough and steam began to rise toward the ceiling.

Then she crossed the room and bolted the door. Fetched the large metal washtub hanging on the wall and filled it. She took off her clothes slowly. As if performing a ritual.

She folded each piece of clothing to hide the bloodstains. As if she wanted to remove them by not having to look at them. Finally, she stepped naked into the steaming water.

The howl began somewhere outside her. Prepared itself in her throat. Broke loose and shattered everything around her. Until Hjertrud came and gathered up the pieces.

Chapter 21

I come to my garden, my sister, my bride,
I gather my myrrh with my spice,
I eat my honeycomb with my honey,
I drink my wine with my milk.
Eat, O friends, and drink:
drink deeply, O lovers!
— The Song of Solomon 5 : 1

*T*he day Dina was away in Kvæfjord, looking at a horse that had been recommended to her, Leo Zjukovski arrived with a small boat that chanced to sail from Strandsted. He did not have much baggage; just his sailor's sack and a travel bag. Peter the store manager, who had just closed for the night, met the stranger on the wharf.

When he realized this was not a late customer but an overnight guest, he told him to go to the main house.

Leo stood for a moment, looking at the rowan trees that lined the road to the house. Their branches teemed with crimson berries. But the wind had already taken all their leaves.

Then he walked between the rows of trees. Their leafless crowns sang softly. He paused at the front steps. And apparently changed his mind. Turned and walked around the house and in the back entryway. After tossing his sack and travel bag on the steps, he knocked. Soon he was inside the blue kitchen.

Oline recognized the man with the scar. At first she was shy and formal, as if she had never received guests at Reinsnes. She invited him into the parlor, but he politely declined. He wanted to sit with her, if it would not be a bother.

She stood for a moment with her hands hidden under her apron, but then she rushed over to him and thumped his chest.

"Thank you for the gift! I haven't gotten a present like that since I was a girl! Bless you. . . ."

433

She was so moved that she had to thump him even harder.

The gesture was unexpected, but he laughed and gave her a kiss on each cheek.

Embarrassed, she turned and began stoking the stove.

"To think you'd give me something so elegant as a lace collar!" she said. Perspiration sparkled on her face as she leaned over the wood hole in the stove.

"Have you worn the collar?" he asked.

"Oh, yes . . . but that's not what matters. I don't go many places, after all. And it's not proper to go around looking so fancy here in the kitchen."

"But you do dress up, now and then?"

"Yes," she said. To put an end to the questions.

"When did you last wear your collar?"

"Christmas Eve."

"That's a long time ago."

"Yes, but it's nice to have something that's not spoiled and worn out, you know."

He gave her a good-natured look behind her back. Then he began to ask how things were at Reinsnes.

The maids poked their heads through the pantry door, one after another. Leo shook hands with them. Oline ordered them to prepare the largest guest room. Brief orders. Just the key words. Which showed that the maids knew what needed to be done. And the real goal was to get them out of the kitchen.

Then she served coffee at the kitchen table. He went out to the steps to get his travel bag. And urged her to have some rum. Oline sat there glowing. Until he asked again how things were at Reinsnes.

"Mother Karen is no longer with us. . . . Died," said Oline, brushing her hand across her eyes.

"When did that happen?"

"Last fall. After Dina returned from Tromsø. Yes, she was in Tromsø to arrange to get flour from Archangel. . . . But of course Mr. Leo wouldn't know that."

Oline told about Mother Karen's death. And about Stine and Tomas, who were married and lived in the cottage and were expecting a little one.

"It seems I always arrive after a death," he murmured. "But that's good news about Stine and Tomas. . . . Strange, I didn't notice when I was here last. That something was brewing."

Oline looked embarrassed. But then she said:

"They didn't know much about it either. Dina thought it was a good solution. So that's what happened. And it seems to be a blessing for all of us. But not all women at Reinsnes are a blessing. . . ."

"What do you mean?"

"The mistress. I shouldn't say anything, I know. She's too hard. On herself too. She's got an iron knot somewhere. And she's not very happy! You can tell that. But I shouldn't say such things. . . ."

"That's all right. I think I understand."

"She killed her horse herself!"

"Why?"

"He was sick. Had a sore under his belly that got infected. He was old too, of course. But that she could . . ."

"She was fond of her horse?"

"It appeared so. But that she killed him herself!"

"Did she shoot it?"

"No; she stabbed it. Huff, huff!"

"But a horse wouldn't allow that!"

"Dina's horse did."

Oline's face suddenly became a wooden wall without a door or windows. She went to the stove to get the coffeepot and poured a cup for each of them.

Then she told him that he had gotten thinner and paler.

He smiled broadly and asked about the children.

"Benjamin is with his mother, for once. She probably needs him more, now that the horse is dead."

"For once?"

"Yes; that child hardly ever gets outside Reinsnes. Of course, many people come here. But a boy who'll be responsible for as much as he will be should see more of the world!"

"He's still young, after all." Leo smiled.

"Yes, yes . . . And Stine's going to have a little one in November. Then there'll be three children in the cottage. But none in the main house. It's not right that Benjamin isn't being brought up according to his status. Mother Karen wouldn't have liked it. She would have brought him back to the main house."

"Benjamin doesn't live with his mother?" Leo asked.

"No . . . he doesn't want to, I guess."

Leo regarded the woman in the apron.

"How are Benjamin and Dina traveling?"

"Oh, she's sailing a small boat alone. She's so stubborn about what she does. If Mother Karen had been alive, she wouldn't have allowed Dina to take the boy to sea without a man to help her."

"And Dina would have respected that order?"

"Respected or not respected . . . I don't know about that. But I'm sure she wouldn't have done it."

Oline suddenly realized she was talking to this stranger about things that should not be put into words. She blinked several times and wanted to change the subject.

It must be the lace collar he gave her? Or the fact that he asked so many questions? Or his eyes? She made excuses for herself and busily began filling a cookie plate and brushing crumbs from the embroidered tablecloth.

"And Johan? How is he?" Leo asked

"He has his small parish at Helgeland. I really don't know how he is. He doesn't write, now that Mother Karen is no longer here. He's become a complete stranger. To me too. But his health is better, I think . . . He wasn't well for a while."

"Are you worried?" he asked.

"Oh, yes. That's all I have to do now."

"Are you working hard?"

"No . . . I have such good help."

There was a pause.

"And Dina? When do you expect her?" he asked.

"Probably not before tomorrow," she said, observing the man out of the corner of her eye. "But Anders is coming from Strandsted this evening. He'll surely be glad to see Mr. Leo! Anders is outfitting both the cargo boat and the longboat for Lofoten fishing. And he's talking about sending both cargo boats to Bergen this spring. He's an enterprising fellow, if I may say so. Now that he's built a cabin on the longboat, he lives like a prince and sometimes fishes himself. Last year he sailed to the Lofotens with equipment and food to sell to the fishermen. And he came home with a full load of fish, liver, and roe, which he had either bought or caught himself!"

Dina rarely sailed alone. But this time it had turned out that way. She had such a hard look in her eyes that no one felt like asking to come along when she did not demand it. So she had only Benjamin for company.

He had been sitting on the flag knoll when she came to watch for the steamboat. Had greeted her the way he greeted people who stayed overnight or who came from the store to have coffee at Stine's.

His blue eyes peered at her. As though she were a thin layer of dust in the air. His face had begun to develop definite features, with sharp cheekbones and an angular chin. And his limbs were awkward and in the way. He had a bad habit of tightening his mouth into a thin line.

"You're looking for the steamboat too?" she had asked.

"Yes."

"Do think any travelers will come today?"

"No."

"Then why are you watching?"

"Because it's so ugly."

"You look at the steamboat because it's so ugly?"

"Yes."

Dina sat down on the flat stone by the flagpole. Politely, the boy moved well over to the side.

"There's room for both of us here, Benjamin."

She impulsively put her arm around his back, but he twisted away. Inconspicuously, as if he did not want to annoy her.

"Would you like to come along to Kvæfjord and look at a new horse?" she asked as the steamboat whistled.

He did not answer until the air was quiet again.

"That might be fun," he said in an artificially ordinary tone. As if he were afraid Dina would change her mind if he showed any pleasure.

"Then it's decided. We sail tomorrow."

They sat for a while and watched the men from the warehouse row out to the steamboat.

"Why did you stab Blackie?" he asked abruptly.

"He was sick."

"Couldn't he get well again?"

"Yes. But he could never be the same."

"Did that matter?"

"Yes."

"Why? You could get another horse to ride."

"No. I can't have a horse just standing in the stable while I ride another."

"But why did you do it yourself?"

"Because it was a serious matter."

"He could have kicked you to death."

"Yes."

"Why do you do things like that?"

"I do what I have to," she said, and stood up to leave.

Dina had asked his advice about buying the horse. They came to an agreement, at her instructions. The horse was not entirely satisfactory. It had shifty eyes and a narrow chest. When Dina sat astride it, the animal was very amenable, and that did not help. They did not buy it.

"Otherwise I'd need someone to sail home with you," said Dina easily. "It was probably intended that we go home together, you and I."

They spent the night at the sheriff's. In peace and tolerance.

The sheriff had gotten a message through the chief magistrate that Leo Zjukovski had been released a short time ago.

Dina received the news behind half-closed eyelids. Then she told Dagny she would like to take to Reinsnes the pictures of Hjertrud that Dagny and she had fought about all these years.

Dagny shifted uneasily. But agreed. It was a good solution.

"And the brooch. Hjertrud's brooch. The one you wear when you want to be elegant. I'd like to take care of that too," Dina continued.

The sheriff and his sons sat on pins and needles. But Benjamin did not seem to be concerned that they were sitting on a powder keg. He looked at everybody, one after another. As if he had discovered something interesting in a picture book.

The moment passed. Like a gust of wind that changed direction.

Dina left with the brooch and the pictures.

It was a bright fall day. With favorable winds.

Benjamin was proud as a rooster. He had been at the helm much of the voyage. Here at sea, the boy seemed content. Almost happy. And they talked about many things on the way home.

Dina saw him! Heard what he had to say. The whole time, she answered his questions very seriously. About Mother Karen. About the horse. About studying for something important when he was old enough. About who made decisions at Reinsnes. About why Anders would get the cargo boat if Dina died. All the things Benjamin had heard when the grown-ups did not think he had been given ears like other people. All the questions they did not answer when he asked.

Dina answered. Sometimes he was no wiser when she finished. But that did not matter. Because she answered.

In a few instances, she said she did not know. When he asked if he could come along the next time she sailed somewhere. Or when he asked if Johan would come to Reinsnes again.

"I don't care whether Johan comes home," he said.

"Why?"

"I don't know."

She dropped the subject and did not ask any more questions.

They sailed almost all the way to the pier.

"You're as good at the helm as Anders," said Dina, when the boat reached the first rocks.

Benjamin beamed for a moment. Then he hopped from the boat like a man and pulled it to a large rock so Dina could step onto the beach without getting her feet wet.

"You're damn good at sailing," he said, and turned to take the travel bags she handed him from the stern.

His smile was a rare gift. But she was no longer accepting Benjamin's gifts. Her eyes were somewhere on the hill.

A man came down the tree-lined road, wearing a wide-brimmed black felt hat. He raised his hand in greeting.

She set down the travel bags in the seaweed. Then, slowly and purposefully, she began picking her way among the rocks. Across the high-water mark. Between the warehouses. Onto the gravel path. Under the arch of trees that guarded the road to the main house.

At the end, she ran. Stopped short, one step away from him. Then he held out his arms. And she was in them.

The boy on the beach lowered his head and pulled the boat onto the shore.

It was heavy.

They had come to the dessert course. The autumn darkness hid in the corners. For they did not spare candles this evening.

The tutor and Peter, the store manager, had taken little part in the conversation. Anders and Leo had done most of the talking. Dina's eyes were a bonfire.

Stine did not sit at the table. Had not done so since her marriage to Tomas. She had renounced that status of her own free will. For Tomas would never be invited to the festive table in the dining room of the main house.

She moved to and fro, made sure nothing was lacking. Despite her large abdomen, her movements were as lithe and quick as an animal's.

Leo had greeted her warmly as a member of the household. But she was politely reserved. As if she wanted to protect herself, to avoid questions.

No one mentioned the prison asylum or espionage activities. But the war came up in the conversation. Inevitably.

"Are they satisfied with the new czar in Russia?" asked Anders.

"Opinions differ about that, of course. But it's a long time since I heard from Saint Petersburg. I'm sure the czar made the best of a lost cause. And unlike his father, he isn't educated simply as a military man. On the contrary, all during his youth one of his teachers was the poet Vasily Zjukovski."

"A relative of yours, Leo?" Dina asked quickly.

"That could be." He smiled.

"You think one's teachers are important?" Dina wondered, with a glance at Angell, the tutor.

"It would seem so."

"I have Lorch," said Dina thoughtfully.

"The man who taught you to play the cello and the piano?" asked Angell.

"Yes."

"Where is he now?"

"Here and there."

Stine was in the room preparing the after-dinner coffee cups. She raised her head for a moment at Dina's reply. Then calmly left the room. Anders looked clearly amazed. But said nothing.

"One realizes that one may have an influence," said the tutor.

"Absolutely," said Leo.

"Do you think the Crimean War was lost in advance because the soldiers hadn't been taught to fight?" the tutor asked with interest.

"A war with no meaning for those who must fight it is always lost in advance. War is the ultimate result of people becoming so frightened they stop talking."

"That's the ethical side of it," the tutor remarked.

"You can't avoid the ethical side," said Leo.

"Wasn't the peace agreement actually a dependence agreement for the Russians?" Anders wondered.

"A thinking Russian is the most independent being in the world," said Leo good-naturedly. "But Russia is no single voice. It's a choir!"

Anders liked dessert, but he put his spoon down for a moment.

Dina's mind was elsewhere. She stared straight ahead and did not respond to the looks they gave her. Finally, she took her napkin and wiped her mouth.

"There must be a key in the door someplace," she said blankly. "It's just that I can't see it. . . ."

"Leo, what do you think of the Scandinavianist idea of unifying the Nordic countries under one flag?" asked the tutor.

"It depends on what you mean by the Nordic countries," he replied evasively.

"There's already enough foolishness on the map. You can't smelt gold and ashes together. They'll separate as soon as they cool," said Anders crisply.

"I'm not so sure. Nations must see beyond themselves. People who see nothing but themselves are lost," said Leo slowly, examining his spoon.

Dina looked surprised and then laughed. The others stared down at the table in embarrassment.

"Will the mistress of Reinsnes perform one last service for an old, battle-worn Russian?" he asked pleasantly.

"That depends on what it is."

"Play some of the music I sent?"

"Yes, if you'll go with me to look for the bear that killed two sheep above the canyon last week," she said quickly.

"Agreed! Do you have a gun?"

"Yes; Tomas does."

Dina rose and gathered her dark-blue Canton flannel skirts around her Joselin corset and sat down at the piano. Leo went with her, while the other men seated themselves inside the open doors of the smoking parlor.

Their hands were thorns and live embers when they brushed each other.

"Some pieces are harder to play than others," she said.

"But you've had plenty of time to practice. . . ."

"Yes; I can't complain about that," she said sharply.

"May I make a request?"

"Yes."

"Then I'd like to hear something for a moonstruck man. The *Moonlight* Sonata by Beethoven."

"You forgot to send that."

"No, I sent it. Sonata number fourteen," he explained.

"You're wrong! Sonata number fourteen is called *Sonata quasi una fantasia*," she countered condescendingly.

He positioned himself between her and the men in the smoking parlor, so he had her eyes to himself. His scar was very pale this evening. Or perhaps it was because the man himself was so pale.

"We're both right. The sonata was originally given the name that's on your music. But an author renamed it the *Moonlight* Sonata. I like that name very much. . . . Because it's music for a moonstruck man."

"Maybe. But I prefer Sonata number twenty-three, the *Appassionata*."

"But play for *me* first," he said in a low voice.

She did not reply. But found the music and began playing. The opening tones were a grating protest. Then the notes floated through the room like caresses.

As usual, the doors to the kitchen and pantry were opened, and all the noisy bustling ceased. Oline and the maids moved like shadows past the open doors.

Dina had closed her face. But her fingers were sly weasels in white winter coats. They flew out of the batiste ruche cuffs with great energy.

The Russian stood behind her, audaciously resting his green eyes on her hair and his hands on the back of her chair.

Anders sat where he could see Dina's profile. He raised a steady hand and silently lit a cigar. His face shone in bright contrast to the dark wall. The furrow between his brows made him impregnable. Though he still looked friendly.

For a brief moment, he met Leo's glance. Openly. Then he nodded to the man. As if they had been playing a game of chess, which Anders had lost with complete equanimity.

Anders had always been an observer. Of his own and others' lives. He calculated months in his head, from the time Leo was last at Reinsnes to the voyage across Fold Sea. Then he bowed his head and let his thoughts rise toward the ceiling with the cigar smoke.

Epilogue

Do not gaze at me because I am swarthy,
because the sun has scorched me.
My mother's sons were angry with me,
they made me the keeper of the vineyards;
but, my own vineyard I have not kept!
Tell me, you whom my soul loves,
where you pasture your flock,
where you make it lie down at noon;
for why should I be like one who wanders
beside the flocks of your companions?
— The Song of Solomon 1 : 6–7

*O*ne by one, candles were snuffed in the buildings at Reinsnes. In the main entry, a pair of wax candles flickered gently in heavy, wrought-iron candlesticks.

Dina and Leo took a late stroll after everyone had gone to bed. The two large aspens by the garden fence already stood naked against the violet sky. The crushed shells around Mother Karen's heart-shaped flower bed were a sea of tiny dead bones in the moonlight. Autumn was in the air.

They turned their steps toward the summerhouse, as if by mutual consent. Raw air met them when they opened the flimsy door. The colored glass panes gleamed in the light from Dina's lantern. She was wearing a coat and a shawl. He was not as warmly dressed. But warm enough for the moment.

The moment she set the lantern on the table, he threw two hungry arms around her.

"Thank you!" he said.

"For what?"

"For giving a false witness!"

Their bodies were trees in a storm. Forced to stand close together.

To bite into each other, deeper and deeper with each gust of wind. Unable to admit pain.

"Was that why they released you?"

"It helped. Plus, the code was just a harmless one."

"That stood for something else?"

"It had to be read by people who know the double meanings in Russian."

He kissed her, holding her head between his hands.

The roof split, and heaven descended on them like a speckled black dove. Red lightning struck in the colored glass panes. And the lantern went out by itself. A seagull was an agile red ghost through the window, and the green moon drifted past. Round and full.

"You came!" she said, when she caught her breath.

"You got the hat?"

"Yes."

"And still you doubted?"

"Yes."

"I've longed . . . ," he whispered, his mouth against her throat. "I sat in prison and longed for you."

"What was the prison like?"

"We won't talk about that now."

"Was it the first time?"

"No."

"When was the time before that?"

"In Russia."

"Why?"

"Dina! Do I need to kiss you all the time, to stop your questions?"

"Yes! Why did you come, Leo?"

"Because I still love a skipper's widow named Dina Grønelv."

She sighed loudly. Like an old farmhand when evening finally comes after a long day in the fields. Then she bit his cheek.

"What does it mean, when Leo Zjukovski loves?"

"That I want to know your soul. And that I want to repeat the blessing from the organ loft through all eternity."

As though he had given a password, she rose and drew him with her.

A darkened lantern remained on the table.

And they went straight to the blessing.

*   *   *

At three o'clock in the morning, Lorch's cello sang in the master bedroom. Anders turned in his bed. The moon cast a lonely shadow of the window crosspiece on him. He decided to take a trip to Namsos to buy lumber before winter. But he did not sleep until early morning.

Benjamin heard Lorch's cello too. The notes floated across the courtyard into the cottage.

He had seen the dinner party through the parlor windows. The tall, dark man with the ugly scar had looked at Dina. As if he owned her.

Stine had called him inside in plenty of time for him to change his clothes and join the group in the main house.

But Benjamin Grønelv had sailed from Fagerness that day. And had been abandoned on the beach.

Dina would have to bring him to the table herself!

He knew she would not do that.

Leo followed her into the master bedroom. Like the leader of an army who finally enters the triumphal chariot, having conquered the largest city in the land. He had already removed her coat and shoes in the entry downstairs.

The black stove rumbled faintly. Annette had started a fire early in the evening.

Dina lighted the candles in the candelabra on the mirrored table. Extinguished the lamp.

He stood watching while she began to undress. When her bodice lay on the floor, he sighed, moving his hands in a circle over her bare shoulders.

She took off her shift, and her breasts tumbled out. Prisoners released into his hands. Shining, each with its dark protrusion growing beneath his fingertips. He leaned over and drank from them.

She fumbled with the waistband of her skirt. There was a soft rustling of material. An eternity of material. Finally, she stood in just her pantalets.

He let his hands glide down her hips and sighed again. He found all the forms he was seeking. Warm skin through the finest East Indian cotton percale. It drove him wild. And they were both still on their feet.

She got free and took off his vest as she gazed into his eyes. Loosened his neck scarf and removed it. Then his shirt.

He stood with his eyes half closed and enjoyment showing in every feature. The wide leather belt with a brass buckle. Leather trousers. She leaned over him and around him. Her fingers were calm and warm. At last he stood naked before her.

Then she sank to her knees and hid her face against his groin. She owned him and took possession. With her mouth and hands.

He lifted the large woman onto his hips. His arms trembled from the exertion. At first he moved his hips only slightly.

A cooing, pleasurable movement. A black grouse pressing its partner before coupling. Then, slowly, he thrust into her. Drew her body close, like a mighty shield against all danger.

She responded by putting her arms and thighs around him. And holding him tight. Until he grew calm. Then she lifted her breast to his mouth and clung to him with strong arms.

He was a cylinder in a huge machine. Gliding. Heavy. Deep.

The ride began. Thirst and hunger.

Desire!

Finally, he laid her on the floor. Waited, then stole upon her.

His hips were so firm! His breathing so exciting! His spear so exhaustive! He rode her toward a corner, seductively forcing all the notes to a crescendo.

When she threw back her head and plummeted endlessly, he held her hips and rode into her.

She welcomed him.

Their trembling flanks merged, and they became one. Bore each other's weight in a Gordian knot as red flames leaped in the black stove.

> Catch us the foxes,
> the little foxes
> that spoil the vineyards,
> for our vineyards are in blossom.
> My beloved is mine and I am his,
> he pastures his flock among the lilies.
> Until the day breathes
> and the shadows flee,
> turn, my beloved, be like a gazelle,
> or a young stag upon rugged mountains.
> — The Song of Solomon 2 : 15–17

When Annette came to light the fire, she found the door locked. She trudged into the guest room and discovered that no one had slept in the bed.

Then she went to the kitchen to see Oline. Stood shyly with her hands under her sackcloth apron.

"Why are you standing there like that?" demanded Oline. "Aren't you going to finish lighting the stoves?"

"The master bedroom is locked!"

"Well, then, light the stove in the guest room, and be done with it! Anders is already outside, so you don't have to . . ."

"There isn't anybody in the guest room!"

Oline turned and looked squarely at the girl. Her eyes flashed behind large, round pupils.

"Well, you can certainly start the fire even if nobody's there! Are you afraid of ghosts, in broad daylight?"

"But . . ."

"No buts!" snapped Oline, giving the coffeepot a shove on the stove that sent coffee grounds sloshing from the spout.

"What should I do about the stove in the master bedroom?"

"What should I do? What should I do?" Oline mimicked. "Have you ever heard of anyone lighting a fire through a locked door?"

"No."

"Well, then! Now stop gaping! And not a word!"

Oline went over to the girl and hissed into her face:

"Not a word to anyone about empty beds! Do you understand?"

"Yes . . ."

Benjamin stopped Dina when she came into the courtyard.

"Are we going sailing today?"

"No; not today, Benjamin."

"Are you going sailing with the Russian?"

"No."

"What are you going to do, then?"

"Go with the Russian. Hunting."

"Women don't go hunting."

"I do."

"Can I come along?"

"No."

"Why?"

"We can't have children running around in the bushes when we're going to shoot a bear."

"I'm not a child!"

"What are you, then?"

"I'm Benjamin of Reinsnes."

Dina smiled and gripped the back of his neck.

"That's true. One of these days I'll teach you to shoot with the Lapp rifle."

"Today?"

"No; not today."

He turned quickly and ran down to the boathouses.

Dina went to the stable and asked Tomas if she could borrow his rifle.

He gave her a long look, smiled bitterly, and nodded without a word. Then he brought the powderhorn and its pouch and took the rifle from the wall.

"The Russian won't get anything with this. He's only used to a pistol."

"So you know all about what weapons Mr. Leo uses?"

"No; but he could hardly be used to a Lapp rifle!"

"But you are?"

450

"I know this rifle in and out. It's got a good sight. And nobody can get a better shot. . . ."

Dina squirmed like a snake.

"Perhaps all that shooting isn't necessary?" she said lightly.

"No; hunting is fine in itself," he said.

"What do you mean?"

She moved close to him. They were alone in the stable.

"I don't mean anything. Just that you're not so particular about shooting what you intended when you're hunting."

"Rabbit hunting," he added, looking her straight in the eye.

She took the rifle and the powder horn and left.

They walked up the path toward the grouse woods. She took the lead. Turned constantly, smiling like a young girl. She wore a short jacket and a homespun skirt that reached to her ankles. Her hair was tied with a ribbon at the back of her head. She carried the Lapp rifle easily, as if it were a feather in her hand.

He observed her from behind. She glittered in the sunshine.

The first frost had left its traces. The lingonberry patches had an iron tinge. Red berries hung heavy with juice among oily leaves.

Neither of them looked for bears. Nor did they see the boy who trudged in their tracks. Well hidden behind scrubs and juniper bushes. They walked here to be alone.

She put down the rifle and waited for him behind a large rock. Sprang at him like a lynx.

He met her. Their embrace was pitch on an open fire. He was the master out here. Tamed her beneath him in the heather, until she whimpered and bit his throat. Then he burrowed himself against her, became heavy as a giant. Spread the wide skirts and found her.

"I love you, Dina!" he murmured from a deep pool. Where water lilies drifted among the rushes. The strong, fresh smell of earth rose from the churned water. Somewhere at its edge, a large animal moaned.

"Do you want to squeeze me to death?" she gasped.

"I'm just continuing what you started," he said hoarsely.

"Didn't you get enough last night?"

"No."

"Will you ever get enough?"

"No."

"What will we do about that?"

"I'll come back again. And again . . . and again . . ."

She stiffened under him.

"Are you going to leave?"

"Not today."

She threw him off in blind rage. Sat up. A large cat that leaned on its front paws and looked its prey in the eye.

"When?"

"On the next steamboat."

"And you tell me that now?"

"Yes."

"Why didn't you tell me yesterday?" she shrieked.

"Yesterday? Why?"

"You don't know?!"

"Dina . . . ," he called softly, and tried to put his arms around her.

She pushed him away and got to her knees in the heather.

"You knew I had to leave," he said pleadingly.

"No!"

"I told you, in Tromsø."

"You wrote that . . . you would come, no matter how bad things got. You've come to Reinsnes to stay!"

"No, Dina. I can't do that."

"Why are you here, then?"

"To see you."

"Do you think that, for Dina of Reinsnes, it's enough that somebody comes to see her?!"

Her voice was a hungry wolf in deep snow.

"Do you think you can just come and satisfy yourself and then leave? Are you so stupid?" she continued.

He stared at her.

"Have I promised you anything, Dina? We talked about marriage, remember? Did I promise anything?"

"Words aren't always what counts," she interrupted.

"I thought we understood each other."

She did not reply. Stood up and brushed off her skirt with sharp claws. Her face was white. Her lips were covered with rime. Her eyes frozen to the depths.

He stood up too. Repeated her name several times, as if asking for mercy.

"Do you think people can leave Reinsnes unless I say so? Do you think they can just come to Reinsnes to sow their seeds and then leave? Do you think it's that easy?"

He did not answer. Just turned halfway around and sat down in the heather again. It seemed he wanted to calm her by letting her tower over him.

"I have to go back to Russia again. . . . You know I'm involved in things that have to be finished."

"Jacob wanted to be here," she said into the air. "But he had to leave. . . . I have him here. Always!"

"I don't plan to die, even though your husband died. If there should be children, I'll . . ."

She laughed harshly, picked up the rifle, and strode purposefully into the woods.

He rose and followed her. After a while, he realized that she had begun to hunt. She was watchful and intent. As if expressing her fury in the fierce concentration of this hunt. She slipped silently among the trees.

He smiled.

Benjamin had seen them from his lookout point. The large aspen above the scree. He sat very still and watched the people embracing behind the big rock. His mouth was open, and he had a deep furrow in his forehead. Now and then the corner of his mouth twitched.

He could not hear what was said down there. And when they finished and began walking again, he lost sight of them for a while.

But he stole after them. Benjamin wanted to see everything, without being recognized.

Leo walked calmly behind Dina, observing her body.

It attracted the setting autumn sun and searched for his shadow against tree trunks and clumps of heather.

When they came to the edge of the woods, she stopped and turned around.

"Jacob disappeared over a cliff because he didn't know who I was."

"What do you mean?" he asked. Relieved that she talked to him.

"He had to go over the edge. Because I wanted him to."

"How?" he whispered.

She took a few steps backward. Slowly. Her arms hung loose.

"I let the sleigh go."

He swallowed and tried to go to her.

"Stay there!" she commanded.

He let himself be cemented into the heather.

"Niels didn't understand who I was either. But he did it himself."

"Dina!"

"The fetus I bled out of me, on the Fold Sea . . . It was safer with Hjertrud too. . . . Because you didn't come!"

"Dina, come here! Explain what you're saying. Please!"

She turned her back to him again and began walking slowly across the plateau.

"You're going to Russia, are you?" she shouted as she walked.

"I'll come back. What's this talk about a fetus that . . ."

"And if you don't come back?"

"Then you'll have been my dying thought. Tell me what happened on the Fold Sea, Dina!"

"Jacob and the others, they stay with me. They need me."

"But they're dead. You can't be blamed for . . ."

"What do you know about blame?"

"Quite a bit. I've killed several . . ."

She turned swiftly. Stood staring at him.

"You're just saying that," she said furiously.

"No, Dina. They were traitors, who might have caused others to die. Still . . . I feel guilty."

"Traitors! Do you know what traitors look like?"

"They have many faces. They can look like Dina Grønelv! Who wants to force a man to wear her skirts."

I am Dina, who sees Leo coming from the shadows. He is bearded and ragged and infested with lice. He holds Pushkin's dueling pistol in front of him so I will think it is a book of poetry. He wants to do something to me. But I keep him one step away. I have loaded the Lapp rifle to go hunting. Leo does not know what is best for him. He wants to tell me something about the new czar, Alexander II. But I am tired. I have walked a long way. I do not have a horse.

I am Dina who says to the thief: "Today you will meet Hjertrud. She will free you from all frightening thoughts, so you need not flee like a traitor."

I point at Cain and mark his head. So I will recognize him again. For he will be chosen and protected. Through all eternity.

I lay him down in the heather so he will always be safe in Hjertrud's lap. I look at him. The green eyes are still trembling. He speaks to me. A beautiful stripe runs from his mouth onto my arm. I hold his head so he will not lie alone in the dark. He has seen Hjertrud.

Do you hear me, Barabbas? Lorch will play the cello for you. No, the piano! He will play the Sonata quasi una fantasia. *Do you see who I am? Do you know me?*

Am I always doomed to this?

Suddenly the boy stood on the cliff. His scream cut a hole in the heavens. Seconds fought in the flickering sun.

I am Dina who sees Benjamin come from the mountain. Born of cobweb and iron. His face is jagged with pain.

I am Hjertrud's eye, which sees the child, which sees myself. I am Dina — who sees!